eden Hudson

DARKENING

SKIES

PATH OF THE
THUNDERBIRD - BOOK 1

PROLOGUE

22 years ago

PURPLE-WHITE TONGUES OF LIGHTNING forked through a midnight sky, revealing for an instant the roiling black clouds over the Shangyang Mountains. A crack of thunder followed, shaking the walls of a teahouse nestled in Kokuji, the fishing village at the foot of the highest peak. Rain poured down all at once as if the lightning had broken open the sky. Storm waves pounded the beach in the village's little cove, and fat, heavy drops battered the teahouse's roof, partially muffling a scream of agony from within.

"Shhh!" a young woman whispered, squeezing the hand of the laboring soon-to-be mother. As one of the few sensha, or entertaining girls, not engaged this night when no travelers would venture out into the rain to traverse the mountain pass, Daitai was standing in as midwife for her friend. With her free hand, she wiped the sweat-soaked black hair from the young mother's bright jade eyes. "You have to stay quiet, Lanfen. If you disturb the guests, Madam will send you out into the streets!"

Lanfen fell back onto the bed mat as the contraction ended, limp with relief. She saw the truth in Daitai's admonishment. Madam was already furious that her most admired sensha had been unable to work these last three months, when it was no longer possible to hide her blossoming stomach. Lanfen would be years in paying back all the silver links Madam believed the teahouse had lost because of her pregnancy. It was enough that her child was coming into the world stained by a house of ill repute. Lanfen wouldn't further dishonor its first breaths by giving birth in the streets like a stray dog.

As the next contraction ripped through her delicate body, Lanfen bit down on the knuckle of her first finger until she drew blood. Sweet singing drifted through the wall, accompanied by the sharp notes of a double-necked lute. One song after another, interspersed with the clinking of fine cups set down too hard by callous, slightly drunk hands and the occasional peal of raucous laughter. Through it all came the angry clatter of rain on the roof and rolling thunder overhead.

The next cry that went up was reedy and small, brought forth by a throat just learning to make sound. Daitai forgot to admonish the infant or the mother in her wonder at seeing life's first moments. It was much smaller than she'd ever imagined, much bloodier. Gently, she bathed the boy with the pile of fabric scraps and the small pot of boiled water Madam had allowed them. Tiny fists, with long, graceful fingers, tipped with scratchy little nails. Scrawny, kicking legs. A head of thick black hair. In the brief flashes that his eyes were open, Daitai saw jade starburst irises brighter than even his mother's.

As she washed the delicate shell of the boy's right ear, Daitai found a moon-mark nestled in the hollow behind his jaw. She wiped the spot clean, then pulled a jasmine-scented oil lamp closer and leaned in to inspect it. Pale white against his ruddy skin, the mark was like a painter's hint at a distant sheet of falling rain.

The more she looked at it, the more the mark reminded her of one of those ancient glyphs from Deep Root, the Old Language, with its multitude of intricate lines layering together to make the words. Babies born marked by those old letters were said to be children of prophecy, their destinies written on their skin. The glyph for *white celery* predicting a beauty who would topple kingdoms, *cicada* foretelling the first of an immortal dynasty, *phoenix* for one who would end a great plague. Or was that cause a great plague? There were so many prophecies that Daitai could never keep them all straight. Lanfen would know—she had such a sharp memory— but the exhausted young mother was dozing so peacefully that Daitai didn't have the heart to bother her over it.

"Who are you, little one? What does your glyph say you'll do for us?" Daitai grinned as she chucked the baby's nose.

He blinked, startled, then opened his mouth.

Daitai giggled. "Are you so hungry? Let's wake Mama."

Daitai took the infant back to Lanfen's mat and knelt at her friend's side.

"Mama Lanfen," Daitai whispered, nudging her friend softly. "Your son is desperate for his first meal."

Groggily, Lanfen pushed herself up and took the child to her breast, whispering soothing nonsense as she helped him find his first meal.

Daitai played with a strand of her hair while she watched the mother and child together. She couldn't recall a destiny for a baby marked by *distant rain fall*.

Could she have been misreading it? She'd never really mastered reading Deep Root. Who needed it these days when the simpler, more civilized characters of the New Script were so much easier to read and write?

"Does Lanfen remember the destinies prophesied by moon-marks from the Old Language?" Daitai asked, twisting her hair around her finger.

"Mm," Lanfen said, nodding without looking up from her son. "Why?"

"Oh, silly Daitai!" She pulled a face that never failed to charm the teahouse's patrons, then gestured to the infant. "He has one behind his right ear."

The new mother lurched upright on the mat and pulled the baby from her breast. He let out a cry of protest as she folded his tiny ear out of the way and studied the pale mark.

"Is it *rain fall*?" Daitai asked. "I thought it might be *rain fall*."

But Lanfen didn't answer. Her bright green eyes sparkled with unshed tears, and she caressed the mark with her thumb.

A tingle of fear crept up Daitai's spine. "What's wrong? Is his prophecy bad?"

"It says *thunder*," Lanfen whispered in a ragged voice.

Daitai's brows furrowed, then soared for her hairline.

"The chosen one? Daitai held the chosen one?" Her voice was rising steadily, both in pitch and volume. Madam would scold her or worse, but she couldn't contain her ecstasy. She leapt to her feet and shouted at the rafters, "This filthy sensha bathed the chosen one with these hands! These hands!"

While Daitai rejoiced over her blessed fortune, Lanfen sat silently on her mat, breathing deeply into the soft, soft hair of her newborn son. The chosen one, the thunderbird. A tear dripped off Lanfen's long eyelashes and onto her baby's cheek, sparkling in the golden lantern light.

力

Months later, a small form trekked up the mountainside of the highest peak of the Shangyangs, an even smaller bundle slung across her chest. Darkness had long since fallen, making Lanfen glad Daitai had insisted she take a lantern along. Eyes shined in the undergrowth when her meager light passed by—not only the greens and yellows of natural beasts, but flashes of demonic magenta, teal, and ever-shifting rainbows. Fearsome guai, demon beasts, roamed these mountain forests, hungry for hunters and lost travelers.

Lanfen carried nothing more than the child in the sling, the lantern in her hand, and a small pouch tucked into her robes for after her errand was done. When her slender, shaking hand was not comforting her infant son, it frequently returned to the pouch in her robes, as if to reassure itself that the contents had not spilled out. She was more frightened of losing it than her life.

She felt no fear for her son's safety. Raijin was the chosen one, after all, and the chosen one could not be eaten by guai before he fulfilled his destiny.

Lanfen had no martial skill or training with weapons, had never even cultivated her Ro beyond what she needed to manifest a pick for her moon zither. In the teahouse, she sang and played and danced and giggled delicately when the patrons said something they felt was clever. Entertaining was her skill, not fighting, and so all she could do as she journeyed through the eye-filled forest was sing. Raijin at least seemed to enjoy the music, and through the night, no wild beasts or guai attacked, so perhaps they enjoyed it as well.

The sun was rising when Lanfen finally stepped out of the tree line and into the light. She had only a few minutes' walk under the caress of its warm rays before she ascended into the smoky cloud layer surrounding the peak. Chilly mist wet her face and beaded on Raijin's eyelashes and hair like diamonds, but the baby only laughed.

Lanfen's hands shook endlessly now, and in spite of the chill, she was sweating. With no need for the lantern any longer, she dropped it beside the path and kept one hand on her son and the other on the pouch. Its contents were for later, not now, not before the errand was complete, but touching it, reminding herself it was there, made her feel safe.

Near midmorning Raijin began to complain for his meal. He'd been a good boy, gone the night through without eating, and Lanfen's legs were unaccustomed to such strenuous use, so she stopped gratefully and sat on a flat rock in the shelter of an outcropping to rest and breastfeed him. Usually these days, Raijin ate rice pudding or soft bits of boiled vegetables, but Lanfen had left too suddenly the day before to think about bringing solid food. Now that she was feeding him, however, she was glad she hadn't brought anything, glad for the closeness. She bent down and kissed his forehead. This would be his last meal with her.

Her shaking intensified at the thought, the nagging ache in her bones turning into an unbearable need. She couldn't wait until the trip back down the mountain. She reached for the pouch.

The deep call of a great rainbird rumbled overhead.

Startled, Lanfen looked up, searching for signs of the creature. A trio of trailing plume feathers as wide as a grown man and twice as long cut through the pale gray mist. Each one shimmered with greens, indigos, purples, and blacks.

Just before the tailfeathers disappeared, a soft indigo barbule drifted down through the swirling fog to land on Raijin's cheek.

Lanfen's fingers trembled so badly that she had to try three times before she successfully plucked the fuzzy barbule from his skin. It was no more than a wisp, so downy she could hardly feel it. She popped it in her mouth.

The barbule tasted of plum blossoms and dissolved on her tongue like a sugar sweet.

Immediately, strength returned to her exhausted limbs, and her blearing vision sharpened. The shaking vanished, her hands becoming as stable and strong as when they were wrapped around the neck of her moon lute or pouring a drink for a wealthy patron. The nagging, aching need battling to take control of her mind dissipated. The pouch remained unopened.

As soon as Raijin finished his meal, Lanfen pushed away from the boulder and returned to her climb. Her delicate feet seemed to fly over the rocky path as if her silken shoes, which had been nearly destroyed by the journey so far, no longer touched the earth. It was as if she had become a storm cloud drifting through the sky. Before she knew it, a dark shape began to emerge from the mist.

Lanfen had been told all her life that the structure at the top of the Shangyangs' highest peak was a monastery filled with monks watching over Kokuji and the mountain pass to the east. These holy men were said to be the reason the village had never been overrun by guai.

As she drew closer to the structure, her jade eyes followed the line of the building's ancient wood porch around each corner. The wooden shakes of the roof had been painted a deep forest green, and its eaves were upturned at the corners in a foreign or forgotten architecture. She counted three sets of sliding doors along this wall, all closed against the pervasive chill. Each panel depicted in golden paint an ornate Deep Root glyph—*wisdom, self-control, improvement.*

Still floating on the essence of the rainbird's barbule, she glided up the steps and let herself into the center door—*self-control*, something she'd had precious little of in her life—sliding the panel shut behind her.

Lanfen found herself standing in a corridor that ran the length of the building. Doorways stood open on the interior wall, and at each end, she could see the hallway turned the corner. A pervasive warmth burned away the cold and wet of the mountain's atmosphere. She could hear the muted din of many voices, but she couldn't tell from which direction they were coming.

She chose one end of the corridor and began walking.

Just before she reached the end, a young man of an age with her came around the corner wearing the loose gray pants and jacket of warrior artists, held closed by a blue-gray sash tied about his waist. The young man stopped suddenly when he saw her, surprise lighting his face. Before his reaction could considered rude, however, he recovered his manners.

He pressed his fists together and bowed deeply to Lanfen, keeping his eyes locked on hers. It was the first time in years Lanfen had been bowed to as one equal greets another, and she thought it unlikely hc would do the same if he knew her occupation. The New Tongue had dozens of speech tones for varying levels of familiarity and respect, and Lanfen was surprised once more when the young man spoke to her in a tone of kind reverence.

"You have traveled a great distance to our school, honored guest," the young man said. "How may I make you comfortable?"

Lanfen returned his greeting bow, one hand holding her baby's head stable against her breast as she bent.

"Gratitude, brother, but I'm confused. Is this establishment not a monastery?"

He smiled at her familiar address. Most men did.

"This is the school of the Path of Darkening Skies, sister," he said, matching her tone. "Are you lost?"

"I am beginning to wonder," she admitted. "In Kokuji, your sister was told of a monastery on the highest peak of the Shangyang Mountains, peopled by an ancient order awaiting the thunderbird of prophecy." She raised Raijin in his sling so that the young man could see the baby inside. "You see, brother, I have him. The chosen one is here."

Rather than burst into throes of ecstasy as Daitai had, the young man just nodded.

"You are looking for Grandmaster Feng. Follow me, little sister. I will bring you to him."

力

The young man led Lanfen down the corridor and into one of the doorways on the interior wall.

Lanterns hung from the ceiling and a hearth stood in the corner, saturating the room with light and warmth. Elaborately woven silk tapestries lined the walls, wafting in a draft too faint to feel, each one valuable enough to set Lanfen up comfortably as the madam of her own teahouse in a much nicer city than Kokuji. A low desk on a thick colorful rug faced the doorway. Sitting behind it was a man with long white hair as fine as spider's silk, ageless skin, and ancient sapphire eyes. As they entered, he looked up from the scroll he was studying.

The young man with the blue-gray sash dropped to his knees before the desk and pressed his forehead to the rattan mat on the floor, just inches shy of the colorful rug.

"Apologies, Grandmaster, but I met with an honored guest in the hallway who needed to speak with you."

"Yes, yes," the grandmaster said, waving a hand heavy with rings.

The young man rose up to his knees and backed to the doorway before bowing his face to the floor once more, then standing and leaving.

Bored sapphire eyes turned to inspect Lanfen.

"Which mud-farm village are you from?" the grandmaster asked in a rude tone she was much more accustomed to hearing. She opened her mouth to answer, but was stopped by another dismissive wave of his hand. Firelight glinted off the precious metals and stones in his many rings. "Never mind, I don't care. I can hardly keep track of them anymore, anyway. Tell me about the latest chosen one. The child is the reason you've come here, is he not?"

Lanfen thought it likely that when faced with this grandmaster's rudeness, most people cowered and faltered, uncertain of how to proceed, but his discourtesy didn't upset her composure. She had dealt with many a merchant and noble so rich they could no longer feel anything but superiority.

She bowed deeply, exposing the back of her neck as if the grandmaster were no more than a fragile elderly man.

"My apologies for interrupting your evening rest, grandfather," she said, her voice a patronizing coo. "Your granddaughter will be quick so you can make your way to bed. This child is the thunderbird. He has a moon-mark of the Deep Root for *thunder* behind his right ear. I will bring him close so your tired eyes can see."

She knelt on the edge of the lavish rug and held Raijin out across the desk. With one finger, she folded her son's tiny ear flat to better expose the pale mark.

The grandmaster snorted. "Have you any idea how many ancient symbols that supposedly say 'thunder' and 'rain' and 'rainbird' and 'storm' I see every year, woman? Never mind that most of you rural bumpkins are too ignorant to tell a moon-mark from a smear of white sauce, let alone read the ancestors' language. How many of them do you think can actually be the chosen one?"

"One, grandfather. This one."

"Get that bastard whelp out of my face and go back to your teahouse, *granddaughter*," he sneered. "I'm sure you have customers waiting."

With that dismissal, the grandmaster spread his scroll across his desk once more and returned to his reading as if she were no longer there.

Lanfen scowled. The weight of the pouch, so reassuring on her journey up the mountain, now hung heavy in her robes. The pipe and sticky ball of brown qajong inside seemed to burn her skin through the layers of fabric. Panic prickled down her arms and into her fingertips, and she saw her son's life stretch out in two parallel paths: one growing up in the teahouse with a mother who entertained men for room, board, and opiate money and the other in this school.

In her heart, she knew Raijin was the chosen one. Whether the grandmaster realized the truth didn't matter. All that mattered was the honorable life her son could lead here.

Holding Raijin to her heart, Lanfen backed away from the desk off the precious rug and pressed her face to the rattan.

"Apologies, venerable Grandmaster. Please forgive this lowly sensha's insolence. She was ignorant and arrogant to assume that her knowledge outweighed the grandmaster's infinite wisdom. She begs you, please do not turn away this child. His mother's sins are not his, and her dishonor should not be his, either." She wasn't surprised to feel tears wetting the mat beneath her eyelids. "Please, revered Grandmaster, if not as a student, then take this child on as a servant. He is weaned and will soon be old enough to complete simple tasks. He need not be a burden, but a boon to your school."

"This isn't a monastery where you can drop off your unwanted bastards," the grandmaster said without looking up. "Find the door and leave by it."

His words struck like a fist to Lanfen's solar plexus. She stifled the sob of desperation that shook her shoulders.

"Please, Grandmaster," she begged. "Please reconsider."

The soft grunt of a cleared throat came from behind Lanfen.

"Apologies for the intrusion," a throaty, elderly voice said.

Lanfen crawled backward once more and turned to the side so she would not be disrespecting either the grandmaster or this new arrival by giving them her back.

In the doorway stood a stooped, balding, wrinkled old man much closer to her imagined monk. Unlike the grandmaster, the old man's brown eyes shined from beneath his wild brows with warmth and barely contained humor.

The grandmaster sighed. "What is it, Master Chugi?"

"If the grandmaster would honor Chugi so greatly as to consider his input, the school could greatly use another servant." The old master smiled at Lanfen, his eyes twinkling. "And if in time this new servant should prove to be the chosen one, then at least we won't have to go looking for him."

Hope tightened Lanfen's throat. Afraid of what she might find there, she turned her gaze to face the grandmaster's face.

"Fine," the grandmaster said as if he were bored of the subject and prepared to say anything just to be left alone. "The boy may stay. But until he's old enough to work, he's your responsibility, Master Chugi."

"Thank you, Grandmaster."

"Feh." Grandmaster Feng returned to his scroll.

On her knees, Lanfen crawled to Master Chugi and handed him her son, the tears rolling down her face now.

In spite of his elderly appearance, Master Chugi took the baby in strong, sure arms. Lanfen swallowed hard as she let her son go. She could already feel his warmth fading from her skin. The cold that replaced it stung like a blade.

"His name is Raijin, Master," she whispered, unable to raise her voice any louder.

Master Chugi smiled down at the boy. "It suits him, granddaughter."

CHAPTER ONE

Present

KOIDA, SECOND PRINCESS OF THE Shyong San Empire, focused her breathing and stilled her mind. She focused on the meagre amount of amethyst Ro at her heartcenter, circling and swirling like a handful of purple sand tossed into a river. Disordered. Unmanageable. Something that would slip through her fingers the moment she tried to grab it.

"Are you ready, Second Princess?" Master Lao asked.

After another moment of intense focus, Koida tried to send the Ro through her shoulder, down the pathway in her arm. Instead, her veins tingled as the energy followed them, seeking out and forcing its way along the easiest routes, traveling down the outside bone of her lower arm and into the heel of her hand. She could feel the Ro manifesting off-balance, but there was nothing she could do to correct it. It was all that she could do to force enough into her hand to manifest a glowing purple bo-shan stick the length of her forearm. By the time she finished, sweat cooled her temples. The stick was barely there, translucent, a ghost of the weapon it should be. The color—still a perfect match for her eyes—was a visual reminder that at seventeen years old her Ro was no more advanced than that of six-year-old.

Koida opened her eyes. "Ready, Master."

Lao stepped forward and swung his glowing red bo-shan stick—this one as solid as stone and the proper color for an advanced Ro—overhanded at her head. Koida sidestepped and countered, then spun and swung a counterattack upward at her master's thigh. Lao blocked as he evaded, the impact of their sticks ringing in the midmorning air.

Across the courtyard, Koida's personal guards looked up long enough to ascertain that she had not been harmed, then returned to their game of Stones and Tiles. It was a ridiculous precaution, being surrounded night and day by guards inside the secure walls of the Sun Palace, but while her father and sister were away, the guards watched over her like a band of mother tigers. Couldn't leave the helpless Ro-cripple alone.

Koida bounced backward, evading another strike, and switched her feet. She stepped in and slashed her amethyst stick up from the reverse angle, this time at Master Lao's ribs. He met her attack, another *thwack* sounding through the courtyard, then a scrape as he shoved her stick off. He sidestepped and dropped to one knee on the colorful glazed tiles of the courtyard, slapping his stick down at her toes. Koida switched feet again to avoid a broken toe and chopped downward at his collarbone. Still kneeling, Lao raised his arm over his head and knocked her attack aside with a hastily manifested High Shield—a glistening ruby shield the length of his forearm. Without a moment's pause, he swung his stick at her shin.

She slid her foot backward, forced to waste valuable attacking opportunities on smacking Master Lao's attack aside with her own bo-shan. She had never been able to manifest a shield. Or anything but a useless stick.

Lao spun away from her, spiraling up to standing once more. Koida snapped her wrist backward, whipping the amethyst stick over to rap her master on the head. He raised his arm and blocked with his High Shield again.

Movement by Lao's left foot caught Koida's eye. A fuzzy black-and-blue wool worm about as long as her pinkie was crawling across the courtyard. The creature looked frantic, as if it were running for its life from the stomping feet of incomprehensible giants.

"Your weapon, Second Princess," Master Lao said, stepping over the wool worm without even noticing it. "Focus!"

In Koida's hand, the bo-shan flickered like a guttering lamp and lost most of the little physical substance she'd been able to give it. Like this, a strike would more likely whistle right through the stick than be stopped by it.

Koida bit her lips together and forced as much Ro as she could manage down through her arm and into the weapon. If she let her mind wander too far, the stick would disappear, the Ro returning to her heartcenter, and there was no telling how long it would take her to remanifest the weapon—or if she even could. She could usually only manage one or two manifestations strong enough to train with per day, and never more than one at a time.

She still wasn't able to force the Ro through the correct pathway to manifest the stick with a perfect fighting grip, but slowly, the weapon regained the lost sturdiness and color.

Koida nodded at Master Lao.

He pressed forward, feet following the zigzagging step pattern common to bo-shan combat, while he slashed the stick at her diagonally from the left and right, left and right. Koida blocked, blocked, blocked, then pulled her body out of line, giving Lao a smaller target, and spun around to his rear. She lashed out with a backfist from her free hand.

It almost landed on the back of Master Lao's skull, but his High Shield arm swooped over his shoulder. Her bare knuckles struck the hard, glowing surface instead of his head. It felt as if they splintered on contact, like she had backfisted a ruby wall.

"Ah!" Koida cried out as much from surprise as the pain. Her bo-shan stick disappeared as she lost concentration completely. A small amount of her Ro prickled back up through her arm and shoulder into her heartcenter, but the majority formed a small cloud that filtered into Master Lao's chest.

"Wait," she said. "I haven't conceded. This match isn't over."

With a terse downward snap of his fist, Master Lao dismissed his own bo-shan and grabbed Koida's hand.

"You are incapacitated," he said, studying the angry red skin along the ridge of her knuckles. They throbbed in time with her heart. "The match is over."

"But I can continue fighting, Master," she protested, forcing her voice to return to the polite student-speaking-to-master tone. In truth, it felt like her hand bones were jagged shards of glass, but she didn't want to quit training for the day. She'd almost had him this time.

Within the Path of the Living Blade, Ro was absorbed through combat. A little through these training matches when one participant was incapacitated or yielded, and a lot through dueling, battle, and war when an enemy or opponent was killed. Though Koida always lost these training matches with Master Lao, she didn't think she had lost this particular match, and she didn't know why her Ro had behaved as if she'd been defeated. She hadn't admitted defeat or been incapacitated; her weapon had just been broken. She could have finished the fight bare-handed—indeed, she would've had to if this had been a fight for her life, as it so often was in the world outside the palace.

"Apologies, Second Princess, but you cannot continue fighting." Master Lao probed the red mark, eliciting a wince from her. "You may have a broken hand."

"I would like to continue training, Master." She couldn't order him to continue their fight outright—even the second princess must respect the rules of the student-master dynamic—but she did infuse her voice with royal authority. She might not be able to remanifest her stick, but there were always hand and foot techniques. Perhaps she would never absorb enough Ro to use the weapon techniques as intended, but to learn them could only do her good.

Master Lao waved at the guards. "Please escort the second princess to the court alchemists. See if they can mix her a salve to repair the damage."

Batsai, the captain of her personal guard, joined them.

"But, Master, I could practice kicks," Koida said. "My legs aren't injured."

"This discussion is closed," Lao said, his voice a stone wall. He covered his closed fist with a flat palm and bowed. "Good training today, Second Princess."

21

"Thank you, Master." Koida mirrored his motion, trying not to grimace with the frustration of being dismissed or the pain in her knuckles when she covered them.

Batsai waited for her to precede him, then fell into step beside her. The other three guards in her escort fanned out behind them.

"That spinning backfist looked good," Batsai said as they stepped into the cool shade of the courtyard portico.

Koida frowned. "For a cripple."

Batsai stopped and turned to face her.

"Do I grovel and fawn over you, Second Princess?" he asked. "Am I known to wheedle your favor through empty compliments?"

Personally responsible for her protection since she was a baby, Batsai was one of the few people in the empire who wasn't afraid to speak to her that way. His honesty was a rare treasure in a sea of courtiers and nobles all frightened of losing their heads to the royal executioner's Falling Blade Wall technique.

"Apologies, Batsai," Koida said. "My anger took control and shamed me. Can you forgive your princess?"

The captain let out a grunt and nodded. "Better learn to differentiate between the honesty of a friend and the sweet lies of a foe, little dragon, before you burn us all."

Before he turned back and began walking again, his hand shot out, and he tweaked her nose as he had when she was still a child. Koida grinned and caught up to him, the rest of her guard following behind.

They climbed the steps from the training courtyard into the cool, shadowed halls of the Sun Palace. As they wound through the mazelike corridors, courtiers, officials, and her father's concubines backed against the walls and bowed to the second princess.

Proper conduct didn't require that Koida return their obeisance with acknowledgement—none of them ranked highly enough or were her blood relations or master—so she ignored them. A nod of her head would only serve as permission to speak with her, and she knew they were all dying to ingratiate themselves so she would plead their causes to her father, Emperor Hao. Over the seventeen years of her life, Koida had become adept at avoiding these smiling traps.

The Eastern tower was the only remaining section of the original castle, a stout stone fortification that the luxurious new palace had consumed long before Koida's birth. These days it housed the court alchemists and eunuchs, far removed from where an explosion could harm one of the royal family.

Outside the door of the Eastern tower, Batsai stopped.

"Wait here," he ordered the other three soldiers. "Guard the tower until we've returned."

"Yes, Captain." They took up spots on either side of the doorway.

Alone, Koida and Batsai climbed the spiraling stairs.

"Why leave them behind?" she asked him.

The captain smirked. "Jun has been desperate to master the Serpentine Spear ever since his brother did. I wouldn't put it past that idiot to try making off with something."

"Oh."

Koida could understand the young guard's temptation. Though most of her visits to the Eastern tower now were for powders to ease her monthly pain, as a child watching her sister Shingti advance from student to mastery of the Path of the Living Blade with seeming ease, Koida had dreamed of a potion or pill that would advance her Ro and make her as strong and capable as anyone else in the empire. Unfortunately, even with all their knowledge and experimentation, the court alchemists had yet to find a concoction that would cure a Ro-cripple like her.

The higher they climbed, the more overwhelming the stink of strange metallic vapors and chemical salts became. Floorboards overhead creaked with activity, and muffled voices drifted down from above.

At the entrance to the laboratory—little more than a hatch in the ceiling—Batsai went in and inspected the room for any hidden threats to Koida, then returned and stood aside, allowing her to enter alone.

Inside, the smell was even more intense. Busy alchemists and apprentices leaned over bubbling cauldrons, dusting multicolored powders from grindstones into phials and dipping precious gems in smoking solutions.

"Second Princess?" An aging alchemist with black dye smudging her hairline and charcoal darkening her eyebrows bowed. She rose gracefully and asked, "You wish for your monthly medicine?"

"Gratitude, Sulyeon, but Master Lao sent me." Koida pulled her arms from her sleeves and showed Sulyeon her hand. "He believed it to be broken and requested that you mix a salve to repair the damage."

In vexation, Sulyeon's false eyebrows attempted to touch in the center of her forehead.

"May a thousand suns burn Lao and his ignorance," she said, prodding Koida's throbbing knuckles. "We have no salve that can repair broken bones in a day. We practice science here. If the fool wants magic, he should send the second princess to the eunuchs." Sulyeon finished her rant and inspection of Koida's knuckles at the same time. "Bruised, not broken. A tincture of distilled Green Haze will soothe the tenderness and prevent discoloration."

While the alchemist went to a long workbench covered with jars and stone boxes and flasks, Koida's attention was drawn to the rough wall of wooden shelves dividing the laboratory into a half-moon. This wall of shelving had not existed on her last visit. She could see movement in the crack between two shelves but couldn't discern what was being done on the other side or who was doing it.

Sulyeon returned with a gritty green ointment that smelled like sharp herbs and salts. She rubbed the concoction onto Koida's knuckles, and within moments, the throbbing subsided.

"That is much better. I think I will tell Master Lao that your science is not far from magic," Koida said, dipping her head to the reluctantly pleased alchemist. "Gratitude, gifted healer."

Koida slipped her hands back inside her sleeves and was about to ask Sulyeon about the shelves dividing the room when a slender, white-haired form ducked out from behind the barrier into the laboratory.

"Cousin Yoichi?"

The young man stopped midstride, clearly surprised, then bowed to her. "Cousin Koida."

She returned his bow. Though Yoichi was not truly her cousin, he was a blood relation. Shyong Liu Yoichi was her father's only known son, a bastard from a harem girl. The version of his story Koida had heard was that, twenty-three years before, Shingti's mother, the late first empress, had been told by the eunuchs she could never have a child. Distraught, the first empress asked Emperor Hao's most beautiful harem girl to stop taking precautions and sent the emperor to her. Two months later, both the first empress and the harem girl were pregnant.

The eunuchs who'd pronounced the first empress infertile were put to death for their blunder. Not wanting her child to have competition for the throne but unwilling to kill a pregnant woman, the first empress sent the harem girl away. Shingti was born the heir, and the first empress died in childbirth. Her death seemed only a tragic accident until Koida was born to her father's fourth wife, the fourth empress, who also died giving birth. One at a time over the following years, the remaining Empresses died of illnesses and accidents. Behind closed doors, citizens claimed the deaths were the result of a curse put on the emperor's wives by the wronged harem girl.

Rumors continued to fly until five summers previous when Yoichi had appeared at court to petition the emperor for his right to the throne. Though his hair was snowy white, Yoichi's high cheekbones, slanting jaw, and purple eyes left no doubt as to who had sired him. He was a looking glass image of Emperor Hao as a young man, but handsomer, nearly beautiful, as if an artist had refined the father's characteristics in the son. His mother, Yoichi explained, had died in childbirth like Shingti's and Koida's, a complication the midwife had speculated came from their shared father. He then revealed his Heroic Record—the tattoos covering his arms and chest that recorded his greatest feats of battle. He had waited to come to the palace until he had advanced himself and mastered the Path of the Living

Blade so that he would be worthy of his place in the Shyong San dynasty.

Though Emperor Hao had refused to take away Shingti's birthright and give it to Yoichi, he had accepted his illegitimate son into the royal household, going so far as to give him the Shyong clan name and legalizing his rank as noble above any other being in the empire excepting the emperor and his daughters. This had suited Yoichi, and to spare his half-sisters the shame of addressing a bastard as an equal, he had suggested they simply call one another cousin.

"What are you doing up here?" Koida asked.

"Ah..." A slight discomfort twisted Yoichi's beautiful features. "That might be a conversation for a more...worldly woman than yourself, little cousin."

"I'm worldly." As she said it, she realized that the declaration made her sound even more childish than if she'd kept her mouth shut. But Cousin Yoichi was in his early twenties and always seemed to be up to something interesting. Whenever he was around, she wanted to impress him so that he would let her in on the secret.

Yoichi faltered. "Don't tell your father that you saw me here or that I told you why I came. He'll hang me for corrupting your innocence."

"I swear," Koida promised. "Not a word."

"Sometimes men—" He cast around for the words. "—visit with women...alone..."

"Cousin, I am not a child. I know what intercourse is." There were plenty of scrolls in the royal library explaining how it was done and giving tips on making the experience more enjoyable.

Yoichi's pale eyebrows arched toward his shaggy white hair. Then a grin broke out on his face.

"Little cousin is already planning her harem," he teased. They both knew that unless Shingti abdicated the throne, Koida would never be the empress and have no right to a harem. "Fine, if you know so much, then you know the consequences a careless night can have?"

Koida nodded. "Pregnancy."

"But there are ways to prevent that." He produced a stone phial from his sleeve. "I'm taking precautions to ensure there will be no more bastards born into our family line. Not by me, in any case."

"Oh." Koida's face colored as she realized the significance this precaution would have for one such as Yoichi. She pressed a closed fist to her heartcenter and gave a remorseful bow. "Apologies, elder cousin. Your little cousin should not have pried."

"It is nothing," Yoichi returned easily. The phial disappeared back into his robes. "What force caused you to brave the stink of the Eastern tower today?"

"I bruised my knuckles training," Koida explained, pushing back her sleeve to reveal the pungent green salve soaking into the back of her hand.

"Training?" Yoichi glanced down at her martial attire as if just then seeing it. "I would have expected you to spend this morning dressing for court."

"Court?" Koida canted her head. "Today? But Father and Shingti are still on campaign."

"No one told you? A messenger came in during the night. The Wungs surrendered. Emperor Hao and the first princess will return home this evening."

CHAPTER TWO

Present

THE LAST CASCADE OF TINY BELLS WAS pinned to Koida's elaborate hair dressing just as the war horns became audible. The sound meant her father and his entourage were passing through Boking Iri, the empire's capital city, just down the Horned Serpent River from the Sun Palace.

Koida clutched her blood-orange shoulder wrap with one hand and the hem of her blue-green silk robes with the other as she sprinted from her residence. The bell cascades were meant to stay silent, proof of her impeccable poise and grace, but they jangled like a troupe of dancers at her father's yearly birth celebration as she ran through the corridors.

In the north gallery of the palace, just inside the doorway to the main courtyard, Koida slid to a halt, stilled the ringing bells in her hair, smoothed her train and sleeves, and slowed her heaving breath. Composed but for a slight flush in her cheeks, she stepped out into the courtyard.

Most of the nobility already lined the golden stairs and were watching the massive gates that stood open to the north. Their finery painted the courtyard in the bright colors of a lush garden.

Near the top of the stairs, as befit his bestowed station, Yoichi stood with his hands tucked into plum-colored robes that matched his eyes. He, too, had changed clothing since their meeting in the tower that morning, though it looked as if his change had been much less rushed. He nodded to her, then adjusted the left shoulder of his robe meaningfully.

Koida hurried to pull the slipping wrap back onto her bare shoulders. Yoichi smiled his wry smile and returned his attention to the gates.

Outside the palace gates, a raucous cheer went up, and the war horns blasted another growling bass note that echoed through the valley. In the distance, Koida could see a great throng of riders, the blood-orange Shyong San banners fluttering overhead. Though she'd seen the same sight many times since birth, her heart leapt. Somewhere near the front of that churning mass of horses and soldiers were her father and sister. They were finally home again.

As the entourage approached the palace, Koida raised her arms in the ceremonial return greeting pose—chin high, eyes forward, elbows away from her sides, palms open to receive her emperor and his armies back into their home.

The bannermen rode through the gates first, followed by the horn bearers. Mounted soldiers came next and pulled up on either side of the gate, creating an equine tunnel.

When Koida caught sight of her sister's personal guard, all wearing Shingti's Green Dragonfly armor, she had to fight to keep the grin from her lips.

Shingti galloped in behind them to the deafening cheers of noble, soldier, and servant alike. The first princess was powerful and strong, the youngest Master of the Path of the Living Blade in nearly a century, and beloved by all her subjects for the honor she brought to the empire. Her long brown hair whipped over her shoulder, and her purple eyes flashed as she wheeled her half-demon destrier and reared him up onto his back legs. Like the mounted soldiers, Shingti and her Dragonfly Guard lined both sides of the courtyard, completing the tunnel to the palace stairs.

The Emperor's Guard trotted into the courtyard next, their blood-orange plumage shifting in the breeze. The men dismounted and dropped to their knees. With equal pageantry, their warhorses—trimmed in blood-orange tack and bearing the emperor's crest—each bent a front leg and lowered their long heads toward the ground.

Last of all, in the position of greatest honor, Emperor Hao rode in on his aging chestnut destrier, another half-demon hybrid. His blood-orange armor glinted fire in the sunset as he walked his horse up to the steps.

Koida brought her palms together and bowed to her father, keeping her head motionless to avoid ringing the cascades of bells.

"Exalted Emperor," she intoned, her voice ringing off the walls, "the Sun Palace welcomes you into its embrace. May your mighty Ro fill its halls with glory once more."

"Daughter, you have kept the palace alive in my absence."

With a thrust of his gauntleted fist, Emperor Hao manifested a glistening ruby scepter crowned with wicked spikes and extended it to Koida. She rose from the formal pose at his invitation, her part in the ceremony complete.

Emperor Hao turned his horse to face the gathered crowd. "After a brave fight on the field of battle, the Wung tribe honorably surrendered! We feast this night in celebration of the enlightenment and peace the Shyong San Empire has brought to a new tribe!"

Nearly everyone in the courtyard cheered. Several of the soldiers threw their helmets into the air, Shingti included.

As the return ceremony ended, palace servants scurried inside to finish preparations for the feast, commoners hurried back to Boking Iri and the surrounding farms to recount the story to their families, and weary soldiers either started their trips home or dismounted and led their horses to the stables. Nobles pressed forward to the emperor and first princess, all attempting to offer the first and most elaborate congratulations.

Koida slipped back into the palace. She wanted to talk to her sister and father, but she would never get near them in the swarm. She would greet them privately when their attentions were undivided.

CHAPTER THREE

Present

BEFORE THE FEAST COULD BEGIN, THE customary signing of the Book of the Empire had to be completed. The chieftain and a small group of representatives from the Wungs came before the raised White Jade Dais, where the emperor's royal table presided, and carved their seal into a steelwood panel. This minor act officially ended the enmity between all Wung villages and the empire, recognized all tribal territory as falling within the empire's borders, and pledged a tithe of crops and tribute of soldiers from each of their villages. As the commander of the Imperial Army and the empire's greatest known Master of the Living Blades, Shingti accepted the finished panel and added it to the Book, clamping the thick rings that bound it back into place.

"Brave warriors of the Wung tribe," the first princess said in a proud, clear voice that filled the feasting hall, "be welcomed by your new brothers and sisters."

Koida sat at her father's left hand, watching this formality unfold. Like most of the envoys from the peoples her father and sister had subjugated and united, the Wungs seemed a combination of sullen and terrified.

Not long ago, Yoichi had confided in Koida that on his travels, he'd heard barbarian tribes claim that Emperor Hao was a cannibal who ate his enemies' heartcenters in arcane ceremonies designed to multiply the strength of his Ro. When she asked Yoichi whether that would work, Yoichi had laughed and said not to try it, for "the human heart carries diseases worse than all other organs combined."

Once the official business was complete, the music, feasting, and drinking started, and the Wung delegation began to relax. They clumped together around a far table near the corner of the hall, talking amongst themselves and glaring at any noble or official who strayed too close. They didn't turn down any of the Sun Palace's famous blood orange wine, however.

Shingti handed off the Book to an official and began to make her way back to the dais, but group after group of courtiers stopped her. Now that the first princess was back in the castle, everyone wanted her ear, but Shingti brushed them aside easily in favor of drinking with her guard.

Servants bowed up the dais to fill the plate and cup of the emperor, then Koida's. One discreetly removed Shingti's place setting and bowed back down the stairs to find where the first princess had landed.

Until the emperor's meal was finished, it was forbidden to approach the dais without being summoned, which meant Koida had him to herself for the time being.

"Your daughter is glad you're home, Father," she said, switching from the formal tones she'd used during the return ceremony to the loving familial speech. She leaned over and pecked his cheek.

This close and without the blood-orange armor covering most of his face and body, her father's age showed in the lines at the corners of his eyes and mouth, the thick wine-barrel belly, and his graying beard and warrior's knot. These signs of passing time caused Koida no distress, however. For as long as she could remember, her father's hair had been graying, but the gray had never quite been able to overpower the black. The vigor in his purple eyes and the power in his weapon techniques were all one needed to see to know this man would outlast the Horned Serpent River itself.

"Your father is glad to rest his old bones and see his youngest child again." Emperor Hao squeezed Koida's hand, then patted it roughly. "She seems to have grown even more beautiful while I was away."

Koida suppressed a wince. The linctus the alchemist had spread on her knuckles that morning had worn off, and she hadn't had time to reapply the gritty green gel in her rush to dress for the return ceremony.

A boisterous laugh went up from the crowd below. Shingti at the center of her Dragonfly Guard. The first princess elbowed one hugely muscled guard in the side and said something, then pretended to preen and admire her reflection in a cup of wine. This sent the rest of them into fits while the offended party shook his fist at her. He, too, was smiling, however. It was clear these men saw Shingti as one of their own rather than as a fragile ward as Koida's guard saw her.

"I've been keeping up with my training," Koida told her father, wanting him to approve and simultaneously feeling small and stupid for trying to curry his favor. "I nearly landed a backfist on Master Lao this morning."

The emperor took a long sip of wine. "That's good, daughter, but have you given any further consideration to what Eunuch Ba-Qu said? I would rather my child leave off the studies of the Path than have her harmed trying to strain toward an advancement she can never achieve."

Koida tugged her sleeve down farther over her bruised knuckles. "But even if I can never advance, learning the techniques—"

"Aha!" Emperor Hao clapped his hands together with delight. "The poets are starting!"

Fighting hard not to show the twinge of bitterness at his dismissal of her, Koida fell silent as the lanterns around the room were dimmed and a single bright light shined on a set of opaque shades at the far end of the room. Her father often did this when she disagreed with him, changing the subject and then pretending he couldn't hear her appeals. Arguing further would accomplish nothing but to make him sullen and spiteful. Resigned, Koida took a deep drink of her wine and watched a performer take his place behind the shade.

The next hour went to the court's poets and the shadow actors as they recounted the most harrowing tales from Emperor Hao's Heroic Record. After this came the Record of Shingti, Dragonfly of the Battlefield, followed by the account of the Wandering Hero, Cousin Yoichi.

Wedged between the sagas of the valiant offspring the Exalted Emperor had produced was a short song called the Beauty of Koida, Lilac of the Valley, a polite attempt at pretending that she had contributed anything useful to the mighty warrior dynasty.

Koida wished they would have forgotten her altogether.

CHAPTER FOUR

Present

THE FEAST CARRIED ON WELL INTO THE night, as the return celebrations often did. When the hard wine was brought out, Emperor Hao announced that he would retire, which allowed Koida to slip away as well. Though her father had given little indication through the night that he noticed Koida's presence, it was still offensive to leave before the emperor did.

The moment she arose from her seat, Koida's personal guard sidled away from the conversations and dances they were engaged in and followed her out of the hall.

"Had enough celebration?" Batsai asked.

She smiled up at him. "I miss the quiet of an empty palace."

"You would make a good soldier's wife," he teased. "Pine for him until he comes home, then wish he would get back to war already."

Koida let this go. She loved having her family home. It was being forced to spend time around the rest of the royal entourage she could do without.

They traversed the mazelike corridors to the royal residence wing of the palace. Once there, they fell into a single file to follow the snaking pattern of boards that would not trigger the shrieking of the nightcaller floors. Nightcaller floors were one of the palace's many precautions against assassins. Should anyone who didn't know the pattern attempt to sneak into a residence at night, the hinged boards' high-pitched scraping would alert every guard within hearing distance and likely wake the sleeping target as well. The serpentine patterns were well-guarded secrets that only the most trusted members of palace staff were privy to.

At Koida's residence, her guard spread out and searched each chamber thoroughly for hidden threats, then inspected her furniture for poisoned needles, deadly adders, and venomous spiders. As usual, they found nothing.

"Be sure you stay closeted tonight, little dragon," Batsai warned her as she walked him to her outermost chamber. He and Jun had the watch that night and would stay in the sitting room until daybreak, when Hyung-Po and Qing would relieve them. "A countryside full of drunken soldiers and unfamiliar faces is a danger to any man, woman, or child, let alone a princess."

"Of course." Koida feigned a yawn. "I am exhausted from the wine, anyway. My ladies should come soon to help me undress. Will you let them in?"

Batsai nodded, then took his post at the door. Koida went into her dressing chamber and rang for her waiting ladies, then stood before the looking glass and attempted to pick bells out of her dark brown, nearly black hair. Her dark hair and purple eyes had come from her father, though her irises were a light violet instead of the deep plum color Hao, Yoichi, and Shingti all shared. Overall, there was very little of her father in her appearance. Her face was as round as the moon and nearly as pale, marked by a measure of the legendary loveliness of her mother. The Fourth Empress had had nearly a full arm's worth of Heroic Record to prove that she had no trouble controlling her own Ro, but perhaps she had been the silent carrier of the Ro-crippling deficiency that plagued Koida.

Emperor Hao's two other extraordinary children were clear proof that he wasn't to blame for his second daughter's uselessness.

Koida was still scowling and picking at the first bell cascade when feminine giggling in the outer chamber announced her ladies' arrival. Jun was an interminable flirt. Batsai showed the ladies into the inner chamber, then let himself back out. The ladies began taking apart Koida's ceremonial robes, hair dressing, and jewelry while hinting at their desire to gossip about the celebration. Koida ignored their obvious leading. Even in the best of moods, she hated idle chatter.

Finally, the chittering monkeys finished helping Koida into her nightdress and left, taking their constant stream of babble with them.

Koida stuck her head into the outer chamber. Batsai was seated on a cushion, reading a scroll, while Jun practiced Pose of the Mountain, holding himself horizontal to the floor on an extended Serpentine Spear Hand. His Ro glimmered red in the shape of a twisted spearhead, the sharp tip lodged in the wooden floorboards. The greatest of artists were said to be capable of holding the Mountain for hours at a time, but

Jun's Ro spear flickered as she watched. He would drop soon and have to begin again.

"Good night, Batsai."

"Good night, little dragon. Dream vast breaths of endless fire," came his familiar reply.

She closed the door and walked to her bed platform, then slid off her velvet residence slippers and climbed up onto the soft layers of feather ticking and luxurious demon beast furs. She put out the bedside lantern and sat in the darkness, eyes adjusting to the scant silver-blue moonlight filtering in around the wooden sliding door closing off her balcony. In the winter, heavy drapes were hung about the door to seal out the cold, but this early in the fall, those were still hidden away somewhere. The stretch of nightcaller floor between the balcony and her bed had no pattern of silent boards to follow.

In the outer chamber, Koida heard the floor squeal and a heavy bump, followed by Jun's muffled curse. Batsai murmured something. Jun groaned and resumed the pose.

As Batsai began to speak again, Koida stood and grabbed the closest of the thick wooden beams crossing her ceiling. Hand over hand, she climbed to the exterior wall, bypassing the unforgiving section of nightcaller floor, then shoved the balcony door with her toe. It rolled open without a sound. She kept the wheels and track heavily greased year-round.

With a swing of her legs, Koida dropped herself onto the stone floor of the balcony, landing as silently as a moth. She slid the door closed behind herself, then found the loose stone in the waist-high wall surrounding the balcony. Behind it, a set of black silks in the style of peasant clothes, but much finer, were folded around a pair of soft leather boots. Working quickly in the chill fall air, she traded her nightdress for the black pants and shirt, then laced on the boots.

Now more appropriately outfitted, she swung herself over the edge of the balcony and scaled the stone wall down to the palace gardens, where numerous fountains burbled into the night. Guards patrolled the perimeter and pathways, occasionally rousting drunken couples out of the shrubbery. Koida crouched and watched, wondering whether Yoichi was somewhere out there with one of the worldly women he'd mentioned, then whether Shingti was. Her sister was never one to brag about her non-martial conquests, but Koida knew there had been several.

Finally, Koida's chance came. The guards were all facing away from the garden wall, sending off a particularly amorous couple who didn't want to leave and who declared so loudly. She darted to the garden wall, ran two steps up the side, and grabbed onto the top, hauling herself over. She dropped to the other side and slid along the wall like a shadow until she came to the royal stables.

A reinforced lantern cast yellow light through the open doors at both ends of the long building. Peering in through the nearest window, Koida could see the stable hands and drivers were all gathered around a game of Stones and Tiles, laying bets and passing the time while they waited for the visiting nobles and soldiers to return and demand their carriages or mounts for a tipsy ride home.

Koida slipped down the stable wall until she came to the right window, then climbed inside.

An enormous black destrier snorted and stamped his wide hoof in fury.

"Shh." Koida leaned into the light shining through his stall doors so the monstrous horse could see her face. "It's only me, you big brute."

When Pernicious saw it was her, he quieted instantly and began to nuzzle her side. Koida dug into her shirt's pockets until she found the candied blood oranges she had stashed there for him. His wide eyes flashed bloody red fire, but he nibbled them out of her palm as delicately as a kitten lapping up milk.

Like her sister's and father's warmounts, Pernicious was half demon, half horse, built out of unholy slabs of thick muscle, bred to ride down enemies in the chaos of battle. The bloodthirsty half-demon could never be tamed, but he could be befriended. He'd taken a liking to Koida when she was little more than a toddler who had wandered into the stables with a handful of candied blood oranges. At the time, her inadequacy manifesting Ro had yet to be discovered, and it was assumed she and Pernicious would dominate the battlefield together with Shingti and their father. Now that everyone knew better, Pernicious mostly spent his time terrifying the stable hands, escaping when he wanted, spreading his seed to every mare he could scent, and smashing small animals that wandered too close. No one but Koida could get near the half-demon safely, let alone ride him. The last person who'd tried had been decapitated with one kick from his broad brimstone hoof.

Candied offering consumed, Pernicious folded his legs and knelt. Koida grabbed his shaggy black mane and lifted a leg to climb on, but he lurched back to his feet, throwing her down.

"Ha ha." Koida scowled up at him. This was a game he found particularly funny. "There's enough meat on your bones to feed the war hounds for a month, you know."

He whickered softly, an almost human chuckle, and lowered himself again. But as soon as Koida moved her leg, he stood back up.

"That's the sort of night this is going to be, then?" she asked in a low voice.

Pernicious tossed his head, his mane flying.

"So be it."

Koida ran up the stall wall and kicked off lightly, launching herself at the warhorse's broad back. With a screaming whinny, Pernicious circled away, his hairy fetlocks glowing with fiery tongues of orange, yellow, and red Ro as he activated his Darting Evasion. Koida hit his spinning haunches and bounced off. Just before she slammed into the far wall, she grabbed a hank of his tail and pulled, snapping her body perpendicular to his and letting her feet land against the wall like a floor. She flipped backward, arms thrown wide, and dropped into place on his back.

Pernicious howled, his scream split into nine minor harmonics, and reared. It was his Petrifying Shriek of Legions, intended to paralyze anyone within hearing distance with fear.

Koida just laughed in victory and grabbed his mane. The beast's demonic scream had never worked against her. Most likely because she knew that all it took was a handful of candied fruit to reduce him to an oversized lapdog.

With a kick of one enormous hoof, Pernicious smashed the stall door open and stormed down the center of the stables. He made straight for the stable hands and carriage drivers.

"No," Koida snapped, yanking sharply with both hands and pulling his head to the left. "We'll find you something bigger to kill."

Mollified by the promise of deadlier prey, Pernicious wove around the terrified servants and galloped out into the moonlit night.

Together, they raced across the countryside, the cold fall wind tearing at their hair. They followed the Horned Serpent River to Boking Iri, then turned sharply into the city, Pernicious's brimstone hooves striking sparks on the paving stones. He let loose another Petrifying Shriek of Legions, rattling the air and ensuring that no late-night busybody would look out their window and see the second princess riding through the city.

They whirled down several streets and switchbacks and a few alleyways almost too narrow for Pernicious's broad body before coming to the beggar's row. Here the Ro-crippled, the addicts, and the insane huddled together around smoldering rag fires and crouched inside poorly constructed shelters of stolen or scavenged boards. These were the empire's untouchables, forced into the dark corners where no one from polite society had to see—or smell—them. And, Koida knew, this was where she would be if she had been born anything but the daughter of the emperor. Forgotten and homeless. Cast away.

She didn't slow Pernicious, just threw the bagful of silver she'd brought along at the foot of the largest group of them as she rode through. Behind her, she heard the mad scramble to collect the shiny links but didn't look back.

After the city, the princess and the destrier crossed the river, Pernicious taking them straight through the deepest part and soaking Koida to the bone. They rode through the forest, searching out prey. Animals were getting harder and harder to come by this close to Boking Iri, and demon beasts were almost nonexistent in the area, hunted off by fur traders dealing in the most tender and resilient of pelts and students of the Path of the Living Blade hoping to advance themselves to masters by consuming the precious stone at the demon's core.

Finally, after an hour's hunt, Pernicious tracked down an ordinary mountain lion to fight. Their competing screams echoed off the trees and frightened sleeping birds from the branches as they circled and brawled. The mountain lion tried to leap onto Pernicious's back, but the warhorse activated his Darting Evasion, kicking at the same time. The mountain lion yowled. The flaming brimstone hooves struck its skull with a splintering crack. The big cat fell dead. Pernicious stomped on the back of its neck for good measure.

A white-gold cloud of Ro filtered up from the mountain lion's chest, lighting up the trampled undergrowth and the clawed and torn trees as it flowed into Pernicious's broad chest. The half-demon's eyes glowed fiery orange as he absorbed the Ro into his heartcenter.

Koida had seen the process many times, both when Pernicious killed another beast and when Master Lao defeated her in sparring, but still she watched with wide-eyed fascination. It was brutal and beautiful all at once, the essence of the Path of the Living Blade. The strong survived, and the victor went on to more victories, until the day they met an opponent stronger than themselves and became the defeated.

With the warhorse's desire for battle satisfied, they followed the river north, out of the forest and into the mountains, climbing higher and higher until they came to a cliff beside the Horns, the twin waterfalls that gave the Horned Serpent its name.

Pernicious folded his legs and rolled in the dewy grass, trying to crush Koida, but she leapt off before she was caught under him. Making a rude gesture at the enormous warhorse, she went to the cliff and dangled her legs off the edge. Stretching out below was the valley, its forest a dark shadow along the silvery strand that was the river. Lights glowed yellow like neighboring stars in the windows of the Sun Palace, and farther downstream, smaller stars marked Boking Iri. Just visible on the eastern horizon, the jagged teeth of the Shangyang Mountains hemmed them in.

It was the entire world to Koida, everything she had ever known. She'd never been outside the valley. She sat up on the cliff's edge and stared down at it, wondering what life was like anywhere else. Uncountable ages later, an inferno of muscle and fur scooted up behind her, head down and eyes closed so he couldn't see over the edge. She leaned back against Pernicious and fell asleep.

CHAPTER FIVE

Present

HOURS LATER, WHEN THE MOON HAD GONE to bed and dawn was beginning to break in the eastern sky, Koida awoke. Pernicious grumbled in his sleep against her back.

She groaned and stretched. "We're late. Get up."

The half-demon flicked his ears, then rolled his head to its opposite side and ignored her.

Koida climbed onto his back and nudged him with her knees.

"Wake up, you lazy nag, or I'll ride you off this cliff."

Pernicious howled, his voice splitting into the nine-tone Petrifying Shriek of Legions. For all of his fire and fury, the destrier was terrified of heights.

"You know that doesn't work on me," Koida said. "Let's go."

The half-demon warhorse inched away from the edge of the cliff first, then stood and tore back down the mountainside, leaping over boulders rather than going around, and following the river back down into the valley. They flew through the palace gates at a breakneck gallop and charged into the stables, frightening the morning hands almost as badly as those from the night before.

Pernicious obligingly went back into his stall and allowed Koida to curry and brush him. Because he was a half-demon, he never broke a sweat, let alone lathered, but he enjoyed the grooming. His wounds from the fight with the mountain lion had healed overnight, a side effect of the Ro he'd absorbed.

When she finished, Koida scratched a note on the splintered remains of the stall door with an old horseshoe nail.

"The beast broke down his door again," she read it aloud to Pernicious. "He'll let workers repair it without harming them—" She glared at the hard-eyed destrier. "—or else he won't get any more candied blood oranges."

Pernicious neighed angrily and pawed the floor, then huffed off into the depths of his stall. Koida leaned the broken door up against the wall with its note facing out where someone would find it, then joined Pernicious in his stall.

She gave him a scratch on his forelock, dodged away when he snapped at her with his iron teeth, then let herself out the window and slipped over the garden wall.

She had to get back up the same way she'd left; she couldn't risk a noble spotting her in peasant's riding clothes when she wasn't technically allowed to ride Pernicious. Her father had forbidden it after word got back to the emperor about the half-demon decapitating that stable hand. If her father found out Koida was still riding, he might go so far as to have the half-demon destroyed. In any case, at this hour, the only witnesses would be the low- to mid-level palace servants, and they would never have the opportunity to tell her father. There were too many layers of hierarchy between them and the Exalted Emperor Hao.

Koida scaled the wall as quickly as she could and pulled herself up onto her balcony. A quick check below seemed to confirm that she'd gone unseen. Only a few servants were outside, and none of them were looking up. Ducking down below the level of the wall, she changed back into her nightdress and folded up the riding clothes and boots before hiding them once more behind the loose stone.

Then she slid aside the door and jumped onto the ceiling beam, ready to climb back over the unforgiving stretch of nightcaller floor and fall into her soft, warm bed.

"Little sister, the inji. Now that is a tale I would like to see on her Heroic Record."

Koida dropped from the beam, the shock making her arms numb, and landed in the center of the floor with a shriek of wood on metal.

Shingti sat grinning on Koida's bed in a shimmering green nightdress and embroidered blue silk robe, legs crossed beneath her. A half-eaten tray of buttered rice, quail eggs, spiced bread, and tea rested on her lap.

"Better a sneaking inji than the Lilac of the Valley," Koida said, standing. "Does Batsai know I was gone?"

"Captain Batsai gave me the mother bear glare when I claimed you were in your bed and I could see you, and oh no, Captain, don't bother coming in, Shingti will wake little sister," the first princess finished in a sickly-sweet voice. She grinned. "But he left without arguing when the morning guard showed up. I think the old man was tired."

"Are you eating my breakfast?"

"I had to do something while I waited for you to return. War is hungry work, little sister, and a Living Blade Master's work is never done."

Koida dusted off her feet on the rug, then climbed onto the bed, snatching the chopsticks and bowl of eggs and rice from her sister. The buttery, starchy, yolky concoction lit up her taste buds so strongly that the bottom of her mouth ached. She was starving.

"Father wants me to speak with you." Shingti pulled a bit of crust off the spiced bread and chewed it while Koida shoveled rice and eggs into her mouth. "It's about your training."

Koida froze, then swallowed the large bite. "He wants you to convince me that the eunuchs are right and training at this age will only lead to injury."

"Father knows I trust the eunuchs' word as far as I can throw my dead mother." Shingti offered her the bread. "In fact, I doubt he even hears their endless nattering except as a handy excuse to stop your training while sparing your feelings. He's worried that you're losing face with the court. It's one thing for a princess to be a Ro-cripple, but to keep beating a dead warmount as you're doing can only send bad messages about not accepting one's place in society. He has to think about what that sort of delusion will do to the citizens of the empire if he continues to indulge it—both our native-born and the tribes we've conquered."

Koida took the bread from her sister and dipped it in the yolk. She popped it in her mouth and chewed, the complexity of the spices blending seamlessly with the egg it had soaked up. What Shingti said was true. If one didn't accept their station and responsibility in society, order would quickly break down, and chaos would follow. But if she quit training and admitted defeat, then what else was there for her? She would truly be useless then, without even a hope of contributing honor to her family or her empire.

Shingti poured herself a cup of tea as if she were oblivious to the second princess's brooding, but Koida recognized her sister's silence. Those who didn't know Shingti thought the Shyong San Dragonfly was a creature of constant motion and noise, flitting from conquest to conquest on and off the battlefield, but in truth, this was only one of Shingti's many faces. She could be just as contemplative and still as a wise old tortoise when she needed to, waiting for others to reveal their intentions before acting, as she was now.

"Do you think I should give up?" Koida asked her. "Stop training to save face?"

"You're seventeen, Koida, and you're still struggling with a novice-level weapon. You've gone through six masters in ten years, and you show no signs of advancing. You're Ro-crippled with no prospect for bringing honor to the Shyong San Dynasty through battle. These are all facts."

The tangy bread and buttery rice turned to ash in Koida's mouth. Her sister had never been one to coat the truth in sugared lies, but this morning the truth felt much harsher than she was prepared to deal with. She looked down at her plate, hoping Shingti wouldn't notice that she was blinking back tears.

"I see powerful, skilled fighters killed every time I ride out to face another tribe. I kill most of them." Shingti picked another bit off the bread, then set the larger piece back in Koida's limp hand. "Their Ro is strong, but there's something else missing in them, some reason they lost on the day I won. A will to survive at all costs or a thin moment's loss of focus that allowed me to strike the killing blow. Or maybe it's only luck, and all my thinking about it is senseless. But if it's not luck—if it's will—then I want my little sister to have more of that than anyone else out there."

Koida swiped away a bit of wetness from her eyelashes and looked up at her elder sister.

"I think you should keep training," Shingti said, rolling the bit of bread she'd torn off into a ball, then tossing it into her mouth. She chewed thoughtfully for a moment, then swallowed. "Train every day until you either advance, break yourself, or die. The eunuchs and the court can go eat destrier droppings."

Koida grinned. "What about Father?"

"Leave Father to me." Shingti bounced up off the bed, her long hair jouncing along behind her. "Come on, let's go train. We'll give Lao the day off, and I'll show you the new Soaring Axe Kick I've been working on."

CHAPTER SIX

10 years ago

THE SUN HAD NOT YET BEGUN TO consider stirring when twelve-year-old Ji Yu Raijin climbed shivering out of bed and hurried into his cloud-gray school uniform. He whipped the loose jacket closed over the pants, then tied the pale blue sash around his waist, the color denoting his rank within the Path of Darkening Skies. Raijin and his currently snoring roommate, Yong Lei, had both just advanced to the third tier, the Wind belt, within days of one another. The boys were of an age, born only a few months apart on opposite sides of the Shangyang Mountains. Both had been brought to the school to study the Path of Darkening Skies, and both had moon-marks which could be an ancient rune marking them as the chosen one.

Unlike Yong Lei, however, Raijin could not sleep in until the morning bell. Yong Lei was from a wealthy family of merchants in a port city far to the south. His father's gold secured his place in the school. Raijin had no family, only a mother who had given him up before he was old enough to remember her face. His place in the school depended entirely on being a good and useful servant. If even one day went by where he didn't complete his tasks, he would be dismissed. It had been this way since his sixth year, and it would continue until he was a full Master of the Path of Darkening Skies.

Raijin eased the door shut behind him so as not to wake his friend, then sprinted down the hallway and outside into the icy darkness. A heavy snow had fallen overnight and blanketed the woodpile, pinning the oiled cloth protecting the sticks under hundreds of pounds of frozen precipitation.

He smiled. An inconvenience, yes. But also an opportunity to use his new Wind-level kick.

Raijin sprung onto his hands in the wet snow and whipped his long legs in a circle. Focused jade Ro, glowing in the early morning dark, whistled across the woodpile, blasting snow away. With the weight removed, he flipped up the oiled cloth easily and gathered an armload of wood.

Back inside, Raijin hurried up the stairs to the masters' quarters. He would have to build fires in each residence, then in the kitchens before he began the rest of his morning tasks, but the first fire always went to Master Chugi.

As soon as Raijin slipped inside Master Chugi's door, a gravelly groan came from the bed.

"Morning comes earlier every day, doesn't it, my boy?" The old man was sitting on his mat in the Resting Meditation position—legs crossed, fists over his heartcenter with only a sliver of space between the opposing knuckles—with his blind eyes open wide and his head cocked so that his ear followed Raijin's movements.

"That's what you keep telling me, esteemed elder," Raijin said, grinning. While he spoke, he arranged a nest of kindling in the fireplace.

Master Chugi chuckled, his belly jumping beneath his robes.

"You laugh now," the old man said, feeling around until he found the staff at his side. He would need it if he were to go anywhere. Having been a master at the school for longer than Raijin had been alive, Chugi did not require assistance finding his way around, but he did need a sturdy stick to lean on. "When you're my age, we'll see if you're still laughing."

In one practiced movement, Raijin struck the fire tool with his thumb and dropped the resulting sparks into the tinder in his opposite hand. The dry wisps of beardmoss flared up immediately, and he set the whole thing in the nest of kindling. He fed the growing fire larger and larger sticks until the flames danced merrily in the fireplace.

With the fire warming the room and his favorite master's woodbox refilled, Raijin bowed himself out of the little residence and set to tending the rest of the school's fires.

Fatty, the school's cook, was just yawning his way into the kitchens when Raijin finished stoking the banked cookfire back to life. Still half asleep, the heavyset man grabbed a pair of cold corn buns and tossed them to the boy.

"Thank you, honored chef."

"Extra water today, Raijin," Fatty said around an eye-watering yawn. "Makin' sprout congee for lunch."

"It will be done." He bowed, maintaining eye contact in spite of the fact that Fatty had already begun pulling down ingredients and baking pans.

The water was Raijin's next stop. He retrieved the yoke and buckets—each one half his height and as wide as his shoulders—from the implement shed, then raced down the southern mountainside to the stream that bubbled out of the rocks. Farther down, the stream became a gushing river, but here it was as wide as Raijn's closed fist, and at the perfect height to set the water buckets beneath.

This was one of the few times during his morning tasks that he had a moment's breath to pass, so Raijin dropped into the Resting Meditation position. He couldn't keep his fists as close together as Master Chugi without accidentally allowing them to touch, but the point was not how close together he could bring them, but to clear his mind and focus on the present. He slowed his breathing, concentrating on the pathways the icy air took rushing in through his nose and down his throat, branching past his heartcenter and the Wind-level Ro that danced there like a jade breeze, then filling and circling in his lungs. He contained the air only long enough to warm it, then followed it back out once more as it left his lungs, passing over the heartcenter, warming his throat and the back of his nose, then turning to mist in the icy air. Four of these deep breaths and the first bucket was full. Four more and the second one was finished as well.

It seemed impossible that he could be strengthening his Ro in such a short time, but he knew that having done so every day for the last six years had to have had a cumulative effect. In any case, it wasn't hurting him to practice his meditation, and he had to use that waiting time for something.

The trip back up the mountainside was much slower with the full weight of both buckets pulling Raijin toward the earth, but he didn't try to rush or use Straight Line Gusts. The Wind students had only practiced the speed-enhancing move once, and Raijin couldn't afford to spill the buckets, not on a morning when he had to carry extra water for the school's congee. When he finally could use Straight Line Gusts reliably, however, this water-carrying was going to take much less time.

It took four trips to fill all the masters' washbasins and pitchers and the kitchen's barrel, another to water Fatty's beloved covered garden, and then a sixth to fill the enormous soup cauldron. Raijin was breathing heavily by the final trip, the muscles in his legs and back protesting, but he couldn't slow down. On his way out of the kitchens, Fatty tossed Raijin another bun—this one piping hot and tasting of delicious honey—and then it was back outside to the raw log stack. Raijin had to cut and split enough of the logs into useable sticks of wood to replace what he'd used that day, stacking it under the far end of the oiled cloth so that it could begin to dry.

This was a task that always took longer during the brutal mountain winter, as the school used much more wood. By the end, Raijin's uniform was soaked in sweat, and his arms and back felt like they were on fire.

The first lights of dawn reached into the sky as he laid the last stick onto the woodpile and pulled the cloth over it, leaning a heavy stick on each corner to secure it against the wind.

The morning bell rang a deep-throated peal that echoed down the snowy mountainside.

Raijin laughed in a great puff of white and took off running for the courtyard. That extra trip to the stream had nearly made him late for morning training.

The rest of the students were already assembled in the courtyard when Raijin raced through the door. Yong Lei stood at the far left of the third row with the rest of the Wind-level students, a place at his side saved for Raijin.

At the front of the rows, Master of Training Palgwe was explaining the cultivation of Ro to a newly arrived student, a girl of about five, but speaking loudly enough that everyone could hear him.

"Ro is the force at the center of your being, the base of all spiritual strength and abilities," Master Palgwe explained. "It can be absorbed from other life forms by violence or death, but that is not the way of the school you've chosen. In the Path of Darkening Skies, we do not seek to steal what belongs to others. We seek to better ourselves, to sharpen and strengthen our own Ro through meditation, both resting and martial, and training our bodies to do what no others can do."

Master Palgwe bent to tie on the girl's white Cloud sash, the symbol that she had just begun her training.

"It is not easy," he continued as he knotted it around her waist. "It is like carrying a bear cub up a mountain every day until he is fully grown. He starts out heavy and only becomes heavier, and at times, he grows claws and teeth and attempts to maul you."

Raijin slipped into the empty spot beside Yong Lei and stood at attention, back straight, fists in front of his sash.

"With each new stage comes increasingly more power, but many do not see advancement for years,"

Master Palgwe reminded them all. "For some, progress through the ranks will come sooner than others. Remember, it is not your fellow students you are competing with, but yourself. You strive every moment to become better than you were the moment before."

From the corner of his eye, Raijin saw Yong Lei look at him. With a grin, Raijin swiped one hand across his forehead as if to say *Made it just in time.* Yong Lei chuckled, then clamped his mouth shut tight.

"The Path of—" Master Palgwe broke off in the middle of his customary new arrival speech. The training master's sharp brown eyes closed in on the two of them instantly.

"Student Raijin, student Yong Lei," he snapped, his voice ringing sharply through the courtyard. "Horse Riding Stance."

They dropped into the low stance, feet spread apart, knees bent until they were nearly sitting, fists at their hips, elbows back, eyes forward.

"Recite the Seventy Principles of the Path of Darkening Skies for your fellow students," Master Palgwe ordered.

As one, the boys began. "All life is sacred and worthy of respect in every form it takes. Ro is the basis of life, and to steal it through violence is to steal life. Bloodshed is a last resort, reached only when protecting a weaker life form from a stronger one who will not be diverted by any other approach…"

While they spoke, Master Palgwe crossed the courtyard and pulled something from the racks in the far corner. Yong Lei groaned quietly between principles.

"Self-control is the mark of enlightenment," they continued. "Training the mind to go against its selfish nature strengthens and prepares the body to achieve unnatural feats…"

The training master returned with a pair of brass ring weights in each hand. As they recited, he tethered them to a strong cord, then hung them over the boys' necks. Yong Lei grimaced with the added weight, but Raijin didn't mind. They were heavy, but not as heavy as the water bucket yoke he carried every day.

By the thirtieth principle—"Serve others before self."—Yong Lei dropped onto his backside, unable to hold himself up any longer.

Sweat rolled down Raijin's back and his whole body shook with fatigue, but he clenched the muscles at his core and continued. Beside him, Yong Lei gingerly repositioned himself on his knees and rejoined the recitation.

"Fear no death in the service of others, but life in the service of self."

The longer they went on, the more the fire raged through Raijin's limbs. His voice grew strained, then weak, but Yong Lei's made up the difference, regaining strength as he rested.

At the fifty-second principle—"Adversity builds strength, but indulgence tears it down."—the pale-haired Yong Lei clambered back to his feet and returned to the riding stance. Raijin's muscles were screaming, and he was shaking like a leaf bug in a tornado, but a goofy grin broke out across his face. He huffed an exhausted laugh as they launched into the remaining principles together.

When they reached the final one—"Always strive to improve, refine, and strengthen the body, mind, and Ro."—Raijin's knees gave out, and he tumbled to the ground beside his friend, brass weights clanging on the flagstones. He felt like his body were made of overcooked noodles.

"Attention," Master Palgwe said.

Yong Lei snapped back to attention—legs straight, fists in front of sash, eyes forward. Raijin stumbled onto his feet to do the same. The weights slapped against his chest as he did. His resulting attention was decidedly less sharp than his friend's.

"Now tell us which of the principles you broke," the training master said.

"Respect others above self," Yong Lei answered quickly.

"Wrong."

Yong Lei's forehead creased in confusion.

Master Palgwe turned to Raijin expectantly. The motion made Raijin's head spin, and he had to shut his eyes to keep from falling once more.

"All of them," Raijin answered. He swallowed around a dry throat.

"Correct." Master Palgwe spun on his heel and returned to the front of the ranks. "Every principle in the Seventy relies on every other. Disregard one and the rest will soon follow."

Now at the head of all the students, the training master turned back to face them.

"If the interruptions are finished, it is time to begin the morning's exercises. Cloud students, stay close to me, and do not stray in the mists alone." He looked down his pointed nose at Raijin and Yong Lei. "The two of you will finish out the training with the weights."

With that, Master Palgwe turned and jogged out of the courtyard, the dozen Cloud-ranked students following close on his heels and the higher ranks falling in behind them. The newest students would run only a few miles, a little more distance added each day, until they could run the full hour the older students were expected to before returning to the courtyard for Moving Meditation.

Yong Lei groaned loudly, then ran to catch up.

Raijin shook his head, throwing sweat like a wet hound, then took off at an uneven lope. The weights thumped against his chest. It was going to be a long morning.

CHAPTER SEVEN

10 years ago

THAT AFTERNOON, WHILE THE REST OF the students were gathering their congee and fried bread from the kitchen, Raijin dragged himself into the dining hall and fell lengthwise onto a bench. Every muscle in his body ached and throbbed and occasionally cramped in excruciating pain. The back of his neck felt like the weight cord had rubbed a hole through his skin and into his spine, and he was certain he had a bruise on each side of his chest where the weights had been hitting.

Running had been bad, but Moving Meditation had been the worst. Stepping at a crawl through every hand and foot technique when his body wanted nothing more than to fall apart had made him want to scream. In fact, he'd done it a few times as they neared the end, the shout ripped up from the bottom of his stomach. He'd had to. Otherwise, he felt he would have just collapsed in a heap on the flagstones.

Raijin threw his arm over his face. If one could have nightmares about exercise, today's training was guaranteed to wrench him from a sound sleep.

The dull roar of conversations filled the dining hall. A girl laughed, her voice musical. A bench scraped. Someone argued for spiritual medicine while someone else claimed there was no substitute for demon core stones. The bench was hard beneath him, and too narrow to span his shoulders, but at least he wasn't moving. And without the weights, he felt lighter than air. If he weren't so tired, he thought, he could leap over the Shangyang Mountains.

A clatter on the table above startled him. He must have drifted off for a moment.

"You always get me into trouble," Yong Lei complained.

"Never that much trouble before." Raijin cracked an eyelid and pushed himself up on one elbow. "I think we hurt Master Palgwe's pride, interrupting him in front of the new student."

Yong Lei sat across from him, scooping a spoon into a steaming bowl. When he saw Raijin sitting up, he pointed at the second bowl he'd brought.

"Eat your congee before I do, laughing bird."

Raijin grinned and gave a half bow. "Thank you, sulking horse."

"Why can't you ever break your leg during your morning tasks?" Yong Lei grumbled. "If you missed training one day, I wouldn't get a punishment."

Raijin sat up the rest of the way and took a huge bite of the piping hot, savory rice porridge. Fatty had used chicken and vegetables in it this time. It was one of his best creations so far, imbued with the chef's natural Strength Restoration ability. With the first bite, Raijin felt energy returning to his exhausted body, flowing down the Ro paths and into his heartcenter like cooling

65

rainwater on a hot summer roof. The edge came off the throbbing pain, and the looming threat of muscle cramps dissipated.

"The weights are good for you," he told Yong Lei between bites. "The harder you train, the stronger your Ro will become. And you'll need all the help you can get if you want to advance to Rain before I do."

Yong Lei looked up from his congee long enough to make a rude hand sign, then went back to eating. "Don't be late for afternoon training, servant boy. I'm not saving you a spot this time."

Laughing, Raijin finished off the rest of his rice porridge and bread, then bolted down his water. After returning his bowl to Fatty and thanking the chef for the wonderful food, he raced upstairs to the masters' quarters to find Master Chugi.

Yong Lei might have been joking, but he was also right. Raijin had afternoon chores that needed tending before he could go to afternoon training, and after that morning, he didn't want to risk being late.

CHAPTER EIGHT

10 years ago

THAT NIGHT, RAIJIN LIMPED HIS WAY TO the massive library. It housed every scroll, tablet, and book the Path of Darkening Skies's practitioners had ever brought to the school, knowledge from both sides of the mountain and beyond. If a student did not already know how to find what they were looking for, they could easily spend weeks searching the shelves and sparrow holes for a single text, but Raijin was well acquainted with the stacks. He visited often on his rare days off training and every night before bed, searching for Master Chugi's requests.

He wound his way through the shelves with a demon firefly lantern. No actual fire was allowed in the most prized room in the school. The glowing green bugs flitted around inside the glass globe, their green lights casting an unnatural amount of illumination onto the scrolls and books around him. Each of the scrolls was stored inside a wooden tube with the name of the story or subject of the text carved onto the side and each end, and the books were slipped into special oiled leather packages with the title or subject tooled into the edges and both covers.

As Raijin searched, the smell of rich leather, exotic woods, ink, and parchment curled inside his head like a calming incense. He loved the library, but the last of his strength was waning, and he still had one serving task to complete before he could return to his room and fall onto his bed mat.

It took longer than he would've liked, but finally, he found the book Master Chugi had requested, a bound volume wrapped in dusty leather. The words *Tale of the Thunderbird and the Dark Dragon* had been worked into its covering.

He dusted the book off and tucked it under his arm, then returned the firefly lantern to Master Tang-Soo at the library's central desk.

"Book?" she asked without looking up from her ledger. Green firefly light briefly illuminated her sunken, papery features. The effect was to make her look nearly as old as Master Chugi, though in many lights Raijin had always thought Master Tang-Soo looked young enough to be a sister to Master Palgwe. That could have been her Ro, however. Many masters looked much younger than they were because their cultivations slowed their aging.

"Tale of the Thunderbird and the Dark Dragon, Esteemed Library Master."

"Studying up on what you have to do to become the chosen one?" she asked, holding back her sleeve as she painted the title into the ledger with the precise strokes of a master calligrapher.

"I am bringing it to Master Chugi, Library Master," Raijin said. He didn't add, *Like I do every night.* He wasn't sure the library master paid enough attention to humans to notice that he had been borrowing a different book every night since Chugi began to lose his sight.

Master Tang-Soo nodded, her hair sliding softly over her smooth cheeks with a sound like whispering pages. "Tell him to have it back by tomorrow."

"I will bring it back tonight when he finishes it, Master Tang-Soo." Like he did every night.

Raijin bowed to her, keeping his gaze on her face though she wasn't looking his way. Politeness dictated that he treat every master as if they could strike him dead at any moment, never exposing the vulnerable back of his neck to them, even if they couldn't be bothered to pay him any attention.

This late, the halls between the library and Master Chugi's residence were empty. Everyone had retired to their rooms except for the library master and him. There were days when Raijin didn't want to do his tasks, days when he wished he could just lie in bed and be expelled from the school, but it was silent times like these that he relished the idea of being one of the last people out at night, knowing that in a few hours, he would be one of the first back out again.

Firelight flickered and danced off the walls in Master Chugi's room as Raijin let himself in. Reclining on his bed mat, Master Chugi at first looked to be asleep, but the old man turned expectantly to follow the sound of Raijin's movements as he crossed the room and lit a lantern.

"Did you find it, my boy?" Master Chugi asked in his craggy voice.

Raijin brought the lantern to the old man's side and sat on the floor beside him. Carefully, he unfolded the protective leather covering the paper book.

"The Tale of the Thunderbird and the Dark Dragon, as requested."

"Well, go on," the old man said, waving his gnarled hands impatiently.

Raijin carefully opened and leafed through the paper book to the beginning.

"The chosen one was born in a village at the foot of the rainbird's nesting mountains…"

Master Chugi settled back on his mat and folded his hands over his frail birdlike chest. The old man listened, enthralled, as Raijin read him the story of tragedy, battle, betrayal, love and loss, though it quickly became apparent that Master Chugi was even more tired than he was. The elderly master's eyelids slowly drooped closed, then his mouth eased open. When the sound of throaty snoring filled the residence, Raijin switched from reading aloud to reading to himself. It was the first time he'd read this book, and he couldn't put it down. He didn't see how the Thunderbird would stop the evil Dragon and save the world, but he had to know.

The fire had burned down to glimmering red coals by the time he turned to the final page. One of the embers cracked loudly, shooting off a burst of popping sparks and announcing another coming snow.

On the bed mat, Master Chugi snorted and sat up, his milky eyes wild.

Raijin took up reading aloud midsentence. "…with all his power and all his might, still the Thunderbird submitted willingly to his death, and in doing so, destroyed the Dark Dragon's world-crushing grip."

Master Chugi tucked his feet beneath himself and rested his hands on his lap.

"The end," the old man said.

In the red-tinged light, Raijin closed the book and folded it back into its leather covering.

"The end," he agreed solemnly, rubbing his tired eyes.

"Uh oh," Master Chugi said, cocking his ear toward Raijin. "My good student doesn't like this story."

"No, Master, it isn't that." Raijin searched a moment for the words to express the thoughts whirling through his mind. "This is the prophecy of the chosen one..."

"Yes." Master Chugi nodded. "And you hope you *are* the chosen one. So, what about your prophecy troubles you, boy?"

Raijin struggled again. "Why is it written as if it has already happened?"

"Because the seer viewed it from a point in time when the events of the chosen one's story had already come to pass."

"When the chosen one was already dead," Raijin said.

Master Chugi smiled, revealing his toothless gums. "Ah, now we come to it! The death bothers you."

Raijin shook his head though he knew the blind man couldn't see him. "I don't understand the Thunderbird's decision."

"Raijin, if you are the chosen one, then it is your decision."

"But how can I make the right decision if I don't understand it?" he asked, tracing his thumb across the tooled leather of the book's covering.

"Tell me this," Master Chugi said, leaning close as if to look into Raijin's eyes. "If you are weaker than I, and I kill you, what have I accomplished worth bragging about?"

"Nothing," Raijin answered immediately, disgusted.

"If you are many times stronger than I, and I kill you, I could brag for years, correct?" The old man waved a gnarled hand before Raijin could speak. "In the view of the world, not the Path of Darkening Skies."

Slowly, Raijin nodded. "It would be a larger accomplishment, so naturally, the self would feel inflated pride."

"And you, as the much stronger party, would seek to save face as well as survive my attack. It would impugn your pride to have a weakling destroy you."

"Yes." Raijin gave another nod, though he didn't see where the master was leading him.

"Suppose that you, the stronger party, submitted to the weaker party, allowing yourself to be killed though an entire world was mocking you for weakness while you did, but in doing so your death defeated the Dark Dragon. You would lose face and never live to see your triumph, but your submission would save the world all the same. A moral victory."

Master Chugi put up a hand as if to forestall Raijin from speaking, though Raijin had no idea what he could possibly say to that.

"Now," the old man said, "imagine instead that you gave in to your pride and avoided a shameful death at the hands of one weaker than you, but when you did, the entire world was swallowed up by the darkness in the Dragon's heart. In that case, showing your superior physical strength would reveal a spirit too weak to save the world. A moral failure."

His milky-white eyes searched the area near Raijin's face.

"Could you do that, good student?" Master Chugi asked. "Could you die a ridiculed weakling to prove your strength?"

Raijin closed his eyes and considered the question for several slow heartbeats. The correct answer was obvious, but to blurt it out just to make an old man think he might be the chosen one would only prove it a lie.

Finally, he looked at Master Chugi and asked, "Why did my mother bring me here when I was an infant? Yong Lei's father kept him at home until he was six years old, even knowing he might be the chosen one."

Master Chugi sat back, surprise marking his wrinkled face.

"Raijin, twelve years ago, I laid these failing eyes on a young woman who climbed a mountain with nothing but a baby and a pouch for qajong smoking. She was beautiful beyond description, boy, but already her bloom of youth was beginning to wither under her addiction. Her hands shook, her eyes watered, her teeth clenched. She sweated and stuttered and winced at the touch of the softest breeze. The drug had taken hold, and though she'd managed to go the trip up the mountain without smoking, she wouldn't go the trip back down without it. The baby she left in my arms screamed for nearly two weeks straight. Perhaps it was that he missed his mother and could sense that she was gone, but the baby also sweated and shook and winced in pain at the softest touch as if the poison were in his body as well. The mother who left you at the school was one who had already seen what your life with her would become and had chosen instead to give you a chance at something much better." He raised one gnarled finger and pointed it at Raijin. "Raijin, that same mother wept as she left her son behind. She held her stomach and stumbled away bent nearly in half, sobbing so loud that it sounded as if the mountain's heart was breaking. Many nights, I hear her cries in my dreams, and I wake up thanking this woman for her selflessness. She brought the world the hope of a rescuer, but more precious to me, she brought a son to an old man who had long since given up all hope of experiencing such a joy."

Raijin swallowed hard, glad Master Chugi couldn't see the tears in his eyes.

"I could do it," Raijin said, his voice escaping his throat in a strained growl. "To save someone like that, I could die in whatever way was required."

CHAPTER NINE

Present

THE EMPEROR HAD BEEN IN RESIDENCE for six days before he sent a summons to Koida. The messenger brought the scrolls to the training courtyard where Koida and Shingti were sparring while Master Lao watched on.

"A summons from the Exalted Emperor Shyong San Hao for the Second Princess Shyong San Koida," the man shouted, his voice ringing off the courtyard walls.

Koida looked over her shoulder at him. The messenger knelt and held the scroll above his head, the wooden royal seals tied to it clicking against one another.

"Ah-ha!" Shingti leapt into the air, swinging her ruby bo-shan stick overhanded at Koida.

Koida flinched and nearly tripped over her own feet backing away. She barely brought her stick up in time to protect her face. Her elder sister spun lightly on the ball of her foot and rapped Koida's wrist, hip, and knee in quick succession.

"You're dead, little sister." Shingti scowled, pressing the end of the bo-shan to Koida's throat. "Concede."

Koida swallowed hard, lungs heaving with effort. "I am beaten."

"If your enemy yet survives, you have no business looking away from them." Shingti's stick disappeared as the first princess let her Ro return to her heartcenter. A generous portion of Koida's amethyst stick followed it, the price of losing.

"The message," Koida panted, swiping her sleeve across her face to wipe away the sweat. "It's from Father."

In spite of having been sparring for the better part of the morning, Shingti looked as if she had done nothing more taxing than calligraph a particularly easy character. She flicked her long curtain of brown hair over her shoulder and waved Koida's protest away.

"He's only holding court. I was with him this morning when he had the scribes make the summonses out." Shingti pointed a finger at Koida. "But even if it was an urgent message about the Sun Palace being engulfed in flames, it's not worth dying over."

Koida conceded the point and pressed one hand flat to her fist, bowing to her sister while keeping her violet eyes locked on Shingti's darker ones.

"Thank you for the lesson, elder sister."

"I hope you take it to heart." Shingti returned the bow, watching Koida as she did. The eye contact was just politeness. The Dragonfly of the Battlefield had nothing to fear from exposing the back of her neck to her Ro-crippled little sister. "Thank you for the exercise."

As Koida went to the messenger, Shingti dropped into Dueling Sword Hands, manifesting a pair of wickedly curved, glowing red blades. "Master Lao, would you like a turn at teaching me? No? Batsai, you old bear?"

Hearing the second princess coming, the messenger bowed his head lower and straightened his arms, extending the scroll once more.

Koida took the proffered item and rolled off the royal seals. "Thank you, gracious messenger."

He pressed his forehead to the dirt in acknowledgement of the dismissal, then backed away.

It was exactly as Shingti guessed, a summons to court, identical to the hundred others that must have gone out to the nobles in residence and the surrounding land. Though it was not for the reading of a new law, to bestow rank on a heroic soldier, or to collect an emergency tribute tax from the nobles.

Koida turned back to her sister, who was furiously dueling her way across the courtyard with Jun. His red serpentine spear was not holding up well against Shingti's Thousand Darts of the Dragonfly technique.

"This says a tribe from the Shangyang Mountains is coming to sign the Book of the Empire," Koida said. "I was not aware you and Father had ridden as far as the mountains."

"That's to the southeast," Shingti said. "We haven't even ridden in that direction yet."

Jun stabbed his Spear Hand at Shingti's ribs. She turned aside easily at the last moment, letting the Ro blade sing past, then slapped Jun on the back of the head with the flat of her left sword.

"Dead," she declared, dispelling her Sword Hands. As Jun breathlessly declared his defeat, a portion of his Ro flowed into Shingti's heartcenter, and they bowed to one another. "Thank you for the exercise, skilled soldier. The Spear Hand is a weak technique on its own. Might I suggest developing your High Shield to be used simultaneously as a complement?"

"Thank you, Master Shingti," Jun gasped. "I will act on your counsel."

The first princess joined Koida. "The Ji Yu tribe. They're sending an envoy to negotiate a peaceful alliance with the empire. Father's going to refuse."

"Why?" Koida asked.

"Because they robe themselves in dishonor by refusing to meet on the field of honorable battle," Shingti said, "and by allowing it, the empire would take that stain of dishonor upon itself."

"Perhaps they heard tales of your conquests and decided it was better to join the empire willingly than to be subjugated by force. Wouldn't it be wiser to accept their allegiance without the loss of life a war would entail?"

"And water down our empire with cowards who won't even fight?" Shingti sneered. She leaned over Koida's shoulder and read the scroll. "Father thinks they're coming to beg for mercy."

Koida canted her head a fraction. "But you don't?"

"I think when a coward's words fail, watch for their blades."

"Surely they wouldn't dare attack within the palace walls," Koida said.

"Anyone would do anything that might benefit them, little sister," Shingti said. "That's why you keep a careful watch on enemies coming within striking distance in the name of peace."

力

Hours later, bathed and dressed for court, Koida stood in the hall outside the Citrine Throne Room while the Exalted Emperor and his Dragonfly general were seated. Unlike the White Jade Feasting Hall, there was no waiting room for the royal family outside the throne room, so noble men and women crowded the area, smiling and bowing when they spotted Koida. Several bared their necks—mostly those whom she had offended repeatedly with her cold disregard in her father's absence—a subtle stab at her harmlessness, though they would likely claim it was out of deference to her place as the second princess and say that, like the emperor, Second Princess had the divine right to kill whomever she wished.

"Cousin Koida." Yoichi pushed his way through the crowd to stand beside her. He bowed to her, and she mirrored the motion.

"Cousin Yoichi, I'm so glad you're here."

He glanced around the hall. "Trapped in the shallows with the minnows who've come to eat the moss off the snapping turtle's shell. Think the old monster will snap any of them up today?"

Koida covered her smile with one sleeve. "One always hopes."

"Today, two do," Yoichi said, waggling his pale brows and sending her into a fit of undignified giggles. When she regained control, he nodded into the throne room. "The gossip says that this new tribe is soiling their robes with fear of our Exalted Emperor and his armies, so they've come to bargain their way out of fighting. Think our—apologies, *your*—father will agree?"

The last trace of merriment disappeared at his correction. Koida hated the flash of discomfort she'd seen in Yoichi's eyes, but propriety wouldn't allow her to dismiss his slip of equating himself to the emperor's legitimate children in eavesdropping distance of all these noble ears.

"It would be foolish for my father not to agree, wouldn't it?" she said, still using the cousinly speech to cushion the possessive declaration. "Negotiating in an afternoon what could be won in month's attrition would save time and valuable lives."

Yoichi nodded. "I only wonder what sort of precedent it will set for dealing with enemy tribes in the future. Will it look like cowardice to bow to a weaker tribe's wishes just to avoid the battlefield? A softness and fear of death setting into the Exalted Emperor's bones as he ages?" Seeing the surprise on her face, he hurried to add, "May he live ten thousand years and rule a hundred thousand tribes."

"Shingti believes they are trying to get within striking distance," Koida said.

"Cousin Shingti is wise to be wary," Yoichi said, cupping his chin thoughtfully. The pronouncement was a rare occurrence coming from him. Much of the time, Yoichi and Shingti gracefully avoided speaking to or about one another, a silent rivalry Koida tried to pretend she did not notice. "In truth, we should guard against their words as much as their attacks. Empires are lost just as often to one as the other."

"You think they come with honeyed lies?"

He frowned at the door as if he could see the tribe in question beyond it. "I think we would be foolish to believe anything they say without first seeing proof of its truth."

The throne room doors opened.

At the head of the room, beneath the blood-orange banners of the Shyong San Empire, her father sat on the glittering Citrine Throne. Shingti stood at his right hand in full ceremonial battle dress, her Dragonfly helmet tucked under her arm. At Emperor Hao's left hand sat the smaller and more delicate Amethyst Throne, Koida's official court placement.

"The second princess, Shyong San Koida, Lilac of the Valley," the court speaker intoned.

Yoichi turned to her and offered his arm.

"Might I have the pleasure of escorting little cousin to her seat?" His smile revealed none of the concerns he had just given voice.

Koida took his arm, steeling herself for lies, manipulations, and assassins.

CHAPTER TEN

Present

WHEN THE LOWEST RANKED OF THE NOBLES were finally seated, the eastern door of the throne room opened. The court speaker stepped forward for the last time.

"Chieftain of the Ji Yu tribe, Ji Yu Raijin."

Koida leaned forward in her seat, watching as a trio of strangers entered from the eastern door. A small, graceful woman with dark almond eyes and white cotton wrappings covering her face from the nose down. A wiry foreigner with close-shaved yellow hair like dry summer straw and a scarred, flat face like a demon-baiting hound. And just behind them, a lean man with a curling mop of unruly black hair cut short instead of knotted back in the style of the empire. His jade eyes were as cold as the throne Koida sat upon, and his skin a dark olive, as if he spent most days toiling outside like a servant. His face was a mask of stone.

The three could not have looked more different from one another. Koida wondered what sort of tribe these clearly unrelated people could have formed up in the mountains.

They came to the long aisle at the center of the throne room and stopped, awaiting the emperor's signal.

With ease, Emperor Hao manifested a glowing Ro scepter and extended it.

The woman with the cloth-covered face and the demon-dog faced man stepped to the side, allowing their leader to pass.

The man with the jade eyes approached the throne. Koida noted that his clothing was well made, but simple and sturdy. A loose traveling jacket and pants more akin to a warrior artist's training attire than a noble's court robes.

At a respectable distance, the man stopped and did something no other chieftain had ever done before. He knelt before the emperor and touched his forehead to the stone floor.

A soft murmur ran through the court. The emperor frowned with disgust. In the front row of the nobles' seats, Yoichi had cocked his head, his sharp eyes narrowing. Though Koida couldn't see her sister's face from her seat on the Amethyst Throne, Koida imagined Shingti's had much the same look on it, weighing and assessing. Deciding whether this was a show of craven groveling or flattery hiding treachery.

When the Ji Yu's leader looked up, however, Koida could find no trace of groveling or trickery in his cold gaze. Nor did she find the fear of a leader driven to beg for mercy. The man seemed relaxed, even at his ease before the mighty warrior emperor who had united a thousand tribes and ended a hundred thousand lives. Even stranger, this close she could see that the leader was young for such a powerful position, of an age with Shingti and Yoichi.

"Emperor Hao," the young leader began, his voice a rough baritone that hardly seemed a match for his lean body, as if his vocal cords had been scoured raw with sand. "On behalf of the Ji Yu, I extend to you an offer of peace."

"*You* offer *us* peace?" Hao boomed in disbelief. "As if we feared meeting an unknown mountain tribe on the field of battle!"

"I have no doubt that you harbor no fear of us, having already turned down my requests to negotiate this alliance in private," Ji Yu Raijin replied. "It's a mistake of pride and arrogance. We wish only to protect the lives of your armies rather than allow you to throw them away going to war with us."

The emperor's face grew steadily redder as the young chieftain spoke, and his shoulders rose and fell visibly. A branching vein throbbed in his temple. Koida braced herself for the eruption.

Hao lurched to his feet. As one, the nobles in the closest seats flinched, but the young chieftain remained still and relaxed.

"I agree to allow this negotiation rather than storming your village and wiping you out, and you dare to insult me in my own palace before my court, before my children? Me, Master of the Living Blade, Exalted Emperor, and Originator of the Shyong San Dynasty!" Hao bellowed. His Ro scepter disappeared. "Kill this puffed-up adder."

Immediately, the Emperor's Guard swarmed in from all corners of the throne room, their blood-orange armor clanking and Ro weapons manifesting.

Koida's eyes widened, her heart fluttering like a panicked sparrow caught in a net. She had thought she'd prepared herself for the worst when she walked into court, but this young chieftain was going to be executed before her very eyes. Nothing in her life had prepared her to watch another human die. The very thought made her stomach sink into a black abyss, but she was paralyzed to the spot, unable to turn away or even close her eyes.

The Emperor's Guard attacked. The Ji Yu leader eased to his feet, dodging glowing ruby blades with the slightest turns of his shoulders and head. He sidestepped one here and knocked its owner's arm aside there with a simple palm thrust. Just as another was about to cut him in half, suddenly he was somewhere else. He hardly seemed to move, and yet, like a whirling leaf on a breeze, he never stopped. The best soldiers in the empire could not even graze him.

"Assassin!" Shingti shouted, planting herself between the assassin and the emperor and manifesting a pair of Dual Sword Hands. "Dragonfly Guard, attack!"

At the word *assassin*, nobles who had been looking on in bloodthirsty excitement a moment before broke out in a panic, some climbing over the benches in their rush to put distance between themselves and the danger.

Soldiers in the iridescent green armor of Shingti's Dragonfly Guard ran into the roiling crowd, their Ro blades, spears, and shields glowing ruby as they rushed the assassin, while Batsai and the rest of Koida's personal guard swarmed around her, manifesting their Serpentine Spears and High Shields

The assassin wove through the Dragonfly and Emperor's Guards like water through rocks, using the soldiers' direction and speed against them, evading and circling, finger-striking the weak places in their armor— the side of the neck, below the left arm, in the lower ribs, then the top of the spine in quick succession. One by one, the Ro blades dissolved until the guards were slashing at him with empty fists and bashing with shield-less forearms, still missing the elusive young man. They growled and lunged and missed, and in retaliation, he planted palm strikes in the center of their backs.

The air crackled with sudden cold and frost spread across the guards' armor, covering it in a thin layer of ice. No matter how hard they struggled, they couldn't budge the frozen joints.

Koida used the arms of her throne to push herself up high enough to see over Batsai's High Shield. The assassin's techniques were like nothing she had ever seen. Even Yoichi, whom she assumed was more well-traveled than anyone, looked on with pale brows furrowed and mouth hanging open, as astounded as she was by this strange and powerful fighting style.

With the guards incapacitated, the assassin turned to face the Citrine Throne.

Shingti launched herself at him, her ruby blades thrusting and slashing in the Thousand Darts of the Dragonfly. The assassin ducked under her dancing blades and dropped to the floor, whirling his leg in a sweeping crescent. A flood of brilliant jade Ro gushed across the colorful stone tiles, knocking the frozen soldiers to the floor in a clatter of armor.

It never touched Shingti. The first princess threw herself into the air, flipping over the watery Ro and the assassin. Her Dual Swords flashed as she passed over his head, one at his throat, the other at his heartcenter.

The assassin threw himself backward, landing on his shoulders, then kicking back up to his feet. He spun around to follow Shingti's arc, but didn't attack. Instead he shifted his weight to his back leg, one fist over his head and the other angled downward in front of him.

Shingti landed with the assassin out of reach of her swords. In a blink her Ro became a Long Spear stabbing at his heartcenter.

The assassin moved with a speed Koida had never imagined a human moving, twisting his upper body out of the way of the whipping Long Spear, first one way and then the other. Shingti backed him across the throne room, but before they reached the wall, the assassin swung to the side of a long thrust, wrapping one arm around the glowing ruby haft of Shingti's spear and pulling.

The Long Spear disappeared, and Shingti wheeled herself into the air, swinging a Hook Kick at the assassin's throat. The assassin arched backward, the deadly hooked blade passing overhead, then stepped behind her as the momentum spun her around. He jabbed his fingers into the armor joint at her neck, then below her left arm. Shingti manifested her Dual Swords, striking at him over her shoulders in a reverse Strikes of the Scorpion, but he dodged them, hands flying. The final finger strikes landed in Shingti's lower ribs and the top of her spine.

Shingti's ruby blades disappeared. Koida watched in horror as Shingti threw her arm up to manifest a simple High Shield, but nothing happened.

The first princess was defenseless. If he attacked, the Ji Yu assassin could kill her as easily as plucking a flower.

The assassin moved.

"Don't hurt her!" Koida shrieked, leaping to her feet.

The assassin's head snapped around to meet Koida's gaze. Taking advantage of the distraction, Shingti slammed an elbow into his cheekbone and spun, raising her leg and then slicing it downward at his neck in a bladeless, yet brutal Axe Kick.

The assassin turned at the last moment, the heel of Shingti's boot caressing his sleeve as it passed. Without touching down, Shingti changed the direction of her kick, swinging it back with enough power to shatter his skull. But the assassin ducked the kick, stepping behind Shingti, and struck out with that armor-freezing palm thrust.

Frost crackled, and a layer of ice locked Shingti in place. She screamed, infuriated, and struggled inside her armored prison.

Slowly, the assassin returned to the foot of the Citrine Throne.

Now it would happen, Koida thought with cold, sick inevitability. Now he would kill her father.

Rather than attack, however, the assassin knelt again and bowed three times to the emperor.

"May we speak in peace now, Exalted Emperor?" Ji Yu Raijin asked in that raspy baritone, raising his voice to be heard over Shingti's cursing. "I am not an assassin. If I were, your guards would be dead where they stand. By the principles of your own Path, a portion of their Ro belongs to me for besting them, but I left them with all they have. I tried to allow you to save face by conducting this negotiation in private, but you rejected my offers. Will you accept them now and allow us to discuss a peaceful alliance away from prying eyes and wagging tongues?"

Koida dropped back onto her throne, numb. She looked to her father. Beneath his beard, Emperor Hao's face had gone a shade of crimson that was nearly purple. Slowly, the nobles who hadn't run—or who hadn't run very far—stilled, their eyes searching the emperor's face, waiting for his decision. Even the guards trapped in their frozen armor quieted.

"Every man, woman, and child in my tribe is taught this art," Ji Yu Raijin said. "We can be a powerful ally or a devastating adversary. The choice belongs to the Exalted Emperor."

The vein in Hao's forehead pulsed, and his fists quivered. With what looked to be all the strength in his body, the ruler forced his scowling lips to move.

"Undo whatever you've done to my first daughter and my guards. Then we will discuss this matter of alliance in private."

Jumbled protests bubbled up in Koida's mind, echoes of Yoichi's warnings about honeyed lies and Shingti's suspicions of treachery, but her mouth refused to open.

"Gratitude, Emperor Hao." With a final bow, the young leader stood and nodded to his small entourage.

Together, the Ji Yu man and woman rose from their knees—Koida only then realizing that the two of them hadn't moved once in all of the chaos—and joined their leader. The three went through the motionless guards, executing a slightly different series of palm and finger strikes.

One by one, the ice-locked armor melted, and the guards began to move again, scowling and wary. Each manifested weapons and shields briefly, as if to test that their Ro was theirs again to command, but none attacked. Last of all, the Ji Yu leader released Shingti.

Watching her sister manifest a variety of blades, commanding her Ro as easily as breathing, some faraway part of Koida's stunned mind wondered how Shingti had felt being as powerless for a few moments as she was every day.

"Rong Rong," the emperor snapped at a dumbfounded official, "prepare the day chamber for a closeted meeting with the Ji Yu chieftain. First Princess, attend me."

Shingti bowed. "Yes, Exalted Emperor."

As Emperor Hao, Shingti, and the envoy turned to leave the throne room, the young chieftain looked back. His cold green eyes caught Koida's, freezing her blood as cleanly as his palm strikes had done to the guards' armor.

She shivered.

The doors closed behind them, and the rest of the courtiers scattered to spread the gossip of this day far and wide.

"Much luck, cousin," Yoichi said, coming to her side.

Koida looked her question at him.

"Nothing seals an alliance as effectively as a bride," he explained, "and there's no bride as handy as a second princess."

CHAPTER ELEVEN

Present

THOUGH IT WAS HARDLY EVENING, KOIDA slipped out of the palace and down to the stables. She was still in her court robes and could not go riding without attracting every eye in the valley, but she couldn't stand to go back to her residence and stew. Her hands shook, and her stomach trembled with every breath. The scene in the throne room played over and over in her mind, the moments when Shingti or her father could have been murdered while she looked on, helpless.

In his repaired stall, Pernicious tried to bite and kick and trample her like always. The familiarity of the demonic warhorse's friendly malice calmed her shaking. Koida battled him for a while, then fed him a handful of candied blood oranges and set to currying his thick black coat and brushing out his inky mane, tail, and fetlocks. From time to time, she pressed her face into the brute's side, breathing in his musky brimstone stench and unnatural heat.

Full darkness had fallen outside by the time she finished the impromptu grooming. She was about to begin the ritual struggle to climb onto the back of the half-demon when a slender form filled the stall doorway.

"Little sister will never pass for an inji in those robes," Shingti said, leaning against the wooden planking. "The stealth warriors are shadows in the night, not beacons of silk and jewels."

Koida turned halfway to face her sister. Full-facing would be less rude, but turning her back completely on Pernicious was as likely as not to get her killed.

"Elder sister is finished with the negotiations?" Koida was trying to sound caustically sweet like Shingti, but her anxiety came through instead. "What was the result?"

"In negotiation, their chieftain shows the inexperience of his youth," Shingti said, though she and the young Ji Yu leader were likely the same age. "He only requested one thing in return for allying the Ji Yu with the empire and contributing the required number of warrior artists to the armies of the Shyong San."

Koida's heart sank, but she couldn't keep herself from asking. "What was it?"

"He wants you as his wife."

Koida fell back against Pernicious's wide chest. The beast held his ground, supporting her easily—and shockingly, without attack.

Finally, she nodded. "Cousin Yoichi said it would be so."

Shingti cursed, then came over and hugged her. "When he asked for a princess, I offered myself, but Father refused. He said a second princess was good enough for a man who wouldn't even meet him on the battlefield."

Suddenly, Shingti's eyes flew open wide. She held Koida at arm's length.

"A thousand apologies," she said, giving a sincerely remorseful bow. "Your idiot sister did not mean to speak so offensively of you, treasured sibling."

"No apologies required," Koida replied. Her emotions were wrung too dry to feel pain at her father's slight. "They were Father's words, not elder sister's. What else happened?"

"Father told Ji Yu Raijin that in seven years, if he and his tribe had proven their worth in battle, he could choose a second wife from the court."

Desperate hope glimmered like a guttering coal in Koida's breast.

"I might see someone I know in seven years, then," she said.

Shingti shook her head. "Ji Yu Raijin said that men in his tribe only take one wife, and that you were more than acceptable."

"Good. I hate all those silly noblewomen anyway." A tremor in Koida's voice undermined her blustering, and the vehemence quickly ran out. She swallowed hard. "When?"

For a long moment, Shingti stared at the half-demon warhorse looming in the stall with them. Koida was sure that she saw her sister longing to suggest that she leap on Pernicious's back and never stop riding. It was certainly what Koida felt like doing. In the end, however, they both knew this was the only filial responsibility the Ro-crippled princess could fulfill. She wasn't a warrior. She couldn't ride into battle or command her father's armies like her sister did. But an alliance bride, Koida could be.

"The wedding rites begin tomorrow," Shingti said. "He agreed to the customary week of feasts. There are tribal wedding traditions he wishes to observe as well, but he said they won't interfere with ours."

"Oh," Koida said because she could not think of anything else to say.

Pernicious stamped his feet and whickered with his usual bad temper. Absently, Koida turned, reopening her stance so that she could keep one eye on the half-demon.

"There are no nightcaller floors in the guest apartments," Shingti said. She balled her fists at her sides as if to restrain herself from manifesting Dual Swords. "I doubt Father would mourn the Ji Yu chieftain's death."

Koida's heart beat cold at the thought of her sister alone and at the young leader's mercy.

"No," she said, stroking Pernicious's shaggy black fur. "You've always protected me, elder sister. You've looked out for my best interests and the interests of the empire. For once, I can do the same in your place."

CHAPTER TWELVE

Present

THAT NIGHT, AFTER SHINGTI RETURNED to the palace and Koida rode out, the second princess caught sight of a strange shape in the sky. It reminded Koida of a river ray, with graceful rounded curves and a long, thin tail trailing behind like a stinger. The creature soared through the air as if it were swimming, diving in and out of the clouds. She thought she detected a halo of silvery Ro shining around its edges, but repeated flashes of heat lightning kept her from getting a clear look.

She turned Pernicious away from the city and the forest beyond. Likely every hunter in Boking Iri had spotted the creature as well and would be out that night trying to take down one of the last few demons in the valley for its hide and core stone.

Instead, the second princess and the warhorse went north along the palace side of the river until they came to the wide pool at the roaring base of the Horns, the twin waterfalls that gave the river its name. The area was as deserted as Koida's favorite overlook, but without the height Pernicious hated so much. She dismounted, and the two of them splashed into the churning water, swimming when they could no longer touch bottom.

Though she knew it was dangerous, Koida swam out to the waterfall. Icy spring water poured down on her like a rockslide, battering her down into the pool and forcing her head under several times.

Pernicious's scream cut through the constant rumble of the falling water, and she heard his teeth clack together just behind her. He had tried to bite her and pull her back.

"I'm not trying to commit suicide," she yelled to the beast between mouthfuls of water, though she wasn't sure how true it was. "I just want to see what's back here. Go back to shore if you're scared."

She ducked under the surface, thinking it would be easier without the deluge pounding the top of her head. It was less painful, certainly, but the crush of the falling water tried to force her to the bottom and hold her there. Her court robes were no help, tangling around her feet and weighing her down. She struggled out of them, her lungs burning for oxygen, then kicked away from the sandy floor at an angle, hoping she was pointing away from the waterfall and not back into it.

Heartbeats later, the hammering of the water stopped, and she found herself in a lazy pool just behind the waterfall. A cave had been carved out back there, its ceiling populated by winking blue, violet, and magenta stars.

She pulled herself up on the gritty floor of the cave and lay back, looking up at the multicolored lights. Wool worms, making cocoons for their transformation to silk moths. She shivered. Not only because the silk moths were said to be spirits of loved ones returned from the afterlife, but because her thin, wet underclothes were no protection against the chill of the late fall air.

A chastising equine scream echoed off the stone walls of the shallow cave, making every light disappear at once.

Koida sat up. Pernicious had swum under the waterfall to join her.

"That was dangerous," she scolded. "And you scared the wool worms. Keep your voice down and maybe they'll return."

Pernicious grumbled low in his throat, pawing and kicking and thrashing until he pulled himself up out of the water and joined her on the cave floor. With another angry grumble, the beast shook his huge body violently, shedding water in every direction. Koida covered her face until he was finished. Satisfied, he folded his legs and lay down behind her, activating his Burning Heartcenter ability with a flash of Ro. Fire lit the warhorse from within, showing his every vein, organ, and bone through his skin and making steam rise from his rapidly drying coat. Koida leaned back against her friend, thankful for his added body heat.

After a while, the wool worm stars winked back on. As they watched the lights blink and shift, Koida wondered if there were places this enchanting where her future husband came from or if this would be the last time she saw something so beautiful. The question kept her from dozing off, though Pernicious had no such problem.

When the waterfall began to glow with the gray lights of dawn, the half-demon and the second princess plunged back into the icy pool and swam out of the hidden cave together. Angry gray storm clouds were gathering overhead.

They splashed out of the churning water and dripped all the way back to the Sun Palace. As they raced inside the walls, thunder rolled and the sky opened up, pouring down rain like the waterfall.

Rather than return to the stables, however, Koida directed Pernicious around the palace and beneath the guest apartments, then dismounted. The half-demon whickered softly at her and shook rainwater from his mane, then trundled off in the direction of his warm, dry stall.

Though each room along this wall was equipped with windows, only the grandest had its own balcony. It only made sense that the Ji Yu leader would be closeted there.

Climbing the palace wall here was much easier even in the rain, as the stonework had been maintained to a much less exacting degree than that surrounding the royal apartments. Within a few minutes' time, Koida stood on the balcony, sliding open the door.

The inner chamber was dark, the brazier down to nothing more than glimmering embers and the storm-dampened light of the approaching dawn too hazy to fight back the shadows. It was much smaller than her bedchamber, and furnished with little more than a bed, wash screen, and wardrobe.

Though Shingti had told her there were no nightcaller floors in the guest apartments, Koida couldn't help but test the fixed wood floor with the toe of one boot. It didn't make a sound.

Reassured, she ghosted forward, her damp boots squishing softly toward the bed. She couldn't see the sleeping occupant, only a pool of black shadow like the yawning mouth of some unknown underworld ready to receive the dead.

The memory of the ease with which the Ji Yu barbarian had defeated her sister and the royal guards froze her where she stood.

This was beyond foolish. Any number of disgraces could ruin her and dishonor her family if she were discovered sneaking into the room of the empire's newest ally like an inji assassin, the least of which would be the breaking of an alliance her father had given his word to. She should slip back out by way of the balcony now.

"What are you doing here?" a baritone voice rasped behind her.

Koida spun to find a tall, lean form silhouetted against the stormy gray light. Her heart battered against the wall of her chest as if it were trying to fight its way free.

Should she attempt to manifest a bo-shan stick? No, that was stupid. If Shingti and the full royal guard couldn't best the Ji Yu chieftain with all the bladed weapons at their disposal, then Koida didn't stand a chance with nothing but a silly stick. In any case, she could barely summon the focus to manifest a bo-shan at the best of times. She would never be able to command her Ro while standing face-to-face with this deadly adder.

"Did you come to kill me?" he asked, genuine curiosity in his gravelly voice.

It was his strange speech tone that Koida's mind finally seized on, the strange combination of the familiar inflections of a lover and the guarded undercurrent of an enemy.

"You have no right to speak to me as an equal, Chieftain," she said, attempting to project the authority of her station rather than her fear. She swallowed hard and pulled herself up to full height, still a head shorter than he. "I outrank you by several degrees."

For a thin moment, his head cocked as if he didn't understand what she meant. Then he nodded.

"A thousand apologies," he said, switching to the formal tone of a commoner addressing a royal. "Has the princess lowered herself to visiting the chambers of a mere chieftain in order to kill him?"

She clasped her hands together to still their shaking.

"No, I have come to suggest you make a different demand on the Exalted Emperor."

"And set aside the marriage to the princess?"

"Second princess," Koida corrected. "You couldn't have known that your demand was unwise, and I doubt my father felt compelled to share the truth with you." In fact, she was certain her father would find it hilarious that the man didn't know he had asked to buy the stable's only lame horse. "I'm Ro-crippled. Any heir I produce will taint your line and tribe, either by carrying the deficiency or by being cripples themselves."

The young chieftain was silent for several seconds. When he finally did speak, he chose his words as carefully as if he were picking his way barefoot across a bridge of swords.

"I won't go back on my word," he said.

"Even to the point of disgracing your bloodline?" Koida asked, desperation leaking into her voice. "That's madness."

In a heartbeat, the Ji Yu chieftain closed the distance between them. Koida stumbled backward a step, hands raised in First Defense Position to fend off his attack. Her back pressed against a tapestry covering unyielding stone. She was trapped.

But the young leader only edged between her and the foot of the bed, stalking deeper into the shadows and opening the door to the outer chamber. An angular bar of firelight fell across his features, showing Koida that his hair and clothing were as wet as her own. What had he been doing out in the rain in the earliest hours of the morning?

"Will the princess take her leave by the door or the balcony?" he asked, bowing respectfully to her.

Trembling, Koida slipped past him. The outer chamber was thankfully empty. She let herself out into the corridor, picking up speed with every shaky step as she left that adder's lair behind.

CHAPTER THIRTEEN

7 years ago

RAIJIN WAITED IN ANTICIPATION WITH Yong Lei and the small group of combat students in the snow-blown school courtyard. The best friends had been the youngest students in a century to advance to Sleet, and now, at just fifteen years old, both were on the verge of advancing to Hail. After much discussion, the grandmaster had finally agreed to allow them to join the combat class with the older students of the same rank. Raijin and Yong Lei were the only ones under thirty, but their youth was taken as a sign of great things. To reach such an advanced stage so young must mean that one of them was the true chosen one.

Master of Training Palgwe swept out of the school's portico, his robes parting the snow behind him. He glared at the newest additions to the class.

"Attention."

The boys and the older students all dropped into the attention position, backs straight, fists in front of belt, eyes straight ahead.

"I argued against adding children to the combat training," he said. "What we do here can easily be misconstrued as condoning violence against another. Far from it. To steal Ro by fighting and killing is a coward's path, the lashing out of a toddler demanding a shiny toy he has no right to." He turned on his heel and paced away. "However, there will be times in your path when an aggressor will refuse to be deterred. Student Raijin, tell me when it is permissible to enter combat."

"To protect someone weaker than yourself or weaker than the aggressor, Master Palgwe," he answered.

"Student Yong Lei, what methods should one attempt first?"

"Everything possible, Master Palgwe," Yong Lei responded. "Reasoning, calming, distracting, befriending, and bribery."

Palgwe stopped pacing and turned to face Yong Lei, one dark brow raised.

"Bribery?"

Yong Lei grinned. "If you've got the money, Master."

Raijin bit back a laugh, but a few of the older students chuckled outright.

"This is no joke," Master Palgwe snapped, glaring from one boy to the other. "This class teaches the art of pitting one's skill against another's in a fight to destruction or death. What you learn here must be your last resort if you are to remain on the Path of Darkening Skies. Once you have deviated by lifting a hand in malice, greed, or revenge, your Ro will be forever tainted. There is no return from that."

This sobered the boys long enough for Master Palgwe to begin the lesson.

"Today we learn a basic Receive Strike and Return Strike drill," the training master said. "One partner will attack—without making contact!—and the other will *receive* the blow with a force-dissipating block." He raised his hands out in a ready position, then pulled them backward to his chest as if catching something. "Then they will *return* with their own attack." He snapped his hands forward in a double downward strike, a sudden blast of wind slamming into the ground before him, blasting away the snow and slicing twin lines into the flagstones. "Again, without making contact! These drills are designed to train your body in the correct speed and motions for real fights, but executed improperly, they can become deadly. Your focus and caution is paramount."

With a last look around the courtyard, Master Palgwe tucked his hands into his sleeves.

"Partner with another student," he said.

When Raijin and Yong Lei paired up, Master Palgwe rolled his eyes.

"Take your fighting stance."

The class shouted as one, raising their hands into Inviting Attack and shifting their weight to the balls of their feet.

"Begin."

Like the older students, Yong Lei and Raijin began to circle one another. Unlike the other students, Raijin shifted his hand position slightly, going from Inviting Attack to Begging Mercy. Yong Lei grinned and shifted to Demanding Attack. There was no name for the position Raijin made in response, but if it were to have one, it would have been called Screaming Hands.

Yong Lei broke first, letting out a sharp snort of laughter. That set Raijin off and attracted Master Palgwe's furious attention.

Soon they both had brass weights hanging over their shoulders. It was not an unfamiliar situation for either of them.

Moving through the kicks and hand techniques at full speed with the weights on, however, was new. Before they had only practiced the slow, deliberate series of techniques as Moving Meditations. It was much different racing through the strikes, blocks, and kicks against another student. The weights bumping against his chest only added to the strangeness.

They soon fell into a rhythm, however. Raijin and Yong Lei struck and received back and forth in their little corner of the courtyard. Hair-thin projectiles of melting ice sliced toward Raijin as Yong Lei executed Driving Sleet. Raijin leapt into the air, spinning out of the way, then received the strike with a double-palmed warm blast of Changing Air. He returned with a series of Driving Rain kicks that Yong Lei slipped and diverted with a Shield of the Crescent Moon, the first block any Darkening Skies student learned. They plied one another with more and more advanced techniques, laughing and occasionally making faces at one another.

Then Yong Lei wiggled his brows at Raijin, turned his back to his friend, and did a backflip. When he landed, his back foot shot out in a Torrential Downpour. It wasn't focused enough for the Ro droplets to do more than sting Raijin's skin. As they landed, Raijin saw his opening for a surprise attack. Yong Lei was facing away and leaning too far forward, unstable on his single rooted foot. Grinning, Raijin bent one leg and swept with the other, executing a perfect Landslide.

The flood of jade Ro swept Yong Lei off his foot. He gave an undignified squawk of surprise and wheeled his arms, but couldn't catch his balance. He slammed flat on his back with a *thud,* his head bouncing off the flagstones.

Raijin leaned in with his hand extended, expecting to help his friend up and receive a few laughing insults before Yong Lei tried to return the favor, but Yong Lei's eyes were closed.

In fact, he wasn't moving at all.

"Hey." Anxiety tingled along Raijin's spine and up the nape of his neck. He shook his friend's arm, but it fell limp beside him. "Yong Lei?"

A sparkling cloud of golden Ro drifted from Yong Lei's heartcenter into the air.

"Master Palgwe!" Raijin's voice cracked.

The training master looked over from instructing a pair of older Sleet students. When he saw the Ro leaving Yong Lei's chest, his eyes doubled in size.

"Everyone close yourselves off," he barked, blurring into a Straight Line Wind sprint. "Raijin, get back!"

Raijin stumbled out of the way, focusing on closing the Ro pathways into his body, another of the first defenses any Darkening Skies student learned in order to protect their heartcenter from tainted Ro or the invasion of evil spirits.

Robes flying like stormy gray wings, Master Palgwe vaulted over Yong Lei, whipping his hands in a spherical technique Raijin had never seen before. The air in the courtyard crackled with the sudden bone-snapping cold. A dome of ice grew over Yong Lei and the Ro, trapping both inside. Real ice, not Ro in the form of ice.

Master Palgwe landed on the opposite side of the dome.

"Class dismissed—except for Raijin." The training master straightened his robes and tucked his arms into his sleeves. "Stay blocked to the Ro until you've made it inside the school. Ming, you will stay posted at the door and let no one through until Grandmaster Feng or I dismiss you. Tae Fin, find the grandmaster and tell him what's happened."

"Yes, Master!" The designated students broke into a run while the others simply walked inside, murmuring amongst themselves.

The older Sleet-level students did not hold Raijin's attention long. Through the cloudy walls of the icy dome, he could see a distorted image of his motionless best friend. The mass of golden Ro drifted along the walls as if searching for an opening.

"Master, is Yong Lei… Did I kill him?"

"Not if the Ro returns to his body." Master Palgwe lowered himself into the meditative position, face turned toward the dome. "Keep yourself blocked to it. Come. Sit."

Raijin followed the training master's order and joined him. He felt heavier than a millstone when he dropped into Resting Meditation, but he held his fists close together over his heartcenter. Already his blocked Ro pathways were sparking and prickling. They did not like to be blocked off for long. Perhaps they could even sense the unprotected cloud of Ro just feet away.

He closed his eyes and tried to focus his breathing, but his gaze kept returning to the dome and the golden light glinting around inside.

Was it the sheet of ice's interference or had Yong Lei's skin taken on the grayish tone of winter skies?

After a time, Grandmaster Feng strode out into the courtyard, his wispy white hair trailing behind him like lines of spider silk on a breeze.

Still struggling to hold his Ro pathways closed, Raijin knelt and pressed his head to the flagstones. The grandmaster ignored him, instead examining Yong Lei through the icy dome, then turned to Master Palgwe.

"If he dies, have this one carry him home," the grandmaster said, stabbing a beringed finger at Raijin.

Master Palgwe gave a seated half bow. "Of course, Grandmaster."

Without another word, Feng swept back into the school.

Raijin's heart thundered painfully at the thought of bringing Yong Lei's corpse to his family. Scenes unfolded in his mind of screaming accusations, weeping women, and furious men.

Before he could dwell on it for very long, however, Master Palgwe spoke.

"You are strong and fast, Raijin. You learn techniques and master them within days, so easily that at times your training seems a game to you. You haven't yet been forced to take the Path of Darkening Skies seriously." Palgwe flicked his long braid over his shoulder. "Wise elders say that we all practice our own art and walk our own path. You find humor everywhere, Raijin, it is your nature. In this way, you have made the Darkening Skies your own Path—but this is to your detriment."

The training master paused as if giving Raijin a chance to speak, perhaps to argue, but Raijin remained silent. Though blocking oneself off was easy to do at first, it was hard to maintain for an extended period of time. The closed Ro pathways in his body were screaming like lungs too long without air. His mind wanted to ignore the training master's words and focus only on keeping them blocked, but he forced himself to pay attention.

Inside the dome, the golden Ro roved the walls frantically. Yong Lei still didn't move.

"We do not practice martial arts to give in to our nature," Master Palgwe said. "We train our bodies and our minds to do the unnatural. Through the control of the self, we become stronger and make ourselves worthy of the great power this path brings. You must learn to control your nature, Raijin, or you will no longer be a part of this school. Do you understand?"

"Yes, Master," he said in a strained voice. Speaking while blocked took a great effort, as the mouth was one of the many Ro pathways in the body. Raijin couldn't believe the training master had spoken for so long without any noticeable effort.

Master Palgwe nodded, then lapsed once more into silence.

Time passed. The sky clouded over, and a misting autumn rain began to fall, dampening and dissolving the fluffy drifts of snow around the courtyard. In time, all had melted under the steady precipitation. The droplets alighted on the hairs of Raijin's shaking forearms and plastered his unruly black hair to his head. He should have been slowly freezing to the ground, but the effort it took to keep his pathways blocked had him sweating. His muscles twitched and spasmed, and his skin steamed in the chilly rain. Master Palgwe said nothing further, a kindness since Raijin wouldn't have been able to answer without losing control of his blocks.

A glance at the training master showed that Palgwe had one arm overhead in a Shield of the Crescent Moon, protecting himself from the rain. He made it look no more strenuous than lifting the lid of a teapot.

Raijin returned to focusing on himself and watching the dome. Obviously, there was a reason Palgwe was a Master of Darkening Skies.

Just when Raijin's heart began to stutter and his chest began to heave as if he were drowning, the Ro inside the dome slid from the walls and rolled onto Yong Lei's chest. Golden light flickered then disappeared as the boy in the ice reabsorbed the escaped Ro into his heartcenter.

Hope burning like the sun in his throat, Raijin looked at the silent training master.

Palgwe's shoulders slumped with relief, and he let out an inaudible sigh. "He's going to live. You may unblock your pathways, Student Raijin."

Raijin let the blocks go all at once, then collapsed backward, his legs and arms flopping out like the vines of a treestar.

When he pushed back up onto his elbows, Master Palgwe was standing, his legs bent in Horse Riding Stance. With the heel of his palm, he struck the dome. The ice sublimated into a gust of steam and blew away in the chilly air.

Yong Lei sat up, blinking and rubbing the back of his head.

"What happened?"

"You were almost killed," Master Palgwe said. "Due in no small part to your own encouragement of Raijin's foolishness."

Yong Lei's eyebrows shot up toward his peaked hairline.

Raijin got to his knees and pressed his forehead to the flagstones by Yong Lei's side.

"Apologies, beloved brother. I was careless and stupid." He bowed again and again, so grateful that his friend was alive. He wanted to laugh and scream and grab Yong Lei by the shoulders and shake him, but the master's words about controlling the self sounded in his head once more, and he force himself to hold those impulses off.

"It's nothing," Yong Lei said, pulling Raijin up by the arm. "Come on, Raijin. Stop that. You're forgiven."

"Innumerable thanks, beloved brother."

"I'm serious." Yong Lei laughed. "Stop the funeral talk or I'll take back my forgiveness."

Raijin sat back on his heels, trying and failing to suppress a wide smile.

"Student Yong Lei, Student Raijin will accompany you to the physicians' hall." Master Palgwe collected the ring weights from around the boys' shoulders. In the chaos and worry, Raijin had forgotten he and Yong Lei were wearing them.

On the verge of exhaustion, but lighter than he'd ever felt, Raijin rose and helped Yong Lei to his feet.

"Student Raijin," Palgwe said, hanging the weights back on the appropriate racks, "as punishment, you will be caned nine times before the entire school tonight."

Raijin bowed solemnly over his fists. "Thank you, Master."

As he helped Yong Lei toward the door, his friend mumbled, "*Nine.* That's rough. Imagine what they would have done if you had killed me."

"Nothing," came Master Palgwe's reply across the courtyard.

"My apologies, Master. I did not mean to be overheard," Yong Lei said with his typical lack of shame.

The boys limped into the school, leaning on one another.

When Yong Lei was sure they were out of earshot this time, he said, "Can you believe that? Nine canings for almost killing me, nothing for finishing me off." He shook his head. "What am I, a burden on society?"

Raijin thought he understood, however. To live with the knowledge that his arrogance had killed his best friend and he had received no punishment in return—that would have been much worse.

CHAPTER FOURTEEN

7 years ago

THE ENTIRE SCHOOL GATHERED IN THE courtyard that night after supper, everyone from the newest Cloud-level student to Grandmaster Feng himself. Fat drops of cold rain spattered from the sky and slapped against the flagstones, turning the dips worn smooth over the years by thousands of feet into dark puddles that reflected the occasional lance of lightning crossing in the sky.

Sheltered from the rain beneath her own Shield of the Crescent Moon, Master Lengu, the smooth-faced elder in charge of discipline, read a recounting of Raijin's transgression, then his sentence.

"Sleet-level student Ji Yu Raijin is to receive three canings on the palms of his hands, three canings on the soles of his feet, and three canings on his back, for a total of nine. One for each level of the path he has chosen. Do you accept this punishment, Ji Yu Raijin?"

Raijin bowed over his fists. "Yes, Master Lengu."

"Hold out your palms."

He did as instructed.

Master Lengu held up the cane. With dispassionate efficiency, she administered the three strikes to Raijin's hands, the water-soaked bamboo bending nearly in half before straightening out with a furious crack across his palms. Angry white welts rose up immediately, burning like handfuls of live coals, the pain burrowing down into the meat of his palms.

He held his shaking hands open to the icy rain, letting the cold drops soothe the stinging. The small comfort was short-lived.

"Kneel with the soles of your feet facing me," Master Lengu said.

In the grim line of school masters beneath the Shields of the younger masters, Chugi tensed each time he heard the whistle of the cane slicing through the air and flinched at the crack followed by Raijin's strangled cries. He loved the boy like a dear grandson, but knew that this hurt was necessary. This was the first of many growing pains. Without them, Raijin could never become the man he was meant to be.

As the rain picked up, Master Lengu was forced to raise her voice to be heard. "Stand, take off your uniform jacket, and present your back."

Raijin did as he was told, his feet screaming in agony as the soles pressed to the stone and his hands shaking violently as he fumbled with the knot in his wet Sleet-gray sash. Each flex and movement of his fingers sent new waves of pain cutting through his palms like phantom cane strikes. Within him, the Ro roiled and churned like violent storm clouds about to burst.

There was no spare fat across his lower back to pad the blows, and the final three strikes drew blood. The moment the last one landed, multiple tongues of lightning forked across the sky overhead and a fervent peal of thunder shook the courtyard. Several of the students and a few of the younger masters jumped.

At the center of the courtyard, Raijin dropped to his knees. This, he realized, trying hard not to laugh, was the only place he could drop without angering any of the cane welts. His entire body was humming with Ro, and he felt himself teetering on the edge of explosion.

In one huge relieving rush, waves of bone-shattering cold began to radiate from his heartcenter and wash down his limbs. The courtyard disappeared, replaced by a sparkling haze of jade energy. At the very edge of his consciousness, he felt small, hard pellets drumming on his skin.

Hail.

He was advancing.

This time, Raijin couldn't hold back the laughter.

Across the courtyard, Grandmaster Feng frowned, a forehead crease marring his otherwise lineless, ageless face.

"Well, we can safely eliminate this reckless child from the list of potential chosen ones," he drawled.

A few of the masters chuckled at his comment, and others hurried to agree. The grandmaster ignored them.

"Many hear foolishness in a child's laughter," Master Chugi said, leaning on his staff. "Few can see the wisdom that lies beneath. But when an entire world is foolish, what more appropriate response than to laugh?"

"You dote on the boy because he was given into your care," the grandmaster said, stroking his white beard.

"It is as the grandmaster says," Chugi agreed, nodding his wizened head. "But one truth does not preclude the other."

"Clever words hung on hopes don't make a chosen one," the grandmaster said.

Positioned behind the two bickering elders, Palgwe abstained from comment. As one of the school's younger masters, he had the task of sheltering Grandmaster Feng and the blind Master Chugi from the rain with his Shield of the Crescent Moon. Palgwe watched Raijin's still form as the raindrops battering it bounced up and turned into hail before pelting him once more. In Palgwe's mind, however, he was hearing Rajin thank him for the punishment with a maturity and understanding he'd not seen in a student so young before.

To himself, Palgwe thought Master Chugi might not be far wrong. If the boy survived his progression to the next level, he just might be the chosen one.

CHAPTER FIFTEEN

7 years ago

RAIJIN AWOKE LYING FACEDOWN ON A raised bed in the same physician's wing he'd helped Yong Lei to only hours before. His hands were bandaged loosely over an amber medicine that smelled like cedar sap, and he could feel more bandages on his back and feet. Layers of woven blankets were draped over his sweat-soaked body, but the one closest to his skin was half-frozen stiff. On the floor beside the bed, Yong Lei sat in Resting Meditation.

The melting ice in the blanket fibers groaned as Raijin pushed himself up onto his elbows, fists balled loosely to keep from angering the cane welts any more than necessary. Unfortunately, curving his spine irritated the welts across his lower back. He hissed through his teeth. He thought he could feel at least one start bleeding again.

Yong Lei's eyes popped open, and his face lit up.

"The showoff is awake." He closed his eyes again and pretended to go back to his meditation, but he was clearly fighting off a smile. "If I'd known all it took to advance to Hail was being caned, I would've almost killed you unconscious ages ago."

"If you do it now, you'll seem like a mirror-mimic," Raijin said.

"I know. I'll have to come up with something else to get in trouble for." Yong Lei cracked an eyelid and nodded at a scroll by the bed. "You've got a message. One of the Winds brought it from Grandmaster Feng."

Gingerly, Raijin picked up the scroll and unrolled it, trying to move his fingers as little as possible.

Congratulations on your advancement. You are the youngest student to reach Hail level in the history of the Path of Darkening Skies. Your daily serving tasks will be awaiting you as always tomorrow morning.

With a groan, Raijin let the scroll drop and pressed his face into the bed.

"What's the matter?" Yong Lei asked.

Raijin handed him the message.

As he read it, Yong Lei's brows came together angrily. "You can't do servant work like this. My father wouldn't even work a borrowed ox like that. It's not fair."

Raijin shrugged, then winced when the motion pulled at his lower back. From past experience arguing with Yong Lei, he knew it would be senseless to try to explain how rarely fairness entered into the ebb and flow of real life.

"I'll just have to do them," Raijin said, setting his jaw. "If I don't, I can't stay at the school. That was the agreement."

"That's what you get for progressing." Yong Lei tossed the scroll aside angrily. "Good job, your reward is more work."

Raijin laughed.

Soft footsteps approached his opposite side. He turned his head to find the physician Akidori marking on a piece of parchment clipped to a wood tablet and lowering herself to kneel by his bed.

"Physical and spiritual exhaustion," she said. "You overworked yourself. Have you eaten anything today?"

"Not since lunch," Raijin admitted. "I was too nervous to eat supper."

"You should have eaten if you were going to advance. Your body needed the fuel."

"I didn't realize I was going to advance." And he'd been anxious enough about being caned that he thought he would throw up anything he ate.

She grunted and scribbled something on the paper. When she finished, she reached into a pouch on her belt and pulled out a pale orange-yellow pill.

"One sunbright pill. Take by mouth and integrate until fully consumed. Usually requires about twelve hours for full integration."

"Sunbright?"

Akidori glared at Raijin as if angry that she had to look up from her writing.

"It mimics the effects of the sunbright serpent's core stone," she said, shoving it between his lips. "They're not as strong as the real demon core, but they're easier to make than to harvest, and they don't require killing a beast. It took years of study to develop these, and they're so valuable and coveted that only the most gifted and trusted of the physician's apprentices are entrusted with the responsibility of bringing them to the newly advanced."

Raijin swallowed hard, forcing the pill down. It tasted like grapefruit and sunlight.

"Does it speed healing?" he asked hopefully. Chopping wood and carrying water were going to be nearly impossible as he was.

"No, it's to purge impurities and diseases from your body and to refine your Ro. It's customary for every Hail student who survives the progression." She rose to her feet, scribbling on her parchment as she turned to go. "A bath will be provided for you when you're finished. You'll need it."

"Gratitude, wise physician's apprentice," Raijin said. He could still feel the pill sliding down his throat like a stone. It was currently in the stretch between his collarbone and his sternum.

Akidori did not look back. "Integrate that pill."

Raijin let his face rest on the softness of the bed once more. He was the youngest student to progress to Hail in history, and he still might be kicked out in the morning.

He turned his head to face Yong Lei.

Yong Lei snapped his eyes closed and pretended to be meditating.

"I admire your commitment to this joke," Raijin said.

"Gratitude," Yong Lei said without opening his eyes.

"How many hours is it until morning bell?"

"Eight."

Akidori had said it usually took twelve to integrate the sunbright pill. But he didn't have twelve hours. On a good day, his serving tasks took at least two hours.

Wincing at the pain in his hands, feet, and back, Raijin sat up on the bed and got into Resting Meditation position, legs crossed, back straight, fists over his heartcenter. The welts in his back felt tight and burnt, and they pulled painfully at the slightest motion. It hurt to close his swollen fists, but he found if he held them perfectly still once they were closed, he didn't cause any new irritation.

He focused on the location of the sunbright pill. It had reached his sternum, just inches higher than his heartcenter. With a focus of will, he sent a thread of Ro to seek out the pill. When the two touched, the sunbright popped like a spark from a fire in wintertime, splitting in two, each progressively smaller spark popping in turn. He sent out new threads to each of the popping sparks, pulling their power into his heartcenter and integrating them into his body.

As he began to draw the sparks in one at a time, his body heat increased until he felt certain his brain would boil. He split his focus, drawing the sunbright sparks in with one level of his attention and using the Sleet ability Dropping Temperatures to keep himself from combusting.

Impurities began to seep through his skin, stinging the welts on his hands and feet and burning like acid in the wounds across his lower back, but he couldn't stop. He couldn't leave the pill unintegrated and hope to accomplish his daily tasks. The sunbright would cook him alive from the inside out. He had to finish integrating it into his body before dawn. He swallowed past a suddenly dry throat and sent out more tendrils of Ro, trying not just to keep up with the multiplying sparks, but to get ahead of them.

At some point, he was aware of Yong Lei leaving. Another set of footsteps, which sounded too soft for his best friend and might have been Akidori, returned and then left. Then again. There were so many sparks by then that Raijin couldn't comprehend the number and send Ro after them at the same time. He just kept his focus on doing what had to be done.

Finally, with innumerable strands of Ro anchoring every single spark, the sunbright stopped dividing. Slowly, carefully, Raijin pulled the Ro back toward his heartcenter. It felt as if he were dragging tiny shards of broken glass along his pathways, but he didn't let go.

The first sunbright spark dropped over the edge into the churning Ro at the center of his being, lightening the load an infinitesimal amount. With it, his Ro grew stronger, brighter. The second followed, lightening the drag again and brightening his Ro. With each new spark he integrated, he sped up. Pulling them along still hurt, but the flare of intensifying Ro was well worth the pain. And then he was dragging them in by the bunch.

The last spark integrated, and his Ro flared in his heartcenter like an exploding star. He opened his eyes, grinning. He felt invigorated. As if he could run through his chores twice at top speed, then every single exercise and technique with the weights—twice the weights!

His grin slipped as a fetid odor like a tannery pit topped with rotting peaches reached his nose. His robes were stained black with expelled impurities. He wiped some off his cheek with his fingers and grimaced in disgust. It was gritty and oily at the same time.

Akidori, passing in her rounds, stopped and stared at him.

"You're finished integrating the sunbright? Already?"

"Did I miss the morning bell?" he asked, wiping the black sludge on his already ruined uniform pants.

"You still have an hour and a half before it rings."

One and a half hours. His mind tried to panic at the thought, but he pushed the worry away. Either he would finish his tasks in the allotted time or he would fail. Fearing the tasks themselves was of no use.

Meanwhile, Akidori recovered herself enough to begin scribbling frantically on her parchment again.

"How do you feel?" she asked.

"Disgusting. You mentioned a bath."

"Of course." She hustled away, still writing. "La-Min! Oni! Bring the impurities bath!"

Twenty minutes later, Raijin limped out into the early morning darkness wearing a fresh gray uniform damp at the shoulders from his still dripping hair. But as he came to the shed where the yoke and water buckets were stored, a moving shadow startled him.

Demon beasts occasionally migrated up from the forest below and attacked unwary students. With a wince, Raijin dropped into a fighting stance, adrenaline flooding his body and Ro coursing through the sunbright-raw pathways.

The shadow stumbled out of the shed with a clatter of metal on wood.

"These things are ridiculous. I can't believe you have to fool with them every day," Yong Lei said. He adjusted the yoke on his shoulders. "Now, where do I get the water from?"

CHAPTER SIXTEEN

Present

BATSAI AND JUN WERE UNDERSTANDABLY surprised when Koida entered the outer chamber from the hall door rather than her bedchamber's door. They stared in confusion for a moment before the older man jumped to his feet.

"Where have you been?" he demanded, sharp eyes scanning her for injury and finding only mud, rainwater, and disarray. "Out riding that hot-headed demon monster, trying to kill yourself? I've half a mind to turn you over my knee and give you the beating you deserve!"

Koida's mouth fell open.

Then she launched herself across the room and into the gruff old captain's arms, hugging him with all her strength. He smelled like hardened leather armor and the parchment of old scrolls, and she loved him with all her heart.

Gradually, the shock seemed to wear off, and Batsai returned her hug.

"Will you still be the captain of my guard when I'm married?" she asked, her voice trembling.

"Your father is my emperor. It will be for him to decide whether I follow you to your new home or remain in his service," Batsai said, rubbing her back with a calloused hand. "But if he decides against it, I may have to resign and become a wandering warrior." He patted her roughly. "Wandering to wherever little dragons might go, watching over them."

She nodded against his chest, the fear finally starting to dissipate. If Batsai was with her, then nothing could harm her, not even chieftains with demonically powerful Ro. Batsai would never allow it.

Though Koida desperately wished to curl up in the safety of her bed, there was no time. Her wet riding clothes were barely stripped off and replaced by a dry nightdress when Batsai knocked at her inner chamber's door.

"Your ladies in waiting are here to prepare you for the first night of your wedding," he said through the door.

The bottom fell out of Koida's stomach.

"Let them in," she whispered, then had to clear her throat and repeat herself loud enough to be heard.

"Hyung-Po and Qin have also arrived to take over for Jun and me," Batsai said. "I'm going to get some sleep, but I'll be back before you leave for the feast."

Koida pressed her palm to the door. "My thanks."

A moment later, her ladies fluttered in like a flock of excitable birds, chirping and flitting about with armloads of fragrant oils, jewelry, skin paints, and fabric. They threw open the balcony door and built up the fire in her brazier, filling the room with light and warmth as they worked.

In the valley, the week of wedding feasts was traditionally seen as an opportunity for the bride's family to show their power and wealth in a display that rivaled any send-off or receiving home of the armies. They brought in the best of foods both from the valley and imported from exotic lands, the most sought-after performers, and extravagant decorations, and they provided sumptuous treatment, not only for the guests, but for the bride and groom as well.

The preparations for the night lasted much of the day. Every luxury of pampering and dress was lavished upon Koida. A silkwater bath to soak in, fragrant oils massaged into her skin and combed into her long brown hair, ground icestone-based skin paint. Tiered white, violet, and green jade necklaces, platinum coils for each of her fingers, and a matching set of platinum bell cascades for her hair. A flowing robe woven of the softest silk, dyed to match the iridescence of a peacock feather.

Koida tolerated the ministrations without protest or comment. Her mind was elsewhere. Was the Ji Yu chieftain undergoing the same indulgences? Thinking back on their interaction just hours before, she had a hard time imagining him doing something as mundane as bathing or dressing. He seemed less like a human to her and more like a demon beast, a wild creature that would attack and kill at the slightest provocation.

Worse, she recalled Shingti telling her that this demon's people only took one wife. If they didn't keep harems, either, that meant she would be the sole focus of his marital attentions. She had always looked forward with excitement to the day she would be intimate with an imagined perfect husband, but now her stomach turned. What sort of awful things might she have to endure at the hands of a creature who could freeze people with a single palm strike? A creature who now knew that he had been swindled by her father into accepting a deficient wife?

"Is the second princess cold?" one of the ladies asked.

Koida realized she was shivering hard enough to jangle the bell cascades in her hair.

"No." She swallowed and spoke with more certainty. "No, I am fine."

The lady nodded and returned to winding the coils around Koida's fingers.

The sound of Batsai's return in the outer chamber was both a great relief and a cause for a new wave of terror. The hour had come.

The ladies helped her slip on the platinum-trimmed shoes, then opened the doors. Koida imagined them as stable hands opening Pernicious's stall so that he could race out into the night. She straightened her shoulders and stepped out.

In the outer chamber, Batsai stood in his shining dress armor with a scowl on his face. The old bear sniffed and looked away, his dark eyes wet.

A different type of panic jolted Koida's heart. She'd never seen Batsai cry before.

When she reached his side, she leaned in close and whispered, "What's wrong?"

"Nothing," he growled. "I didn't expect this day to come so soon is all." He cleared his throat, then spun on his heel. "Fall in!"

The rest of Koida's escort, their ceremonial armor polished to a dull glow, jumped into action, startled out of their awed gawking by the razor's edge in Batsai's order.

Silently, the small procession made their way out of Kodia's residence and through the winding corridors to the royal waiting room outside the White Jade Feasting Hall.

The emperor, Shingti, and Cousin Yoichi were already there. All of her family members looked as if they had spent the day undergoing much the same lavish attention Koida had endured. If they shared her frayed nerves, they didn't show it. Shingti lounged on an embroidered couch, cooling herself delicately with a silk fan. Rather than the usual ceremonial Dragonfly armor she wore to court, tonight the first princess was draped in layers of aquamarine and violet fabric, set off in places by jewels and platinum. A silk wrap hung off her shoulders, exposing the portion of her vividly colored Heroic Record between her collar bones and the top of her dress robes.

On the opposite side of the waiting room, Yoichi and Emperor Hao, the first in handsome white and plum robes and the second in gold-threaded ebony, were deep in discussion over an issue on which they clearly disagreed on. Yoichi spoke in low but forceful tones while their father shook his head.

"No, absolutely not," Hao said. "I won't hear another word of it."

"But if you were to declare—"

"As your emperor, I tell you no. The matter is closed."

Yoichi face went calculatedly blank. "Yes, Exalted Emperor."

For a moment, jealousy rose like bile in Koida's throat. When her father didn't want to argue with her, he changed the subject and pretended not to hear any further protests. He'd been doing the same since she was a small child. Yoichi, however, he respected enough to treat like any other adult who might appeal to his ruling on a matter.

Then Koida remembered that she had less than a week's time left with the people in the waiting room. The bitterness fled, and a desire to run to each of her family members in turn and hug them took hold. Everything was happening so suddenly that none of it felt real. Or perhaps it was just the lack of sleep skewing her perception.

"Ah!" The emperor stood, taking her hand. "You're well named the Lilac of the Valley, second daughter. Tonight, your beauty seals a powerful alliance."

Koida sunk into a bow. "It is an honor to serve my empire, Father."

"Of course it is," Shingti said, rolling her eyes. "The sacrificial offering is here. Can we go put her on the altar now? I'm starving."

Yoichi snorted.

The emperor scowled. "I can banish you to live with one of the elderly dowagers retired from court, first daughter."

"Banish me to one who's fat," Shingti said. "She'll know how to serve a meal on time."

This drew a smile even to Koida's lips, though it vanished as soon as the waiting room doors opened. The court speaker's voice scraped down the back of Koida's neck as he announced the decorated hero, Shyong Liu Yoichi.

Like the return feast, there was a hierarchy to the seating of the wedding guests, but it began with the lowest ranked and climbed until it reached the emperor, then finally the bride and groom. On this first night, the bride's father would bring her to the wedding table, symbolizing his intention to give her to the groom at the end of the seven nights.

As Emperor Hao walked Koida into the feasting hall, the second princess felt much like the sacrificial offering Shingti had called her. The young chieftain of the Ji Yu stood on the dais in front of the silk-draped wedding table, hands clasped severely behind his back and his cold jade eyes boring into Koida's. She had expected him to be dressed in elaborately tailored robes, as lavish as the nobles filling the hall, but once more he was dressed in the simple clothes of a traveling warrior artist, as if to imply that the extravagance of the occasion was nothing more than a joke to him.

Perhaps it was his way of acknowledging that he had been tricked into wedding a Ro-crippled second princess. His stony face certainly appeared to mask a simmering anger.

Emperor Hao squeezed her arm, and Koida wondered whether she had unknowingly tried to pull away.

When they came to the foot of the platform, the Ji Yu chieftain descended the pair of steps to meet them.

Though for most in the empire, bowing deeply enough to show the vulnerable back of the neck was either a sign of familial love and trust or an insult to a person's strength and power, to the emperor it was a sign of submission, an acknowledgement that his will held the ultimate authority over life and death.

When the barbarian chieftain Ji Yu Raijin bowed to the emperor, however, he kept his eyes locked on the older man's, showing that he considered the emperor his equal.

Koida felt her father stiffen at her side, but Hao did not immediately call for his guards to execute the younger man.

When the Ji Yu chieftain straightened again, he reached out to take Koida's hand from her father, but Hao didn't relinquish it.

"Ji Yu Raijin, Shyong San Koida," the Exalted Emperor addressed them, "your joining is a seal on the promise of alliance between our peoples. See that you maintain it."

"I will protect and defend her with my life," the young chieftain said, his deep rasping voice low enough that it wouldn't carry beyond the three of them. The words had the ring of an oath, though it was not customary for such a thing to be promised at a wedding feast.

Koida lowered her eyes, afraid to meet the Ji Yu chieftain's glare. His long fingers felt like tongues of ice against her burning skin as he took her hand, and her father's reassuring presence withdrew.

They ascended the steps together and took their seats behind the wedding table. The Citrine and Amethyst thrones had been replaced with a pair of elaborate goldwood chairs with intertwining arms to symbolize the linking of the couple and their peoples. Ji Yu Raijin pulled out the second princess's chair as was fitting of his lower rank, finally releasing his demonically cold grip on her hand. Koida sat, noting that the goldwood was still damp, likely cut and carved that very day by master artisans in Boking Iri for this occasion.

Around the feasting hall, servants rushed to fill wineglasses, pour tea, and load plates from the emperor down through the ranks. The nobles, her father and Shingti included, turned their attentions to the food and drink.

A cupbearer and a maidservant bowed up the dais and began to fill Koida and the Ji Yu chieftain's plates and wine cups. Thinking this distraction might provide a safe moment to observe her betrothed without being observed in turn and perhaps gauge his mood, Koida glanced the young man's way. Instead of finding him focused on his food, however, she found him watching her. A feral hunger blazed in his eyes, frightening in its intensity. A thin moment later, it was gone, replaced by that emotionless chill. There was no transition from one to the other and no trace left behind.

"Apologies, Princess," he said, his tone that of the lower addressing a better. "Your future husband is not used to this kind of pomp and ceremony. It is disorienting."

Koida stumbled a bit seeking the appropriate address for her response.

"Please, Ji Yu Raijin—" She decided on a tone of spousal respect, hoping that the approach would repair whatever damage their earlier interaction had done and save her untold harms down the road. "—there is no need to speak up to your future wife. Especially if you feel her father, the Exalted Emperor, is your equal."

He smiled. The sudden warmth of it softened his face from hungry demon to nothing more than a young man. The transformation was startling.

"Self-exalted," he said as if correcting her.

A flame of anger leapt to life in Koida's stomach, and she forgot her caution. She switched back to the cold formal tone. "Apologies, Honored Chieftain, but your emperor is exalted by the battles he has won and the tribes he has conquered. His title is no empty claim."

"Your father the emperor is a great warrior." Though Ji Yu Raijin said this like an agreement, Koida could tell it was the opposite, and his evasion brought back Yoichi's warning about honeyed words felling empires as often as swords. Before she could decide how to respond, however, the chieftain continued, his tone now familiar. "There's no need for you to speak up to me, either, Koida."

He said her given name as if testing whether she would ask him to use her royal address instead. It was within her rights to do so, she did outrank him, and a contrary part of her angered by his dismissal of her father's greatness urged her to, but it would be bad courtesy to so quickly rescind a request to speak informally.

"I would be honored if you would call me Raijin," he said.

Koida searched his face for some hint that he was toying with her, but she could find only sincerity. Either he truly wanted to make peace or he was incredibly good at hiding his intentions.

"Gratitude," she said finally, and only a bit of ice remained in her tone.

A manservant bowed up the stairs with a small silver tray containing two cups and a pair of orange-yellow pellets. With one final bob, the servant set the tray between their plates and backed away.

Koida's brow furrowed. This wasn't part of the wedding traditions.

The young chieftain saw her confusion.

"These are sunbright pills," he said, picking one up and holding it out for her inspection. "It works like the core stone of the sunbright demon serpent, purging impurities and disease from the body and refining the Ro."

"But it *isn't* an actual core stone?" Koida picked up the second pill from the tray and rolled it in her fingers. The little orange pellet was warm to the touch.

"No. The physicians made it to replicate the effects without killing the serpent. It's not as strong as a demon core, but it works in the same way."

A real, Ro-altering medicine! Koida's heart sang, so excited that she forgot her wariness of the young man beside her.

"Will it advance one who consumes it?" she asked, looking him dead in the eyes.

For the briefest moment, a strange expression crossed Raijin's face. Pity? Disgust? Then it was gone. Her excitement had reminded him exactly what sort of wife he was getting in return for the pledging of his tribe's valuable soldiers and crops.

"It won't help you advance," Raijin said, any hint at his thoughts hidden behind that cold mask once more, though his rasping voice had taken on a softer note. "Sunbright's only use is to cleanse the body and the Ro. My people don't hold lavish feasts for weddings, but medicines like this are part of our rituals, to prepare the bride and groom for one another."

Out in the sea of noble faces, she saw her father tipping back a cup of blood orange wine. Did he know the Ji Yu tribe had alchemists so advanced? Most likely. That must be one of the many reasons he was so intent on sealing this partnership quickly.

She would just have to resign herself to the marriage. Raijin clearly had. At least in this way, she could contribute to the strength of the Shyong San Empire. She might never be spoken of when the histories were read, but knowing that she had brought invaluable medicines to help strengthen her people would be enough. Shingti might scorn their father for selling Koida off in exchange for these advantages, but then Shingti had never felt the gnawing ache of being dismissed as worthless.

"Do you know how to integrate demon core stones?" Raijin asked.

Koida shook her head, moving slowly enough that the bell cascades in her hair stayed silent, while she tried to decide how much of her disability to reveal. Dozens upon dozens of core stones had been wasted on her as a child, brought in from the farthest reaches of the valley by hunters, masters, and Living Blade warrior artists hoping to win the emperor's favor by helping his youngest daughter advance, but none had ever done more than give her a day or two of fever and stomach sickness until she threw them up. Back then, she'd even had a dedicated alchemist whose entire job was to mix soothing medicines whenever a new stone was brought to her.

"I fall sick when I swallow them," she said. "Will this pill do the same?"

"Yes," Raijin said. "But you have to stop your body from rejecting it. Use your Ro to break the sunbright down and pull its components into your heartcenter. It's exhausting and not a very pleasant sensation, but it can't be avoided or lessened. Focus helps, so it's best if you take the pill when you leave here, then spend the night meditating. And—" He shifted uncomfortably in his seat. "—you'll want a bath when you're finished. The results are a bit disgusting."

"Gratitude for your honesty." Koida set the pill back on the tray.

Raijin nodded and fell silent.

Though the White Jade Feasting Hall was filled with conversation and music from the performers in the corner, the table on the dais seemed enveloped in unbearable quiet. Koida took a long drink of the palace's best blood orange wine. Raijin toyed with his cup, not drinking and not speaking.

Koida set her cup down and looked out into the crowd, hoping it would provide a distraction.

Her sister was deep in discussion with their father. As if she could feel Koida's eye, Shingti turned and caught her gaze. The first princess raised an eyebrow, nodding subtly toward the young chieftain, then made a stabbing motion with one hand.

It took Koida a moment to realize her sister was asking if she wanted her future husband murdered. When she shook her head, Shingti scowled. The first princess mouthed two words clearly: *Be careful.*

Koida nodded, her eyes falling on the sunbright pills.

"How do I know these aren't poison?" she asked her future husband.

Raijin's brow furrowed. "Why would I poison you?"

"If I were to die, you wouldn't have to suffer the disgrace of your stubbornness and your bloodline would be protected," she said.

The smile returned to his face.

"That was a well-crafted twisting of keeping my word into an insult," he said. "I would never poison someone, especially not…" He faltered. "I pledged to protect you with my life."

She saw white hair in the crowd. Cousin Yoichi sipping his wine and listening to the musicians.

"Honeyed words mean nothing," she said. "Take your sunbright pill now and I'll believe you."

"No, you won't. You'll say one is poison and the other safe, and only I know the difference between them." Raijin pushed the platter toward her. "Pick one. I'll take whichever you choose."

Though she tried to search for a trap in his words, Koida couldn't find it. Finally, she picked up both pills, rolled them around in her fist, their heat tracing invisible lines across her palm. Satisfied they were well mixed up, she pulled one out at random.

Raijin accepted the orange pill and popped it into his mouth and swallowed without hesitation.

Koida watched like an eagle to make certain he didn't have an opportunity to spit the pill out, but he didn't reach for a cup or bring his hand to his mouth. He seemed to be waiting for her to say something.

"Are you holding it under your tongue?" she asked.

Raijin sighed and opened his mouth, lifting his tongue out of the way so she could search for the sunbright. His mouth was empty. The pill was gone.

"Fine," Koida said reluctantly. "I concede that these might not be poison."

He laughed. "If that is the best the treasured princess is willing to part with, the lowly chieftain will have to accept it."

"It is," she said. "For now."

They lapsed back into silence once more, though the musicians didn't make it through a full song before Raijin spoke again.

"From your wariness of poison, I take it you've heard of the Path of the Water Lily?" All trace of teasing was gone from his gravelly voice.

"Batsai—the captain of my guard—used to tell me stories of them poisoning young princesses, then he would say to always watch my food and drink carefully so as not to become a cautionary story myself."

"It's sound advice," Raijin said, his face once more becoming the cold mask of the demon. "The Water Lily school doesn't only teach their students the art of poisoning, however. From the shadows, they plot assassinations, stir up rivalries and war, and create unrest to topple dynasties, all so they can steal Ro from the casualties. There's no telling the number of rival paths they've destroyed. They purge every practitioner and all evidence of the schools they target. They're a blight eating away at the world."

Koida flinched at the icy venom in his voice.

"I-I thought they were just a legend," she said. "An object lesson for royal children."

"They're real," he said. "And they have to be stopped."

Koida searched the room until she found Shingti. The first princess was in a far corner, surrounded by soldiers, guards, and a few rougher nobles, speaking to the yellow-haired foreigner from the Ji Yu envoy. She and the foreigner dropped silver links into the hand of a soldier, then tipped back their wine cups and drained them. Without stopping, Shingti reached out and pushed the bottom of the foreign man's cup skyward while the spectators laughed and jeered. But even while she played this drinking game, Shingti's eyes watched shrewdly, missing nothing in the feasting hall.

Nearer the head of the room, Yoichi had taken Shingti's place at their father's side. The two were busy trading Heroic Record stories over their wine, sleeves rolled up and pointing at the colorful scenes depicted in their flesh. Several other decorated noble warrior artists around the hall were engaged in the same pastime. There was no shortage of heroic deeds in the empire, most of it gathered in this very room.

"Water Lilies would never attack here," Koida said, watching her sister pound the foreigner on the back heartily as he coughed and spluttered.

Raijin didn't answer. She turned to find the young chieftain glaring into his cup.

"We're too strong for them," she insisted, though in truth the words were a question, begging for reassurance. "My sister is a master—the strongest in decades—the Dragonfly of the Shyong San Empire. Shingti would kill them all."

Raijin's eyes met hers, as cold and hard as stone.

"If she saw them coming," he said.

CHAPTER SEVENTEEN

Present

L IKE THE RETURN HOME FEASTS, THE wedding festivities carried on well into the night, growing more boisterous with every hour. Nobles excused themselves to the private rooms on the far side of the hall to drink phials of medicine the alchemists always prepared for these occasions. Stomachs emptied, they returned and continued the feasting.

When the first few rounds of eating concluded, and Koida and Raijin's plates were cleared away, nobles began to approach the dais, bowing and offering congratulations and compliments on the emperor's lavish hospitality. Koida accepted these with the required graciousness. Her future husband didn't seem inclined to speak. He watched each interaction with an incomprehensible expression, though his bright green eyes sparkled strangely. Koida felt certain that beneath that cold exterior, Raijin was laughing at them all.

Not long after the first cask of hard wine was drained, the Exalted Emperor declared that he would retire. Immediately, courtiers across the hall began yawning and speaking about the lateness of the hour.

At Koida's side, Raijin let out a sharp laugh.

"It must be exhausting to be a member of the royal court," he said, the barest hint of a smirk on his lips.

"It's good news," she said. "Because it means I can retire now as well."

"Your future husband plans to do the same," Raijin said, standing. He handed her down the dais, and at the bottom, pressed the sunbright pill into her hand. "Don't forget your poison. I mean, sunbright pill."

Koida laughed in spite of herself.

"It can take up to half a day to fully integrate it into your heartcenter," Raijin continued more seriously. "It might be painful and unpleasant, but you can't allow your body to reject it or take any medicines to dull its effect."

"You took one at least an hour ago, and you don't seem to be in pain," Koida said, though she wasn't certain she had a firm grasp on time through the warm haze of the blood orange wine.

He smiled. "There are some people for whom seeming not to be in pain becomes second nature."

Koida frowned and studied him more closely. Had his olive complexion gone waxy underneath? And how had she not noticed before that sweat had begun to shine on his temples? She took his hand. The ice that had been in his fingers was now a burning fire nearly as hot as her own skin.

A tingle of fear prickled across the nape of her neck.

Raijin must have seen it because he added, "Just remember that you're not going through this alone."

Koida looked down at the sunbright pill pinched between her fingers, then put it in her mouth and swallowed. The taste of sun-warmed grapefruits filled her mouth.

Nothing happened.

"I don't feel anything," she said.

"That won't last long," Raijin said, concern touching his expression. "I suggest getting to privacy sooner than later."

Koida nodded. They bowed goodnight to one another, then Batsai appeared at her side to accompany her back to her residence.

Koida and her personal guard walked in silence, her mind on what a strange night it had been. The demon chieftain had turned into nothing more than a young man, and she had begun the process of leaving her life as the second princess to become his wife. What sort of conditions did the Ji Yu tribe live in? She knew they lived in the mountains, and Raijin had claimed that he wasn't used to extravagance. What if she was leaving behind the Sun Palace for a village of mud huts?

The sunbright pill lodged at the base of her throat. She swallowed hard, but couldn't force it to move.

When they reached her rooms, Jun waited at her side while Batsai and the rest of her guards conducted their routine search for hidden dangers. Finally declaring it safe, Batsai allowed her in. She stopped at the water pitcher and took a long drink to unstick the sunbright pill. It came loose reluctantly.

Her ladies met her in the inner chamber, so excited about the wedding feast that it seemed to Koida they didn't stop to breathe the entire time they helped her undress. She remained taciturn while they gossiped. A feeling of nausea swelled in her stomach, the familiar sickness of core stone rejection she'd felt so often as a child. Her mouth watered as her stomach threatened to force up everything she'd eaten and drank that night.

She cupped one hand over her lips and pressed the other to her stomach.

"Second princess, are you unwell?" one of her ladies asked.

If she spoke, she would vomit. That Ji Yu snake had poisoned her. He must have spit out his own poison when she wasn't looking or somehow tricked her into choosing the safe pill for him. He'd also sent her conveniently back to her rooms to die so he couldn't be accused of her murder.

But she'd seen the sweat beginning to form on his temple and felt the fire burning in his skin. No one could fake that, could they?

"Do you wish me to call the alchemists, Second Princess?"

This ailment had all the familiar sensations of core stone sickness—the nausea, the pressure at the back of her throat willing her to vomit, the whirling and twisting of her vision.

Koida managed to stumble across the room, making the nightcaller floor squeal repeatedly in her clumsiness, and dropped onto her bed. The furs and silks felt like wool worm feet prickling against her skin. Millions of them marching over her body. She could hear the nightcaller floor creaking under them, marching, marching.

"Hurry! Get an alchemist!"

"What in blade and death is going on here?" Batsai demanded. "Koida?" His voice sounded so far away, as if he were shouting through the waterfall cave to her. His battle-roughened hands grabbed her by the shoulders. "Koida!"

"Nnno," she groaned, rolling her head on her neck.

"Hold on, little dragon, Batsai will protect you," the captain's rough voice promised. His rough hands felt cold as he pushed the sweat-damp hair off her face.

"No medicines," she tried to say, though her voice sounded strange to her ears. Muffled and thick. "Raijin said—"

"Did that barbarian do this to you? I'll kill him!" Batsai's icy hands left her face, and she fell back to the bed from thousands of miles up.

Ruby light glowed through Koida's eyelids. Was it blood or fire? She felt as if she were burning alive. But Batsai would never let her burn. The old bear always protected the little dragon. Unless she had set this fire. What if the little dragon had burned up the old bear? What if she was all alone now in this sea of fire and blood?

"What did you do to my sister?" Shingti's voice bounced around the inside of Koida's skull like a ball of Ro, setting off angry sparks everywhere it touched.

"It's part of the Ji Yu wedding rites," Raijin answered her in his scratchy rumble. The sound of it made Koida's throat ache in sympathy. "Her body is trying to reject the sunbright. She has to use her Ro to pull it into her heartcenter."

"Water Lily!" Batsai's face twisted until he did look like an angry old bear. He sprinted at the young chieftain, wielding a glowing red Serpentine Spear and Low Shield.

Instead of attacking Raijin, however, Batsai fell on Shingti's Dual Swords. The Dragonfly princess screamed with fury, hacking the captain of Koida's guard apart.

But when Koida blinked, none of them were there. Two of her ladies stood in the corner wringing their hands, and the third was showing a group of the palace alchemists into her room.

"The second princess collapsed holding her stomach, and she hasn't stopped moaning since."

The alchemists crowded around her bed, reaching for her with fingers that looked like venomous adders. She tried to scramble away from them, but she felt her arms and legs do nothing more than flail weakly.

"What did she eat at the feast?" one of the alchemists asked before bursting into a cloud of brightly colored silk moths. Or perhaps he had only been overwhelmed by the countless number of wool worms wandering over her skin as they spontaneously transformed. Whatever had happened, he was gone now, nothing more than a swarm of motion.

As one, the creatures swirled around Koida in a tornado of blues, purples, and greens. They were horribly beautiful, a parade of ghostly color that made her feel as if her heart was broken beyond repair. She choked on the tears pouring from her eyes, unable to contain the inexplicable sadness the sight inspired in her.

Someone screamed, frightening the moths away. The scream came again, a noise like wood scraping against metal, then again and again. Something about the sound triggered recognition in Koida. When she heard that sound in the night, it was a warning. But of what?

"Stand back!" Batsai snapped. "Out of the way. She's with the Ji Yu envoy. The chieftain says she knows how to help the second princess."

Koida tried to ask Batsai why Shingti had run him through with her Dual Swords, but her throat was so dry that all she could manage was a low croak. Fire burned in her skull, hollowing out her eyes and mouth until only blackened holes were left behind.

"A pill that mimics a core stone?" That sounded like one of the alchemists. Koida searched her mind for his name, but came up with nothing. "Impossible! No one can create medicines such as that!"

"I didn't ask you what was possible," Batsai growled. "I told you to get out of the way."

A cool, slender hand pressed against Koida's forehead. Soft, icy fingers plucked her eyelids open one at a time. The face staring down into hers was far, far away, down a pinhole of light, but she could see that the nose and mouth were covered in cloth wrappings.

The face disappeared as her eyelid snapped shut again.

"Why didn't you bring the chieftain with you then, if he knows so much?"

"He's ill, too," Batsai growled. "Same as the princess, shivering and sweating and burning with fever. But he said his physician knows how to help her."

The cool hands wrapped around Koida's shoulders and pulled her to a seated position. The soft shake they gave her was an order to stay sitting up. Koida tried to concentrate on remaining upright, but it was hard to tell up from down just then.

Had Batsai said that Raijin was suffering from the same sickness or had she imagined that? Before they left the feast, he'd told her to remember she wasn't going through this alone. Apparently, he'd spoken the truth. If that was true, then perhaps he was telling the truth about the pill. What else had he told her about it? To use her Ro to break it down before her body could reject it?

His face appeared before her, carved in black ice. "Pull it into your heartcenter."

"I can't," she said. "I'm Ro-crippled. I've never advanced in all the years I've been training."

"Excuses." His voice rasped like dry leaves skittering across pitiless, inflexible stone. "This can't be avoided. Focus helps. You're not going through this alone."

An icy thumb pressed against the burning flesh over Koida's sternum, drawing her attention to her heartcenter. She followed the focus point inward and found the sunbright pill shining like a citrine catching the morning light. It had lodged just above her stomach.

How was she supposed to use her Ro to break that down? Try to create a tiny Ro knife and chop it in half?

With a colossal effort, Koida forced Ro toward the sunbright. As usual, it refused to follow the correct pathways in her body, instead reaching right through the walls of her heartcenter and skewering the pill through its midpoint. She gasped at the sudden pain and clutched her chest. It was like being stabbed.

From far away, she heard Batsai shouting again, but she couldn't focus on him. She had no attention to spare. The moment her Ro pierced the sunbright, it burst like a dying star, exploding outward in billions of sparkling orange-yellow shards.

They were going to escape.

Koida grasped at the pill shards instinctively, her Ro snatching them up like greedy hands. Each one she grabbed exploded again into infinitely finer pieces. Grabbing them wasn't working. There were too many, and they were too small. She needed a net.

Concentrating, she manifested an amethyst seine from her Ro and began netting the sunbright dust together.

"Good," Raijin's voice said. "Now pull it into your heartcenter."

Koida tried to pull the seine full of sparkling orange-yellow dust into one of the Ro pathways, but it refused to budge. Always. Always, her Ro had to disobey her.

Setting her jaw, Koida took a deep breath and then jerked as hard as she could with her mind. With a crack like breaking bone, the Ro and sunbright tore through the sheets of muscle tissue and organs, slamming into the roiling cloud of amethyst energy in her heartcenter. The Ro crackled and hissed as it consumed the pill dust. A brilliant lilac flare burst outward from her heartcenter, then settled in rings around her Ro like a tiny planet. Every so often, the rings sizzled with orange arcs like lightning.

She felt…good.

The orange arcs tapered off until they stopped completely.

She felt better than good. Incredible. Like she could run for miles or fight a dozen demon beasts on her own. Had she advanced? Could she manifest bladed weapons now?

Koida opened her eyes, eager to try every technique she had ever seen Shingti or Batsai use. But bright midday sunlight poured in from her open balcony, illuminating an inner chamber filled with alchemists, eunuchs, ladies, and her personal guard, each face displaying differing levels of concern, apprehension, and outright curiosity. On the bed before her sat the woman with the cloth covering her nose and mouth, her legs crossed and her fists pressed together, her dark almond eyes staring into Koida's intently.

When the woman saw that Koida was coherent once more, she bowed over her fists and climbed off the bed. The nightcaller floor screamed beneath her feet.

The inner chamber erupted in a storm of questions and demands. Alchemists and eunuchs crowded the woman, all shouting at once about core stone medicine and magical properties transmuted into pills. The woman made no effort to respond, and suddenly, Koida realized why.

"She can't speak," Koida said. She swallowed past the dryness in her throat. "That's why she wears the face mask. Your questions are pointless. She can't answer you."

The woman caught her gaze, then bowed once more, her horsetail of black hair sliding over her shoulder.

"Apologies, Second Princess." One of the eunuchs stepped forward. It was Ba-Qu, the one who had advised her father to stop her training before she hurt herself. "But if this physician can write, she can answer our questions. Learning about her tribe's advanced magics and medicines is too great an opportunity to throw away just because she cannot speak."

The stink of rotting peaches and a backed-up private room turned Koida's stomach. Her disgust grew as she looked down and found her nightdress soaked through with a foul, tarlike substance.

"Everyone but my ladies get out," she said, infusing her voice with authority. "I need to bathe."

Reluctantly, the alchemists and eunuchs bowed to Koida and backed out of the room, Batsai hurrying along anyone who lingered overlong. The silent woman left as well, no doubt to be barraged with more questions the moment she stepped from the outer chamber into the hallway.

The trio of ladies bowed their way out of the room on promises to return immediately with a steaming bath. They still looked sick with worry. No doubt they had feared retribution from the emperor if the second princess died while they were in the room, but had been unable to leave until she recovered or risk being dismissed in shame for failing to tend to her.

Koida watched them all go, relieved to see her inner chamber emptying of so many bodies.

"Batsai?" she called before he could close the door behind himself.

The battle-scarred old captain turned back to her, his dress armor dull with a night's wear.

"Was Shingti here last night?" she asked. The image of her sister murdering Batsai in a twisted fit of rage seemed etched onto the backs of her eyelids.

"No, though I imagine by now the first princess will have returned to her rooms from wherever her post-feast festivities took her. She'll most likely be along as soon as the gossip reaches her."

"Were you truly going to kill the Ji Yu chieftain or did I dream that?" she asked.

Batsai scowled. "I was. Luckily for him, he explained what he'd done before I ran him through. The words came dear, though. He wasn't doing much better than you were when I broke down his residence door."

"You could have been killed," Koida said. "If not by him or his guards, then by my father when he learned that you endangered the empire's first chance at a tribe who can make Ro-altering medicines."

Batsai snorted.

"If you think I care more about that than your life, then you don't know me at all, little dragon." He hesitated a moment, then said, "A father's life is of no concern to him when his daughter is in danger, whether she is the true blood of his blood or only the blood of his heart."

Before Koida could reply, her ladies bustled into the chamber with buckets of steaming water, leading young servant boys from the kitchens wearing yokes carrying more of the same.

Batsai bowed himself out. Koida watched the gruff old bear go, the image of him dying horribly on her sister's ruby Ro-swords playing out again in her mind.

"But to the daughter, the father's survival is everything," she whispered. "She'll protect you in any way she can."

CHAPTER EIGHTEEN

6 years ago

R AIJIN SPUN INTO A BACK KICK, FIRING a Battering Volley at Yong Lei. His friend received the storm of Ro-hail with a single-handed blast of Changing Air, then struck out in return with the other hand, a Hammering Rain backfist.

Raijin had grown cautious over the past year, maturing with his abilities. As the first solid stage in the Path of Darkening Skies, Hail techniques hit much harder than anything he had learned in the previous ranks, and since the day he had almost killed his best friend, he'd gained a healthy respect for his art. Yong Lei still occasionally struck too close, but Raijin was always quick to counter and careful never to do the same.

Today, Yong Lei was flagging, his attention waning. Raijin could see it in his friend's poorly timed motions. This happened often on the days Yong Lei helped Raijin with his serving tasks. Though he joined Raijin in hauling the wood and water at least once a week now, Yong Lei's body had yet to become accustomed to the added strain of serving the school on top of their daily training.

Yong Lei sliced his arms through the air in his favored Driving Sleet technique, hurling a barrage of hair-thin, icy projectiles at Raijin like needles made of Ro. But Yong Lei's knees buckled as the strike left his hands, and he went down, sending the shots flying wildly in every direction. Raijin lashed out with a quick Shattering Crescent Wind, his foot smashing the projectiles with a focused sheet of Ro-wind before they could hit any of the other practicing Hail students.

Threat to others averted, Raijin turned back to help his friend up. But Yong Lei had not fainted from exhaustion like Raijin guessed, he had dropped into Resting Meditation. Now he sat on the flagstones shivering with cold while the hot summer sun beat down from above. His body steamed, and the sweat on his skin turned immediately into tiny balls of ice that bounced upward, then pelted back toward him, gaining mass from the moisture in his skin and the air around him.

"Master Palgwe," Raijin called. "Yong Lei is advancing to Hail!"

The training master, who clearly expected to hear that his two youngest combat students had finally killed one another, relaxed visibly when his eyes landed on the shivering Yong Lei.

"Continue on your own," Master Palgwe told the pair he had been working with. "I'll be back to check on you." He tucked his arms into his sleeves and joined Raijin. After a moment's study of the shivering Yong Lei and the little balls of hail bouncing around him, the training master said, "He doesn't seem to be having any serious trouble with it. His collection is good, and his Ro is strong. The only concern would be hypothermia. It's much more likely in an autumn or winter progression than summer, but it still happens at times."

Raijin remembered the bone-shattering cold of his last advancement. "What if I were to keep blasts of warm Changing Air focused on him, Master?"

"It is the Ro inside Yong Lei freezing, Student Raijin," Palgwe said. "Changing Air can't penetrate that deeply. Yong Lei must either survive or perish on his own now. The progression belongs to him alone."

"May I have special permission to stay with him until he finishes advancing?" Raijin asked.

"I can only release you from your classes," the training master said. "The grandmaster has full authority over your serving tasks."

"Yes, Master."

The rest of the day, Raijin stayed at Yong Lei's side, only leaving twice—for the noontime tasks and again for the night tasks. The sun beat down on them from overhead and not a breath of a breeze blew through the courtyard, but cool air surrounded Yong Lei like a cloud, turning the moisture that entered there into hail. While Raijin soaked his uniform with sweat, his best friend shivered.

Other students and masters came and went throughout the process, Grandmaster Feng included. When Master Chugi joined them, he released Raijin from his nightly reading.

"Yong Lei never left your side when you advanced to Hail," the old man said. "He deserves as much of the same in return as you can give him."

Fatty, the school cook, even showed up with a bowl of rice noodles for Raijin's supper.

"You got to eat, Raij," Fatty said. "Going without won't get Yong Lei to the other side any faster."

Though concern for his friend made the noodles feel like slugs in his mouth, Raijin accepted Fatty's wisdom and forced himself to eat.

The night seemed to last forever. Raijin meditated on and off, but couldn't focus on cultivating his Ro while Yong Lei was still in danger. Though Raijin could remember the feeling of his own progression to Hail, he had never seen anyone else do it. From the outside, the process was extremely unsettling. Yong Lei's shivering increased for long periods of time, sometimes growing so violent that he toppled over and flopped against the ground like a fish out of water. His teeth chattered, and once his skin turned to a deathly gray-blue for almost a full minute before it began to return to a normal color.

Finally, just before Raijin would normally wake up and begin his morning serving tasks, the cold air surrounding Yong Lei dissolved into the summer heat, and the cloud of accumulated hail cycling and bouncing off him dropped to the ground and began to melt.

Yong Lei slumped forward, asleep.

Raijin leapt to his feet in excitement and relief. His best friend had made it. They were Hail brothers!

"If the two of you keep this up, you may become the youngest masters of Darkening Skies since its founding."

Master Palgwe's voice startled Raijin. He'd thought he was alone with Yong Lei in the dark courtyard. He turned to look at the training master.

"I'm only here to check on you two," Palgwe said. "Now that it's clear you'll both survive, I can return to my meditation."

"Master?" Raijin asked before Palgwe could leave. A question had been forming in his mind through the night. "Yong Lei was exhausted from helping me with serving tasks. I thought he was going to faint, but instead he advanced."

"Yes?" the training master said, his tone indicating that Raijin should continue.

"And I advanced on the night I was caned for my negligence," he said.

Palgwe canted his head to the side. "What do you make of that, Student Raijin?"

"Is physical exhaustion required before one's Ro can reach the Hail stage?"

"Not exhaustion. Consider the fifty-second principle."

"Adversity builds strength, but indulgence tears it down," Raijin recited.

The training master nodded. "We don't know exactly what causes a person to advance from one level to the next. If we did, we could give each student a list and they could advance to master in as long as it took them to accomplish the tasks on it. But we do know that a certain level of maturity must be reached before the Ro advances, and it's well known that hardship often breeds maturity."

Raijin looked down at his snoring friend as he digested this. When viewed in this way, his quick progression from Sleet to Hail made sense. Though he hadn't often thought of his life as having hardships in it, nearly losing his friend had driven the point home.

"Perhaps Yong Lei would have reached this point at such a young age on his own," Master Palgwe said. "Or perhaps he learned this maturity by watching his friend go about his daily responsibilities without complaint. It's not possible to say for sure."

On the ground, Yong Lei groaned and rubbed his eyes. Raijin rushed to help him up.

"Am I still alive?" Yong Lei asked, eyeing the puddle of melting ice chips at his feet. "Did I advance?"

"Yes on both accounts," Raijin said, grinning. "Though I didn't think you would do either."

Yong Lei laughed and thumped Raijin's back. "You mean you hoped I wouldn't because you knew that once I did, I'd you beat to Thunder in no time."

"Even the strangest things happen on occasion," Raijin agreed.

"Take Student Yong Lei to the physicians for his advancement pill, Student Raijin," Master Palgwe said, striding back toward the school's open door. "You should have just enough time to get there and back out to begin your chores."

CHAPTER NINETEEN

6 years ago

THAT NIGHT, RAIJIN SEARCHED THE library for one of Master Chugi's favorite books, *Medicines of the Northern Grasslands*. He found the text unbearably boring, but Master Chugi had insisted Raijin pick their reading material for tonight, and he wanted to make up for having left the old man without a story the night before while Yong Lei was advancing.

Yong Lei had finished incorporating the sunbright in time to assist Raijin with his nightly chores. With the added energy from the purged impurities and the refined Ro coursing through his system, the newly ranked Hail was a welcome help to Raijin carrying water, refilling wood boxes, and replenishing the woodpile.

The reading, however, was a task only for Raijin. A small thanks for the master who had worked out a way to ensure that Raijin could study at the school and raised him from an infant. Master Chugi loved reading as much as he loved to meditate on the path. Going blind had been a terrible blow to the old man. When he was a child, Raijin had asked Master Chugi why he aged and

Grandmaster Feng didn't, but the elderly master could only shrug.

"Grandmaster Feng has learned a trick I can't," he'd said.

Bitterness shriveled Raijin's heart on his master's behalf. "But that's not fair. You're both on the same path."

"There come times while we walk the path when one rises and another falls," Master Chugi had said contentedly. "This is life. You may as well say that the changing seasons or the height of a tree is unfair."

While he searched the shelves, his mind wandered, and he wondered whether there would come a time when Yong Lei learned a trick that he couldn't. Would he envy his best friend or would he accept it as Master Chugi did? Raijin wasn't sure he could be as understanding as his master.

Finally, Raijin found *Medicines of the Northern Grasslands*. Someone had mis-shelved it beneath a stack of heavy carved panel books. Lucky for whoever had read it last that Raijin found it before Library Master Tang-Soo realized it was out of place.

He took the stack of panel books down, intending to hold them only long enough to pick up Medicines, but an ivory inlay on the cover of the top panel caught his eye. It was a water lily. Raijin had never seen this book before.

As much as Master Chugi loved *Medicines of the Northern Grasslands*, the old man would want to know what was in this new book more. Each wooden panel was much thicker than the usual parchment pages, but Raijin thought the novelty would more than make up for its brevity.

Carefully, he returned the other panel books to the shelf, then put Medicines in its proper place. He worried that the library master would refuse to let him leave with such a new addition to the stacks, but the implacable Tang-Soo didn't bat an eye when he told her it was the one he wanted to borrow.

Back in Master Chugi's quarters, Raijin guided the blind old man's hand to the front panel so he could feel the ivory inlay.

Master Chugi nodded gravely. "So soon, so much sooner than I hoped. But isn't it always?" Raijin opened his mouth to speak, but Master Chugi waved him off. "No, no questions now. Later. Please begin, my boy."

Obediently, Raijin opened to the first written panel. The text was Deep Root, the Oldest Language and the common ancestor of all modern languages. Each character had been gouged so deeply into the wood that the lantern cast them in pools of shadow.

"Among the ancient paths, there exists one which threatens to undo all. The Path of the Water Lily." Raijin ran his fingertips over the words as he read, the silken smoothness of the panel attesting to the book's age. "Hidden so frequently behind the fairest of faces, this poisoned bloom sits in direct opposition to the Path of Darkening Skies. One destroying what the other would save, tainting what the other would cleanse. The Water Lily cannot be defeated by clouds and rain or any of the other ancient ways. A day comes when its toxic touch will wither the Paths of the Falling Leaf, Endless Day, Hidden Whispers, and Darkening Skies, and wipe from the earth every other path the ancestors left us. War will rage on the end of the Water Lily master's puppet strings, feeding life energy to the deadly bloom, strengthening it with every sip."

Tonight, there was none of the usual dozing or snoring while Raijin read. The old man sat rapt, his frail bird's chest rising and falling with each breath.

"That character is interchangeable with Ro," Master Chugi said, though he spoke quietly, almost as if thinking aloud. "The shape of the character is where we get the modern word. Over the years it evolved into the letters we use for Ro."

Looking at it, Raijin could see how the intricate lines of "life energy" had grown together and simplified to become the stylized "Ro" of New Script.

He returned to reading. "Deliverance may never come. The world may well expire in the poisoned grasp of the Water Lily. Not even the combined wisdom of the ancestors can save us. Whatever hope there might have been lies at the end of a broken path, the cost greater than any man or woman could ever pay."

Raijin closed the bleak text and stared down at the beautiful inlay in the front panel. Master Chugi didn't speak a word, but the pattern of his breathing and the fidgeting of his gnarled hands told Raijin the old man was still awake.

Finally, Raijin could take the silence no more. "Is it… Is it a prophecy?"

Master Chugi shook his bald head.

"Much surer than that," the old master said sadly. "The detail, the names. None are open-ended placeholders. This is certain. It will happen."

"Why wouldn't all the paths join forces to destroy the Water Lilies?" Raijin asked. "This book has been worn smooth with age. They've had decades—maybe longer—to eradicate the Water Lilies."

"Ask any inji," Master Chugi said. "You cannot defeat that which you cannot find."

"Then why do any of the paths still exist? Why bother following them if they'll just be destroyed and nothing can save them?"

"I cannot speak for any path but my own." Master Chugi straightened up on his bed mat. "The Path of Darkening Skies, however, remains as a gateway for the chosen one. Without it, the Thunderbird will never come."

Raijin's brows furrowed. "Are Water Lilies the Dark Dragon that the Thunderbird is destined to defeat?"

"In truth, my boy, I don't know. But I have always hoped the two were one and the same."

"It has to be done," Raijin said, making up his mind. "They have to be stopped, no matter what an old book says." He looked up at the old man. "Whatever price is necessary, I can pay it."

A tear slipped down Master Chugi's deeply lined cheek. He wiped it away with one gnarled hand.

"Your time here is at an end," he said in a thick voice.

"What?" Raijin shook his head, though the blind master couldn't see him. "That's not right. I'm just a Hail. I'm nowhere near mastering Darkening Skies."

The old man took Raijin's hand in both of his and squeezed. "This is your last night at the school. You must leave."

Shock and confusion turned to anger in Raijin's chest. "But I've done everything required of me. From the day my serving tasks began until now, I've never shirked my duties." Then a thought occurred to him. "If

Yong Lei isn't supposed to help me, I'll have him stop. I promise. I can do them alone easily."

"You can't continue to walk the Path of Darkening Skies," Master Chugi said, his voice hard as burled steel. "Those on it must never absorb Ro taken from another in violence after their first purge of impurities."

"But, Master, I haven't—"

"Listen to me!" Master Chugi shouted, dragging Raijin closer with surprising strength. "Are you the chosen one or not, Raijin? Because this night is the night that decides. If you can't take the burden upon your shoulders, tell me now. The entire world depends upon it."

Raijin's brain stuttered and fought to catch up.

"I can shoulder whatever burden has to be shouldered," he said. "Whatever needs to be done, I'll do it."

"That is good," Master Chugi said, his grasp on Raijin's hand easing a degree. "Because what needs to be done is something no one in this school can do. It's so much. So very much. The Path of Darkening Skies has prepared the way for the chosen one, but the path he makes from now on will have to be his own."

"What about Yong Lei?" Raijin asked. "He's advanced at almost the exact same pace as I have. What about all the students with moon-marks who might be the Thunderbird? How do you know they aren't the ones you should be speaking to instead of me?"

"Can they carry the weight you can, Raijin? Can they serve the world or can they barely serve themselves?"

Raijin faltered. He knew the truth, had seen it several times since his best friend began helping him with his daily tasks.

At his silence, Master Chugi's face softened, the wrinkles going slack. "You've taught Yong Lei well by your example, but he will never be able to shoulder the burden you will be called to." The old man gave a phlegmy sniff. "My boy, you think I'm bestowing some great honor upon you, but in truth, I'm doing quite the opposite. The chosen one must suffer and die horribly to save this world. His end will draw out until he himself questions whether it was worth the pain, and when all is said and done, he may have defeated the Dark Dragon only to find that it was never the Path of the Water Lily at all, and the threat to all other ancient paths still remains. If I could place the burden on any other student in this school, I would do it. You are like a son to me, Raijin, and I would protect you with my very soul if I could. But there is no one else."

Raijin inhaled deeply, then released the breath, steeling himself.

"Tell me what I have to do, Master."

Multiple tears now tracked down the old man's wrinkled cheeks. He patted Raijin's face with one gnarled hand.

"You have to go down to the foot of the mountains, into Kokuji, the village where you were born, and find your mother. Leave immediately. Pack nothing. Tell no one." Master Chugi pressed a small stone into Raijin's hand, its surface a swirl of blue and gold. "Swallow this. It will protect you against malicious attack for one full day."

Raijin stood, his mind reeling. "How will I find her? My mother."

"She works in a teahouse, I've told you that, haven't I?" Master Chugi nodded. "Of course I have. Her name is Lanfen." He gave Raijin a soft shove toward the door. "Go now. Remember to take the pill. The forest is full of guai, and I need to know that my student-son is protected."

"Yes, Master," Raijin said, his throat suddenly constricting at the thought of leaving behind the man who had been like a father to him all his life.

Though Master Chugi couldn't see him, Raijin pressed his face to the cold stone floor three times, then backed away, still scraping his face along the floor. The old man deserved more than that, but it was all Raijin had to give. Respect and obedience.

CHAPTER TWENTY

Present

"WHERE IS MY SISTER?" SHINGTI'S demand thundered through the walls, carrying easily to the inner chamber as Koida climbed out of the bath.

In the outer chamber, Batsai's reply was a low grumble, but before he finished speaking, Shingti slammed open the door.

"Koida?"

"In the screen," Koida replied. She took a linen from her attending lady and wrapped her wet hair up, then reached for another and began drying herself.

The nightcaller floor screamed beneath Shingti's angry tread as she crossed the floor between the bed and the bathing screen.

"Are you well, little sister? Do you feel all right?"

"I feel better than I have in..." Koida set the linens aside and stepped into the silk robe the lady was holding out. "Well, I can't remember ever feeling this well. Energized. That pill did something to my Ro. Maybe I advanced."

Shingti didn't look convinced. "You would know if you had advanced."

"How?" Koida asked as she tied her sash. "I've never seen it done, and I don't know what it feels like."

"You would just know. It's not easy to mistake."

Koida walked out from behind the screen and to her bed, where the elaborate dress for the second wedding feast had been laid out. Rather than begin the arduous task of dressing, she went to her wardrobe and found a clean set of training clothes.

"In any case, I want to see if I can manifest a bladed weapon now," she said.

"So try," Shingti said, gesturing with one hand.

"Not here." Koida realized it was faulty reasoning, but she felt like she had a better chance of success in the training courtyard where she'd seen Shingti and so many others manifest blades. "I'll do it outside."

The first princess raised a dubious eyebrow at her.

"I know it's silly," Koida snapped, changing into the training clothes. She sighed. "Just let the Ro-cripple be silly for now. You can say you told me so later."

"If that's what it takes." Shingti shrugged. "Let's go, little sister. I'll walk you down."

Though they clearly wished to protest, the ladies held the door to the outer chamber for the princesses. Koida's personal guard fanned out on her side while Shingti's Dragonfly Guard filled in on the first princess's side. There were too many of them to go single file, so the nightcaller floors squealed and squeaked like a herd of angry pigs as they walked the winding corridors connecting the residences.

Eye-watering afternoon light filtered through sandglass windows in the ceiling.

"Is Master Lao expecting you today?" Shingti asked. "Shouldn't you be dressing for your wedding feast?"

"I dressed for your return home ceremony in less than two hours," Koida said. "I'll be finished training in plenty of time for my ladies to manage the wedding clothes."

They descended the stairs and stepped out onto the portico. But as Koida's eyes adjusted to the blinding light, she realized they weren't the only ones in the courtyard. The Ji Yu entourage—if two could be considered an entourage—rested in the shade, reminding her that she needed to find their young leader and thank him for the sunbright pill.

The silent woman who had helped her the night before sat with her back to the palace wall, legs crossed beneath her, fists on her thighs, her entire body perfectly still. If her dark almond eyes hadn't turned to the princesses, prompting her to give them a respectful bow, Koida might have imagined the woman was dead and in the late stages of rigor.

Koida returned the silent woman's bow with one deeper than required for the woman's unknown rank. "Endless gratitude for your aid last night, gifted physician. Without your help, I don't think I could have survived."

Smile lines appeared around the woman's dark eyes and she pressed a palm to her heartcenter as if graciously accepting Koida's thanks.

Nearby, the yellow-haired foreigner with the squashed, demon-baiting dog face lounged on the thick balustrade running between the portico's stone columns. Unlike his fellow Ji Yu tribeswoman, he swayed slightly like a charmed snake or an early drunk.

"Lysander," Shingti greeted the yellow-haired foreigner informally, boosting herself up onto the balustrade beside him. "I see you survived the night as well."

The foreigner, Lysander, chuckled. Koida caught sight of a carved ivory flask disappearing into the man's robes.

"How's your head this afternoon, Princess?" he returned. Koida couldn't tell whether the strange lilt to his words was the product of an accent or the result of his drinking. He wrapped an arm around the column to steady himself.

"First princess," Shingti corrected, a smile tugging at her lips. "I could have drunk twice that and been on the battlefield this morning. I only went easy last night out of respect for your delicacy. What is all this?" Shingti waved at the courtyard, drawing Koida's attention out into the bright sunshine. "Does the Ji Yu's leader need training in a proper warrior's art?"

At the center of the colorful tiles, Master Lao and the young chieftain of the Ji Yu bowed to one another, then stepped back. Raijin raised his hands, arms outstretched in a strange fighting stance she had never seen before. Opposite him, Master Lao manifested glistening ruby Double-Crescent Knife Hands and crouched in First Attack. Though both men stood relaxed, waiting calmly, as if there was no hurry to begin this match, tension seemed to crackle in the air.

"Raijin would've sought out the Dragonfly of the Shyong San Empire if he wanted instruction in the Path of the Living Blade," Lysander said. "Not this fraud."

"Fraud?" Koida asked, turning back to the man. "You cannot mean Master Lao."

"I can mean whatever I say," the foreigner said rudely. "That *Master*—"

A sharp finger snap drew their attention to the silent woman. Her dark almond eyes glared a warning at the foreign drunk.

Lysander rolled his eyes. "Yeah, yeah, whatever you say, Hush."

Koida, however, wasn't ready to let the insult to her master pass. She might frequently find herself frustrated and even angry with the man, but as his student, she was honor bound to defend his reputation.

"That is my master you're offending—" she started.

But before she could demand an apology, the match in the courtyard began, and all of their attentions returned to the combatants. Master Lao lunged first, the attack swift and calculated. It was a move that often threw Koida off balance during their sparring matches and pushed her into ill-considered reactions, but Raijin simply slipped the Ro blades with a twist of his shoulders, then gave the older man a two-handed shove.

Master Lao stumbled a step, causing Lysander and a few of the watching guards to snicker. Raijin's face betrayed no hint of pleasure at his opponent's misstep, but remained the stony mask of the demon. Calm, cold, alert. Waiting.

Lao recovered his balance and squared with the young chieftain once more, this time rearing his Double-Crescent Blades back in Second Attack.

When it became clear that Raijin wouldn't strike first, Master Lao leapt into the air, bringing his heel around in a glowing ruby Axe-Blade Kick that could easily decapitate a man.

Raijin pivoted at the last second, slapping Lao's kick aside with a forearm. The redirected momentum carried the master full circle this time, the sudden spin causing Lao's grounded leg to slip out from underneath him.

As Lao hit the ground, laughter and jeers filled the air. The master was losing face in front of both the princesses' personal guards.

Snarling, Lao sprang back to his feet, Double-Crescent Knife Hands raised once more.

Raijin raised his hands in an obvious invitation to attack, his face devoid of emotion. He looked no more pleased with or angered by the progression of the match than the palace walls did.

Master Lao's tenuous composure snapped at the sight. He roared a fearsome battle cry and wheeled into the air, whipping his legs and hands in turns in a series of Soaring Axe Kicks and Double-Crescent Knife attacks. Calm as the gray autumn sky above, Raijin continued to slip the older man's strikes by mere fractions of an inch, his hands clasped behind his back. He moved with a graceful precision and economy of motion Koida had only ever seen Shingti approach. If he didn't have to move, he didn't move. When he did move, it was almost faster than the eye could see.

Just yesterday she would have given anything to see Master Lao thrash the Ji Yu barbarian soundly. The longer she watched, however, the more she found some small, petty part of her hoping to see the master who beat her in every sparring match on the losing end for once.

"Defense and evasion is no path to victory." Shingti's words filtered slowly through Koida's fascination. "Eventually luck will fall on Lao's side."

"I wouldn't worry myself overmuch about Raijin, Princess," Lysander said. "I've doubted the kid for years now, but somehow he always manages to come out on top. It's disgusting."

Raijin showed no signs of fighting back, however. Lao's continuous attacks pressed him backward across the courtyard. The young chieftain waited for each ruby blade to slice within cutting distance before sliding back another step, swinging his lean body aside like an opening door. Lao had grown tired and frustrated, as Koida herself so often did when fighting the master. His attacks were sloppy enough that even she could see his errors, but still Raijin only evaded.

With a start, Koida realized that Raijin had yet to manifest any weapons or shields in this duel. So far, he hadn't used his Ro at all. Every move he made was a motion of the bare hands or feet.

They were all techniques she could use.

She leaned in closer, determined to commit every detail to memory. Master Lao might refuse to teach her when she couldn't manifest a weapon, but perhaps she could learn on her own.

In the courtyard, Master Lao backed Raijin into a corner where the palace walls met. Lao attacked, slicing his Double-Crescent Knives at the younger man's throat and stomach.

Raijin spun and ran up the corner, feet springing off of each wall alternately, until he flipped over the master's head and landed easily behind him. With a hook of his leg, he swept Lao.

The master landed flat on his back. Though the air woofed from his lungs, Lao managed to keep the glowing Double-Crescent Knives solid. He rolled up to his feet, lunging at the young chieftain.

Raijin slapped each of the attacks away with open hands. Lao overcommitted to a final dual swipe aimed at the young chieftain's flat stomach and exposed throat. Raijin knocked both aside, then lashed out with bare fists so fast that Koida almost couldn't follow them. She saw him hit Lao in the face once, then deliver two blows to his exposed ribs, but she thought she heard at least four more strikes land.

Beside her, Shingti cursed in awe.

"Yes," Lysander agreed.

In the courtyard, Raijin's body went as still as a stone column, his fingertips poised at Master Lao's throat.

"Admit defeat," he said, his rasping voice little more than a growl in the otherwise silent courtyard.

Master Lao's shoulders heaved as he panted for air.

"I am defeated," the older man wheezed. He pressed his fist against his palm and raised it to Raijin.

A cloud of glistening ruby Ro filtered from Lao's heartcenter and into Raijin's chest. The Ji Yu chieftain scowled as if disgusted.

"Now admit your crimes," Raijin ordered, his hand still at Lao's throat.

The master's face turned red. "I have done nothing—"

"Imir Ikindi'i," Raijin said. "Cold Sun, firstborn of Jaguar Three-Eyes. And now Second Princess Shyong San Koida."

Even from her place on the portico, Koida saw Master Lao pale at the foreign names.

"I don't know what you're getting at, spouting nonsense, Chieftain, but I can assure you—"

"Do you think I challenged you to a duel to pass the time?" Raijin snapped. "I know what you are, leech. You don't deserve to call yourself a master."

"What are these accusations you're slinging, Chieftain?" Shingti demanded, her tone carrying every ounce of authority the Exalted Emperor's did. The first princess hopped down from the balustrade, a glowing ruby sword manifesting in one hand. "I will hear the facts before you spill any blood in my palace."

Raijin didn't look away from the cringing Master Lao. "This man is a known predator of those with Ro deficiencies. He teaches them nothing, then spends all his time sparring them in order to steal their Ro. It's an exploitation of your sister, your path, and the position of master over student."

"That's nonsense," Koida blurted, stepping into the sunlight. "Master Lao has been my teacher for four years."

"You see!" Lao jabbed a finger at her.

"Name a single technique he's taught you, and I'll rescind my accusations," Raijin said.

Koida opened her mouth to list off the strikes and steps of the bo-shan stick, but each of those had come from the master before Lao. Hand and foot techniques and stances she had learned from her earlier masters and drilled with Shingti. Koida couldn't remember a single occasion when Lao had even corrected a stance. Since he had arrived at the palace, all Koida had done in training was spar.

"There must be something," she said stubbornly. "I only can't think of it because I wasn't prepared."

But even as she spoke, doubt whispered at the back of her mind. What sort of master would use any minor excuse to end their training, but only after he had absorbed some of his student's Ro?

"What's in your head, little sister?" Shingti asked, her sharp purple gaze narrowed.

"It's nothing," Koida insisted guiltily. These weren't thoughts someone should be having about their master.

"You don't have to protect him," Shingti said, voice low enough that it wouldn't carry beyond the two of them. "It's only honorable to defend your master if he is worth defending."

Without provocation, Master Lao shouted, "The Ji Yu chieftain is mistaken! This is a misunderstanding of Paths! His barbaric notions can't grasp the nuances of the Path of the Living Blade. Everyone here knows I would never prey on the second princess. Tell them, Second Princess!" As Lao spoke, he tried to force his way to his feet, but Raijin put a foot on the man's chest and pushed him back down to the tile.

"Do not address her," the Ji Yu chieftain growled.

"Ignore them," Shingti whispered, stepping in front of Koida and blocking her view of the men. "Both owe their allegiance to you, not you to them. Help me find the truth in this matter so no one can say justice was miscarried in our father's palace."

Koida gave her sister the smallest of nods, then stepped around Shingti to face the master and the chieftain.

"It's a simple matter," she said, her gaze jumping from Lao to Raijin. "If you both submit to a divination by the court eunuchs, they can tell us who is telling the truth."

Raijin nodded, a glint of approval in his jade eyes. "I submit to a divination."

175

Lao spluttered furiously. "I will stoop to no such low! I have been your master for years, Second Princess, and yet you allow this snake to whisper lies into your ear? Are you so easily manipulated into disloyalty by a fair face? If the Exalted Emperor Hao in all his infinite wisdom has seen fit to retain my services for his beloved youngest daughter for this long without incident—"

From the portico came a drunken hoot of laughter. The yellow-haired foreigner, Lysander, slapped his knee. "Keep talking, Ro-thief! Your innocence will be judged by the length of your argument."

Raijin silenced his drunken friend with a look.

"It was not a question, Lao," Shingti said, manifesting a second sword and creeping closer to the men. "The second princess's decree carries the same authority as mine or my father's. You have no right to refuse her once she's given a royal order."

At this, Shingti sent a meaningful glance at Koida.

"As second princess of the Shyong San Empire, I order Master Lao and the Ji Yu chieftain to accompany me to the Eastern tower for a divination. If the master is found to be the victim of slander, then Ji Yu Raijin will repay him with whatever price he sets on his honorable reputation. If not, you'll be subject to the laws of the empire."

Lao's face twisted into a grimace. Under the law, Ro-thieves were not given the benefit of a quick death at the hands of an executioner, but drawn and quartered by demon beasts. After a moment's hesitation, however, he nodded.

"It will be as you wish, Second Princess," the master said in a tone of formal respect for royalty.

Raijin let the man up, and together, he and Shingti escorted Lao to the portico.

Koida followed, forcing her face to show nothing but determination. Half her mind claimed she was betraying the master who had given up four years of his life trying to teach an unteachable Ro-cripple. The other half wondered why Lao was sweating so heavily if he was innocent. And what of Yoichi's warning about being wary of Raijin? Was she allowing a liar full of sweet words to destroy her father's empire from the inside out? Both men had submitted to the divination, where she had expected the guilty party to steadfastly refuse and make the answer obvious.

As their small procession ascended the steps into the shade, Koida desperately hoped that the eunuchs truly did have a magic that would reveal the liar.

Without warning, Master Lao whirled, locking an arm around Koida's neck. A glowing Double-Crescent Knife appeared an inch from her eye. She didn't even have time to shriek in surprise.

Ro blades lit up the shade of the portico. Armor clinked and boots hit the ground as members of both princesses' personal guards sprang into action.

"Stay back!" Lao shouted. He jumped off the stair, pulling Koida with him. She clawed at his arm, and her soft-soled shoes scrabbled for purchase on the glazed tiles, but Lao tightened his grip until her vision blurred and her head pounded. He dragged her along easily. "Keep your distance, or I'll shear her face off!"

With detached awareness, Koida watched the palace soldiers freeze where they stood, looking to Shingti for orders. The first princess nodded at one of her Dragonfly guards, and he gave a signal to the rest. Slowly, they began to fan out, but didn't approach Koida and her captor.

"Dismiss your weapons," Lao demanded.

When the soldiers didn't immediately move to obey, he pressed the cutting edge of the Double-Crescent Knife to the hollow below her bottom lip. Koida tried to pull her face away, but Lao's grip tightened until it felt as if her eyes would pop out of her head. Shingti scowled and raised up on her toes but didn't take another step. Koida thought it looked as if her elder sister was trying to calculate whether Master Lao could kill her before Shingti killed him.

Finally, the first princess growled, "Do as he says," through gritted teeth.

The guards didn't look any happier about it than the first princess, but they dismissed their weapons. Hyung-Po caught Koida's eye, his round face frantic, probably imagining the fury he would have to endure when he told Batsai that he'd allowed the second princess to be diced and scattered to the winds.

As Lao pulled her across the courtyard, movement near the back of the soldiers drew Koida's attention.

Raijin was circling around them, and it looked as if he held some sort of black butterfly sword down at his side. Koida only glimpsed it through the gaps in the guards, but it certainly wasn't made of Ro. Rather than glowing, the wide blade seemed to absorb the light around it.

And then the guards opposite Rajin's position stumbled and cursed.

"Apologies, apologies," Lysander slurred drunkenly as he wove in and out of the tense crowd, shouldering into them as often as going around. "But I wouldn'ave to apologize if some people would get outta my way."

Koida looked back toward Raijin, but he was gone. She searched the sea of faces, but didn't see a hint of that strange blade or his unruly black hair.

"Stay back!" Lao thundered in Koida's ear, digging his Double-Crescent into the hollow below her lip.

A trickle of warm blood rolled down Koida's chin. Her heart raced, and she was certain she was about to have her lips cut off at the very least. She tried to hold still to minimize the damage, but a terrified shaking had taken hold of her entire body. As much as she had always hated being known throughout the empire as nothing more than a passable face to look at, she didn't want to be horribly disfigured.

"Let's all juss calm down," Lysander slurred in reply, still tripping tipsily forward. He stumbled and grabbed onto one of the Dragonfly Guards. "Oh, ah, whoops. I think you've had too much to drink, there, friend. Might wanna—"

A force like a charging bison hit Koida in the ribs, knocking the air from her lungs and tearing her out of Lao's grasp. All she saw was a blur of black and sun-burnished skin. Then she slammed to a stop, her cheek thudding into the hard wall of Raijin's chest.

Behind her, yelling and running boots.

"He's going to run!" Lysander's shout cracked across the courtyard like a breaking branch.

Koida twisted in Raijin's grasp, turning in time to see Lao backing impossibly *up* the wall, his legs and left arm moving like a spider's over the stonework. His right arm—sliced cleanly off below the elbow—lay hugged against his stomach, gushing blood. Hyung-Po and a few of the Dragonfly Guard sprinted to the wall and tried to climb up after him, Shingti hurling ruby Flying Knives, but Lao skittered up onto the wall without stopping.

A dark streak blurred across the courtyard and up the corner where the walls met, knocking aside a climbing guard. Lao disappeared below the roofline. The blur following him slowed just enough for Koida to see the cloth face wrappings and long horsetail of dark hair.

The silent woman's head snapped from side to side, then she changed directions abruptly and shot below the roofline.

"Dragonflies, surround the palace!" Shingti was shouting. "Move!"

Koida stared at the splashes of red marking Lao's escape route. It looked as if a calligrapher had slung red ink at the wall. Absently, she touched her bottom lip where Lao's Double-Crescent Knife had been pressed. Still just a trickle of blood running down her chin, nothing major missing. Raijin had saved her, somehow ripping her from Lao's grasp with inhuman speed, then spun them around just before she slammed into the wall, taking the impact himself.

"Are you all right?" Raijin asked, his rasping voice right next to her ear. "Did I hurt you?"

Koida untwisted, turning back to face him. "No, I'm—"

She broke off as she realized that she was still cradled against Raijin's chest.

As if he'd just realized the same thing, Raijin straightened up and eased his right arm from around her rib cage. A wave of dizziness swept through Koida and she wobbled slightly, but he grabbed onto her elbow so she could steady herself.

Her gaze lighted on the black butterfly sword. Just as she'd thought, it was no Ro construct, but made of a glassy black stone. Raijin held the blade safely away from his side, the tip dripping blood on the courtyard tiles.

Except he wasn't holding it. From his elbow to his hand, his arm *was* the butterfly sword. When he saw her staring, he cleared his throat and tried to pull the blade behind his back.

Without thinking about the rudeness of her action, Koida caught his arm and held it in place. Before her eyes, the blade shifted from the black stone butterfly sword back to his hand and forearm, the sleeve falling in place over it as if nothing strange had happened at all.

Then Shingti was at their side, pulling her away from Raijin.

"What a mess," Shingti growled, prodding at Koida's chin and bottom lip. "That scum. I'll execute him myself."

"I'm fine." Koida pulled her head out of her sister's hands. "Raijin saved me."

Assured of her sister's wellness, Shingti turned to the Ji Yu chieftain. "What technique was that? How did you manifest a blade from real stone? Was that a Ro technique? Or, no, is it a constructed mechanism?"

"It's living lavaglass from the lower reaches," Raijin said. "Not exactly a mechanism, but not a Ro technique, either."

Koida's brows nearly touched. There was nothing in the lower reaches but savages. What business could the civilized leader of a mountain tribe have there?

181

A hand smacked down onto Shingti's shoulder, making Koida flinch. Lysander had appeared behind her sister.

But the hand on Shingti's shoulder wasn't his.

Koida's stomach lurched. That yellow-haired drunk was holding a forearm that had been cleanly amputated just below the elbow. It was covered in an array of colorful tattoos Koida recognized from Master Lao's Heroic Record.

Shingti swiped the dead hand off her shoulder as if it were nothing more than a bothersome insect.

"Stop that," the first princess snapped. "I am attempting to speak to your leader, one warrior artist to another."

"So am I," Lysander said, the slur miraculously gone from his words. He turned to Raijin. "You let most of him get away." Lysander used the dismembered arm like a Sword Hand, slashing it casually through the air. "Should've cut horizontal instead of vertical, taken his head and shoulders off."

"I didn't want to kill him," Raijin said. "Not until after he told us what he knew, anyway."

Lysander pointed the hand at Raijin. "Wipe that smug look off your face. Just because you were right about that Ro-sucker Lao being here doesn't mean that Youn Wha is, too."

"Hush thinks it does," Raijin said, glancing toward the rooftops again.

"Her going after him doesn't prove anything," Lysander said. "She probably just wants to dissect him and see what's inside."

Raijin looked as if he were about to protest, but Shingti interrupted.

"Which hidden pocket did you pull your information from, Chieftain?" the first princess asked. "His actions betrayed him, but how did you know what he'd done? He'd obviously never seen you before or he should've run the moment he saw you, not stay around to spar."

"The abbreviated answer is that we've walked in on Lao's aftermath more than once. He's a…" The Ji Yu chieftain stopped suddenly, frowning, then said, "Lao has stolen Ro from two of my friends and allies—three, counting your sister. One of his former victims is a student of my path now. I have a responsibility to bring him to justice."

"My Dragonfly Guard will stop him before he leaves the palace grounds," Shingti said with certainty.

"I wouldn't count on it." Lysander held up the dismembered hand, reigniting the queasiness in the pit of Koida's stomach. "One lost arm isn't going to slow him down much. That pest has slipped through our fingers before minus bigger chunks of himself."

Shingti scowled. "You're mistaken."

"I might be, but Hush never is."

"Then you're exaggerating," Shingti said.

Koida nodded. "Lao has been whole and healthy as long as we've known him."

"Lao's got some nasty secrets, princesses," Lysander responded. "The least of which is leeching Ro from those who can't afford to lose it."

"Lysander," Raijin said, his low rasp a warning.

"Have it your way, Raij. But while we sit here following your closed-mouth nonsense rules, he's getting away." Lazily, Lysander scratched his chin with the back of the dead hand.

Koida felt the color drain from her face and pressure rise in the back of her throat.

“Give me that.” Shingti snatched the appendage from Lysander, much to Koida’s relief. “If you’re so sure Lao will slip past my guard and outrun your woman, then go to my father and tell him I want messengers dispatched to every city with Lao’s description. He can’t outrun or out-hide every citizen in the empire.”

From the corner of her eye, Koida caught Raijin giving the yellow-haired man a nearly imperceptible nod.

Lysander bowed. “It will be done, Princess.”

“First Princess,” Shingti corrected. Then she pointed the dead hand at Koida, sending Koida’s stomach reeling once more. “We need to see the alchemists. With skin like yours, you’ll have a scar twice the size of the wound if you leave it untreated.” She beckoned to Koida with the limb. “You can talk to your future husband at the feast tonight. Come on, little sister. Elder sister will accompany you to the Eastern tower.”

CHAPTER TWENTY-ONE

Present

WHEN THE ALCHEMISTS SAW KOIDA'S tiny cut, they had to hear the story. It wasn't every day—or even every year—that the second princess came to their tower for real wound care, superficial or not. Shingti was all too happy to recount it, using Lao's dismembered arm to illustrate several points. By the time the first princess finished her account of Raijin's strange technique and how the arm was severed, Koida needed a powder to settle the sickness in her stomach.

With the nausea powder consumed and the tincture for the cut applied to Koida's chin, the princesses departed the tower to dress for the wedding feast. Thankfully, Shingti left the arm with the alchemist Sulyeon, who had expressed great interest in experimenting on it.

As with the day before, Koida's ladies invaded her bedchamber and spent the next several hours bathing, combing, dressing, and decorating her, all the while fretting over her shallow cut as if her bottom lip were a loved one who had been murdered horribly.

Koida ignored their endless chatter, her mind wandering to what Raijin had said about the Ro-cripples he knew following his Path. Had he taught them that Ro-less fighting he'd used against Master Lao? And if other cripples had learned Raijin's Path, could she? Was it even possible to switch Paths? She'd never heard of such a thing outside the old legends.

The next Koida saw of her betrothed and her sister was in the royal waiting room outside the White Jade Feasting Hall. The nobles were all being seated from lowest ranked to highest for the second night's celebration, while she, Shingti, Yoichi, and the emperor waited. Raijin was there as well. Tonight and each night after, the bride and groom would walk to the dais together, the final two to be seated.

By the time Koida arrived, the Exalted Emperor Hao was raging at the young chieftain, his voice thundering through the halls.

"You dismembered and chased a perfectly good Master of the Living Blade from my palace without royal permission," the emperor bellowed, his face so dark red that it was nearly purple. "The only master in the valley who would take on a Ro-crippled child, and you dismissed him!"

Koida's brow furrowed. Clearly her father had forgotten that not so many nights ago, he had suggested she abandon training altogether. The sudden shift wasn't a good sign. Her father became petty and argumentative whenever he was sinking into a low mood—usually when he had remained away from the battlefield for any stretch of time.

Raijin stood silently through the emperor's diatribe, his cold jade eyes betraying not a hint of fear at the ruler's fury. But Koida knew the chieftain wouldn't know how best to handle her father when he was like this.

When Hao paused to gather more fuel for his fury, Koida stepped between them.

"Apologies, beloved father," she said in a respectful filial tone, bowing deeply enough to expose the back of her neck to her father and remaining bent. The cascades of bells slid a little, but did not ring. "But Ji Yu Raijin was only obeying a royal order. Your adoring second daughter gave it when she learned that Master Lao was a Ro-thief who sought to make a fool of the Exalted Emperor by living off of his good graces. When apprehended, Lao stooped yet lower and used your second daughter as a hostage and a shield against your first daughter and her personal guard. The chieftain of the Ji Yu saved me from Lao's clutches and exacted a steep price paid in the man's flesh."

Raijin's eyes caught hers for half a moment. She looked away. She hadn't technically lied; it didn't matter that the royal order Raijin had obeyed was to submit to a divination by the eunuchs, not capture Lao.

"But he didn't catch the degenerate, did he?" the emperor retorted, taking a sharp right turn from his original tactic of bemoaning the loss of her master. "If he could move fast enough to snatch you back when Shingti couldn't, then he should have had plenty of time to bring Lao back for execution."

"Raijin was concerned for my well-being." Koida pouted. "Doesn't Father care more about Koida than drawing and quartering some good-for-nothing false teacher?"

"Of course." Emperor Hao crossed his arms over his wide stomach. Though his face did not show it, he was softening.

Over her father's shoulder, Koida caught Cousin Yoichi's gaze from his seat on the lounge. She expected a conspiratorial smile from the white-haired young man acknowledging the way she had turned aside her father's anger, but the smile Yoichi sent her never touched his plum-colored eyes.

Yoichi stood and joined them. "The chieftain saves the second princess from a false master with one hand, then disrespects her by withholding a bride price with his other." He glanced from Koida to Shingti to the emperor. "Surely I am not the only one who sees this discrepancy."

"Apologies," Raijin said, "but it was my understanding that the custom of the groom giving gifts to the family was no longer observed in the empire."

Yoichi snorted. "You must have gathered your information from among the commoners, Chieftain. The previous second princess was married off for no less than a pristine demon stallion from which all royal destriers today are descended."

"Wasn't that Father's great-aunt?" Shingti asked with open incredulity. "That was nearly seventy years ago."

"Father had yet to even be born," Koida said. "There is no precedent for a bride price in these modern times."

"The wagging tongues of the court say otherwise," Yoichi insisted, expertly exploiting the emperor's concern for saving face. "This chieftain is making a mockery of you, treating you as no better than a peasant, and I refuse to stand for it."

Koida's heart sped up a step when she realized this was the perfect opportunity to bring up an idea she'd been turning over all afternoon.

"In truth, elder cousin, I care less about saving face for those backbiters than I do about continuing my training," she said. "I've just learned that I spent the last four years under Master Lao for nothing, and he was the last teacher to be found who was willing to tutor a cripple. But perhaps Ji Yu Raijin could teach me and count it as the bride price."

"Him?" Emperor Hao's dark brows pulled low over his plum-colored eyes.

Yoichi let out a sharp laugh. "He doesn't even follow the Path of the Living Blade, little cousin."

Koida's face burned, but she ignored Yoichi's scoffing and turned to Raijin. His face was unreadable stone.

"Will you teach me?" she repeated.

"If you wish, I can teach you the Path of the Thunderbird, but your cousin is correct, my Path is not like the Living Blade," Raijin warned her. "The training begins hard and only gets harder as you climb through the ranks. Progress comes slowly, and with your deficiency, you'll have to work harder than any of the other practitioners."

"You'll teach her." Emperor Hao snorted. "Bold words are easily spoken, Chieftain, but Koida has been Ro-crippled since birth. The best masters in the empire have been unable to advance her."

"Apologies, Exalted Emperor," Raijin said, "but that means nothing. Strength comes from facing adversity, not the indulgence of weakness." His eyes locked on Koida's as if she were the only one in the hall with him, and he switched to a familiar spousal tone. "Are you certain this is what you want, Koida?"

"She is still my daughter for five more nights," Emperor Hao said, annoyed. "You may address your request to me."

But neither the second princess nor the chieftain was paying attention to the emperor.

"I want to learn the Ro-less fighting you used against Lao," Koida said. "Can you teach me how to do it?"

Raijin dipped his head in a nod. "It's one of the first things you'll learn."

"Master!" Koida dropped to her knees in her dress robes, her bell cascades calling out her loss of poise, and bowed her head, pressing her fist to her palm.

Raijin returned the bow, then helped her back to her feet. In the tangled lengths of her dress robes, the maneuver would have been impossible without his assistance.

Emperor Hao glowered, but seemed to realize that, at best, he could forbid Koida to train under Raijin for five more nights, no longer.

The waiting room doors swung open, revealing a feast hall filled with nobles and officials.

In a resounding voice, the court speaker announced, "Decorated hero Shyong Liu Yoichi."

With one last cold, condescending glance at Raijin, Yoichi departed for his seat. Koida promised herself that she would speak to her white-haired half-brother alone at the first opportunity and convince him that there was no offense in the lack of bride price, and the training was what she'd been after all along anyway. She was certain he would back her once he knew how she felt.

"Dragonfly of the Battlefield," the court speaker continued, "First Princess Shyong San Shingti escorting the Exalted Emperor Hao, Conqueror of a Thousand Tribes."

As Shingti led their father into the feasting hall, Koida inhaled deeply, trying to contain her excitement. It was trying so desperately to escape that she could hardly hold still.

"Are you all right?" Raijin murmured at her side. So quiet, his gravelly voice was nearly a growl. "You're bouncing."

A radiant smile broke free. "When can your student begin training, Master?"

"Are you talking up to me again?" he asked, a smile tugging at the corners of his lips. "If the cherished second princess insists on formality, her lowly chieftain husband will do the same."

"Groom, Chieftain Ji Yu Raijin escorting bride, Lilac of the Valley, Second Princess Shyong San Koida," the court speaker said.

As she and her betrothed walked side by side to the dais, Koida told him, "I will speak familiarly to you outside of training if it pleases you, but I won't be disrespectful of your superior rank in the Path while you instruct me."

"Gratitude for the compromise," Raijin said, pulling out her chair as was expected of his lower rank.

"Gratitude for the seat," she clipped off smartly.

His lips twisted into a grin. "It was your unexalted husband's pleasure."

Koida covered a traitorous giggle with her sleeve.

Servants spread through the feasting hall, filling cups with the palace's signature blood orange wine and carrying golden and jade platters of fattened calf, towering displays of exotic fruits and vegetables, and elaborate braids of spiced breads. They served first the emperor, then down through the ranks, a waiting servant bowing up the steps to do the same for the bride and groom.

Koida watched them go, wondering if everything had been as beautiful and appetizing the night before or if she had been too occupied with fear of her future husband to notice it.

"May we begin training tomorrow morning?" she asked. In the royal waiting room, Raijin had spoken as if her crippled Ro would not be the barrier she'd always been told it was, but only a hindrance. If it took years to advance on the Path of the Thunderbird, then she wanted to begin immediately.

Raijin shook his head. "My sincere apologies, but we can't begin tomorrow. I have something very important to see to. When I return, we'll begin."

Courtesy would not allow Koida to ask where Raijin was going, but she was only concerned with his destination insofar as it affected her future training, anyway.

Instead, she asked, "Is there anything I can do until you return to prepare myself?"

"Do you know how to meditate at rest?"

Koida shook her head, taking care not to disturb the bell cascades. She had read about meditation in ancient legends, but had never known anyone to practice it in modern times.

"I can ask Hush to teach you the correct form while I'm gone, but the important part of meditation is cultivating your Ro. The first exercise most students learn is Pouring Ro into Itself."

At her confused look, Raijin smiled.

"It sounds strange, but it's actually fairly easy. Focus some of your Ro into a ring. Send the rest into the hole at the center, then catch it on the other side, and cycle it back around. Try to get it circling continuously, so that it looks as if you have two rings linked together."

"I think I understand. I'll begin practicing tonight if Hush can spare the time." Koida realized that in her excitement about the new Path she'd forgotten to inquire about the woman's rooftop pursuit. "Is she well? How did Lao escape her? Did he defeat her?"

"There aren't many warrior artists who can defeat Hush in a fight, and Lao isn't one of them." For a moment, he fell silent, as if deciding how much to tell Koida. "We think—well, I think and there's a good chance Hush agrees with me—that he had a secret way into and through the palace."

"You think he planned for a day when he would need to escape."

"This isn't the first time he's needed to disappear. Hush has been hunting him for years and gotten much closer than I have."

Koida twisted her wine cup as she considered this. "It's eerie knowing someone for such a long time only to learn that you never knew them at all."

When she looked up again, she found Raijin staring at her.

He smiled, clearly embarrassed. "Imagine meeting someone and feeling as if you already know them."

A blush heated Koida's face. She took a sip of wine to hide it.

"How long will you be gone?" she asked afterward. This time, she wasn't asking entirely out of eagerness to begin training.

"Not long, I hope," Raijin said, his jade eyes searching the sea of faces below. They fell on Yoichi's plum gaze. Neither man made any effort to convey the slightest amount of cordiality, and neither man looked away.

Another servant bowed up the steps, this one carrying a silver platter like the one that had contained the sunbright the night before. Tonight, however, the cups were the only things on the platter.

"Is this another of the Ji Yu wedding rites?" Koida asked as the servant set it on the table between them.

The question tore Raijin's attention from the stare down with Yoichi.

"Breath of the Underwater Panther," Raijin said, lifting one cup for her inspection. Inside, an eddy of liquid swirled, blue and gold battling for control of the surface. Koida could hear the trickling babble of a shallow creek against the sides and bottom of the cup. "It isn't an imitation like the sunbright pill, but the real thing, from the Dead Waters Kingdom. It will protect you from malicious harm for seven days. More than enough time to—" He faltered. "—to complete the wedding rituals and make it back to my village safely."

Koida lifted her cup. She could feel the whirling of the current in her finger pads.

"Will it make me sick?"

"Not this," Raijin said. "It isn't like a demon's core stone. Your body consumes this, not your Ro. You don't have to do anything except drink it."

With both hands, he raised his cup to her, then swallowed the eddying liquid inside. Koida spent a moment watching Raijin for signs of illness before she did the same. The Breath of the Underwater Panther was cold, and it tasted like the icy melt that ran down from the mountains and swelled the river and creeks during the spring.

Belatedly, she remembered the pill from the night before.

"I forgot to thank you for the sunbright," she said. "It was awful, but I feel like it changed my Ro somehow. Made it stronger."

"Sunbright cleanses and refines the Ro," Raijin said. "There are certain items that will strengthen Ro enough to speed progression, but those are of no use until the higher levels. Most are potentially deadly to anyone who hasn't advanced, and each one affects the Ro differently."

"Levels?" Koida asked.

Raijin shook his head. "In the Path I follow, the students are ranked based on how many times their Ro has advanced."

Now she was utterly confused. In the Path of the Living Blade, there were no ranks, only students and masters.

"But Ro can only advance once," she said. That was common knowledge. Ro advanced one time. In the Path of the Living Blade, that advancement allowed the student to manifest the bladed weapons that gave the Path its name.

"Apologies, Koida, but you've been misinformed. Depending on the Path you've chosen, Ro can advance many times, each new level granting the student new abilities. In the Path of the Thunderbird, there are nine stages of advancement."

"The Path of the Thunderbird is not one I've heard of," she said.

"It's an offshoot of the Path of Darkening Skies." He hesitated, then added, "I couldn't complete my training on that Path, so I had to create a new one."

It was as if he couldn't stop making unbelievable statements.

"What? How?" Koida demanded.

"Largely by trial and error." Raijin grinned sheepishly and cleared his throat, though the gravel in his voice remained the same. "More error than I'd like to admit, honestly."

"But all Paths were created by the ancients millennia ago," she said. "You can't just create a new one."

Raijin laughed. "Every Path was young sometime."

"And what about other students and masters? If you're the only one who follows it, then it's just another Path executed incorrectly."

"The people of my tribe are all students of it," he said. "Though I only require them to learn enough to defend themselves. Whether they choose to study it further is their decision. A great many of them do. As for other Thunderbird masters, there are two besides me. Both mastered it much faster than I did, though Hush was already a full master of another Path when we began training together. I think it becomes easier to master secondary Paths once you've mastered the first…if you can swallow your pride enough to start over at the bottom of a new one, that is."

"What about Lysander?" Koida asked, nodding at the yellow-haired foreigner. Shingti had left their father's side to join the raucous group gathered around the man. The two of them seemed to get along strangely well, perhaps helped along by the fact that as soon as he saw the first princess, the foreigner offered her a drink from his ivory flask. "Is he the other master of your Path?"

Raijin shook his head. "Lysander could follow the Path of the Thunderbird if he chose to, but he's not convinced it's a real Path yet. So far, you and he agree on that much."

"If you can teach me to fight as well as you do, then you'll change my mind," she said.

He grinned. "If you work as hard at training as you do trying to disprove everything I say, then you'll be besting me in no time."

They turned to their food for a time in companionable silence, Koida turning over and over all that she was learning about her future husband.

"Your parents must have been very proud to leave the tribe in the hands of a son who created his own Path," she said.

Raijin finished his bite, then took a sip of wine. He seemed to be in no hurry to speak.

"The tribe wasn't left to me," he said.

"Did you defeat the previous chieftain?"

"There was no previous chieftain." Raijin twisted his wine cup. "I'm the first. I didn't intend to start a tribe…" He shrugged. "It just happened."

Koida raised an eyebrow at him. "You accidentally started a new tribe?"

"People kept coming," he said. "People who were missing something or searching for something. We couldn't turn them away."

"You started your own tribe, you created your own Path." She could hardly comprehend having the power to change not only your own life, but the world. "You're like the heroes from the old legends."

"Let's hope this hero doesn't fail."

Raijin looked so grave that Koida grabbed his hand.

"He won't," she said. "Whatever his journey is, his future wife will help him to the end."

A strange shadow crossed Raijin's face then. His eyes bored into hers.

"I know," he said, his cool fingers squeezing hers.

CHAPTER TWENTY-TWO
6 years ago

A MISTY DRIZZLE BEGAN TO FALL AS Raijin made his way down the mountainside. With the thick scrim of clouds covering the moon, the night was dark and lonely. Once he passed outside of the area that could be reached in a thirty-minute run, the well-worn paths around the school disappeared. Grass and small shrubs carpeted the earth between massive, moss-covered boulders, their odd shapes casting strange shadows by the light of the lantern Raijin had taken on his way out of the school.

Though Master Chugi had insisted he leave without packing, Raijin had little besides spare uniforms to take with him. The only personal possessions students of the Path of Darkening Skies kept were the sashes denoting their rank and the sturdy martial meditation uniforms given to them by the school. With the addition of the lantern and the pill Master Chugi had pressed into his hands, Raijin now had more possessions than he'd ever had in his life.

Closer inspection told Raijin the capsule was a Breath of the Underwater Panther pill. It would mimic the protective properties of the water demon's exhalation, shielding him for a full day from anything malicious that might try to harm him.

As he reached the tree line of the forest, his lantern light reflected back at him from the eyes of unseen creatures. It was well known at the school that these woods were filled with deadly guai. Raijin considered taking the pill then, but told himself it would be better to wait. The journey down the mountain was long. It could take days. If he wasted the protection now when there was no immediate threat, he might find himself in peril and empty-handed later.

The undergrowth and trees seemed to close in behind him, the canopy overhead easing the drizzle slightly. Rain pattered against the leaves overhead. The loam squished beneath his feet like a springy wet cushion. No night animals called to one another in the darkness, but he heard them scamper through the brush now and again.

The sun would rise in a few hours, he realized. His daily tasks would go undone for the first time since he was six years old. Once that agreement was broken, he would never be allowed back in the school. That part of his life would be over. Sixteen years of training and work done. What would he do with the next sixteen?

Raijin pulled his robes tighter against the cold. He wished he could have woken Yong Lei to say goodbye. Would Master Chugi tell his friend where he had gone? Would they ever meet again?

As he traveled deeper into the woods, the eyeshine and movement sounds of the smaller forest animals disappeared. The hairs on the back of Raijin's neck prickled. It felt as if he were being watched. When he turned to look, however, he found nothing. Perhaps it was only his imagination. Thoughts of the demon beasts frightened him out of his wits. He swallowed and continued walking, one hand on the blue-and-gold pill in his robe's pocket.

Then he heard it—the rattle of a branch scraping over a wide back. Using a burst of Cyclone Speed, he whirled.

A huge ray, with a wingspan easily the length of a bison, drifted in the air behind him, the creature identical to the river rays that filled the muddiest waterways in the mountains. Except, of course, that it was swimming through the air rather than water. Its scar-crossed skin shined with silver-gray Ro, and on the top of its head, its eyes glowed like molten platinum. Raijin could smell the beast's musk, the salty, wet, burning ozone stink of a lightning strike on the ocean. A long, deadly stinger trailed the ray like a barbed cane pole, razor sharp and crackling with electricity.

The raw, deadly power of the sight made Raijin's heart stutter and his bowels weak. He was standing face-to-face with a guai—a demon beast—the type of creature that had killed more humans wandering the mountains than anything else, and there were no masters about to help him fend it off. He forgot the pill in his hand, forgot his purpose in the forest, forgot even his name in that sudden wash of terror.

The guai-ray sensed his fear. It shot toward him, slashing its stinger through the air.

Just before he was impaled, Raijin remembered Straight Line Winds. He sprinted, his speed boosted by the Wind technique. He nearly bashed into the trunk of a dead evergreen, but escaped the ray's wicked stinger.

The beast gave no howl of chase as it cut through the night behind him, but Raijin heard the crackling sizzle of the ray's electrical appendage slicing madly through the air. The hair on the back of his head stood up as the stinger's current passed too close. A moment later, he smelled singed hair.

Raijin's mind churned frantically. How could he escape this creature? Demon beasts never tired and didn't require sleep or food. It could chase him to the school and back easily. At best, he could sprint Straight Line Wind speed for ten minutes before his Ro exhausted itself. But then what? Even if the exhaustion of Ro wouldn't leave him weak and fatigued, this was as fast as he could run, and still he could feel the creature just over his shoulder, could see its silvery Ro lighting up the trees and undergrowth just ahead.

A Shield of the Crescent Moon would only protect so much of his body from the razor-bladed stinger, and an electrical current could travel through his body and stop his heart no matter where it struck.

Raijin dodged the knotty bole of an ancient oak, then leapt over a fungus-covered deadfall. Funny, in his panic he could see the lacy pattern of every lichen and the velvety texture of the resident mushrooms as if he'd stopped to study them for hours.

Through the trees to his left, he caught sight of a tight stand of white birches and tangled briars, their pale bark ghostly in the darkness. Raijin grabbed the trunk of a rafter pine, using it to turn his momentum sharply, and sprinted toward the birches. He ducked under a low-hanging branch and into the brambles, thorns and cutleafs tearing at his skin and uniform. Immediately, he dropped the speed-enhancing ability and skidded to a stop.

The ray slammed into the ghostly birch trunks with a splintering crash, and for a brief, thunderous heartbeat,

Raijin thought the beast would smash its way in, but there were too many of the trees spaced too close together. It couldn't break through with sheer brute force.

Raijin dropped to the ground, his head spinning with relief. He was safe.

Thwack! Thwack! Thwack!

The guai-ray chopped at the brambles and trees with its bladelike stinger.

Raijin scrambled back to his feet. Run or stay?

If he ran, the ray would flit around the side and catch him. If he stayed, it would cut its way into the thicket and catch him.

Thwack! The scent of burning birch filled the air as the demon ray's lightning stinger blackened the trunks. *Thwack!*

If he hesitated much longer, the decision would be made for him.

"Please!" Raijin yelled. Shaking, he pressed his fists together and bowed, keeping his eyes on the creature's lashing, sizzling stinger. "Honored ruler of the Shangyang Forest, please do not kill this pathetic child! I cannot provide any challenge for your hunting and would only be a waste of your great might!"

The ray froze mid-swing of its arcing stinger.

Encouraged, Raijin went on. "If I have done something to offend, I apologize and declare my debt to the honored guai. Is there no way your servant can make amends?"

This proved to be the wrong thing to say. Wings flapping with rage, the guai-ray slammed its head and shoulders against the trees, trying to batter its way in once more.

"The legged creature kills and butchers my mate and destroys my nest, then it asks to make amends?!" the demon roared in a voice like a mountain crumbling into a sea.

The ground shifted beneath Raijin's feet as the trees' roots strained against the ray's pounding. He stumbled back against a cutleaf bush, so startled that he hardly noticed the waxy leaves slicing into his arms and back through his school clothes. Not only a demon beast, but one that could speak. Through his panic, his mind spit out a fact he'd read in the Tiered Demons scroll: to have developed that ability, this guai-ray must be a hundred years old at least. Rarely did demon beasts live to fifty years before hunters or battles for territory killed them.

"Apologies!" Raijin's voice cracked with fear. "Ten thousand apologies, honored ruler of the forest, but I have never seen your mate or nest!"

The thrashing stopped.

"The legged thing is lying," the ray growled, wings rippling. "Its partner will sneak up behind Zhuan now and kill her with their armies of poisoned wasps."

"Your servant has no wasps, great and honored mountain ray," Raijin said. He turned out his pockets, then untied his uniform jacket and opened it to show nothing but his lean chest and stomach. "No traveling partner, either. In fact, your servant is realizing more every moment just how alone he is."

"Prove yourself," Zhuan the guai-ray demanded, pressing in against the trees and brambles. Her snout poked between two of the widest spaced trunks. "Put out your hand and let me sense your body's electrical signature."

"Will the honored guai give an oath to assure her servant's survival?"

"If you are neither of the legged creatures I have been tracking, then no harm will come to you," she said, pressing closer. The birches at her shoulders groaned.

"Apologies, honored ruler—" Raijin bowed over his fists once more to offset any perceived rudeness of his insistence. "—but that is no oath."

Zhuan snapped her wings down hard, indignant. "My every word is an oath older than your people, legged thing. I will not dilute my speech with many words for your comfort. Put out your hand."

Raijin couldn't see that he had any other choice. He'd done nothing to this beast or any other. That alone should exonerate him.

However, his hand still shook as he stretched it toward her snout. She raised her body at a slight angle. On either side of her flat, crushing mouth plates, Raijin could see a set of branching ridges running beneath her skin. He flinched but forced himself to keep his hand extended. Blue lights like tiny fireflies ran along the branching ridges, spreading out to follow his fingers.

With a low growl, Zhuan backed away from the thicket.

"You spoke the truth, legged thing. Zhuan will not harm you."

Though he'd known all along that he was innocent, Raijin slumped as the tension in his neck and shoulders disappeared. He bowed again, his entire body loose and jittery.

"Thank you, honored—"

The demon ray interrupted, uninterested in his courtesy. "Have you seen two-legged creatures like yourself with poisoned wasps? Their electrical signatures are male. I tracked them from the destroyed nest in my cave. They were moving this way."

"Poisoned wasps?" Raijin asked, retying his sash over his jacket. "Humans—legged creatures like me—cannot command wasps."

Zhuan turned an imperious circle in the air.

"Their stingers protruded from what was left of my mate's thick hide," she said. "They could not bury themselves as completely in him as they did in my cubs' tender flesh, but their poison worked just as effectively. The stingers were long and thin. Silver. Numerous."

An image of a needle blowgun appeared in Raijin's mind. He'd seen such a thing illustrated and described as the weapon of choice for many fictional villains in the wandering warrior stories he and Master Chugi enjoyed.

"Were the stingers metal?" he asked.

Her snout dipped. "Their signature was iron with a small amount of carbon."

"These sound like the poisoned needles evildoers shoot from a blowgun over a distance when they cannot best an opponent in a close-up fight. It is a cowardly weapon."

"It must be so," Zhuan agreed. "If my mate had sensed these vile legged things stalking our nest, they could never have killed him. He was mighty."

"Your servant—"

"Stop that nonsense talk that hides your self behind words!" The demon beast fluttered her wings with frustration. "Speak out in the open or not at all."

Raijin took a moment to compose himself. If anyone had ever asked him when might be an ideal time to speak in the highest tones of formal respect, he would have said when face-to-face with a force of nature like this guai-ray. Obviously demon beasts had different ideas about manners. He still couldn't bring himself to speak familiarly to her. He settled instead on the respectful address of an honored relative, a tone somewhere between familiar and formal.

"I am sorry, Zhuan, so sorry for what these legged creatures have done to your family."

Another flap of indignation. "You cannot apologize for what you had no part in, and there is no time to mourn for what has not been avenged. Will you bring death upon them with me, legged one?"

Something moved at the edge of the demon ray's silvery glow, but it was gone before Raijin's eyes could focus on it.

"Apologies, but I can't," he said, returning his gaze to the guai-ray. "To bring violence on another is against the teachings of my master unless it is to save a weaker creature from death."

"Aha. This is why you did not fight me," she said, her tail ticking back and forth as if reenacting the attack. "Because there is nothing weaker than a legged creature in my forest."

The memory of that mind-blanking fear prickled at Raijin's heart, even now trying to send panic racing through his veins. He hadn't even been able to remember his own name in that moment; there was no way he would have been able to remember the central code of his path.

"My master says that, in danger, one does not rise to the level of his hopes, but falls to the level of his training," he said, hoping she would accept this as agreement. Then he remembered the Breath of the

Underwater Panther pill Master Chugi had given him. He reached into his pocket and pulled it out. "But I can give you this. It will protect you from their poisoned needles and any other malicious harm someone might try to do to you for one full day."

He came out of the thicket, trusting the demon beast would stick to her word not to harm him, and offered the blue-and-gold pill to her. Zhuan descended on his palm, pressing her flat underside to his hand and crushing the pill between her jaw palates without damaging his flesh.

A ripple ran through the guai-ray from snout to barbed stinger.

"Thank you for the gift," she rumbled. "In return, no harm will come to you from demons or natural beasts while you move through my territory."

"Thank you, Zhuan." He bowed to her, this time deep enough to expose the back of his neck and make himself vulnerable. He wanted to show the guai-ray that she had his full trust.

"I would know what you are called, legged one."

"Ji Yu Raijin."

"The thunderer who stops the rain," she mused, interpreting the ancient meanings of his names. "I cannot see how this will come to pass on your current path, but I could not see legged ones killing my mate while I was hunting, either. Go in peace, Ji Yu Raijin."

Without waiting for his response, Zhuan the demon guai-ray swam off into the darkness. Once more, something flickered at the edge of Raijin's vision, but when he turned the thing was gone.

Deciding to take the hundred-year beast at her promise that he would not be harmed by animal or demon, Raijin turned back down the mountain and returned to his walk.

CHAPTER TWENTY-THREE

6 years ago

DAWN PAINTED THE SKY IN GRAYS, blues, and purples as Raijin walked out of the Shangyang Mountains' treacherous forest unharmed the next morning. His mad run the night before had brought him farther down the slope than he'd estimated. As the sky lightened, he could see a cloud of salty mist rolling in from the ocean. One by one, squares of yellow light appeared below. Fire shining through the windows of Kokuji's houses. Servants going about their morning work.

Raijin's stomach sank. His serving tasks were now officially undone for the day. He was no longer allowed to train with the school. The only home he'd ever known was closed to him. There was no turning back now.

With no other options available, Raijin continued down toward the yellow fires.

Until it grew light enough and he drew close enough to see each individual building in the coastal village and every tiny boat pulled up on its beach, Raijin didn't realize how nervous he was. He had been focusing all night on leaving behind his school and best friends, on stepping off the Path of Darkening Skies and what he would do next. Focusing so hard that he'd hidden from himself the anxiety of finally meeting the woman who had given him up.

What if she looked at him and said she wished he hadn't come? What if she told him to get away, leave her alone, that she hadn't wanted him then and she didn't want him now?

For some reason, this frightened him on a more primal level than the rampaging guai-ray had. Every step grew harder to take, as if he were walking uphill rather than down.

It occurred to him that he could sit down and spend some time meditating. He usually did that in the morning while he waited for the water buckets to fill, and his Ro could always use the exercise.

But he knew that was only the seized-upon excuse of a frightened mind. If he stopped now, he would never complete the climb down to the village. Master Chugi had told him that he must find his mother if he would become the chosen one and protect the other potential chosen ones—Yong Lei included—from terrible suffering. There was no other way. He couldn't let his friends suffer in his place. If his mother rejected him, then he would bear that burden, as he had promised Master Chugi he could.

The sun had risen fully over a wide gray horizon when the slope began to level out beneath Raijin's feet. He passed through a neatly kept vineyard, plucking a few heavy purple grapes for his breakfast. They were warm with the summer heat and sweeter than that first moment stretching out on the bed mat after a hard day of work and training. He savored them with true delight, their juices renewing his exhausted body's energy, but he was careful not to pick more than the common laws of civility would allow a hungry traveler. To do more would be the same as theft, and he had read stories of angry farmers requiring a finger or two in exchange for the extra grapes.

At the vineyard's edge, he found a rutted road to follow. A sea breeze ruffled his unruly hair and the tang of salt grew stronger in the air as he drew nearer the village. The sun seemed to shine on him from every angle at once. He tried to focus on the world outside of himself as he walked, push aside the fears of what might lie at the end of this road, but they refused to be ignored.

After a time, he turned his focus inward to the pinging Hail-level Ro in his heartcenter and began putting it through the various strengthening exercises. It was strange to cultivate outside of the school. Over the years, he'd gotten so used to the familiar paths and places of his home that he hardly needed to pay attention to his surroundings while exercising his Ro. Walking this unfamiliar road, however, required him to focus as much on the new surroundings as on the exercises. The effort of doing both at once wore him out quickly, but it also managed to shoulder aside his anxiety over meeting his mother long enough to make it to the village.

Kokuji's streets were alive with the bustle of farmers coming in from the northern road Raijin now walked and fishers hauling their daily catch in from the beach to the south. Travelers of every shape, color, and size, wearing a multitude of styles, stood out from the locals in their drab robes and wooden platform-strapped shoes crossing muddy, churned-up streets inches above the muck.

Raijin soon found himself in a central market crowded with people purchasing food, spices, wine, cloth, ivory, fish, meat, vegetables, fruits, and pots. There were jars of liquid that sellers shouted would advance Ro, but these were made of nothing Raijin had ever heard of. Hunters hawked piles of cured hides and tiny cloth bags they claimed contained true demon core stones. Raijin looked to see if any of the hunters had the skins or core stone of a guai-ray and its pups, but saw none. Good. He would hate to see what sort of carnage Zhuan could wreak in this busy market before the hunters killed her.

After a while wandering the boardwalks, Raijin finally admitted to himself that he was unable to find the teahouse on his own. None of these buildings had signs declaring their name or purpose; the locals all just seemed to know where they were going. Unsure where else to turn, Raijin stopped at the nearest fish stall, where a bored-looking, sunbaked man sat on a wooden crate, carving intricate designs into a thick, yellowed bone of some kind.

"Excuse me, uncle," Raijin said politely, "but can you tell me how to find the teahouse?"

The man looked up from his work. His eyes were a gray-blue like the sky over the ocean, surrounded by crinkles, and perpetually squinted from too much time in the sunlight.

"You're too young for that, little nephew. Why don't you go find a nice girl and see if she'll let you hold her hand?"

Raijin's face heated. "I wasn't going for…that. My mother is there."

The man's sun-bleached eyebrows climbed toward his graying hair. He squinted at Raijin with new eyes, taking in the scratches and bruises and tears in his clothing that he'd obtained the night before on the run for his life.

"She rent you off for qajong money?" the man asked.

This sparked a memory of what Master Chugi had said about his mother's addiction. A dull pang of anger shot through Raijin's stomach that this man would guess such a thing without even knowing her.

"No, uncle," Raijin said, straining to keep his voice civil. "I'm trying to find her. I've never met my mother."

"Oh," the man said, nodding as if in understanding. "Her apothecary found out she had a baby and is trying to wring what she owes out of you and your adopted family."

"No. You see, her name is—"

"Better I don't know." The man held up both hands to stop Raijin from speaking. "Don't want to be thinking about her having a kid your age running around if I'm ever with her."

Raijin fought off the urge to scowl. It was becoming harder and harder to be polite to the man. But it was as Master Palgwe had said—he hadn't trained his entire life to give in to his nature.

He took a calming breath, released it, then asked, "Can you tell me where the teahouse is, uncle?"

With a groan, the sunbaked man stood and stretched his back.

"You take that street over there until it runs out," he said, pointing with his carved bone. This close, Raijin could see a tiny scene taking shape on the bone, dozens of little fishermen hauling intricate nets full of fish into boats on a foaming sea. "Get to the end, you take a left. It will be the last building on your left, the doors are painted with all sorts of pretty flowers and what have you. The red lanterns won't be lit in the middle of the day, but you'll still be able to see their shades. No mistaking them."

Raijin bowed to the man. "Thank you."

The man nodded over his own hands, then plopped back down on the crate and returned to his carving.

Raijin followed the man's instructions down the street, took a left, another left onto a boardwalk, then came out at the end of the street in front of a garish yellow-and-green two-story building. Its door was decorated with night glories, ghost lilies, blood blossoms, and beauty berry clusters. At one time the painting had been a vibrant sight, but now it was faded and peeling with age.

He stood staring at the peeling paint for a long time. His mother was in there. What would she be like? Master Chugi had remembered her as beautiful, but troubled. Would Raijin recognize her by sight? Would she recognize him? What would she say? Master Chugi had said she wept as she left her baby behind. But she had still left him behind. What did that mean?

Raijin waited out on the boardwalk for so long that the door opened.

A plump little woman with a brightly painted face sauntered out onto the porch, tucking a stray hair up into her bun and pinning it in place with a decorative stick.

Raijin's legs went weak, and his heart raced, blanking everything in his mind in a bright flare of adrenaline. Was this...? Could she be...?

The little woman saw him and shook her head.

"Too young!" She flapped her hands at him, shaking expensive bracelets and sending the sun glinting off gilt-painted nails. "Get out of here. Don't try to peep. No free shows. Go!"

Raijin opened his mouth, but no words would come.

"Go, little boy, shoo!" she snapped.

He had to say something. He had to ask her. If she was the one and he didn't say anything, if she sent him away before he even spoke… But he couldn't force his voice to work.

"Now or I'll shout for my security man," she threatened. "Have him drag you all the way home to mama."

"Uh—that's why—apologies, honored aunt—that is why I—you can't send your nephew home because I live at the School of Darkening Skies on the top of the mountain—or I did live there, but now I can't go back because I didn't do my serving tasks this morning because Master Chugi made me leave because he said my time was over following that path, and they won't let me back in because of the chores—oh, I already said that…" His flash flood of words finally tapered off. Raijin tried to collect himself. Bowed. "Honored aunt, I am looking for my mother. She gave me to the school on the mountaintop when I was a baby. Her name is Ji Yu Lanfen."

The little woman's dark eyes doubled in size, and her painted black lips dropped open.

Tears filled her eyes. Rather than engulfing him in a hug, however, the little woman dropped to her knees and pressed her forehead to the dirty boardwalk.

"The chosen one! This old madam is not worthy to look at the chosen one!"

It took several seconds for Raijin to realize why the woman was kowtowing to him. In the school, nearly every student had been a potential chosen one and every master a former potential, and no one fell on their knees before any of them.

He bent down and pulled her up. "Please, aunt, stop. You are worthy. I am no better than you. Please."

When she finished crying out that she wasn't worthy, the little woman pulled a square of intricate lace from her robe and dabbed her eyes, careful not to smudge the already streaky paint lining them.

"You don't understand," she said, sniffling. "I was there, chosen one. I was at your birth. I held your mother's hand. I caught you as you came into this world. I heard your first cries. Me, a worthless sensha, and I have been blessed by fortune ever since. I used to be the lowest girl in this teahouse, and now I own it."

A combination of disappointment and relief filled Raijin as he realized what the little woman was saying. This was not his mother.

She patted him on the back as fondly as if he were her son and beamed up at him with that painted smile. "Daitai will take you to Mama Lanfen. We'll go right now. It's time I saw her, anyway. Just let me put on my walking shoes."

She slipped back through the peeling flower door. A minute later, she reemerged wearing the wooden platforms Raijin had seen on other locals, hers gilded gold. He glanced down at his own bare feet, realizing for the first time how out of place he was here in the seaside village.

Daitai didn't leave him time to dwell on this, however. Her plump little hand slipped into his long fingers, and she pulled him across the muddy street.

"Come, come. Mama is this way, chosen one."

They stepped from the street onto the boardwalk opposite the teahouse, Raijin's bare feet and Daitai's platforms tracking mud on the planks. Though his legs were much longer than the little Daitai's, Raijin had to hustle to keep up. The madam was giddy with excitement. She pointed out businesses and gossiped about their owners and clientele, maintaining a constant flow of words as they walked. They took a right, then a left, then followed a street to the farthest south edge of the village. The businesses thinned out and the houses grew smaller and rougher, until finally they were in a neighborhood of shacks made of scavenged boards, castoff boat pieces, driftwood, and broken roof tiles. The boardwalk likewise died out, and the mud turned to sand beneath their feet.

Outside one shack, a pair of filthy toddlers screamed at each other while a girl no older than Raijin sat nearby staring down into the sand and chewing on her bloody thumbnail.

Farther in, a dirt-crusted elderly man missing his right arm and leg leaned against a rock, his remaining hand outstretched.

"Anything the honored young man can spare? Perhaps esteemed business lady can spare a coin?" he begged.

Raijin's chest felt tight. He couldn't look away from the beggar, but he didn't want to look at him, either. It wasn't right for an elderly man to speak up to a child. He should be the one shown honor and respect. Where was his family to provide for him in his old age?

"Esteemed young warrior, a coin for a worthless beggar?"

"I-I—" Raijin stuttered, bowing sloppily in his haste. "Apologies, revered grandfather, but your grandson has nothing."

Daitai hissed at the old man and pulled Raijin away. "You have to ignore them, Raijin. They'll never stop asking for more."

But they were everywhere he looked, begging, filthy, defeated, suffering. Running sores, hollow eyes, and starving potbellies were the norm among these people. Legions of sand fleas leapt whenever one of them moved, gnats swarmed in the hot air, and tiny crabs wandered in and out of the doorless holes in the sides of the thrown-together little shacks. The farther they walked, the less Raijin felt he could breathe.

Where was Daitai taking him?

As if she had heard his thought, the little painted woman stopped at a lean-to built against the back of another building's latrine. It wasn't even a shack; it didn't have the necessary number of walls, just the slanting ceiling of foraged and salt-faded tiles that didn't look as if it would keep anything dry in a rainstorm. Through the nearest opening, Raijin could see a threadbare blanket lying on the sand bundled around a small pile of sticks. Nothing else.

"Lanfen!" Daitai called cheerfully, rapping on the roof. "Your beloved sister is here bringing your medicine and a surprise!" The little woman ducked inside, then leaned back out to beckon for Raijin to follow. "So tall. You'll have to crawl in. Come now, chosen one."

Something in the lean-to croaked.

"Yes, yes," Daitai said, slipping back into the lean-to. "After I show you who is visiting."

Not sure what else to do, Raijin knelt down and walked into the makeshift home on his knees. It smelled awful. Unwashed flesh and human excrement mingled with a stale chemical odor.

Daitai was sitting next to the threadbare blanket, holding one of the bundled sticks with one hand while she patted it with the other. Raijin could see her painted mouth moving, but the words had ceased to make sense.

At the top of the blanket, he realized, was a skull covered in withered gray skin and dusted with wisps of greasy, colorless hair. Dull green eyes burned in the hollows of the skull's sockets, alight with madness or fever or both. They blinked, and Raijin flinched. The skull was alive. It was connected to the stick Daitai kept patting, and the stick wasn't a stick at all but a skeletal hand.

"I need my medicine," the skull croaked at the painted woman. "Please, Daitai, good sister, always so good, give me my medicine, please I'm crawling with it, I need out of this pain, please, Daitai, fix your sister's pain, help me, give me the qajong, take care of your sister, please give it to me."

"Yes, Lanfen, but listen first. Do you recognize this boy?" Daitai said, gesturing to him. "Why, he is practically a man. Isn't he so handsome all grown up?"

The feverish green eyes focused on Raijin. Cracked white lips opened.

"I'm hallucinating," the skull croaked. "He's not here. You did this to me, Daitai, by not giving me my medicine in time. You're torturing me because you love to see me in pain! You hate me! You are a bad sister!"

"Oh, you hush," Daitai scolded as if there was nothing sickening about the skull screaming at her for drugs. "You're not hallucinating anything. He's really here."

The feverish green eyes lit up for a moment, going a rich, brilliant jade with happiness. Tears spilled down the skull's emaciated cheekbones. Except it wasn't a skull, it was a woman. A woman no older than Daitai. He could see that now, as her wasted face stretched into a smile.

"Raijin?" she whispered. "My baby?"

His heart stopped. The world pitched violently beneath his knees, and he felt himself drop onto his backside in the stinking sand.

The woman—his mother—reached skeletal arms toward him like a child asking to be picked up.

Trembling harder than he had when he offered his hand to the guai-ray, Raijin crawled over to the stinking, filthy bundle of blanket and bones. The stench gagged him. He leaned down into her arms, and they closed around him. It was like being hugged by a foul-smelling cedar sapling. His skin buzzed like furious bees, both repulsed and confused.

"My baby," she whispered, squeezing him with all of the meager strength in her frail body. "I love you, Raijin, my baby boy."

Then warmth like the first hot wind of the springtime exploded from his heartcenter. His throat ached with unshed tears. This was his mother, and she didn't want him to leave.

"My boy," she cooed, petting his thick black hair. She kissed his ear, then whispered, "Mama is in so much pain, Raijin. She needs her medicine. Will you be a good son and go to the apothecary and buy a ball of qajong for Mama? It will help her stop hurting. You can go do that for Mama, go ahead."

Like that, the warm wind was gone, replaced by icy winter.

Raijin felt a paper packet stuffed into his fist. When he glanced over his shoulder, Daitai gestured toward his mother. The skeletal woman was still coaxing and cooing at him, begging him to go buy her something to take her pain away.

He held the packet out to the skeleton.

She kissed his cheek and squeezed him again. "Mama knew her Raijin was such a good boy! You are a good son, such a good son, taking care of Mama."

Her sticklike arms released him, reaching instead for the pipe tucked away under the lowest corner of the lean-to. Raijin watched, frozen, while she shoved the little brown ball down into the bowl with shaking fingers and lit it.

Raijin lurched backward onto his hands in the sand and scrambled out of the stinking little hovel like a crab. He turned over onto his hands and knees just in time. Vomit spewed out of his mouth as if it were coming up from the depths of his soul.

CHAPTER TWENTY-FOUR

Present

ATE THAT NIGHT AFTER THE SECOND wedding feast concluded, Hush came to Koida's chambers as promised to model the proper position for meditation. Unable to speak, the woman brought with her a scroll from Raijin explaining her purpose—mainly, Koida thought, to set Batsai's mind at ease at having a stranger closeted overnight with his ward.

The mute woman led the second princess to the foot of her bed platform, then pulled her down onto the nightcaller floor and took a seat facing her, their knees nearly touching. When the scream of wood on metal stopped, Hush folded her legs, straightened her back, and pressed her fists together in front of her heartcenter.

Koida mimicked the pose. At least, she thought she had until Hush shook her head and took hold of her wrists. The mute woman pulled Koida's fists apart half an inch.

"But your fists are touching."

Hush shook her head. She brought her own fists together, then held them up for Koida's inspection. The thinnest rift remained between the woman's sharp-looking knuckles.

Koida tried to get hers as close but found she couldn't keep them from bumping into one another.

Hush shook her head again, the black horsetail of hair sliding over her shoulders, and pulled Koida's fists back to the half-inch distance.

"Will they get closer with time?" Koida guessed.

The woman nodded, her dark almond eyes crinkling with the smile hidden beneath the cloth mask covering her nose and mouth. Then she pressed her fingertips to her chest. She sucked in a long breath, the cloth sucking tight to her nose, then breathed it back out, pushing the cloth away from her mouth.

Koida tried it. Hush nodded in approval. They practiced breathing together for some time before the woman got Koida's attention once more and pointed to her eyes, closing them gently.

They spent the next hour practicing. Now and again, Hush reached out and pulled Koida's bumping fists apart or pressed burning fingertips to the hollow of Koida's chest to slow her breathing.

When Koida felt that she had gone long enough without bumping her fists together, she opened her eyes.

"Ji Yu Raijin mentioned an exercise," she said. "Pouring Ro into Itself. May I try it?"

Hush nodded.

Koida turned her concentration inward, finding the roiling cloud of amethyst energy at her heartcenter. Rings of pure, dense lilac surrounded the Ro cloud like planetary rings. She couldn't begin to imagine how she would turn that mess into a single cycling waterfall while holding the Resting Meditation position, not when she had never yet been able to send her Ro down the pathways it was supposed to follow instinctively from birth.

Inhaling through her nose, Koida focused on the dense rings and roiling cloud, trying to ball them together forcefully. It was as if she were trying to lift the Sun Palace one-handed. She strained until sweat ran down her face, but nothing happened.

Hush's burning fingertips tapped Koida's chest. She had stopped breathing altogether in her struggle. She refocused her attention on inhaling and exhaling, then returned to the Ro at her heartcenter.

Maybe she couldn't ball the disobedient cloud and rings together. Their densities seemed so different, the rings so compressed, the clouds sizzling and arcing all over the place like electrified mist.

What if she poured the Ro cloud into the center of the rings and cycled it around them instead? She would have half a dozen rings, but that would still count as Pouring Ro into Itself, wouldn't it?

Koida straightened her back and—after an adjustment of her bumping fists from Hush—concentrated on sending the purple energy at the center of the rings swirling around it. At first the Ro tried to scatter in all directions away from her heartcenter, but she reined it in like she would her headstrong half-demon warhorse, chasing it down and fighting it until her Ro reluctantly started to do as she ordered.

A trickle of airy purple energy slid over the edge of one dense lilac ring. So little that it was almost nothing at all, and yet it was everything.

Koida seized upon the tiny victory, dragging the airy, sizzling Ro around the ring and forcing it over the edge again. It felt like mist from a waterfall. The rest of her rebellious Ro was sizzling along her limbs, not escaping or manifesting, but traveling up and down just out of her reach. She ignored it. She would deal with it if she could just get Pouring Ro into Itself to work.

From the center of the ring, she pulled the slender finger of sizzling Ro mist around and repeated the process. And again. And again.

Her muscles shook from the physical strain, and her nightdress was soaked with sweat, but she watched the scene in her heartcenter with satisfaction and fascination. She was doing it. She was exercising her Ro.

Koida giggled with exhilaration and immediately lost her grip on the sizzling misty Ro. It scattered as if grateful to escape. All at once, the rest of the amethyst energy rushed back into the center of the dense lilac rings, returning to the messy, roiling cloud.

She sighed and opened her eyes.

Hush, still seated before her, raised her thin black brows.

"I had it," Koida said. "I was doing it."

Eyes crinkling with a hidden smile, Hush pressed her palms together and tipped them to Koida in a gesture of praise.

"Gratitude," Koida said, though the word had come instinctively and without conviction. Her mind was elsewhere. "Perhaps if I…"

She closed her eyes and returned her fists to their position over her heartcenter, but Hush pulled them apart and rested each fist on one of Koida's thighs.

Koida frowned at the silent woman in confusion. "What's wrong?"

Hush pointed at the bright morning light glaring through the cracks around the balcony door, then at Koida's bed. She pantomimed sleeping by laying her head on one palm and shutting her eyes.

How long had she been wrestling with that single strand of Ro? Hours, at least.

Exhaustion hit Koida all at once. Her body was stiff and achy from sitting in one position for so long. The muscles in her arms and legs and back burned as if she'd torn each and every fiber apart. A blinding lance of pain flashed through her temple, and in its wake, she felt the dull ache that had built up in her skull while she fought with her Ro.

Suddenly, she thought she might topple over backward in a dead faint.

Either her face betrayed her or Hush had expected this when she urged Koida to rest. The mute woman grabbed Koida's hands, then hooked Koida's arm over a shoulder knotted with muscle and lifted her onto the bed platform.

Koida had time to think that she should change out of her sweat-soaked nightdress and wash her face. Then she fell over the edge into the black hole of sleep.

CHAPTER TWENTY-FIVE

Present

KOIDA WOKE LATE IN THE AFTERNOON. She hoped Batsai had sent a page to tell Master Lao she would not be training that morning—he often did so when she slept late—until she remembered that Lao was gone, exposed for his deceit and replaced by her future husband only a day before. Raijin was her new master, and she was on the Path of the Thunderbird now, her stiff, screaming muscles the proof.

Remembering the small victory of the night before, Koida focused on the roiling amethyst Ro surrounded by the dense lilac rings at her heartcenter. It didn't look any different. She raised one protesting arm. Her hand shook as she forced the Ro down her shoulder and into her hand—as usual, it ignored the correct pathway, scraping along the inside of her arm the whole way—and manifested an amethyst bo-shan stick.

The stick looked like it always did. Not quite all there. Weak. Just a stick.

Koida let her arm drop back to the bed. Raijin had said it could take years before she saw progress, but it was still disappointing. Last night, she'd felt so exhausted that she was sure she'd made leaps and bounds forward.

"What's all that sighing?" Batsai's gruff voice demanded. He cracked her door open and leaned inside. "Are you complaining yourself awake, little dragon?"

She sat up and stretched, groaning at the million throbbing aches and pains shouting at her from her strained muscles.

"I wish I wasn't," she told him.

"Well, get up anyway so I can be free of your ladies," Batsai said. "They've been flirting with Hyung-Po since dawn, waiting for you to wake so they could dress you for the wedding feast. Though I don't see how we'll have a feast without the groom."

For a moment, the comment confused the second princess. Then she remembered Raijin saying he had important matters to attend to and would be gone today.

"Surely he will be back by tonight," she said.

He wasn't.

Koida sat on the dais and ate by herself, pretending nothing was amiss while her father, sister, and the nobles and court officials looked on. After the meal, several of the courtiers came to tell her how beautiful she looked and made poorly veiled attempts to wheedle out information about the missing groom. She turned aside their curiosity and vindictive glee until her father finally declared that he'd had enough of the feasting and would retire. Infinitely thankful to end the torture, Koida withdrew to her residence.

Shingti burst into the inner chamber while the ladies were unwrapping the second princess's embroidered silk sash.

"Where was he, little sister? Where was your groom?"

"Do I know everything?" Koida snapped, raising her arms while one of her ladies pulled the dress robe over her head. She wasn't in the mood for the accusatory tone in her sister's voice. "Raijin said he had important matters to attend to. They must be taking longer than he expected."

"That old dog Lysander is gone, too."

"But Hush is still here," Koida countered. "I saw her at the feast."

The mute woman had stalked the perimeter of the hall with the palace guards, not touching food or wine, her dark almond eyes roving constantly.

Shingti acted as if she hadn't heard Koida. "Do you know what they're all saying? They're saying he realized the runt of the litter was being pawned off on him and broke the agreement." She manifested a flanged ruby mace not unlike their father's Ro scepter and tested a barbed flange with one thumb. A bead of blood welled up immediately. "I nearly had to knock the asinine grin off Duchess Ongri's face. And she's not even the worst of them! If that scum hasn't slithered back by tomorrow morning, I'll hunt him down myself."

"You can't leave the palace," Koida said, massaging her throbbing temples. The exhaustion headache she'd started the day with had only gotten worse over the last four tense hours of pretense. "If you go off after him, they'll assume the rumors are correct and that Raijin did break the agreement. You'll be confirming it for them, and it isn't true."

At least, she hoped it wasn't true. He wouldn't have lent her Hush or promised to train her if it was all a lie, would he?

"Well, what do we do, then?" Shingti snapped.

"We wait," Koida said. "He'll be back by tomorrow night."

He wasn't.

Once more Koida sat alone on the dais, trying not to imagine the cruel things the painted and decorated nobles were saying behind their wine cups about her. By then the rumor had spread far and wide that Raijin had rejected her, and they were only carrying out the wedding feasts because the emperor had promised a week of feasting and would lose even more face if he reneged. A scowl attached itself to Batsai's face and would not come loose. The old captain muttered that he should have killed Raijin the first night of the feasting, when the young chieftain was sickly. Shingti seethed and vowed to Koida that Ji Yu blood would be spilt. Their father went on with his drinking and feasting as if he hadn't even noticed the absence. Koida wondered whether the emperor felt this embarrassment was her just reward for disobeying him and taking on Raijin as a master.

Strangely, it was Cousin Yoichi who made Koida feel slightly better.

Late into the wedding feast, after the second cask of hard wine was opened, a drunken duke let slip blunt speculation about Raijin's absence a little too loudly.

"Found out she was Ro-crippled." The duke was practically shouting, his voice carrying over the general din of the celebration. "No man in his right mind would want that tainting his bloodline."

Koida cringed. The hall fell silent, expectant. Surely there would be retribution for speaking so bluntly about the second princess's disgrace.

But Shingti was nowhere to be seen, and Emperor Hao seemed content to pretend that he hadn't heard the slighting of his youngest daughter.

"Sit down, Fi-Ping," Yoichi said in a loud voice. "We all know no man in his right mind would forfeit a treasure like the second princess. You yourself have been eyeing her since I came to court—since far before it was proper for a man to admire her that way."

As he spoke, Yoichi sent Koida their secret conspiratorial glance. She smiled gratefully down at him, relieved to know that he still backed her, no matter what his feelings about her betrothed were.

Emperor Hao let out a braying laugh at Yoichi's cutting reprimand.

"It's true!" the emperor shouted, sloshing wine onto the table as he banged down his cup. "I've turned down half of these fools' offers for her, Fi-Ping included. He thought he could buy her as a third wife! My daughter, this white jade ghost lotus of a child, second princess to the whole empire, a third wife!"

The guests lapsed into hilarity, and the humiliated duke slunk unsteadily back to his seat for more wine, mumbling about making offers out of altruism. With Yoichi's stance on the matter heard and cheered on by the Exalted Emperor, the nobles stopped their blatant gossip and returned cheerfully to matters of eating, drinking, and purging in the private rooms.

If Yoichi hadn't been on her side, Koida thought, it would be frightening how much sway her white-haired half-brother held over the court's opinion.

That night, when the feast ended, Koida returned to her chambers, changed into her hidden riding clothes, and slipped off to the stables.

Pernicious was in a vile mood, but then so was she. The half-demon and the princess fought and stamped and bit and kicked and screamed at one another until they had exorcised the venom from their systems. Then Koida leapt up onto the huge beast's back, and they stormed from the palace stables like a hart from a burning forest. They could find no demons or even regular predators in the forest for Pernicious to kill, so Koida turned him toward the mountain and they rode up to her overlook spot.

Koida dismounted and sat down with her feet hanging over the edge. Below, the lights of Boking Iri slowly winked out as the people went to sleep. Probably all laughing about the rejected second princess. She should face the fact that Raijin had lied. He was gone and wasn't coming back. Even Hush had disappeared. Probably off to rejoin the chieftain. There would be no training, no new Path, no marriage.

A yellow-orange spark popped in her heartcenter, causing her to jump.

Pernicious screamed and pawed the earth with one enormous hairy hoof. He didn't like it when she sat on the edge like that.

"Settle down, you scared kitten. I won't fall."

Pernicious snorted and shook out his mane contemptuously.

Koida ignored him and turned her focus inward. The spark had been the very last of that sunbright pill, a bit of it she must have missed integrating finally being consumed. That pill alone was a treasure worth half the silver in her father's treasury. And the Breath of the Underwater Panther Raijin had given her the second night of wedding rituals, that was worth all of it, if not more. Who would waste riches like that on a lie?

No, Raijin was coming back. And when he did, he would begin training her in the Path of the Thunderbird. He would teach her to fight without Ro and maybe even to eventually overcome her deficiency altogether. For that, she could endure whatever embarrassment waiting might cause her.

Mind made up, Koida folded her legs and raised her fists to Resting Meditation. She may as well exercise her Ro while she waited. Maybe she could surprise him with her progress.

CHAPTER TWENTY-SIX

Present

SHARP PAIN BIT INTO THE SOFT FLESH over Koida's left shoulder blade. She shrieked and tried to jerk away, her eyes flying open. She was thousands of feet above the ground, dangling over a sheer drop to the thundering water of the twin Horns' pool in the valley below. She stopped struggling, scared stiff.

But she was moving. Something was pulling her backward, away from certain death.

Pernicious.

The half-demon horse's big, square iron teeth were digging into her skin through her black riding shirt as he dragged her away from the cliff face. A look over her shoulder showed her the huge beast on his belly, slowly slinking backward to safety.

She had spent the night Pouring Ro into Itself. Still just that airy, sizzling strand, but she had managed to do the exercise nonetheless. She hadn't wanted to quit the first time she dropped the strand, had gone directly back into the arduous process of threading it around and around the lilac ring. At some point, the strain must have become too much, and she must have passed out. Only Pernicious's Demonic Speed had saved her.

When they were safely away from the edge, the big brute dropped onto the grass, shivering. Koida had never seen him sweat, but the half-demon's fear and panic had worked him into a lather. She crawled over to him on trembling arms and legs and fell on him. Her arms barely reached halfway around his thickly muscled neck, but she hugged him as if she were still dangling over the drop and clinging to him for dear life.

After her shaking calmed to a tolerable level and she could see her surroundings again, Koida realized that she hadn't just stayed out past sunrise this day. The sun had passed its apex and was falling; she had stayed out past noon. Batsai would have burned half the empire down looking for her.

Still jittering, Koida pulled herself up onto her half-demon warhorse's back, and they began the climb back down to the valley.

When they arrived at the palace, the stables were filled with the banging and bleating of unfamiliar stock.

One frazzled stable hand ran out to meet her. "A thousand apologies, adored second princess, but this lowly stable hand begs you to put Pernicious in the paddock today." He dropped to his knees and held up clasped hands. "They're full-blood demon beasts, each and every one."

Through the open stable doors, Koida saw war rams as tall as Pernicious butting heads in the throughway while hands threw themselves out of their path. The impacts sounded like great trees shattering to splinters. Farther in, a giant gecko walked across the ceiling while a pair of stable hands followed along on the floor, trying to coax it down with an apple.

Pernicious let loose a Petrifying Scream of Legions, prancing in place. He smelled them. Koida sawed on his mane. He fought, turning in a tight circle, but she didn't loosen her grip. Giving him the slightest freedom now would only end in bloodshed and even more chaos.

"Whose mounts are these?" She had to shout to be heard over the gecko's barking and Pernicious's whinnying.

"Your father the Exalted Emperor's," the stable hand answered. "We haven't had time to sort them into different stables yet, they only just arrived."

Before she could ask anything further, a cry went up inside the stable and someone shouted, "He's loose! Shut the doors!"

The ground shook as an enormous brindled bull with glowing red eyes charged toward them.

Pernicious reared, shrieking for blood. Koida held her seat by throwing her arms around his huge neck and squeezing his shoulders with her shaking knees.

The stable hand ran to the open door and threw his weight against it. Several others added their bodies to the pile just before a boom rocked the entire structure.

"Please, Second Princess!" the stable hand begged.

Koida wheeled the obstinate Pernicious, fighting him every step of the way.

"All the fillies and mares will be in the paddock," she yelled into his flattened-back ear. "Get us there before that demon bull breaks free, and you can impregnate as many as you want."

The half-demon destrier took a few lunging steps toward the stable, then turned toward the paddock.

Clearly, the temptation to fight his own kind to the death was as strong as the one to spread his seed. And these strange demons were trespassing in his territory.

Koida leaned up to his ear and shouted, "I'll bring you so many candied blood oranges you'll make yourself sick!"

That decided it. With a toss of his head, Pernicious galloped off toward the paddock. In eight months, the hands would have their hands full of quarter-demon baby warhorses, but for now the bloodshed had been averted.

With Pernicious safely stored with the rest of the non-demon mounts in the paddock, Koida limped back to the palace. She was too exhausted to drag herself over the garden wall, let alone make the climb to her balcony. If she wanted to rest today, she would have to walk through the front entry of the palace wearing her riding clothes.

Well, her father couldn't get that much angrier than he'd already been. And if he did, she would only have to put up with his cruel moods until the wedding feasts and rituals were complete. Just three more days.

Koida trudged wearily in through the front doors, ignoring the scandalized looks on the faces of the servants. She met no nobles or court officials in the halls. Odd. They should be in their best robes by now, parading themselves around the lower floor for the entire palace to see.

She was plodding past the throne room when its huge double doors were thrown open by pages.

Courtiers bustled past, talking amongst themselves so eagerly that they did not even notice the bedraggled second princess in her disgraceful peasant's riding clothes. She backed into an alcove behind a jade statue of a demon dog and watched as the flood of people dispersed down the hall in both directions.

After the courtiers came a cluster of muscle-bound wild men, each one a head taller than the tallest noble and twice again as wide. Clothed only in furs draped over their shoulders and around their loins, their skin was a deep umber, and their chests, arms, and legs were bare. Bright red clay had been worked into their hair and beards, smoothing it into long ropes decorated with bones and teeth. Every savage had a double-line of shiny black stone on the back of their left arm, cutting through their Heroic Record from shoulder to elbow, surrounded by jagged lines of pale pink scar tissue.

At the center of these hulking barbarians stood tall, lean Ji Yu Raijin, like a rangy wolf leading a group of well-fed bears. As Koida watched, the young chieftain showed the savages politely down the hall toward the guest residences.

She slumped back against the wall, too tired to feel anything but a weary relief that Raijin was back. The gossips would have to start some new rumor about her father or Shingti tracking him down and dragging him back to complete the wedding rituals. Koida found she didn't care much. This meant they could begin her training today.

A wave of blackness washed over her, and she woke on the floor, looking up at the demon dog statue. She'd fainted.

Tomorrow. They could begin her training tomorrow.

Checking for nobles, officials, or her father, Koida slipped out into the hallway and turned toward her residence. Maybe she would collapse on Batsai; forestall the inevitable tirade before he managed to start.

When she opened the door to her outer chamber, however, the furious captain of her guard only pointed. In the corner, a distraught-looking messenger dropped to his knees and held a scroll over his head.

"S-summons from the Exalted Emperor Shyong San Hao for the Second Princess Shyong San Koida," the man announced, his hands shaking so that the wooden seals dangling from the scroll twirled and clacked against one another. "For th-this morning…immediately after the fast is broken."

From his seat, Batsai's expression somehow managed to convey both rage and a grim satisfaction.

Koida's mind and body were exhausted. She wanted nothing more than to fall into her bed. Or a sitting cushion. Or the floor. The floor was starting to look quite comfortable.

"Gratitude, gracious messenger," she said, taking the proffered scroll with clumsy hands. "Inform my father the Exalted Emperor that the second princess sends her regrets, but she is ill and will not be attending court."

Batsai gave an indignant snort. "You were summoned to a morning court, Second Princess. Hours ago. It will be over by now."

So that was what she had seen on the way in. But if that had been court letting out, then who were those barbarians with Raijin? More of his tribe? They hadn't looked or behaved like he did, but then neither did Hush nor that drunk Lysander.

"Well?" Batsai snapped, returning Koida's slipping focus to the outer chamber. "Are you going to give this man a writ explaining your absence, or are you going to allow your father to behead him for neglecting his duties?"

The already terrified servant blanched as the captain addressed the second princess in the tone of a disappointed caretaker to a wayward child. Even a Ro-crippled princess outranked the lowly captain of a royal guard like the stars outranked the Earth.

The man couldn't know that Batsai's predictable disciplinary tone was far more welcome to Koida than her father's cruel mood shifts.

"Of course," she answered.

The nightcaller floor squealed as she crossed the room to the calligraphy desk, too tired to pick her way across the solid boards. She rolled out a small length of parchment, weighted its ends, and scrawled a formal apology to Beloved Father, making it sound as if her monthly pain was the cause of her absence and exonerating the messenger by claiming she had sent him to the alchemists for her powders. She sanded the ink, cut the parchment free, and bound it with the royal seals from the summons.

"Apologies, dutiful messenger. Take this reply to the Exalted Emperor."

The messenger pressed his forehead to the floor and backed out of the room, scroll in hand.

When she and Batsai were alone, Koida raised a weary eyebrow to him. "Is there more or may I retire to my bed now?"

The old bear opened his mouth to growl out some further castigation, but as he did, the door to the hall opened again and a trio of chattering ladies sashayed into the outer chamber, their arms draped in dress robes, bell cascades, and jewels.

Rather than being surprised at Koida's deathly tired and bedraggled state, the eldest among the ladies took the bells from the youngest. "Go find the kitchen boys and order a bath. And find those lilac oils and the strong-toothed comb. If it pleases the adored second princess," the lady said, hustling Koida into the inner chamber, "I will have her dressed and ready for tonight's feast in the fall of a raindrop."

As the nightcaller floor shrieked beneath their feet, Koida looked over her shoulder at the captain of her guard. Batsai didn't look as if he were about to berate her anymore. Instead, a smug smile cracked his scar-crossed face.

Obviously enjoying her misfortune, the old bear returned to his favorite cushion and picked up the book on the low table beside it.

CHAPTER TWENTY-SEVEN

Present

BY THE TIME KOIDA WAS BATHED, combed, perfumed, painted, dressed, and decorated for the fifth night of her wedding, the sun had set, and the muffled din of nobles traveling from their residences to the feasting hall filled the palace's winding corridors. She had fallen asleep twice—once in the bath and again on her feet—but neither interlude had restored her energy.

As her personal guard escorted her through the winding residence halls, Koida hoped with all her might that her father would retire at an uncharacteristically early hour. He'd never done so before on a feast night, but anything could happen once.

"You look a touch peaked, little dragon," Batsai teased, his face a funereal mask of concern over a barely restrained grin. "Didn't you get enough sleep last night?"

"Go perfect the Seat of Vertical Blades technique," she snapped.

The old bear chuckled.

Koida entered the royal waiting room expecting reproach and more cold cruelty from her father for missing court. What she found instead was the Exalted

Emperor pounding her betrothed on the back like a proud father.

"And you got all that from looking at the maps in the war room?" The emperor shook his head in gleeful disbelief. "We couldn't have been in there negotiating the alliance for more than an hour. Youngest daughter, you missed the show! Your future husband is brilliant."

She caught Raijin's eye. He smiled as if all the praise were making him uncomfortable and dragged a hand through his unruly black hair. Her own hair had taken no less than an hour to comb, pin, and dress, and she wouldn't dare touch it for fear of ruining her ladies' hard work. Raijin's hair looked as if he'd climbed out of his bed and walked directly to the royal waiting room, and still he looked wonderful. It was the worst sort of injustice.

"Apologies, Cherished Father," Koida said, bowing familiarly since the emperor seemed to be in a good mood. "How did Ji Yu Raijin prove his brilliance?"

"Your betrothed saw the tribes we'd conquered for the empire on the map in the war room and inferred that our next conquest would be against the savages from the lower reaches. What does he do then? He travels to their chieftain and negotiates allegiance to the empire without manifesting a single weapon! Saved our soldiers the ride there and back, all without a single casualty! Not even a single punch!"

Savages from the lower reaches? That was the same place Raijin claimed to have gotten his living lavaglass blade. Koida raised a brow at the mysterious young leader. He glanced away quickly.

"Apologies, Emperor," Raijin said. "Their tribe is called the Uktena, and far from being savages, they are widely accomplished scholars."

Koida couldn't suppress her skepticism. "Those barbarians in the furs and bones?"

"Yes, little cousin, we're all astounded," Yoichi drawled from his seat on the lounge. "Both that these savages can read civilized New Script letters and that the Ji Yu chieftain made what should have been a four-day trip all the way there and back in half as much time."

The stable full of enormous war rams, the giant gecko, and the enormous bull flashed through her mind.

"I've seen the mounts of the Uktena delegation, elder cousin," she said, frowning at his thinly veiled accusation that Raijin was deceiving them. "Demon beasts, each and every one. To run for two days at a speed that would kill a natural creature would be no hardship for them."

Only when Yoichi raised a pale eyebrow at her did she realize that her rebuttal was as good as a confession that she'd been in the stables, from which it was only a short jump to guess she'd been out riding Pernicious. She glanced fearfully at her father, afraid she would see anger and disapproval darkening his expression, but Emperor Hao went on as if he hadn't heard either his illegitimate son's insinuations or his daughter's admission.

"Those are royal stock now, Koida," her father said, his plum-colored eyes twinkling with mirth. "The mounts, the savages—"

"Uktena," Raijin corrected.

"—Ji Yu Raijin brought them all to the palace as your bride price. I asked the court recorder, and it's the most valuable bride price in the recorded history of the valley." The emperor chuckled. He shook a finger at Raijin. "You've got a heavy set on you, boy, walking into that village alone. It's well known throughout the valley that those savages kill and eat any man they meet and enslave the women."

"My only concern was finding a gift worthy of such a treasure as Shyong San Koida," Raijin said.

"So you settled on a tribe of filthy savages," Yoichi said caustically. "You must think the world of her beauty."

"Apologies," Raijin said, his rasping voice like the grinding of burled steel against a whetstone, "but the Uktena are advanced in many sciences the empire's alchemists are not, as well as brilliant strategists and some of the most powerful combatants in the known world."

"So powerful that you were able to talk them into an alliance," Yoichi sneered. "Perhaps your tattoo artisan can ink a babbling mouth in honor of your brave exploit."

"Cousin Yoichi!" Koida gasped. To call into question one's Heroic Record was unforgivable. Warrior artists killed one another for far less.

"There is no offense taken," Raijin assured her. He turned to Yoichi with an icy smile. "Gratitude for your suggestion, many-times celebrated warrior. However, I have no Heroic Record."

To prove it, Raijin pushed back the sleeves of his robe one at a time, baring sun-darkened skin, marked by nothing more than white scars.

Koida stared dumbfounded at the flat straps of muscle moving beneath her betrothed's unmarked flesh. Raijin didn't have a single deed of note tattooed on his arms. Nothing at all. Anyone could accuse him of cowardice, and he could do nothing but agree and slink away in disgrace.

Blade and death! She was the student of a master without a Heroic Record! Even Lao had had a Heroic Record.

"For Ro's sake, cover that up," Emperor Hao snapped, jerking the sleeve of Raijin's exposed arm back down. The older man looked as if he couldn't decide whether to be embarrassed or furious.

Koida stepped back and dropped into a seat on the fainting couch opposite Yoichi's lounge as Shingti dismissed her Dragonfly guard and breezed into the waiting room.

The first princess glanced from the rapidly shifting expression of her father to Koida's bewildered face to Cousin Yoichi's viciously self-satisfied smirk. Raijin stood stoically at the center of it all as if he hadn't only seconds before suffered the humiliation of all humiliations.

"What did I miss?" Shingti asked.

CHAPTER TWENTY-EIGHT

Present

AS THE SEATING FOR THE WEDDING FEAST had been altered to accommodate the traditions of the signing of the Book of the Empire and the Uktena's subsequent acceptance into the imperial fold, Koida found herself seated at the left hand of her father and unable to speak with Raijin, who had been given a seat of honor among the nobles below.

Koida found this separation was almost preferable. So much doubt and confusion was buzzing around in her mind that her skull felt like a wasps' nest. She felt much as her father looked while he praised the young chieftain's peaceful conquest of the Uktena to the court. Almost mystified.

As if Raijin could sense the direction of her thoughts, he kept his distance. It would have been within his rights as both the groom and an honored guest to approach the dais to speak with her, but he sat solemnly amidst the celebration, his jade gaze rarely leaving Koida's face.

Focusing on everything around the hall except her betrothed, Koida saw from the corner of her eye courtier after courtier talking to Raijin, many of them beautiful and influential noblewomen. She wondered what those noblewomen would do if they knew the handsome chieftain they were fawning over had no Heroic Record.

Finally, Raijin excused himself from their attentions and joined the Uktena at their table, which seemed to be surrounded by an invisible barrier repelling all nobles and officials. Even the royal guards gave it a wide berth. In spite of his new position and what looked like an engrossing conversation with the savages, Koida still felt Raijin's eyes on her.

As usual, her father remained at the feast until the earliest hours of the morning. Koida was nodding over her wine cup—though still pointedly looking away from Raijin—when the emperor finally announced that he was retiring, and the nobles quickly took up the echo.

Koida slipped back to her residence, avoiding contact with any chieftains who might have been staring at her the entire night.

As soon as she was in her nightdress and alone in the inner chamber, Koida clambered across the beams of her ceiling and leapt onto the balcony. She felt weary to her heartcenter, but she would never sleep like this. There was only one way she knew to quiet the churning anxieties and disappointment plaguing her.

A change of clothes, a quick climb down the side of the palace and over the garden wall, and a trek to the paddock brought her to Pernicious's temporary quarters. The half-demon warhorse stomped and snorted in indignation when she threw her arms around his neck and pressed her face into his inky black coat, but he didn't attack. Not immediately. Koida breathed in his warm, comforting stink and relaxed against his overly muscled chest before he sniffed out her lack of candied blood oranges.

Then he attacked.

Rearing up on his powerful hind legs, the beast pawed the air. His hooves flared up in fiery orange Ro. Koida dodged them and ran up the fence, sprinting along the top rail. Pernicious screamed bloody torture and wheeled, trying to batter her with his enormous head.

Despite her fatigue, Koida welcomed the fight. It was clean and honest. Pernicious wanted to kill her for forgetting her promise. She wanted to go for a ride or be trampled to death. No deceptions or manipulation, just candid violence.

Finally, she vaulted off the rail and landed on the furious destrier's back. Pernicious reared once more, trying to throw her off, then crashed through the fence.

They blazed across the countryside, the half-demon's flaming hooves nothing more than a blur of fire in the darkness. The wind screamed in Koida's ears, tore at her hair, and made her eyes water, but she gave her mount free rein, letting go of his thick black mane and throwing her arms wide like wings. The only thing keeping her from tumbling off the beast's back was her knees clamped to his heaving sides.

Pernicious tossed his head and screamed at the sky, a sound like a pack of rabid wolves on the hunt. The half-demon was enjoying the breakneck pace so much that he didn't head immediately for the forest where he liked to hunt. Instead, he splashed through a shallow point in the Horned Serpent River and cut out across open fields surrounding Boking Iri, screaming some more. No doubt the peasants in the area would be shivering in their beds and clutching their children tight at the horrible sound.

Koida laughed off the Petrifying Shriek of Legions and howled with the beast. She wasn't as frightening, but it still felt good to disturb the peace and quiet with so much noise.

They had almost made it to the place where field met forest when a shadow flitted across the corner of her vision. The flapping, rippling motion was alien to anything she had ever seen around the empire's capital city. She steadied herself with one hand in Pernicious's mane and twisted at the waist to get a better look at the thing.

The wide silhouette of a river ray too big to be plausible skimmed through the air beside Pernicious. It was easily the destrier's size and looked to be keeping up without much effort.

Pernicious screamed a challenge and wheeled on the creature. In response, the ray's wide wings lit with silvery Ro.

On the creature's back knelt Ji Yu Raijin. Though the light was low, the disorderly hair and sinewy body could belong to no one else.

Pernicious reared, lashing out with his hooves.

"No!" Koida twisted both hands into Pernicious's mane and pulled, squeezing her knees and wheeling him away from the young chieftain's mount at the same time. "It's not for you to kill, you overgrown baiting-dog!"

In response, the half-demon warhorse curved his neck to the side, snapping his iron teeth at Koida's leg, but she planted her soft leather boot on his jaw and held him off.

Pernicious danced in place, protesting with every step in a low, threatening grumble.

The ray descended closer to the ground, creeping toward them on rippling wings. Its stinger was up under its belly, ready to strike if Pernicious attacked.

"Gratitude for the protection," Raijin called, giving her a kneeling bow.

"It is nothing," Koida replied. "Were you following us?"

"Yes."

"Why?"

Raijin was silent for so long that Koida thought maybe he hadn't heard her over Pernicious's stamping hooves. Slowly, the half-demon seemed to realize he would not be allowed to attack the strange oversized ray any more than he'd been allowed to fight the demon bull in the stables, and he stopped his angry dancing. Koida didn't let go of his mane or relax her grip with her knees. There was always the possibility that Pernicious was just waiting for her to let her guard down. She was about to repeat her question when Raijin finally spoke.

"Pride," he said.

Koida cocked her head slightly, wondering if this was some sort of insult to her or her destrier.

"What is?"

"The reason I followed you from the palace grounds. It was pride," he said, scratching the back of his neck. "The act of tattooing your flesh with self-proclaimed deeds of bravery so you can brag about them is arrogance itself. But then so is wanting to explain to you why I have no tattoos. I should accept your scorn and allow you to find out in time what sort of man I am by my actions." He looked down at the back of his mount, then met her eyes once more. "But I find I care a lot about how you perceive me now."

Stumped for words, Koida's grip on the half-demon beneath her eased a fraction. The moment Pernicious sensed the slack, he threw his enormous head, bashing his skull into her nose and throwing her off.

Koida braced herself to hit the hard ground but landed instead on a strangely smooth, velvety surface. Strong arms locked around her stomach, stopping her from rolling off the edge.

"Are you all right?" Raijin asked.

She was on the back of his enormous ray. Just over the edge of the creature's fluttering wings, she could see Pernicious jumping and kicking, furious that the ray had escaped his reach.

"Bloodthirsty nag," she muttered.

With a start, Koida realized she was sitting in Raijin's lap with his arm around her. The young chieftain seemed to realize this at the same moment. Both jumped apart, though Raijin grabbed her wrist to keep her from falling from the ray's back. It was hard to keep a seat on the creature.

"You keep rescuing me," Koida said. "You must be growing weary of it."

Raijin shook his head. "Not yet."

Heartbeats passed with nothing but the sound of the warhorse's furious screams and stamping hooves tearing up the grass. Koida pressed gingerly on the bridge of her nose and traced it to the tip.

"It's not broken. How can that be?" She wiped her fingers below her nostrils. No blood or mucus leaked out, and she could taste nothing like the coppery, salty tang of the bloody noses Pernicious had given her in the past. "My face should be a fountain right now."

"Breath of the Underwater Panther," Raijin said. "It protects you from malicious harm for as long as your body is processing it."

His words sank in slowly. When they finally settled, Koida laughed and clapped her hands.

"I barely felt his head hit me! If I'd known it would be so effective, I would have let Pernicious trample me just to show him it had no effect. He would've been furious."

Raijin gave her a strange look. "You have a bizarre relationship with your demon."

"If you got to know him, it would make sense." She glanced down at the destrier, then back up at Raijin. "You said you came out here to tell me why you don't have a Heroic Record. Could you do so now or is the noise from below too distracting?"

"It's not," Raijin said quickly. But after the initial swift start, he faltered. "The path I come from…is very different. We don't value… Or perhaps the way we value… Apologies, but I don't know how to say this in a way that won't insult the path of everyone you've known your whole life."

"You've already called Heroic Records the definition of arrogance," Koida said. "If you say something more insulting than that, I'll let you know."

Raijin smiled. "Gratitude."

The ray dipped down then rose back out of Pernicious's reach before the half-demon could strike. Pernicious screamed and reared, his hooves pawing the air ineffectually.

"Don't taunt him, Nael," Raijin admonished the ray. Obediently, it rose a few feet higher. Raijin turned back to Koida. "The path I was raised in had a very strict code of honor. I based the Path of the Thunderbird on that code because I believe it to be right about many things. One of those things was the destructive power of pride and the wisdom of humility. Both paths would consider recording your heroic deeds on your skin so the world can read them equivalent to declaring yourself Exalted."

Koida laughed. "That was insulting. The last bit."

"A thousand apologies, Cherished Princess," Raijin said, bowing low over his fists. "You did, however, laugh, which I'm afraid only encourages me."

This tickled Koida even further. She covered her mouth demurely with one hand as she giggled. Raijin's serious façade broke up, allowing through a roguish grin.

When she'd gotten the giggles out of her heartcenter, Koida said, "You could be lying to me. How do I know you're not just a disgraced coward?"

"Anyone with enough money could find a tattoo artisan and have a false Record inked into their skin," he said. "You don't know that I'm not a coward. You can't know what kind of man I am until you've seen me at my best and at my worst." He took a breath as if to say more, but pressed his lips into a thin line instead.

Koida thought through the fight between her betrothed and Master Lao. Shingti had been watching, as had half a dozen of the Dragonfly Guard and Koida's personal escort. Any of these battle-hardened warriors would have spotted rehearsed or play-acted combat, and all were loyal enough to have told her if her future husband was a fraud.

On the day he'd arrived at the Sun Palace, Raijin had single-handedly defeated not only every member of the Emperor's Guard, but Shingti's Dragonfly Guard as well. The Ji Yu chieftain had brought the empire to peace with a formidable enemy whom the rest of the valley feared, and he'd even rushed in to catch her when

Pernicious threw her. These weren't the actions of a coward.

Koida eased herself up onto her knees, careful not to tip backward off the ray's gently waving wing, and pressed her palm to her fist, bowing to Raijin.

"Master," she said.

He returned the gesture. "Gratitude for giving your future husband the opportunity to prove himself, Cherished Princess."

"Second Princess," Koida corrected him.

"Not to me," he said.

CHAPTER TWENTY-NINE

Present

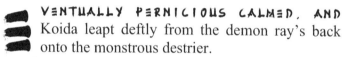VENTUALLY PERNICIOUS CALMED, AND Koida leapt deftly from the demon ray's back onto the monstrous destrier. From his seat on the ray, Raijin clasped his hands and extended them to her in a show of admiration. She thanked him with a seated bow as Pernicious danced and whinnied.

"Shall we return to the palace?" she called up to Raijin. "You've only just come back from the lower reaches, and you're certainly tired after such a long trip made so quickly."

"The work of traveling was all done by Nael," Raijin said, patting between the ray's eye bumps. "I would enjoy a tour of the countryside if the cherished princess would lower herself and her beast to ride along with a mere chieftain."

Koida laughed. "If you can keep up."

Without another word, she gave Pernicious free rein. The inky black half-demon tore off across the field and into the dark forest.

Branches and vines whipped by on either side of Koida. At first she thought they had lost Raijin at the forest's edge, as his ray's wingspan was too wide to fit between the dense foliage, but soon a glimmer of silvery Ro filtering through the canopy overhead caught her eye. The ray skimmed above the trees, keeping pace with them easily.

They bisected the forest from east to west in under an hour, a testament to Pernicious's determination to lose their guests. Finding no prey for the half-demon—or in any case, no prey he felt worth trampling while a much bigger challenge flew overhead—they turned south and galloped out of the forest once more.

Raijin and the enormous ray fell in beside them now that they were out in the open. Inspiration struck when Koida saw the silvery strand of water to the east. She nudged Pernicious toward the Horned Serpent River until they were racing along its winding banks.

The demon ray skimmed out over the surface of the water in obvious delight, dragging its tail and throwing up huge sprays as its wings rilled. Once it even dove under, exploding back out of the water with Raijin sputtering and shaking off droplets like a wet horse.

Seeing someone else's demon get the better of him for once set Koida to laughing again. Raijin grinned and rose up to his knees on the ray's back, reaching up and behind his head with both hands, then bringing them down and slamming his palms forward in a technique she'd never seen.

A wall of water laced with Ro raced up the banks after Koida. Still laughing, she leaned low over Pernicious's head and whispered, "If you don't want to be soaked, you'd better run faster."

The proud warhorse triggered Demonic Speed, his hooves' flames flaring brilliantly in the darkness, and blurred ahead of the watery construct. The wave splashed harmlessly behind them.

Raijin was laughing as his ray caught them up with a burst of its own Ro-enhanced speed. He made the sign for admiration once more.

"You two work well together when you aren't trying to kill one another," he called to Koida.

"It's a rare occurrence," she responded. "You must be blessed by fate to have seen it with your own eyes!"

The moon was leaving the sky when they reached the base of the waterfalls where the Horned Serpent River poured down from the cliffside. By unspoken agreement, they dismounted to let Pernicious drink and the ray swoop in and out of the falling spray. Koida leaned against one of the huge moss-covered boulders on the bank. Raijin wandered aimlessly nearby, picking flat stones among the myriad of river rocks and skipping them across the surface of the churning pool.

The thrill of riding through the night with another person had boosted Koida's flagging energy, but it wasn't enough to stave off the bone-weary exhaustion that had been threatening to drag her down all day. She wanted to talk to Raijin about cultivating, how she had spent the night before Pouring Ro into Itself, but her lips felt heavy and uncooperative. The inside of her eyelids felt as if they were coated with a thin layer of sand and her eyes as if they were roasting over a bed of coals. She blinked to wet them, and the world dissolved.

She woke being lifted onto the glowing silvery back of the demon ray.

"My apologies," Raijin said, laying her gently on the velvety surface. "I was afraid you would be thrown if I sat you on your demon asleep." He grinned. "I also couldn't get close to him without being kicked."

"Now you're starting to get to know him," Koida said.

"Would you like to ride back to the palace with Nael and me?"

"I would love to." She sat up. A jingling weight in her robes bumped against her stomach. The silver links for the beggars. "I have an errand to do before returning, however. Do you mind going into the city? I could ride Pernicious if you're in a hurry to reach your bed."

"It would be our honor to escort you," Raijin said, bowing deeply. "Just tell us the way."

As they skimmed back over the river to Boking Iri, Pernicious kept pace with them, loudly making known his displeasure at being ignored. Following Koida's directions, Raijin guided his mount down the canal and into the city. They twisted and turned through the streets until they reached the beggar's row.

Koida pulled the bag of silver out of her robe and made ready to throw it into the largest crowd, a group of six clustered around a smoldering fire.

"This is where you were going?" Raijin asked.

A strange note in his rasping voice made Koida lower her arm and turn to him. His face wore a stricken expression. Only then did she realize how bizarre it must seem for the empire's second princess to have business with untouchables.

"I wasn't planning to stop," she said defensively. "Just to leave this with them."

Raijin shook his head. "It's just that this isn't how you were when…I mean, how I imagined you would be."

Koida's face heated. She wasn't sure she could explain to him her need to carry out this errand. Someone as talented as Raijin would never understand what it was like to be given so much in spite of having no real worth.

Raijin directed his demon ray to a stop in the alley.

"What are you doing?" Koida hissed.

He didn't answer. Instead, he hopped down from the ray's back and offered Koida a hand.

"Raijin, these are—we can't—if someone found out…"

"When you're ready, I'll be over there," he said, then left her behind on Nael while he approached the fire.

The untouchables cowered, the ones still mostly in their right minds disappearing into piles of rubbish and unseen escape routes. One frail old man remained, raving in an endless stream of babble about chosen ones and great darkness until a thin woman stepped forward, pushing him behind her. In her fist, she brandished a plank torn off a crate, a trio of bent, rusty nails poking from its larger end.

"Stay back!" she snapped at Raijin. "We ain't got any more silver, so you mongrels can just go torment someone else!"

"Apologies, aunt," Raijin said, bowing respectfully to the woman. "I am not here to collect from you. I only seek to share your fire."

The woman cocked her head at him warily, then pointed her plank at Koida and the ray. "That thing yours?"

"It is, aunt."

"What is it?"

Raijin laughed. "A great help when I don't want to walk, but an overgrown nuisance when he wants to swim. Might my friend and I stand by your fire until we're warm?"

"You ain't soldiers?"

"Neither of us," he said.

"You're welcome to it, such as it is," the woman said, shrugging. She went back to kneeling beside the bank of coals.

Raijin nodded at Koida as if to assure her there was no danger, then went to the fire and knelt beside the filthy woman.

Koida swallowed hard and looked around. Did Raijin not notice that these people were hunkered in a back alley filled with refuse? They were untouchables. Half of those who'd scattered had been covered in the weeping sores of addicts, and to pick up a plank of wood rather than manifest a weapon meant that the woman was either Ro-crippled from birth or had broken her heartcenter in some sort of trauma.

The old man was tottering down the alley toward Koida, pointing a gnarled finger at her. She recoiled.

"Thunder of the clouds says yes to look down the tunnel of seconds at the great destruction end of war-peace at the war piece the dragon became in the wake of the water lily so thunder of the clouds throws himself an arrow at the dragon to change the path and change the great destruction and the war piece to bring war-peace on the water lily when the silk moths fill the sky swimming on air all those loved ones! All those souls," he screamed, spittle flying from his toothless mouth.

"Ha-Koi," Raijin called from the fire. It took a moment for Koida to realize he was talking to her, shortening her name to the diminutive so she could remain anonymous. The sound of his voice broke the old man's insane hold over her. Her betrothed gestured for her to join him and the woman.

Cautiously, Koida slipped off the ray and edged around the old man.

"The dragon piece," the old man crowed, following her to the fire. "Dragons, like moths to flame, run to the thunder!"

"Come sit, grandfather," the kneeling woman coaxed gently. The old man staggered over to her and sat, suddenly docile.

Koida knelt on the opposite side of the fire from the lunatic. Her muscles jumped and hummed, ready to flee at the first sign of movement.

Apparently, Raijin and the woman had been talking before the interruption, because he leaned forward and gestured for her to go on.

"Please continue, aunt."

"So then they go on and kick the lice right off Pai-Leng," she said, "laughing all the while. I think there's bleeding in her stomach from it, as if she didn't have enough trouble with the qajong. I swear to you, we ain't had one night of peace since the emperor and his legions got back. Wish the whole lot of foul wolves would march back to war again and die, every last one of 'em."

Koida was too startled by the venom in the woman's voice to even gasp.

"Surely you don't mean the Exalted Emperor Hao's soldiers," she said.

The woman spat into the fire. "Don't know no other armor-wearing, rotten-Ro containers spoiling for an easy target. I sent a couple off all tore up and down their arms by my trusty club. May they get the locked jaw for their crimes."

Someone hissed behind Koida. She jumped and twisted around to find a man with a leathery face scratching open sores.

"You oughtn't talk like that, Ni," the addict said, digging into a bloody spot on his arm. "They're masters. Masters do as they like, and it's good and right that they do. Yeah. Just shouldn't act better than your place around them. Yeah."

"Go drum up some currency for you next fix, Sin-An." The woman—Ni—dismissed the addict with a wave. "I'm not so defeated yet that I'll accept all that untouchable talk. I wasn't born broken, and I don't allow for this being my rightful destiny. Was an accident that broke me, a split second of unlucky when I could've used luck. Could've happened to anybody." She turned to Raijin and pointed a finger at his face. "I'll fight that destiny nonsense to my pyre, don't care who's spouting it."

Raijin nodded. "You should fight it, aunt. There are only a handful of people whose fate is written in stone—" He sent Koida an enigmatic smile. "—and even they can surprise you now and then."

"Exactly." Ni thudded a dirty fist onto her thigh.

"If you would like," Raijin continued, "I know a healer who may be able to help you, and a place where you can live as everyone else, not as an untouchable. You and any here who wish to go with you."

Ni made a rude sound. "Keep wasting that honey, nephew, and you'll get all the bees angry."

"It isn't a lie," he said. "There's a village up the pass, in the Shangyang Mountains. My tribe lives there, and among them are masters of many paths, one a healer who surpasses any other. But you don't have to believe me. Right now, it sounds like your greatest need for healing is Pai-Leng. If she really is bleeding inside, she'll need help immediately or she'll die. I can give you silver. Do you know of a healer in the city who will see you?"

Ni shook her head. Her filthy hair, dry as twigs, scraped over her shoulders with the motion. "You really ain't from Boking Iri, are you, nephew? No, no apothecary or healer in this city will see us. Untouchable, you get it?"

"What will you do?" Koida whispered.

Ni shrugged. "Guess when the time comes, we'll try to get together some of this rubbish for a pyre."

Koida felt her stomach lurch at the unfairness of it. No healers would see this Pai-Leng because of her status. The woman would die in this filthy alley, the victim of a soldier who could do whatever he liked to a Ro-crippled untouchable peasant without fear of retribution. Meanwhile a Ro-crippled princess could sit in the palace at her wedding feast, where legions of alchemists who kowtowed to her mixed vomiting potions so she and her subjects could gorge themselves with more food.

Koida's hands shook as she held out the bag of silver links she'd intended to throw the beggars.

"Do you think they'd see you if you had this?"

Ni glanced down at it hungrily, but a grim acceptance settled across her face. She shook her head.

"Not for all the coin in the empire, niece," she said. "Ain't no respectable body out here willing to lose that much face. Though the soldiers will be glad to take all that shiny off our hands tomorrow."

Raijin stood suddenly. "I have a friend who might be able to help. I'll send her along as soon as I can. She'll have a mask over her nose and mouth. She doesn't speak, so please don't attack her when she shows up."

Ni shrugged. "She don't attack us, we won't have no reason to attack her."

"Gratitude for your hospitality," Raijin said. With that, he bowed respectfully to their hosts. "Aunt Ni, Uncle Sin-An, Grandfather—"

At the appellation, the old man stirred back to life. "Thunder clouds the sky over its head and rains justice on the flowers, but never can if you let the darkness take her. Time is shorter than you think."

Koida shifted uncomfortably. The old man's insane rambling made her skin crawl. On the opposite side of the fire, Ni shushed the old lunatic, rubbing his back like a mother with a fussy baby.

Rather than an understandably confused expression, however, Raijin wore a look of concern.

"How much shorter?" he asked the old man.

"Yes, that is true." The old man shook a finger at him. "Don't lose the dragon to the darkness, grandson."

"I won't," Raijin said. Once more, the low rasp of her betrothed's voice rang like a vow. He turned to Koida. "Ha-Koi, are you ready?"

"Yes." She stood and bowed to the untouchables just as Raijin had, as if they were her equals. Because if her title and fortunate birth were stripped away, she was no different from them.

When she rose again, she pressed the bag of silver into Ni's hand. "Please, aunt, take it. Maybe if you give it to the soldiers, they won't hurt you."

Ni sighed, a defeated sound.

"Gratitude, niece," the woman said. "May we one day live in a world where we can all afford to be so naïve."

CHAPTER THIRTY

6 years ago

"WHY AM I HERE?" RAIJIN wondered aloud.

He sat outside his mother's shabby hut in the burning heat of the afternoon in the place where he had taken to sleeping at night, scratching the sand flea bites on his legs and arms and neck—everywhere he had skin, really—and wondering why Master Chugi would send him away from the school he loved to find this dying woman who'd given him up at birth.

Half of the time she was in such a stupor that she didn't even know he was there. The rest she was either raging at him for not giving her more "medicine" or screaming in agony. At least twice a day he feared that she had reached her last breath. And yet every day, she breathed on.

After the first day spent with Lanfen, Raijin had begged Daitai for fresh clothes and blankets for his mother. The madam was all too happy to give the chosen one anything he would ask for. Raijin had thanked her—not bothering to point out that she hadn't extended the same courtesy to the chosen one's mother, whom she proclaimed a sister—and gone back to burn his mother's

268

soiled rags on the sand. Over the next few days, he'd washed Lanfen, tried to coax her to eat the food Daitai sent, scooped out all the stale, disgusting, packed sand she'd been lying on for one couldn't know how long, and refilled the lean-to with fresh sand from farther down the beach.

There were a few good times. There seemed to be a magic level of the drug where Lanfen could feel relief and yet maintain enough mental awareness to speak to him like a mother. She'd told him the story of his birth, that stormy night when they'd first met, how the madam was furious with her for not getting rid of the child the moment she realized she was pregnant. Lanfen showed him the white scar on her finger where she'd bitten her knuckle in an effort not to scream too loudly and disrupt the performance in the next room of the teahouse as she gave birth to him. Or she talked about the pompous Grandmaster Feng trying to refuse her entreaty to take her son—and she did a wonderful impression of the man—then asked about the kindly Master Chugi and listened with rapt attention to Raijin's account of the sweet old man. She would sing him a song, stroke his hair, and grin at him with an unbearable pride, and in those moments, Raijin could see the beauty his mother had once been. It shined through her dying body like a trapped sun.

A boy a few years younger than Raijin passed by the lean-to. The space between the latrine and the back of another outbuilding was a common thoroughfare for the people who lived down in the beach shacks, a shortcut between their little neighborhood and the city proper. This boy was limping, one eye already swelling, and his lip split. He hugged his willow-switch-thin arms around himself defensively, staring down at the ground as he walked. When the boy saw Raijin, he glared and kicked sand at him.

Raijin conjured Shield of the Crescent Moon to block the spray, a weight like a boulder sitting on his heart. The boy and his mother lived just a few shacks down. She was a qajong-addict as well and often rented him to anyone who could fund her next high.

That boy could very well have been him, Raijin thought. In another life, if Lanfen had chosen to keep her son, she could have turned to using him to pay for the bliss she found in her pipe. She could have sold him. She could have sent him out to find work, and living in this forsaken area with nothing but a family-less sensha as his mother, he would have turned to thievery and killing like the gangs he'd learned roamed the streets. She would never have had to work again.

But his mother had taken her life in her hands, climbing the mountain through a forest filled with dangerous demon beasts to the School of Darkening Skies. She'd fought with the grandmaster for his admission. Weeping, she had stumbled away from the one thing that could have made the rest of her life easier, giving him up so he could have the luxury of growing up safe and honorable rather than caring for an addict mother in a place that would wring the morality from anyone by slow, torturous degrees.

Long ago, he'd told Master Chugi that he could die for a person like that. Now he saw that to die would be a simple thing, too easy to do, and very little help to anyone. His mother had given up everything she could have had so he could live a better life. What was a few hours of own his life bathing her and enduring her drug-craving rants in return for a gift like that?

CHAPTER THIRTY-ONE

6 years ago

VENTUALLY, RAIJIN LOST TRACK OF how many days he'd been with his mother. The cycle of her addiction continued unabated by weather, sand fleas, or her own illness. She worsened so quickly that it was like watching a banana go brown in the hot sun.

One evening, while Raijin was sitting outside his mother's lean-to in a lax Resting Meditation and enjoying the cool breeze rolling in off the ocean, his mother called out to him.

"My beautiful son, are you here?"

She always asked the same question, as if she were certain that some day there would be no answer.

"I'm here, Mother." Raijin crawled into the lean-to and knelt beside her. Though he tried to bathe his mother every few days and change the sand beneath her as often, the place still smelled like an uncovered waste pit. He'd gotten used to it, however. Mostly. "What can your son do for you?"

He expected her to beg for her medicine. It would be a chore telling her that she had already smoked all the day's supply from Daitai and there would be no more until the next morning. She would scream, rage, accuse him of evil lies and smoking it himself, and eventually let him hold her while she wept herself to sleep.

Instead, however, he found Lanfen with eyes bright and alert. Pale pink mists decorated her sallow cheeks as if she were finally regaining her health. She reached out with a skeletal hand and touched his cheek, then reached up and ran her fingers through his shaggy hair. He'd been due for a haircut when Master Chugi sent him away but hadn't yet found the time.

"You have hair like I used to," Lanfen said fondly through dry, cracked lips. "Little waves like a black ocean on top of perfect jade eyes. So beautiful. I gave you the one good thing I had, my beauty, and you wear it better than I ever did."

"I think you're beautiful, Mother." He meant it, too. Since the day he had realized how much his mother had sacrificed for him, Lanfen had grown more and more dear to him, even in the worst moments. "Can I get you some water? Are you thirsty? Would you like to try to eat?"

"My son, my Raijin," she whispered. "You are my gift to the world."

The words had a ring of finality to them that Raijin didn't like. Lanfen's eyes drifted nearly shut.

Raijin grabbed her hand as it fell and pressed it back to his cheek.

"Amma?" For reasons that he didn't understand, he used the address small children used for their mothers. It was the first time he had spoken the word in his life.

Lanfen's eyes remained shut, but she spoke.

"What little that I have, let it pass to you."

As she sighed out her last breath, a cloud of sparkling white jade Ro, the most brilliant and beautiful thing

Raijin had ever seen, rose from Lanfen's heartcenter and flowed into his. He could feel it within him, flowing around and around his own green jade Ro, the two colors dancing wildly together like reunited spirits.

He stared down at the body that had once been his mother. Now it was empty. Dead.

On numb hands and knees, he crawled out of the lean-to. Slowly, stiltedly, he began to dismantle the boards that made up the roof and wall of his mother's death house. The sparkling white Ro danced inside him, free of pain, overjoyed to see its offspring, and his own jade Ro whirled around it, ecstatic.

Raijin didn't want to leave his mother's body alone for even a moment, but there wasn't enough wood in the lean-to to build a proper pyre. When he finished dismantling it, he kissed her cold cheek and promised he would be right back. Using Straight Line Winds, he sprinted past the latrine, through the town. He gathered armload after armload of wood from the forest at the farthest northern edge of the city, each time promising the body he would be back soon.

Raijin built his mother a funeral pyre while her final gift to him swirled in his chest as if it were happy to finally be home.

CHAPTER THIRTY-TWO

Present

KOIDA ROSE WITH THE SUN THE NEXT morning. Before they had parted the night before, Raijin had promised that her training could begin at dawn, and she was not going to miss even a second of it. As soon as she woke, she dressed in her training attire and bolted past Batsai and the nodding Jun.

"Training," she called over her shoulder in explanation. She could hear the sound of the guards scrambling to follow, the nightcaller floors screaming under their rushed, clumsy steps.

The first rays of yellow were piercing the sky when she stepped into the training courtyard. Raijin was there already, standing at the center facing the east, moving through strange flowing motions at a glacial pace.

She stopped at his side and knelt, fist pressed to her palm and raised over her bowed head while she waited for him to finish. His breathing was slow and deliberate, and without thinking, she began to mimic it. It was calming and yet also energizing. Mesmerized, she watched his bare feet scrape the dirt in front of her face.

Finally, his feet came to a stop and turned toward her.

"Master," Koida said, lowering her head even farther.

His feet snapped together, and when Koida looked up, Raijin was bowing over his fists.

"You don't have to kneel," he said, his voice noticeably hoarser than it had been before. "Please, stand up."

"What were you just doing?" she asked, getting to her feet.

"It's a moving meditation Hush taught me," he said. "You can learn it if you want, but it would be better for her to teach you. I tried to learn as much of her Path as I could and only hurt myself." He gestured to his throat.

"Your voice?" she asked.

He nodded. "Not every Path is for every person."

"Then why do you practice it?"

Raijin scratched at the back of his neck, a gesture she was coming to see as a nervous or self-conscious habit.

"The Path of Hidden Whispers is one of... Restraint isn't quite right. More like containment. Containing words, thoughts, emotions. Holding them inside." He cleared his throat as if it were raw, then continued. "I'm doing a poor job explaining it. As you can imagine, it's hard to learn the core principles of a Path from someone who can't speak. Lately, however, I think I'm beginning to understand."

"Why?" Koida's brow furrowed. "How?"

Raijin didn't seem bothered by her clumsy inquiries. He stared into the emptiness between them as if he were considering the best way to answer.

"There are some things you have to hold inside. Things no one else can know." His eyes snapped up to meet hers, a jade fire burning in their depths. "For their protection or for the protection of others."

"You could tell someone," Koida insisted. "If you were going to marry them anyway, and you knew they wouldn't tell anyone else. They might be strong enough to bear it with you."

His expression softened. "Not if it wasn't a question of strength."

"What else could it be?"

Raijin shook his head, then looked up at the lightening sky.

"Our morning's being eaten away and taking our chance to train with it. If you want to study the Path of the Thunderbird, we should start now."

"As you say, Master." She bowed again, promising herself to bring the matter up again that night at their wedding feast when he would have no excuse to evade it.

"It's important to know that the Path of the Thunderbird is in direct contrast to the one you've grown up in," Raijin said. "Your sister and father and even your guard fight other warrior artists to absorb pieces of their Ro, either in open warfare or duels, growing stronger by filling themselves with what belongs to others."

Koida nodded. "This is the nature of the world."

"We don't train to give in to our nature, we train to overcome it," Raijin said. He cleared his throat once more, though it didn't improve his rasping voice. "The Path of the Thunderbird seeks to strengthen and refine what Ro you already have, to make you worthy of the power and responsibility you gain as you progress. It's still permissible to absorb Ro from others if you're forced to defeat them, but unless you're fighting to protect a being weaker than yourself or to see justice done, then fighting others is nothing but a sign of laziness."

Koida tried not to bristle at his words and failed.

"What if I'm near death, and I need their Ro to live?" she asked defiantly.

Raijin cocked his head slightly. "Is it better to take from another so you can live or to give up your chance at life so another can live?"

For some reason, the question brought to mind the untouchables from the night before.

"Did you send Hush to the untouchables in the city?" she asked, her voice tinged with concern. "Was she able to help Pai-Leng?"

"Yes," Raijin said. "Now focus. Get into this stance."

He spread his feet, bent his knees, and brought his fists to his hips. Koida did the same.

At least, she thought she did until he circled her, making minor adjustments to the width of her feet, the angle of her legs, the placement of her fists, even the tension in her shoulders.

"That's good," he said. "You're better at keeping your back straight than I was when I started. My training master used to slap our spines with a staff whenever he saw them bending."

Raijin didn't have a staff, and Koida didn't think he would slap her with one if he did, but she straightened her back more all the same.

Satisfied with all the trivial changes he'd made to her stance, Raijin sank back into his, facing her.

"This is Horse Riding Stance, just like riding your demon. We're going to work on this, your fighting stance, and your set stance today. Probably for most of the first few weeks."

Koida frowned. "But you said I could learn how to fight without Ro first thing."

"One is a building block of the other," he said. "If you can't get these right, your foundation will be worthless. Don't forget to breathe."

They stood in the riding stance, breathing in and out together until Koida felt ridiculous. Then until she felt a little dizzy. Then until her legs started to shake. Then until she felt better. Then until her legs started to shake again.

"Okay, up." Raijin popped back up to standing smoothly.

Koida tried to do the same, but her motion was filled with jerks and silent groans.

Raijin stood with his back straight and his fists closed in front of his waist. "This is Set. It's a position of attention, a way of showing that you're ready. Try it."

Koida did, then he walked around her adjusting the width of her feet, the angle of her wrists, the tilt of her chin.

They went from Horse Riding Stance to Set over and over again. After those first times, Raijin didn't make any adjustments to her stances, only told her they were wrong and forced her to stay down in the riding stance or up in the set position until she'd made the appropriate adjustments herself. Her legs shook and sweat dripped into her eyes, but he always had her switch stances just before she collapsed.

The sun was climbing over the eastern wall of the courtyard before he told her to relax.

"The Path of the Thunderbird seeks to better your body and mind as you cultivate your Ro. The Ro is as good as useless if the other two aren't strong. Your mind is already quite sharp, so to strengthen it, first we have to work your body to exhaustion."

They sprinted up and down the length of the courtyard fifty times. Then Raijin had them switch to running halfway and back followed by the full length and back. This he counted as one divided sprint, and he said they would do another fifty of those.

After the first ten, Koida went from running to jogging, and over the course of the next ten, she went from jogging to limping. Every muscle in her body burned, and most twisted into knots.

On their thirty-ninth divided sprint—which was more of a slow shamble by then—her legs refused to hold her any longer, and she dropped into the dirt like a sack of lentils.

A shadow fell across her vision.

"I should stop you," Raijin said. "Your other masters probably did when you reached your limit before. But I can't do that. I can't be the soft master, not if you want to have any chance of advancing. Adversity builds strength, but indulgence tears it down. Think back. Your limit isn't good enough for what you want to achieve, is it? So you'll have to force yourself beyond that."

Koida groaned and pushed herself up onto her hands and knees. Gasping for air, she crawled toward the courtyard wall. She had eleven of the divided sprints left to go. That sounded like a lot, but she couldn't give up. Not if the price of failure was her one hope at advancing.

When she finished the divided sprints—at that point resorting to dragging herself across the courtyard tiles—

she collapsed beside the portico stair. Her delicate palms were bleeding and torn from the fine grit and dust she'd never noticed covering the courtyard tiles, and the knees of her training clothes were filthy.

Raijin took a seat in front of her, legs folded.

"Do you think you can keep this up?" he asked.

What she truly thought was that the physical exertion alone would probably kill her…and that if he asked her to get up and run some more, she would cry.

"I will," she said. Her throat was dry, but her words were unnaturally loud in her ear as they bounced off the tiles beneath her cheek.

Raijin smiled at her deflection of the question. "Show me what you learned of Resting Meditation."

Grateful to do anything that included sitting, Koida pushed herself up with shaking arms and crossed her legs. Her bleeding palms stung as she made them into fists and spread them a half-inch apart over her heartcenter.

Raijin adjusted her chin, her shoulders, her fists, even the place where her shins crossed over one another.

"When you're tired is the perfect time to cultivate your Ro," he said. "The mental effort it takes to force yourself to exercise your Ro when your physical body is on the verge of collapse—"

Koida grinned.

"—well, when it's past the verge of collapse, too," Raijin amended. "That effort sharpens your mind and strengthens your will. Let's try Pouring Ro into Itself."

Drained beyond anything she'd felt in her entire life, Koida closed her eyes and focused on the sizzling, sparking amethyst Ro at her heartcenter, surrounded by its dense lilac rings. She tried sending a finger of the misty energy from the cloud to cycle around one of the rings.

And immediately blacked out.

CHAPTER THIRTY-THREE

Present

RATHER THAN STOPPING THE TRAINING and sending Koida to the alchemists for some sort of treatment, Raijin woke her gently and sat her up, and they began Resting Meditation again. Three times she blacked out with no success. But on the fourth try, she finally forced her Ro to begin pouring into itself.

Then she blacked out.

When Koida woke again, Raijin was beaming down at her.

"You did it," he said.

She nodded. "For almost a full second."

He helped her sit up, then pulled her up to standing.

"That's the perfect amount for your first day," he said. He pressed his fists together and bowed to her. "Thank you, Shyong San Koida, for this training."

She returned the bow unsteadily. He caught her as she started to tip.

"Thank you, Master Ji Yu Raijin, for not asking your student to quit."

"As long as I live, I won't," he said, his rasping promise carving itself into her mind like letters etched in stone.

Batsai and Jun helped Koida limp back to her residence, where she promptly fell asleep. It wasn't even noon yet, but her body simply refused to stay awake.

When the door to the outer chamber opened, Koida assumed it was her ladies come to bathe and dress her for the sixth night of her wedding feast. Instead of a yammering whirlwind of gossip, however, someone took three running steps and leapt onto her bed.

"Koida!" Shingti shouted.

Koida lurched up from her doze, a scream in her throat. When she saw that it was only her sister, she scowled and dropped back onto her bed. Her muscles ached and jumped individually as if they were being struck at random by tiny tongues of invisible lightning.

"Please go fall off a cliff, elder sister," she groaned. "I'm trying to sleep."

Shingti cackled, clearly pleased with her entrance.

"I heard you had your first training day with the Ji Yu chieftain," the first princess said. "Tell me about it, teach me things. Did he tell you how his construct blade works? Does his Path suit you? Did you learn its basic principles? Did it undo your deficiency?"

Though Koida was fairly certain Shingti was joking with the final question, Koida focused inward, probing at her heartcenter. Her Ro looked and felt the same. She couldn't tell if it was stronger. She opened her eyes and tried to manifest two bo-shan sticks, one in each hand. As always, only her right one would manifest. It didn't look any more solid than usual.

"I don't know," she admitted. "But he said it could take years before I start to see any progress."

Shingti poked the purple stick. Koida was too exhausted to hold its form. The manifestation vanished, and the Ro retreated painfully back up the wrong paths to her heartcenter.

"What sort of techniques did he teach you, little sister?" Shingti asked. "Anything I should try? Show me something."

"We didn't work on any techniques, only stances."

Shingti looked a combination of skeptical and disgusted. "You spent all morning working on stances?"

Koida's shrug was barely more than a twitch of the shoulders, and even that hurt.

"Well, I can't understand his teaching methods, but his fighting speaks for itself," Shingti said. "If my little sister can match half of that ability in her lifetime, I'll never worry about her again."

"If I survive the training," Koida mumbled, rolling onto her stomach.

Shingti laughed. "You'll survive, little sister. You're stronger than people let you believe."

"If you really wanted to encourage me, you would send for one of the masseuses."

A commotion in the outer chamber startled them both silent. The door opened.

Koida propped herself up on her elbows. It was Batsai, with a soldier from Shingti's Dragonfly Guard leaning around him.

"Apologies for the interruption, adored second princess and annoying old hag," the soldier said.

Shingti threw Koida's pillow at the soldier with all the force of a Master of the Living Blade. The soldier swung his leg up into an Axe Blade Kick, the cutting edge manifesting in the blink of an eye, but Batsai snatched the pillow out of the air.

"No messes in the second princess's residence, you children," he growled.

Shingti and the soldier grinned at one another.

"Well, get on with your message, Ym-Luan," the first princess said. "Before it busts your gut."

"There's a tournament in the courtyard," the soldier said, excitement lighting his square features. "The chieftain of the Ji Yu has issued an open challenge to the empire's soldiers."

It was the sort of event that Masters of the Living Blade in the Shyong San Empire lived and breathed for. Shingti bounced off the bed and grabbed Koida by the wrist.

"Come on, little sister! Maybe we're not too late to join the fun."

CHAPTER THIRTY-FOUR

Present

THE LAST THING KOIDA WANTED TO DO after the morning's exertions was sit through a tournament when she could be resting in comfort, but as Shingti dragged her through the halls back to the training courtyard, she had to admit she was eager to see Raijin fight again. His duel against Master Lao had been pure beauty in motion, and his battle against her father and Shingti's personal guards as thrilling and terrifying as standing inside a tornado.

When they reached the courtyard, Raijin and the first of his opponents had stripped away their outer robes and wore only the loose pants common to a formal duel. The soldiers and guards who weren't preparing to fight were pointing at the young chieftain's unmarked arms and chest, elbowing one another and letting out the occasional guffaw of laughter.

Koida wanted to demand all their attention and explain to them that Raijin wasn't a coward as his tattooless skin would make it seem, but that it was in opposition to his Path to proclaim all the feats of valor in his past.

But her anger quickly burned away at the sight of Raijin's bare shoulders and arms. Sinewy muscle stretched as taut as lute strings over his lean frame. With his back to her, she could see a series of red, stringy scars wrapped around his nape, right arm, and shoulder blade like tangled jellyfish tentacles. A double line of black caught her eye, stretching from Raijin's shoulder socket down the back of his left arm to his elbow. For a moment, she thought he did have a tattoo, but the lines were too polished and shiny to be ink. Unconsciously, she leaned closer. It looked as if he'd had a pair of lavaglass canes embedded in his flesh. The skin that bordered it was ragged scar tissue like that she'd seen on the Uktena envoys.

A thousand questions rushed her at once—when and how he'd become acquainted with the savage tribe, whether getting those canes embedded had hurt as badly as it appeared to have, what had caused the multitude of winding scars on his arm and shoulder… Then she remembered that soon she would have every right to ask him such prying questions and anything else she might dream up. In only two more nights she would be Raijin's wife.

A little thrill of pride sang through Koida. In spite of his lack of Heroic Record, the strange scars, and the pair of embedded lavaglass canes, her future husband was a handsome man. He might even rival Yoichi for beauty. For strength and ability, she couldn't say who would come out on top; she'd never seen Cousin Yoichi fight. But she found she felt a very strong—almost proprietary—bias toward Raijin.

"Am I too late to participate in the tournament?" Shingti asked cheerfully, her voice ringing off the courtyard walls as she and Koida stepped off the portico into the sunlight.

Raijin turned and bowed over his fists, his jade eyes locked on the first princess's purple ones.

"The honored first princess is welcome to join the tournament, though its purpose is to settle a matter of grave importance," he said. "This soldier and at least six others have been extorting from, abusing, and generally terrorizing the homeless in Boking Iri since the army's return."

"Nonsense!" Shingti snapped. "My soldiers would never waste their time terrorizing untouchables. What honor would they have to gain from bothering cripples?"

"Apologies, wise and all-knowing first princess," Koida said, her voice clipped with irritation. Did Shingti not realize that if not for Koida's lucky birth, she would be one of those untouchables? "But little sister happens to know that the soldiers in question did not escape unscathed. Many of them bear a trio of scratches from being attacked by one untouchable wielding a nail-studded board." She pointed across the courtyard at the small grouping of soldiers waiting for their turn to duel Raijin. "Look them over yourself if you do not believe."

"It's on his left," Raijin said, raising the man's muscled arm for him and displaying the grooves scratched by Ni's board. The soldier jerked his arm out of Raijin's hand, glaring at the young chieftain. Raijin went on, unconcerned. "I found the men who had the scratches and asked them to pay for the damage they caused. The tournament was their idea. Each one I can best without using my Ro will give a month's wages or a month's care to the injured. To each one who can best me, I'll give a month's wages."

"And you believe this is necessary?" Shingti asked him, still clearly skeptical. "You're going to stake your honor in battle on the behalf of untouchables?"

"Within my chosen Path, the well-being of those weaker than us is the most important matter," Raijin replied. "There is no greater honor than defending them."

Koida's heart thundered in her chest. That earlier wash of pride at her betrothed's beauty was nothing like the pride she felt at his answer.

"Then I will fight you on my soldiers' behalf, as they are weaker than I." Shingti's purple gaze jumped from one accused soldier to the next. None of them were from her Dragonfly Guard, but as she commanded the imperial army, they still answered to her, and their behavior fell under her responsibility. "Do any of you object?"

The soldiers all agreed, many of them eagerly. A few grinned as if the duel had already been won. The great Master of the Living Blade, the Dragonfly of the Battlefield taking their place against a man without a single tattoo to mark a valiant deed—how could they lose?

Koida decided these men must not have been present when Raijin disabled Shingti and more than two dozen of the best warriors in the empire.

As if the first princess were thinking the same thing, Shingti turned to Raijin.

"I'm fine with you using your Ro, but what's your stance on outlawing that cowardly Ro-blocking finger technique for this duel?" she asked.

"I'll use only techniques from the first path I studied, if that seems agreeable to you. It was the Path of

Darkening Skies. The blocking technique is from the Path of Endless Day."

Shingti nodded. "That is agreeable."

As the first princess prepared for the duel, Koida went back into the shade to find a seat. A watching soldier hopped down from a barrel leaning against a wall and bowed to her.

"Please, Adored Second Princess," he said, gesturing to the vacated spot. "Take this seat."

"Gratitude," she said, inclining her head to him.

But when she tried to pull herself up onto the barrel, her arms did nothing more than shake. They were exhausted from training. Solicitously, the soldier shoved over a crate. Koida thanked him again, then used it as a step to climb onto the barrel top. Finally seated, she surveyed the scene in the courtyard.

Shingti had stripped down to loose pants and the binding shift covering her chest. Through the thin cloth of the binding shift, the brightly colored ink of the first princess's Heroic Record showed that she was tattooed from wrists to navel, a sharp contrast to Raijin's inkless skin. To anyone watching, it would appear as if a seasoned warrior were about to fight a cringing child.

"Be warned, Chieftain." Shingti spread her feet, pulling one fist back to her hip and pressing her other palm out, fingers curled into claws. It was a fighting stance of her own invention. "I have no heavy ceremonial armor to slow my movements today."

"I will do what I can to keep up, First Princess," Raijin said, sinking into a fighting stance different from the one he'd spent the morning teaching Koida. One open hand bent inward toward the middle of his forearm, the other outstretched as if in invitation.

Like striking lightning, Shingti shot toward Raijin, a Serpentine Spear Hand manifesting a moment before impact. Raijin wheeled himself into the air, flipping away from the attack. When he landed, Shingti was already there, Spear Hand dismissed, slashing down at an angle with a brutal Axe Blade Kick.

Raijin pivoted away from the blade and dropped. His leg swept in a circle. A landslide of jade Ro moved beneath Shingti's feet.

Like the insect of her namesake, Shingti flitted into the air, leaping over Raijin's head as if she could truly fly.

From her seat in the shade, Koida imagined she saw a hint of thoughtfulness in Raijin's eyes as he turned to follow her sister's trajectory. It was almost as if he were having an internal argument with himself about whether he should attack before she landed. His dark brows gave the tiniest of facial shrugs, the decision made, and he leapt into the air as well.

Rather than soar like Shingti, Raijin's leg shot out straight, sending a circular blade of icy jade Ro singing through the air at the first princess's back. Shingti spun around in midair, then chopped through the circular blade with a bare backfist. The icy blade shattered like glass.

Both combatants hit the ground in ready stances.

Almost faster than Koida could see, Shingti fired off Flying Knife Hand after Flying Knife Hand, a technique that sent thin Ro-blades like daggers screaming toward the target. Rather than knocking the blades out of the air as Shingti had done to his construct, Raijin pulled his open hands behind his back, then thrust the palms outward, blasting them out of the air with hot wind that

Koida could feel even on the portico. Several of the spectators beside her murmured in surprise, squinting to avoid the grit being blown at them.

Prevented from reaching her target and unwilling to waste the continued focus required to maintain the projectiles, Shingti let the Flying Knives dissipate. She darted at Raijin, manifesting her favored wickedly curved Dual Swords.

Once again, Koida caught sight of Raijin's thoughtful expression. It was as if he had all the time in the world to consider how to respond to Shingti's attack.

He bent one arm in front of his face and the other over his head, a jade crescent shield manifesting along each. With the front shield, he knocked aside the first of Shingti's Thousand Darts of the Dragonfly. She spun, attacking mercilessly, one curved sword flashing after the other. Raijin mirrored her spin, knocking aside the blades one shield after the other.

They twirled and danced across the courtyard, the constant clatter of slashing blade against bashing shield filling the air. Shingti's swords blurred as her Thousand Darts technique picked up speed, but Raijin disrupted each attack with his shields and spun away to meet the next. It almost looked to Koida as if he were measuring Shingti's strength and speed with each blow.

With a start, Koida realized the courtyard and everyone in it had gone completely silent but for the ringing of Ro on Ro. Bodies leaned in unconsciously, fists clenched, and heads jerked in response to the observed blows. No one blinked.

Suddenly, the jade crescent shields disappeared. Shingti's next dart shot in at Raijin's chest. He turned like an opening door, the tip of her ruby sword cutting through the space where his heartcenter had been. Her follow up dart was already falling, but before it landed, Raijin struck, his hands a blur. A hail of battering jade fists streaked toward Shingti's head and chest.

The first princess threw herself backward, arching her spine until her long hair caressed the tiles, and let the hail pass overhead.

At the same moment, Raijin dropped and swept his leg out toward her feet. A wall of watery jade Ro rushed at Shingti like a flash flood. As if she could sense it, Shingti continued her own motion, flipping over and landing in a powerful push stance. She slapped her palms together and thrust her fingertips at the wall of jade, manifesting a blade as tall as she was in a technique Koida had never seen before. The blade split Raijin's jade wave as if it were made of real water, but the force of the impact forced Shingti backward, sliding her feet across the tiles.

Immediately the first princess returned to the offensive, leaping into a Spinning Hook Blade Kick. One after another, she sliced the deadly Ro-hooks at Raijin's shoulders, head, and stomach, even coming down at an angle to take out his knees and up at an angle to slice across his groin, but the Ji Yu chieftain slipped each lethal blow by the thinnest of margins. The loose material of his pants took the only damage, thin cuts opening here and there like claw marks from some invisible demon cat.

Teeth bared in a snarl, Shingti returned to her favored Dual Swords and flew at Raijin, the Hook Kicks and Sword Hands slicing at him from every direction.

Raijin ducked under the deadly assault and streaked to the first princess's side. He grabbed Shingti's neck and shoulder with both hands, then slammed his knee into her heartcenter.

Thunder cracked through the courtyard like a breaking ice floe.

Koida and many of her fellow spectators flinched. All except for Hush and that yellow-haired drunk Lysander, whom Koida noticed for the first time sitting across the courtyard next to a small pile of robes. At the sound, both the silent woman and foreigner only grimaced as if they had been on the receiving end of that kick before and neither remembered it fondly.

At the center of the courtyard, Shingti dropped to her knees, coughing blood onto the glazed tiles. Raijin stood over the first princess, sinking once more into his strange fighting stance.

Koida leapt off the barrel and ran to her sister's side, weariness forgotten.

"Shingti, are you all right?" She shot a glare at her betrothed. "What did you do to her?"

The first princess waved her hand at Koida, nodding her head. A gurgling sound rolled from Shingti's blood-filled throat. Koida was nearly frantic until she realized that her sister was laughing.

The first princess spit a mouthful of red—not so different from her ruby Ro—onto the tiles.

"You were fighting down to me," Shingti said, raising her head to look at Raijin. "Making it look as if I were a match for you, then pretending to exploit an opening."

"You are a force of nature, Shyong San Shingti." Raijin pressed his fists together and bowed, his eyes locked on hers. "I'm honored that you lowered yourself to fight me."

Shingti laughed again, louder this time, and lurched to her feet. She returned his bow exactly.

"I am defeated," she said. "And it was truly my honor, Master Ji Yu Raijin."

A cloud of vibrant ruby Ro filtered from Shingti's heartcenter to Raijin's. He accepted it graciously.

Shingti winced as she straightened up. "Be aware, Chieftain, that I hold you personally responsible for seeing that my little sister learns everything you know."

"I will do everything within my power to see it done," Raijin promised.

But Koida saw a flash of concern in her betrothed's jade eyes and realized with a pang of unease that what he was promising was not the same as what Shingti was demanding.

Before Koida could say anything—before she'd even considered what she might say—Shingti had turned to face the accused soldiers.

"You are responsible for delivering one month's pay or one month's care to the untouchables you wronged." Shingti scrubbed away a dribble of blood from her chin with the back of one tattooed wrist, then raised her voice until it rang through the courtyard like a war horn. "It will be announced through the ranks of the emperor's armies that anyone who has abused their power over a weaker party in a time of peace has one month to make the same restitution to that party if they still live. If they don't, the restitution will be made to their family. Failing their having a family, the offending soldier will make the restitution to the community. Any soldier under my command who does not comply within the allotted one-month period will be divined by the court eunuchs and sentenced to forfeit one limb to the Exalted Emperor's executioner. First Princess Shyong San Shingti, Dragonfly of the Battlefield, declares it so and so it will be."

It was much grander than the royal order Koida had given Raijin and Lao in this same courtyard only days before, but Shingti did have more practice issuing them.

Slowly, shocked soldiers filtered out of the courtyard to begin seeing the word spread and amends made.

"Gratitude," Raijin said to the first princess.

Shingti smiled brightly.

"It is nothing." She rubbed the binding shift over her sternum. "By blade and death, I could've sworn you shattered my heartcenter. I thought I'd start vomiting bits of my own Ro all over the courtyard."

Seeing the horror on Koida's face once more, Raijin hurried to explain. "It's temporary, no more than a disabling technique. The Ro is still in her body, just scattered throughout. Someone as talented as Shingti probably won't take more than a few minutes to gather it all back into the right place. The impact point won't even bruise."

"In that case, imagine that I'm limping off to begin dressing for my sister's wedding feast, and not because I'm in incredible pain," Shingti said. "Koida, would you mind sending for that masseuse we were discussing earlier?"

CHAPTER THIRTY-FIVE

6 years ago

THE RETURN CLIMB UP THE MOUNTAIN from Kokuji passed in a haze of confusion and conflicting emotion for Raijin. His mother was dead, but he felt her Ro frolicking with his own. He had never absorbed Ro before, hadn't even known that one could gift theirs to another. Master Chugi had said that his time with the school was over, but Raijin couldn't think of anyone else who might know what this gift meant or what he should do with the strange new addition to his heartcenter. Perhaps if he begged, Grandmaster Feng would allow him to speak with the elderly Master Chugi.

The sun was sinking into its evening bed, painting the sky above in a bloody magenta light, when Raijin stepped into the forest. The tree line closed behind him, the birches' white trunks almost glowing in the eerie sunset light and blocking his last view of Kokuji. In truth, he was relieved not to be able to turn back and see the funeral pyre burning on the beach below.

"You stink of smoke and death, Ji Yu Raijin," an inhuman voice rumbled.

Raijin jumped. The guai-ray had come seemingly out of nowhere.

"Apologies, Zhuan," he said, his legs beginning to walk once more. "I should have washed before I left the town."

The enormous beast swam along beside him.

"Did you kill the ones who killed your mate and destroyed your nest?" Raijin asked.

Her snout dipped. "It is done. They sent their poisoned wasps flying at me from long tubes of bamboo, but the pill you gave me protected me from their cowardly attacks. I spitted one on my stinger and cooked him through, then I decapitated the other."

Raijin nodded. He couldn't congratulate her for taking revenge on the men who'd murdered her mate—such conduct was strictly against the Path of Darkening Skies's central philosophy—but he thought it likely that justice had been served in this case.

"Tell me why you stink of death, legged one," Zhuan prompted when Raijin had gone a great distance without speaking.

"My mother is dead," he said. The words cut like a knife to the stomach. They were so simple to blurt out, and yet so impossible to grasp, so bloody and slick.

"You are unable to mourn her because her murderer still lives," the guai-ray said as if this explained everything. "Zhuan will help Ji Yu Raijin find his mother's killer and take revenge."

For several steps, Raijin remained silent, trying to order his thoughts.

"You can't," he said. "She was her own murderer."

"What does that mean?"

"My mother killed herself with qajong."

Zhuan fluttered her wings in agitation. "Why do you keep speaking nonsense? Tell me who your mother's killer was."

"She was."

"She who?"

"My mother."

"What does it mean?" the guai-ray hissed, clearly frustrated. "Why do you say that your mother is the killer? Who did she kill?"

"Herself," Raijin said.

"Enough!" The demon beast snapped both wings down at once. "Your circular talking makes no sense! Just tell me how we will find the one who killed her."

Raijin rubbed his gritty, tired eyes. The lids felt chapped from the tears he'd cried as he set the fire under his mother's pyre. This concept of a being killing or harming oneself must be unheard of in the world of guai. Trying to explain it to Zhuan would be a waste of time; the idea simply wouldn't translate.

"We can't find her killer," he said. "The killer is already dead and gone."

"If vengeance has been enacted, then you are free to mourn, Ji Yu Raijin."

"I think I am mourning, Zhuan," he said.

The guai-ray made a skeptical noise, but seemed content to let the subject fall to the wayside as they continued up the mountain.

Raijin walked through the night, the enormous ray accompanying him. Zhuan talked of the sensation of letting blood and the healing satisfaction of killing her mate's murderers as if the details might entice Raijin to admit that he knew who his mother's killer was and agree to seek out revenge. Raijin's attention wandered back and forth from the strange conversation to the double Ros swirling in his heartcenter.

"Zhuan, how long have you ruled the mountains?" he asked.

She undulated through the air with obvious pride. "Many times your own years, legged one. I was born on this mountainside in the same cave where my mate and I made our nest. A double century we ruled this territory together."

"Do you know of Ro?" Raijin tapped his heartcenter. He knew all creatures had it, but he didn't know whether they used it instinctually or were aware of its properties.

"More than a legged one can learn in his short lifespan."

"What does it mean when someone has two Ros? What should you do with the second one?"

"You mean when you've absorbed Ro from your enemy," the guai-ray said. "So you did kill your mother's murderer!"

"I promise you, I didn't." Hoping not to let Zhuan become distracted, he returned to the question. "My mother gifted her Ro to me as she died. Have you ever heard of a creature doing this before?"

Zhuan floated along thoughtfully for many long seconds.

Then she said, "Were you your mother's murderer?"

"No," he answered wearily. "Does this mean you've never heard of a creature giving their Ro to another?"

"It is the way of things," she said, irritation creeping back into her voice. "One creature kills another, and the dying surrenders their Ro to the victor."

"What I'm talking about is different. My mother gave it to me as a gift. I didn't win it from her, she gave it to me."

"Gift, *gift*," Zhuan repeated as if testing the word with the sensor branches around her jaw palates. "What is it?"

Raijin struggled for a definition that would suit the guai-ray. "When you give something to someone— something they're not expected to repay—or that they can't repay—for no reason other than that you want to."

"Gift. When my mate or I hunted food for our cubs, we brought the prey back and gave the cubs its meat. They could not repay us, but we wanted to give them the meat. Is that gift?"

Raijin felt a smile tug at his lips.

"Yes, I suppose so," he said.

Before he could steer the conversation back to Ro, however, Zhuan darted ahead. With a start, Raijin realized they were within running distance of his school, the ever-present mountain mists painted in shades of blue and gray by the rising sun.

What was Zhuan doing? Her shadowy form darted at the ground over and over again.

Raijin craned his neck to see better through the mist. Her stinger was tucked under her belly and jabbing at something lying on the trail. Lightning from her stinger crackled and popped each time she made contact.

As he drew closer, Raijin realized the thing she was stabbing was a decapitated human body. Just beyond it was a crispy husk of another. The combined smell made him shudder.

"These were the legged ones who killed and butchered my mate," Zhuan explained happily when

Raijin stopped beside her. She hovered low over the corpses and let loose her bowels on them. "You should do the same to the remains of the one who killed your mother, Ji Yu Raijin. It is healthy for the soul."

Raijin decided against replying. Both because he knew he couldn't make her understand and because his stomach was threatening to spill its contents. His mother was the first lifeless body he'd ever seen. Hers had been strangely peaceful in spite of its wasted appearance. These, however, were the product of brutal violence, and Zhuan's continued desecration of their corpses was disturbing on a level Raijin could hardly comprehend.

He circled wide around the bodies and continued on his way toward the school. The grandmaster might never allow him back inside, not after breaking his serving agreement, but he would be glad just to stand in its familiar shadow once more. If he could just make it back there, then everything that had lurched out of true square since he'd left would fall back into place.

The sun was peeking over the horizon when the school's hulking form emerged from the mists.

Immediately, Raijin felt the weight lift from his shoulders. There were the fading forest green tiles of the roof, the upturned eaves, the wooden porch. Off to the side was the implement shed housing the water buckets, around the corner he would find Fatty's beloved covered garden, and in the very center of the structure was the courtyard where he'd spent the last ten years of his life training.

Raijin started toward the nearest set of sliding doors, which displayed the Deep Root character for *wisdom* when closed. As it was the middle of a harsh summer, however, the panels had all been left wide to capture any stray breeze.

"Wait," Zhuan hissed. Her wings fluttered in sudden agitation, and the branching organs surrounding her crushing jaw palates flashed with blue lights as she sensed the air. "Something is wrong."

"What is it?" Raijin asked, searching for anything awry. The only unusual thing he could see was that a few of the lanterns had scorch marks on their paper, as if someone had let them burn too long.

The guai-ray cautiously swam closer to the school. "Your stench nearly masked it, but this close I sense the signature of the poisoned wasps that killed my pack. Many, many more of them."

Raijin was about to ask if she could be sensing extra needles stored in the robes or pouches of the bodies on the trail behind them, but the words died on his tongue.

There was a bare foot sticking out of the school's open doorway.

CHAPTER THIRTY-SIX

Present

THAT NIGHT, KOIDA RUSHED HER LADIES through the routines of dressing, then hurried off to the royal waiting room outside the White Jade Feasting Hall, hoping to be the first to arrive. She wanted a moment alone to speak to her betrothed.

As it happened, Raijin was already there. At his look of surprise, a smile broke across Koida's face.

She pressed her palm to her fist and bowed to him in greeting. He returned it.

"I was hoping to speak to you before my family arrived, Ji Yu Raijin," she said.

"Nothing would please me more, Shyong San Koida," he said, using the same tone of spousal respect as she.

"I wanted to convey to you my sincerest gratitude for what you did today." Koida hesitated, frustrated by her inability to express the earnestness she felt. "Not only for beginning the training of a student no master in their right mind would accept, but for fighting my sister on behalf of the untouchables." She shook her head. "No, more than that! You didn't just fight for them, you talked to them. You treated them like humans. Even I didn't

305

treat them like humans, and I'm one of them. If I had been born a peasant instead of a princess, I would be out there with them, starving and cringing and dying alone. Who would ever fight for me like that? Who would care enough to right the wrongs done to me then?"

Raijin grabbed her hand, his cool fingers closing around hers.

"I would do it," he said, the low gravel of his voice once more making the statement sound like a sacred oath. "Princess, beggar, untouchable, royal—I would find you, and I would fight for you, no matter what you were born."

The intensity of his promise and the cold fire burning in his jade eyes made Koida look away, suddenly embarrassed.

Raijin started to speak, then stopped himself. Indecision warred across his sun-burnished features. He squeezed Koida's hand, the strength in his grip evident even in his restraint.

"What is it?" she asked.

He shook his head. "You've already done so much I didn't expect. You're so different than I thought you would be. Who knows if this is even the right variation?"

"You aren't making any sense," Koida said. "What are you talking about?"

"There are things that you don't understand," Raijin said. "Things I can't tell you. But you have to know that I would find you, no matter who you were. I would do anything within my power to save you. It's why I was born."

Koida's mind scrabbled for purchase and found nothing. "Please just speak plainly. I can handle whatever you think you're protecting me from. I can help."

The waiting room door slammed open, admitting Cousin Yoichi and his small contingent of personal guards.

Raijin and Koida stepped apart guiltily as the soldiers searched for any threat to the white-haired young man. Yoichi went to his accustomed spot on the blood-orange lounge and kicked his tooled leather boots up onto the rest.

"Please excuse the interruption," Yoichi said, flipping a lock of hair out of his plum-colored eyes. "Better me than the Exalted Emperor, though. Hao's angry enough that he was duped into betrothing you to this Recordless scum, there's no telling what he might do if he saw you cozied up to the man just days after you pledged yourself as his disciple against your father's will."

Koida drew herself up until she towered over Yoichi, easy enough to do when her taller illegitimate brother was lounging on a couch.

"Ji Yu Raijin has proven his worth to the empire a thousand times over," she said, forgoing the polite familial tone for the harsh language Shingti used when intimidating someone. "I notice you didn't conquer the Uktena single-handed, elder cousin. Were you too busy in your life of luxury here at the palace *not* making more bastards?"

Koida knew she shouldn't take the argument down such a hateful road, but Yoichi's rudeness toward Raijin offended her as she hadn't known anything could.

Rather than retaliate in anger, however, Yoichi stood and stretched his slender form into a polite bow, fist pressed to his heartcenter.

"Apologies, little cousin," he said. "I forgot my place in our family. A brother would have every right to call out the betrothed of his sister if he perceived the man to be undeserving of her. Can you forgive me?"

Koida realized she was standing as still as death, staring at Yoichi in shock. She grabbed his folded hands and pulled him into a hug.

"It is nothing. Little sister bears no ill will toward her elder brother."

CHAPTER THIRTY-SEVEN

Present

AS THE FEASTING BEGAN AND SERVANTS bustled through the ranks of nobles pouring wine and filling plates, Koida shifted in her goldwood chair. Raijin was busy glaring out at the sea of faces, his cold jade eyes following something diligently.

Was he angry that she'd dismissed Yoichi's insults so easily? She did feel a bit guilty about that now, realizing that it hadn't been very loyal to her future husband, but Yoichi's admission that he felt more like a true brother to her than a bastard relegated to the rank of cousin had touched her.

Koida studied Raijin's stony mask. She didn't know whether what she felt for him was love or infatuation, but she didn't want him to be angry with her. There had been a hunger in his eyes when he swore that he would fight for her no matter who or what she was that made her heart gallop like Pernicious using his Demonic Speed.

Beneath the table, Koida took Raijin's hand. He turned his focus to her, his gaze like jade ice.

"Will you come riding with me again tonight?" Koida asked, her throat suddenly dry. She switched to a tone she had no experience using, that of a lover, and the words tumbled out in one quick breath. "I know a place where two could be alone without being observed."

Raijin's mouth dropped open, stunned. He shook his head and leaned closer as if he hadn't heard her, but before she could repeat herself, he answered.

"No."

That was it. Just a blunt rejection.

Fire blazed Koida's cheeks, her skin suddenly too tight for her body. She turned away to look out over the crowd, the embarrassment making her movements jerky and awkward. The cascades of bells in her hair jangled to signal her loss of composure—though composure loss was the least of her humiliations at the moment.

"A-apologies," she stammered, slipping back into the respectful spousal tone of speech. "Your future wife thought perhaps…because we will be husband and wife tomorrow night…and the honored chieftain seemed as if he…as if he was interested in…but that was so ignorant of this silly child to think." She tried to force a laugh, but the sound caught in her throat. "A man of Ji Yu Raijin's age and experience would prefer someone more worldly."

Raijin did laugh, though it was tinged with self-deprecation rather than malice.

"I'm not that much older than you, Koida, and I…I don't have any experience. Not of that sort." His long fingers cupped her chin, turning her face back toward him. His eyes were burning with that feral hunger once more. "Believe me, nothing sounds better to me than finding a secluded place with you. But it's like training. We force our bodies to do what they never would on their own, without regard for what they want. That self-discipline makes us stronger. No matter how I feel, no matter what I want, I won't treat you like a sensha in a cheap teahouse. If—*when* our marriage is sealed, I'll take you to my home—your new home—and in comfort and safety, I'll show you what you make me feel."

Koida's face burned now for a different reason. As the cupbearer bowed up the stairs to fill their wine cups, Koida ducked her head. Beside her, Raijin had fallen silent again.

When the servant bowed away, Raijin asked, "Is that woman one of your regular servers?"

Koida glanced up, catching a glimpse of the woman as she disappeared into the crowd.

"She must be," Koida said. "She's wearing the royal livery of the palace servants."

"You've seen her before during these wedding feasts?" Raijin pressed.

Koida tried to remember the woman's face. Except for Batsai and a few others she spoke to on a regular basis, she rarely looked past a servant's identifying garb. They were just another staple of life in the palace, like the statues or the furniture. She searched the crowd, but any of the females with wine could have been the one to serve her only moments before.

"Which one is she?"

When Raijin didn't respond, Koida turned back to him.

His brows nearly touched, and his face had gone pale beneath its sun-burnished tone.

"It's here?" he whispered.

"What is?" Again he didn't respond. Koida touched his arm. "Raijin—"

"I thought we would have more time together," he said, his eyes finally meeting hers. "I don't know if it's been enough. I tried."

"What are you—"

"Please, just listen. There's a certain way this has to go. There have already been so many deviations from what I saw in the Dead Waters, but there's only one sequence in which you and the world both survive, and it's the same every time."

Raijin grabbed her wine cup and tossed the drink back in one quick gulp.

Confused, Koida reached for his full cup, but Raijin's hand shot out like a striking adder and grabbed her wrist.

"Don't," he said, his voice strained. With his free hand, he made a signal in the air. "In some of the variations, it was poisoned, too."

"Poison?" Koida meant to whisper, but the word came out much louder.

The merry rumble of feasting and laughter cut off in a collective gasp. Faces went gray, the Exalted Emperor's included. There was nothing nobles feared so much as poison.

Chaos erupted. Someone screamed. Plates and cups clattered to the floor. Nobles and officials ran for the private rooms, snatching at the vomiting medicines the alchemists had mixed for the night, knocking one another out of the way in their desperation and panic.

"Now see here!" Emperor Hao shouted, standing so quickly his heavy chair toppled over backward. A spire cracked off and rolled across the floor.

Shingti climbed onto her chair and manifested her Dual Swords.

"Bar the doors!" she ordered. "Seize every cupbearer! No one leaves this hall!"

Before she finished speaking, the Dragonfly Guard was already running to do her bidding.

The emperor cried out, a wordless howl of rage.

At first, Koida thought he'd been bumped or disrespected by some panicking noble. But in the next moment, her father manifested a pair of sinuous ruby Scythe Blades along his thick forearms and turned on the closest court official.

"Hellfiends!" the emperor howled. The official screamed as the emperor's scythe chopped into the intersection of his throat and shoulder, nearly decapitating him. "To arms! Hellfiends in the castle!"

Then Shingti's scream filled the feasting hall, making Koida's eardrums shudder with its force. She had never heard her sister make a sound like that. It was terrifying, insane and agonized. That scream paralyzed Koida in a way Pernicious's Petrifying Shriek of Legions had never been able to. Suddenly, Shingti's Dual Swords were flashing through the crowd, cutting down nobles, servants, and soldiers alike with the Thousand Darts of the Dragonfly.

"Rally to me, Dragonflies!" the first princess shrieked, chopping her way through the room. "To me, rally to me!" But as the confused Dragonfly Guard flocked to Shingti, the first princess cut them down, screaming, "Die, hellfiends!"

The remaining Dragonfly Guards gaped at their princess as if unable to comprehend that it was her Dual Swords cutting down their brethren.

Blood fell like rain as Shingti danced across the feasting hall floor, hatred and fury twisting her beautiful face into something unrecognizable. Nobles tried to run, but none could escape her. The Dragonfly Guard tried half-heartedly to fight, but none could stop her. She slaughtered them mercilessly, alternating between opening their throats and running them through with ruthless efficiency.

On the opposite end of the room, the emperor, too, had lost his mind. Heads rolled as he swung his glowing ruby scythes, cutting through every noble and official within reach. A hysterical part of Koida's mind shrieked that the emperor was finally exercising his divine right to decide whether they lived or died, but no one was exposing the backs of their necks and accepting it quietly.

Clouds of Ro, all varying shades of red, filtered through the confusion, leaving the dead and searching out their new, living homes.

Shingti's insane purple eyes locked on Koida's.

"Hellfiends!" the first princess screeched. She changed direction and began to slash her way through the terrified crowd toward Koida. "Die, hellfiends!"

Koida couldn't move. She had never seen so much blood before. Massacre. The word echoed in her head. This was a massacre. She was going to be slaughtered by her own sister, but she couldn't move. She could only watch as Shingti's twisted, blood-splattered face chopped its way through the forest of bodies to her.

Batsai seemed to appear from nowhere. The captain of Koida's guard threw himself in front of the raging first princess. He matched Shingti blow for blow, staggering her with his powerful High Shield and even piercing her side with his Serpentine Spear. But Batsai was aging, and Shingti quickly wore him down. When the twin tips of

Shingti's Dual Swords burst from Batsai's back, Koida finally regained enough sense to start screaming.

"No! Batsai, no!"

Raijin jerked her out of her chair.

"I'm sorry," he said, his voice strained raw, tendons standing out in his neck. "No one else can stop them. It has to be me. Please forgive me."

He shoved her roughly into the arms of the foreigner from his entourage. Koida couldn't remember the yellow-haired man's name. Fear had wiped her mind clean. She could, however, remember that the woman beside him with the cloth wrappings over her mouth was called Hush.

"Get her to safety," Raijin ordered them.

"What about you?" the foreigner demanded.

"Go!"

Koida stared, mystified, as Raijin leapt over the table and off the dais. Time slowed to a speed that couldn't be possible, as if it wanted her to see everything in perfect gory detail so that she could never forget.

Shingti lunged, blood flying from her ruby blades as she tried to run Raijin through. He sidestepped the blade, but his motion stuttered and he nearly fell. Raijin pulled himself upright just in time to avoid being disemboweled by Shingti's Dual Swords. His palms slammed into the first princess's shoulder, using her insane recklessness against her. She spun off course, and Raijin followed, finger-striking where the weak points in her armor would have been if she hadn't been wearing dress robes. He finished the technique by thrusting an open palm into her back, over her heartcenter.

Ice crackled and Shingti's Ro blades disappeared. She whirled on Raijin, clawing with her fingernails.

Thunder shook the walls as Raijin intercepted her with a brutal kick to the stomach. A jagged bolt of jade lightning leapt from Shingti's heartcenter, leaving behind shredded fabric and blistered skin. Raijin stumbled away from her motionless form.

A thin moment later, Shingti dropped to the floor. A cloud of glowing ruby Ro filtered into the air over her body.

Strong hands grappled with Koida, and she realized with detached awareness that she was trying to break free and run to her sister. A foreign voice shouted in her ear, but she couldn't understand the words.

Out in the sea of blood and death, Raijin's quick, graceful movements had devolved into a tripping stagger. His hair was soaked with sweat and clinging to his temples, but he fought on to the emperor.

Hao saw him coming and turned away from the court speaker whose limbs he'd been furiously hacking away at.

Raijin ducked under the emperor's glowing Ro-scythes and kicked the older man's legs from beneath him. As he fell, Raijin slammed his knee into the emperor's heartcenter. Thunder boomed once more, and the Exalted Emperor's scythes flickered, then disappeared. Hao scrabbled to grab hold of Raijin, howling the whole time, but Raijin slipped behind him. The younger man's left arm shifted into a long, thin lavaglass blade no wider than an awl. The black blade pierced the emperor's spine, just below his skull.

The emperor sprawled facedown, dead. His Ro left his body, but it didn't filter to Raijin as it should have.

Instead, it flowed through the air toward the back of the room, meeting up with many more like it on the way.

Koida tried to pull free of Hush and the yellow-haired foreigner, but they were too strong. They dragged her kicking and fighting toward the servant's exit in the far wall.

A familiar voice rose above the wailing and screaming.

"Murderess!" Cousin Yoichi stood near the back of the room, his robes splashed liberally with blood. His finger stabbed into the air, accusing someone Koida couldn't see. "She conspired with the Ji Yu to poison and murder our family!"

Raijin's sinewy form stumbled into Yoichi's path. Her betrothed's back was to her, but Koida could see that he was barely holding himself upright. His dark complexion had gone an ashen gray. Sweat soaked his robes and matted his hair to his head in wet, black spikes. He dropped to his knees on the stone floor, shoulders heaving with effort. He lurched, trying to throw himself at the white-haired Yoichi, but fell to his hands and knees instead.

The poison, Koida realized. Raijin was dying.

A cloud of radiant dark jade Ro like none Koida had ever seen before rose from Raijin's back, over his heartcenter. Brilliant tongues of green flashed through it like a lightning storm.

Yoichi's purple eyes locked on it.

"What I have," Raijin shouted at the floor, corded muscles standing out in his neck, "let it pass to you, Koida!"

Raijin's arms spasmed and gave out. The moment he hit the ground, a chunk of ice encased him like a rough-cut diamond coffin.

All the while, Hush and that yellow-haired foreigner pulled Koida toward the servant's door. Just before they managed to drag her through, the flashing cloud of dark jade Ro slammed into Koida's chest and cut its way into her heartcenter.

CHAPTER THIRTY-EIGHT

6 years ago

THE BODY IN THE DOORWAY WAS YONG LEI. Silver needles stuck out of his hands and face. Looking at them, Raijin could see his friend standing with his hands raised in Inviting Attack. The yoke and two empty water buckets lay on their sides behind Yong Lei as if he'd thrown them off in the midst of returning to the spring for another load.

The corpses of a few higher ranks and several masters were scattered around the corridor, but Raijin could only see his best friend.

Floating beside him, Zhuan dipped her snout to Yong Lei. Raijin flinched, fighting back the instinct to shove the demon beast away from his friend. Blue lights flashed along the branching sense organs on her underside.

"Yes," she said. "These needles have the same electrical signature as the ones used to murder my mate."

"But you killed those men." Raijin's voice sounded foreign to his own ears, harsh in the silence.

"I killed the ones whose signature trespassed upon my nest and surrounded my mate's butchered body," she said.

319

But Raijin wasn't listening. If Yong Lei had been bringing in water, doing Raijin's serving tasks, then whoever had done this had struck early in the morning, before the rest of the school was awake. They planned to take the school by surprise, but Yong Lei must have raised the alarm. That was why Library Master Tang-Soo and Training Master Palgwe lay dead in the corridor, along with many higher-ranked students. They had died defending the school.

But the longer Raijin stared, the less likely this looked. The bodies of the higher ranks seemed to spread out in waves from Palgwe and Tang-Soo. Needles gleamed in the masters' flesh.

"Master Chugi," Raijin said. "He must have escaped with the rest of the students."

Raijin knelt beside Yong Lei and touched his face to the floor three times, then did the same facing each of the dead masters.

"Ji Yu Raijin, I do not sense any living electrical signatures large enough to be legged ones like you in this lower section," Zhuan said. "Nothing but insects and mice living in the walls."

"That's because everyone else escaped while Yong Lei and the masters held the attackers off," Raijin said, bowing his face to the floor one final time. He stood. "We'll make a pyre for them after we find Master Chugi and the rest of the students."

"And kill those who murdered them," Zhuan said.

Raijin didn't respond. There was no time for thoughts of vengeance, not when Master Chugi and who knew how many students were out on the mountainside, perhaps still running for their lives.

Raijin had to pick his way through the corpses to traverse the corridor. Zhuan swam along beside him at shoulder height, floating above the dead like a ghostly silver cloud of Ro.

In the dining hall, they found the side door to the courtyard hanging open, letting in bright yellow sunlight and illuminating even more students, these surrounding and piled on top of the Master of Letters. A few of the students were no higher ranked than Wind or Rain, barely a decade old. Their blood had splattered the benches away from the master.

Raijin shut his eyes and swallowed. That couldn't mean what it seemed to.

Through the doorway into the kitchen, he caught a glimpse of a scene much worse. The swell of Fatty's stomach and a group of Cloud students. None were older than six, and none had been spared. One small head still had the cook's cleaver lodged in it.

Turning away from the kitchen on numb legs, Raijin wove through the dining hall and stepped out the courtyard door.

More dead, young and old, students of all ages and ranks. At the center of the carnage lay the broken bodies of Master Chugi and Grandmaster Feng. Silver needles gleamed in the sunlight.

Raijin dropped to his knees.

This couldn't be right. It looked as if the entire school had turned on one another. It was like a nightmare.

In fact, that must be what this was. Master Chugi would never harm a student. He would never harm anyone. And Grandmaster Feng had found the trick to immortality; he couldn't die. This was all just a nightmare brought on by inhaling too much of his mother's qajong smoke. All Raijin had to do was wake himself, then he would be back in the sand by her lean-to, scratching at sand flea bites and waiting for her to call him inside.

"Legged one." Zhuan floated in the doorway, her wings flapping with agitation.

He wanted to feel fury, outrage that the master who had raised him had died in such opposition to his chosen Path. The very idea of hurting a student would have broken Master Chugi's heart. Raijin bowed to the old man's body. When Raijin rose again, he used the back of his sleeve to scrub away the dirt sticking to his wet face.

"I hear footsteps above," the guai-ray said.

Raijin sprang to his feet and sprinted through the dining hall back out into the corridor. As he ran for the stairs to the second floor, he ran through the faces he could remember seeing. Who had he missed? Who was still alive? The physician's hall—he hadn't checked there! Perhaps Akidori was still alive. Perhaps she could tell him who had done this.

He didn't stop to ask himself why a physician and student of the Darkening Skies would have fled upstairs to the library when the fighting began. He couldn't.

As he ran through the upper corridor, he saw bodies through open doors into the students' rooms. Many were tangled in blankets. A few lay on their mats as if they had never woken at all. Who had killed these?

Raijin rounded the corner. Shadows moved in the light cast through the library door.

He sprinted toward it, but a wall of velvety smooth skin flew in front of him. He tried to dart past Zhuan, but she corralled him, herding him backward.

"No," the ray hissed, her voice low enough that Raijin could barely hear. "You are still the weakest creature in the forest, legged one. If you swim in on these, they will kill you."

The shuffling of parchment and scrolls filtered out into the corridor from the library. Hearing it, Raijin stopped struggling and strained his ears to listen.

"The sheer amount of knowledge here…" The voice was one Raijin had never heard before. A man. "If we could keep just a few scrolls—"

"No," a feminine voice snapped, thin and nasally. "It all burns. Bodies, monastery, everything."

The clinking of scroll cases bumping against one another filled the air.

"I'm just saying, the price these things would fetch from the right buyer… And these cases? We should be able to keep a few of these for our trouble. Call it reimbursement for losing Do-Nang and Olil."

"Those morons killed themselves when they deviated from their orders so they could go after that guai. They got what they deserved. You will, too, if you don't follow your orders exactly."

"Probably Olil's idea. Stubborn mule," the man said. Wood scraped against wood as if whoever was in the library were pushing a table across the floor. "Imagine, though, the kind of amazing things we might learn by reading even a fraction of this pile."

"Read as many texts you like," the nasally woman's voice said. "But if you do, you burn with them. You heard Grandmaster Youn Wha—no trace of this path or its practices can remain. Or did you think we risked our lives so we could let some knowledge of it survive to be rediscovered later?" More scraping, then an exasperated sigh. "Are you going to help me with this or not?"

"Oh, quit your posturing. I was only talking."

"As if you ever do anything else."

Liquid glugged and splattered as if poured from a jar. A moment later, firelight flared up, casting shadows through the library's doorway.

From his place in the corridor against the top of Zhuan's flat body, Raijin's mind reeled. These strangers were casually setting fire to hundreds and thousands of books and scrolls, the combined written knowledge of the Path of Darkening Skies, everything the school had gathered.

All the stories Master Chugi had loved so dearly.

Fury boiled in Raijin's bones, finally emerging from wherever it had been hiding. His fists balled at his sides until it felt as if their tendons would snap. In that moment, the wrongness of what these strangers had done—the evil of it—all seemed to be exemplified by the simple act of burning the library full of books Raijin had read to the old man as his sight dimmed and then disappeared altogether.

He wanted blood.

Once a practitioner caused violence in the name of revenge, they could never step back onto the Path of Darkening Skies. Their Ro would be tainted forever.

But these strangers were murderers. They hadn't just killed the masters and students, but tore them from their Path, denying them an honorable death in protection of the weak and shaming them in their last moments. Now they were destroying Master Chugi's favorite books. How could they do such evil to such a kind old man?

What righteousness was there in allowing offenders like that to go free?

"They killed my master," Raijin whispered to Zhuan, his voice shaking with rage. "They killed my best friend and everyone on my Path."

Fire crackled in the library, obviously finding good tinder in the many shelves of books and parchment. Glass shattered, and the light burned brighter.

"You aided me in ending the legged creatures who killed my mate," Zhuan said, her low rumble just barely audible over the flapping smack of parchment tossed into the flames. "Let me destroy these creatures for you. I am their equal in strength. Together two of them will provide just enough challenge that I will gain some honor by their deaths."

Raijin swallowed hard and shook his head. Only a lazy man or a coward would lay his responsibility on the shoulders of another.

When Master Chugi had told Raijin that his time with them was over, he had assumed the old man meant his time with the school. But no, Master Chugi had meant the Path of Darkening Skies itself.

Raijin pushed past the huge guai-ray.

The time had come for him to step off the Path for good.

CHAPTER THIRTY-NINE

Present

"I DON'T UNDERSTAND." KOIDA realized she was whimpering, but couldn't stop herself. "What happened? I don't understand."

She and the yellow-haired foreigner stood in the shadows of the palace garden beneath her bedroom balcony. Hush had left them behind and climbed up to Koida's room.

"Nothing happened," the foreigner said, showing her a casual smile. It was terrifying in its authenticity. He gave her a wink and lifted his ivory flask to her. "We're just three wealthy folk out for an evening's ride. Nippy out this time of night so close to winter, but we've got a sip or two in us keeping the Ro burning hot."

He tossed back the drink.

Koida stared. This foreigner was out of his mind, spewing drunken nonsense about cold weather. Maybe the shock of the mass slaughter they had just escaped had pushed him over the edge.

A shadow moved in the corner of her vision. Koida flinched, adrenaline flaring to her already overloaded heartcenter. She drew in a lungful of breath to scream, hysteria painting the night around her in garish, oily colors, but a hand closed over her mouth.

"It's only Hush," the yellow-haired man said, tucking his flask away. "Breathe. Calm. If you'll keep quiet, she'll let you go. Nod your head if you understand."

Koida obeyed his instructions. Breathed. Nodded. The hand came off her mouth, then Hush stepped in front of her, holding out her black silk riding clothes.

"How did you find these?" Koida asked, her voice flat and emotionless. "I keep them hidden in a loose stone on my balcony that no one but I know of."

Hush pressed the clothes into Koida's hands.

"Get changed," the foreigner said, turning away and leaning his forehead against the wall as if the drink had already gotten to him. "Every second you waste brings the executioner's axe a little closer."

"Lysander," Koida remembered. "That's your name."

He chuckled humorlessly. "Glad I made such an impression. Now get dressed before we're all arrested and put to death for your supposed crimes."

Koida tried to comply, but she couldn't figure out how to loosen and take off the many layers of her dress robes and sashes. Hush's hands picked and pulled at them, unwinding here and untying there, but this wasn't fast enough for Lysander.

With sigh of frustration, the drunken foreigner turned around.

"She's not going to need those where she's going." He produced a burled steel dagger from his sleeve with one dangerously unsteady hand.

Koida's eyes widened, and she backed away only to bump into the stone wall of the palace. Before she could bolt, however, the knife sliced down the front of her robes and undershift, the cold metal caressing her stomach as it parted the layered fabrics with barely more than a whisper.

She grabbed her falling robes, instinctively trying to preserve some semblance of modesty, but the drunk had already spun around and turned his attention to the lights spilling from the windows farther down the wall.

Koida's stare fixed on the weapon as it disappeared into Lysander's robes.

"I don't understand," she whispered again.

Hush shook her head and helped Koida out of her ruined dress robes, then into the black riding clothes. When that was finished, she began pulling bell cascades out of Koida's hair and wadding them in the remains of the second princess's wedding robes.

The only princess now, Koida realized. The thought seemed to come from far out past the moon and stars. So far away, it couldn't be felt at all.

Koida didn't remember climbing over the palace walls or getting Pernicious out of his stall and mounting up. All she could remember, when she thought back later, was Lysander's weaving feet and drunken slurring about Stones and Tiles, demanding the attention of everyone in the stable, while Hush slipped away. Then everything went black, and confused shouting filled the air.

Sometime later, Koida blinked and the sun was coming up. On the horizon, the sky transitioned from a rim of pale yellow to a soft peach, then a cold blue. She was sitting on Pernicious's back, trotting through a forest next to one of the palace's best destriers, a roan named Linebreaker. Lysander swayed along in the roan's saddle.

"Where's Hush?" The sound of her own voice in the silence of the forest startled Koida.

Apparently it surprised Lysander, too, because his head snapped around as if she'd shouted.

"Can you keep it down?" He squinted and held up a hand to shield his eyes from the weak rays of the sun. "Some of us haven't had the opportunity to sleep off last night yet."

"Was she killed, too?" Koida asked. Perhaps she'd only imagined Hush coming with them. Or perhaps the silent woman had died in the dark confusion at the stables.

"Hush is fine. She's off making a false trail to confuse any unwanted trackers."

Koida turned this over for a moment. "Are there any trackers we do want?"

"For crying out loud." Lysander pinched the bridge of his nose between his eyes. "I'm saving your royal highness hungover, half-starved, and sleep-deprived. This isn't the ideal climate for me to put up with sarcasm, Princess."

Koida blinked. She wasn't being sarcastic. She wasn't anything. With a nothing shrug, she let her mind return to the safe blackness.

CHAPTER FORTY

6 years ago

RAIJIN STEPPED INTO THE LIBRARY, his hands raised to Inviting Attack. Though the fire had been burning for a few minutes at most, already ashes and scraps of smoldering paper flitted through the air.

On the far side of the room, a heavyset man in black with a stringy mustache leaned over a flaming pile of parchment, board books, and scrolls, dumping lantern oil in a line from the fire to the nearest shelves. Much closer to the door Raijin had just entered, a thin woman with a pointed, birdlike nose stood frozen in the act of flipping a low table end over end toward the flames.

She blinked.

In the space of that blink, Raijin took in the sweat wetting the hair at her temples, the sleeves rolled up to expose her freckled forearms to the air, even a faint scarring on her inner wrist.

And then she attacked.

She shot toward him at a speed faster than Straight Line Winds, so fast he could hardly see her. Then he couldn't see her. She disappeared into the shadows thrown by the dancing fire as if she were made of nothing more than a wisp of smoke.

Frantic, Raijin manifested a Shield of the Crescent Moon in each hand and covered his back and front. A rain of needles pattered against the shield behind him.

He dropped and spun, lashing out with his leg and sending a Landslide of Ro in the direction the needles had come from, but the woman was gone.

The heavy footfalls of running feet caught his attention. Raijin turned just in time to catch an oil lantern on his forward-facing shield. The lantern's glass shattered, and oil dripped down his uniform jacket and pants.

Flames raced along the trail of oil on the floor, up Raijin's pants and his shield.

Panicked, he dismissed the needle-studded and oil-covered crescent shields. The fire hung in the air before his face for a moment, seeming to burn the very oxygen from his lungs. He whipped his arms around, directing a gout of Torrential Downpour at himself and drowning the flames.

"Beware, legged one!" Zhuan shouted. "The female attacks from behind you!"

Raijin threw himself into a roll. The poisoned needles flew across the room and thudded into burning shelves.

A net of glowing black strings of Ro slapped down over Raijin's right side, tangling around the back of his neck and shoulder. In less than a second, the strings had melted through his jacket and into his skin. Everywhere they touched, his flesh bubbled and burned as if he were being stung by a curtain of jellyfish tentacles. He screamed and ripped at the Ro net with both hands, trying to tear it off.

It wouldn't move. More needles whistled through the air.

Throwing himself to his feet, Raijin shoved both palms forward in a Flash Flood Wall. A wall of jade water flung the acidic net off him. Some of the needles flying toward him should have pierced his watery Ro, but immediately behind the jade floodwaters flowed another wall, this one of glimmering white jade. The few needles that made it through the first were taken down by the second.

On the opposite side of the double Flash Flood Walls, Raijin saw Zhuan dart like an enormous round hornet at the thin woman from behind. The woman danced and spasmed as the guai-ray's stinger pierced her heartcenter and sent lightning singing through her body.

Behind him, the floorboards creaked beneath a heavy tread. Raijin used Cyclone Speed to spin around. The man hurled his stringy black Ro net. With a burst of Straight Line Winds, Raijin shot to the side. He sliced his arms through the air in Yong Lei's favored Driving Sleet technique, sending a barrage of hair-thin ice projectiles at the man in black's face.

The man manifested a defensive shield from that foul-looking black Ro. The Driving Sleet shattered against it, but already Raijin was twisting into a devastating back kick. Battering Volley of Hail struck the man's shield with overwhelming force and threw him backward into a burning shelf.

Before the man could recover, Raijin struck again with a Shattering Crescent Wind kick. The man's black shield flickered but held. Raijin lashed out with a straight kick that so far as he knew had no name, his heel just missing the man's high shield and slamming into his heartcenter.

Thunder boomed, deafening in such a small space. The man slammed into the floor, his black shield disappearing. He clutched at his heartcenter, coughing in big, wet whoops. Flecks of blood dotted his face.

Raijin crept closer, fists raised and legs ready to spring.

The man reached toward his hip with both hands as if to grab something from the air, then whipped them forward. Clearly the move was meant to manifest a weapon of some sort, but his Ro didn't respond. Whatever Raijin's unnamed technique was, it had disabled this man's Ro.

As if realizing that at the same moment, in one swift motion, the man slipped a bamboo blowgun from his sleeve and lifted it toward his mouth.

Raijin drove himself to one knee beside the man, throwing every ounce of his weight and momentum behind a vertical punch to the heartcenter. He'd seen the technique practiced by the masters and some of the highest-ranked students during moving meditation, but it was always executed with an open palm.

Raijin struck with a closed fist.

On impact, the air around them crackled with frost. The man's heartcenter froze solid, then shattered into a hundred pieces under Raijin's knuckles.

The man's hands dropped limp at his sides. The needle blowgun rolled across the floor. He stared up at the burning ceiling. Dead.

A cloud of foul-looking black Ro filtered up from the man's splintered heartcenter and floated toward Raijin.

Raijin fell onto his backside trying to avoid it, but the black cloud of Ro oozed into his chest.

Immediately, the glimmering white Ro attacked the black, encircling it and tightening down like a clenched fist. His jade Ro closed over both, snapping shut on them like the jaws of a hungry beast.

Raijin could feel the toxic black Ro trying to burn its way out of the dual jades. With every move the black made, the white and green clamped down harder. A tentacle of black Ro burned through the white. Raijin panicked and grabbed at it with his jade Ro, but rather than tightening around the whole structure again, the jade sunk through the white like green sand through a sieve and enclosed the black.

The movement made Raijin's head spin, and he had to stick out his arms to catch himself. In desperation, he turned his focus outward. It was overwhelming enough to feel the jade and white switch places and repair itself whenever the black burned through one. If he kept watching, he would pass out.

All at once, the injuries of the fight caught up with him. His temples throbbed, and the snaking lines of acid-blistered skin twisting around his neck, shoulder, and upper arm screamed with pain. That momentary blast of frost from the deadly heartcenter strike had soothed them, but now they were cooking in the heat from the library-consuming fire.

Some small, rational part of Raijin's brain was still functioning, however. He stumbled up to his hands and knees and leaned over the man. He had to know who these strangers were. Quickly, he searched the man's robes for something identifying. Finding nothing in the pockets, he pulled back the man's sleeves, searching the compartment that had hidden the blowgun. Nothing. He was about to drop the man's arm when he noticed a series of white marks on his wrist almost too pale to see.

Hadn't he glimpsed something similar on the woman's wrist? He turned around, looking for the second corpse.

The woman was still impaled on Zhuan's stinger, but her clothes, hair, and flesh had been cooked to ashes. No answers would be found there.

Zhuan, for her part, was no longer swimming through the air above the floor. The huge guai-ray lay folded over on top of her right wing, the left rippling slowly.

"Go, legged one," she said. "Your kind cannot survive a fire."

"Neither can yours," Raijin said.

"I cannot survive either way," Zhuan said. She lifted her body enough to show him an underbelly full of poisoned needles, then dropped back to the floor. "I will not go mad and kill everything within my reach as your pack members did, but I will die all the same."

Raijin grabbed hold of the enormous creature's left wing and began to pull.

"What are you doing, stupid child?" she rumbled. "Did you not see that I've been stung by their poisoned wasps? To waste your time doing this is nonsense!"

The smoke was starting to choke Raijin, but he didn't think he could answer even if his lungs had been clear. He just focused on dragging the guai-ray out of the burning library. He had to. He couldn't let anyone else die in the only home he'd ever known. So many had already.

The burnt body scraped the floor, still impaled on the stinger, adding weight to Raijin's burden and slowing their escape.

Raijin flattened Zhuan out on the floor, then pulled the crust of ash and bone off the ray's stinger, careful not to shock himself by touching it.

When he was done, his hands were covered in soot that had once been human flesh. He swallowed against the disgust and wiped his hands on his uniform pants before going back to the task at hand.

Zhuan was several times heavier than anything he had ever carried alone, and her awkward shape didn't make things any easier. Seeing that he wasn't going to give up, however, she tried to help with what little strength she had left. With heaving flutters of her wings, she lifted herself an inch or two into the air. She would lurch forward, jerked along by Raijin's pulling, then slam back to the floor again.

By the time they made it down the stairs, the entire second floor was engulfed in flames. Raijin's shoulders and back cramped and protested, and the blisters from the toxic black Ro pulled and popped as he dragged the enormous guai-ray down the corridor. He tripped over bodies and stumbled into walls, but he wouldn't leave her to burn.

Finally, he made it to the open door and pulled Zhuan through. She managed to lift herself one last time, and together, they collapsed off the school's porch onto the verdant late summer grass.

"You did well, legged one," Zhuan wheezed, her eye bumps closing. "You avenged your pack."

Raijin fell back onto the grass beside her, looking up at the billowing black smoke filling the sky.

"You helped me," he said.

"In the trees swims my only surviving cub, Nael." Zhuan's rumbling voice was fading quickly. "Take him, protect him. Will you do this, Ji Yu Raijin?"

Raijin leaned up on his unblistered elbow and looked into the trees. In a sun-dappled stand of sumac trees, a slight fluttering movement caught his eye. He had seen motion like that before, in the dark forest along the edges of the thicket. But if this was a ray, then it was much, much smaller than its mother. Maybe less than a forearm's length.

"I will," Raijin promised.

"Then my last debt I pay now," she whispered. "My core...it's yours. I swim into the afterlife to my mate and cubs, free of all my debts in this world. Many are not so blessed as I."

Then, like the last wisp of fog burning away under a harsh sun, the enormous guai-ray dissolved into a silvery mist and blew away. Every bit except for her left eye. That turned into a glowing platinum bead the size of Raijin's smallest fingernail and dropped onto the grass.

CHAPTER FORTY-ONE

Present

WHEN KOIDA RETURNED TO AWARENESS once more, she was sitting beside a waterfall's pool, leaning against Pernicious's muscled side. The sun was high overhead, and though she was sitting in the shade of the cliff, she felt the beginnings of a sunburn tightening the skin on her face.

At first, she thought she and the half-demon had spent another night out by the twin waterfalls that gave the Horned Serpent River its name. Batsai would be furious.

Then she saw Shingti run Batsai through, impaling him on her Dual Swords.

This wasn't the Horned Serpent River. There was only one small waterfall here, and the stream at the base was too shallow. She didn't recognize this place, but she found that fact barely mattered to her.

Everyone she loved was dead. Shingti, Batsai, Father, Raijin…

I'm the only one who can stop them. Please forgive me.

Koida pulled her knees up to her chest and hugged her arms around them. She was shivering as if she were the one encased in ice rather than her betrothed.

She focused inward, into her heartcenter. There Raijin's dark jade Ro and her sizzling amethyst Ro cloud surrounded by its lilac rings were circling one another like panthers trapped in a pit together. Koida had never before seen an advanced Ro that wasn't as red as blood, and now she had one in her heartcenter. With the bright, flickering streaks shooting through it, Raijin's Ro looked like a deep jade pool that was being struck by lightning.

He'd meant for her to absorb it. The first Ro she'd ever absorbed. Now that she had it, what was she supposed to do with it?

Splashing and a litany of curses dragged her attention outward. Lysander stood in the stream with his pants rolled up to his hairy thighs, slapping at the water.

Koida watched this for a while, then went back to looking inward at the two different types of Ro. How was she supposed to navigate this new development with her master dead? She hadn't even had enough time with Raijin to learn how to stand the right way. They had barely talked about Ro.

The gentle thump of hooves brought her back to the world outside her heartcenter. Koida searched for the source of the sound.

The sun had moved an hour closer to its bed in the western sky, and Lysander's clothing was soaked all the way up to his chest. Time, it seemed, had passed without her notice. No fish lay on the shore, however.

Hush rode out of the tree line on a handsome chestnut stallion stolen from the palace stables like Lysander's.

The yellow-haired man looked up from his splashing. "Just in time to scare the best prospect I had away. I assume you released the rest of the horses?"

Though Koida didn't care about the conversation, she looked from the very wet foreigner to the silent woman with the cloth over her nose and mouth.

Hush nodded. She gestured to the water, then made a sign Koida didn't understand.

"In my guest room with the rest of my things," Lysander said. "I'll get another one when we get back to town. Meantime, I'll catch us a little dinner by hand."

With that, Lysander's arm shot into the pool up to his shoulder, but he came up with nothing more than a handful of rocks. When he saw Hush and Koida staring at him expectantly, he threw the pebbles at the far shore in disgust.

"Well, I don't see either of you filling our bellies," he growled, turning his back to them.

Hush rolled her dark almond eyes and went to Koida's side.

Pernicious gave a warning whinny, a sound halfway between a whicker and a Petrifying Shriek of Legions. Koida pressed her face into the warhorse's thick black coat, breathing in his familiar musky brimstone scent. She didn't know how she had gotten the half-demon to come with her—she was certain they hadn't stopped for a pocketful of candied blood oranges on the way out of the palace—but she was glad to have him there. She wished she could follow his scent back through memory twenty-four hours and stay there forever.

A soft touch on Koida's shoulder made her jump.

Hush sat in front of Koida as if she would suggest practicing Resting Meditation. Instead of encouraging

Koida to get into the meditative position, however, Hush took both of Koida's hands in hers and looked at her. No, looked *into* her. The woman's dark almond eyes plumbed hers with a compassion and kindness that made Koida feel strangled. Numbness and shock melted away like snow under a warm wind, and in its place some small measure of the horror and loss of the past day tried to peek through.

Koida ripped her hands away and sprang to her feet. She couldn't feel that pain, couldn't hold that huge awfulness inside her. No one could. It would kill a human.

Hush didn't grab her hands back or force her to sit down, only sat patiently. After a moment, the silent woman got up and drew closer to the shore. There she sat on a large rock, watching Lysander slap ineffectually at the water.

"We're all impatient to get on the road, but you don't hear me complaining about it," Lysander huffed. "We need food or we won't make it much farther."

As usual, Hush said nothing.

Lysander threw up his hands in irritation. "Well, if you're so sure you can do better, by all means."

The silent woman slipped off her boots and waded into the water.

Koida let their one-sided bickering roll over her mind like the river over stone. It was nothing but meaningless noise to her. She kept coming back to the same few thoughts—slaughter, poison, Ro, murder. None of it made any sense.

The memory of Yoichi pointing at someone and shouting, *Murderess!* surfaced. His plum-colored eyes, so like their father's, had locked on hers. *She conspired to poison our family!*

A wet, wriggling mass of slime and spines flopped onto Koida's lap. She jumped, and the slippery creature went slapping across the grass. Pernicious leapt to his hooves and triggered Darting Evasion, spooked by the sudden movement.

It was a fat mudcat. A second landed at Koida's feet, then a third to her right.

Hush slogged out of the water and gave Koida an apologetic bow. The silent woman picked the closest mudcat from the grass and faced the water, holding the fish's wriggling body up for the yellow-haired foreigner's inspection.

In the river, Lysander shook his head. "Beginner's luck. If I had a drink or two in me, you'd see who the real fisher was in this group."

CHAPTER FORTY-TWO

6 years ago

ITH ZHUAN'S GLOWING PLATINUM CORE stone clutched in his fist, Raijin moved back to the tree line and sat down in Resting Meditation. Before him, the school that had been his home burned.

Between his own jade and his mother's sparkling white jade Ro, the foul black of the man in the library was soon broken down and absorbed into his own. When it was finished, the jade Ro pulsed with evil-looking black veins, and he felt a deep sickness so strong that it was almost a well, a type of grief and despair he couldn't hope to understand. The sickness throbbed in his pathways, the despair threatening to consume him.

Then his mother's brilliant white Ro bumped up against the tainted, vein-crossed jade energy, almost a question or a loving offer of help. The jade Ro slowly oozed around the white, swallowing it. A flash of white light shined through his contaminated Ro, burning away the black pollution. When it was finished, the white Ro had integrated into the jade, leaving his Ro the refined light green of his mother's eyes when she smiled. No longer was it the pinging, jumping Hail-level Ro of a

Darkening Skies student, but as calm and liquid as a deep pool in a slow-flowing river.

Raijin sat there for the rest of the night and most of the next morning, alternating between watching the flames consume the building and looking inward at his Ro's new properties. The blisters from the black Ro net seemed to crawl with stinging needles. Now and again, from the corner of his eye, he caught glimpses of the tiny guai-ray, but it never came close enough for him to look at it directly.

Though he had much to think about, his actions in the library not the least of them, he found there was nothing on his mind but the name the thin woman had said: Grandmaster Youn Wha.

This grandmaster had given the order to destroy all knowledge of the Path of Darkening Skies and kill all its practitioners. But there was no possibility that he would be able to face a grandmaster at his current level. He was no more than a Hail, only halfway through the ranks of Darkening Skies. He would never be able to advance further down that Path because of what he'd done in taking vengeance.

He didn't regret his actions. At least not yet. But he would need a new Path he could follow to its conclusion if he was ever going to bring this Grandmaster Youn Wha to justice.

Master Chugi had told Raijin that to become the chosen one, he would have to leave them. This advice had kept him alive while the rest of his schoolmates and masters murdered one another. Sometime in the future, if Master Chugi had been right, Raijin would have to die, too. Would have to do so willingly to defeat the Darkness. If this Grandmaster Youn Wha was the evil

Darkness the prophecy had spoken of, then Raijin would gladly die to see her stopped.

As night fell on the second day, the final section of wall still standing of the school turned pyre buckled and collapsed in on itself. The fluttering shape in the undergrowth to Raijin's right recoiled.

Raijin looked down at the glowing platinum core stone he'd been clutching for the last two days. In spite of his body heat, it was cold to the touch. There was no telling what sort of gifts a demonic river ray's core would grant him, but it would be a running start on his journey.

Lightning flickered beyond the mountainside, followed by a distant roll of thunder. Not the sharp crack that signaled the beginning of a sudden downpour, but the gentle rumble of a gathering storm.

In time, a cold rain began to fall, its icy caress soothing on his blisters. The bed of embers the school had become sizzled and died as the shower picked up strength. Rivulets of ashy water ran from the smoldering ruins, and lightning showed the contours in the thick blanket of clouds overhead. The deluge showed no signs of slowing.

As the thunder crept closer, Raijin swallowed the core stone, then raised his soot-stained face to the rain.

CHAPTER FORTY-THREE

Present

HUSH SET TO GATHERING WOOD WHILE Lysander pulled his knife and slit the belly of the first mudcat. Koida watched him with eyes that felt as wide as wine cups. She had never seen an animal butchered before.

Inside the mudcat's body, its heart still beat, and a translucent pink bladder filled and emptied of air. Lysander reached into the belly cavity, grabbed the gut sack, and sliced away the connective tissue. These inedible bits he tossed into the river. Blood and slime covered his thick, blunt-fingered hands as he worked.

After the first was finished, Lysander noticed Koida's intense scrutiny. He sighed and stopped his work, resting an elbow on his knee.

"There's no shame in turning away," he told her. "Not today." When she didn't respond or do as he said, he pointed toward the trees. "Go help Hush gather wood, kid."

Koida shook her head. What was it Raijin had said? Adversity built strength, but indulging weakness tore it down? She swallowed. She couldn't indulge her weaknesses anymore. She needed strength. What little she had been born with wasn't enough, especially not if she wanted…

The thought trailed off. If she wanted what? What could she possibly want after her father—Shingti—Batsai—Raijin—after what had happened to them?

To kill whoever had done this to her family.

Thinking that didn't stir up any dangerous emotions that might undo her. All she felt was a calm, cold thirst for vengeance.

Lysander pulled the gut sack out of another mudcat, slicing away the connective tissue with his dagger.

His burled steel dagger.

"Why aren't you manifesting a Ro-knife?" Koida asked.

Lysander didn't look up. "Because I'm not."

"Can't you?" In her numb stupor, the rudeness of the question didn't occur to her.

Luckily, the foreigner was being just as rude. "I liked you better when you were in shock. We should talk to Hush about teaching you the Path of Hidden Whispers."

"What happened?" Koida asked softly, though she was asking it of herself as much as anyone else. "What happened to my sister? Why did she…"

An armload of wood dropped to the ground to her right, and Hush crouched beside it, setting up the fire.

Lysander looked up from washing his hands and knife in the river. "The Screaming Death."

The silent woman nodded, striking a spark into the tinder.

"It makes you hallucinate." Lysander began whittling at a thin stick. "Everyone and everything around you becomes a fiend of hell bent on ripping you apart. Eventually, your heart gives out from the strain—

347

though not before a well-trained artist could take out most everyone around them."

Like Shingti and her father had done. Until Raijin stopped them.

Please forgive me.

"It was the Water Lily," Lysander continued, using the stick he'd carved to prop open the mudcat's empty belly. "Youn Wha, the grandmaster Lao is always trailing around, or one of her students. They must've realized Raij was onto them."

"Raijin switched our wine cups," Koida said. "The poison was in mine. He knew it was in mine."

Lysander propped open the next fish with a whittled stick.

"Must've seen something suspicious, then," he said. He thought for a moment. "If they weren't out to get him, then this Water Lily was probably hoping to implicate him in your death, start a war between your empire and the Ji Yu. Lots of nice, tasty Ro there for them, with all those warrior artists killing one another. But when Raij switched the cups and drank your poison, their plan went sideways." He glanced over at Hush. "That would explain the Flying Needles."

The silent woman nodded.

"Usually they use a blowgun, but this time the needles were probably thrown to avoid anyone seeing the weapon," Lysander said. "Dosed your father and sister with poison using the needles and used the ensuing chaos to cover their escape. It was a well-executed alternate route. I think Raij would've caught up to the scum if the poison hadn't gotten him first."

"Raijin killed my sister and my father," Koida said, marveling as she spoke at the emotionless quality her voice had taken on. "Then he went after Cousin Yoichi."

Lysander grunted. "Anybody who survived that massacre owes Raijin their life. I know you probably don't want to hear this, but your sister would've butchered everyone in the palace if he hadn't stopped her."

"Is it painful?" Koida swallowed. "The Screaming Death? Did Shingti suffer?"

The foreigner blew out a long breath and checked a fish that hadn't had nearly enough time to cook. Koida looked to Hush. The silent woman squeezed her forearm gently and nodded once.

"He killed them quick and clean," Lysander said, stabbing at the fish. "They probably didn't feel a thing from him. The poison, though…"

Koida took a shaky breath and looked up at the falling water casting mist over the huge boulders on the hillside. She couldn't think about that. Couldn't think about their final, agonized moments.

Murderess.

Yoichi had been accusing her, the only legitimate heir.

Then Raijin was on his knees in front of Yoichi. Her betrothed had tried to attack her half-brother, but by then he'd been too close to death. With his final heartbeat, he'd sent his own powerful Ro crashing into her.

Then Koida felt her head shaking, back and forth almost as if she had no control over it.

"Raijin drank the Breath of the Underwater Panther with me," she said, a spark of hope flaring to life in her mind. "He was protected from all malicious harm until after our wedding was over." When she tried to remember how long ago that had happened, time seemed to run together, as if there were three time periods— Before the Feast, During the Feast, and After the Feast. She couldn't tell one day from another, but she knew that the Breath of the Underwater Panther had come Before the Feast. "I…I don't know what day that was, but he said it would protect us until the wedding rituals were over, with enough time to get back to his village."

"No." Lysander sliced one blunt hand through the air. "We saw his Ro leave his body. He's dead. That's it. There's no sense in holding out some ridiculous false hope when we all know he's dead."

Koida turned to Hush. The silent woman's dark almond eyes held only pity, as if she knew Koida were grasping for solid ground in a landslide.

From a lifetime spent with the Exalted Emperor, Koida knew there was a time to press one's case and a time when arguing would gain nothing. Both of Raijin's associates thought she was building up pretty lies to keep from falling apart, trying to pretend that at least one of the people she loved was still alive. Arguing now would only serve to convince Lysander and Hush that they were right.

Koida turned her focus inward to the swirling jade and amethyst Ros at her heartcenter. If the Breath of the Underwater Panther was powerful enough that Pernicious's headbutt the other night hadn't even made her nose bleed, then some poison couldn't have killed Raijin. Why had he sealed himself inside that icy coffin? Had it been to protect himself from Yoichi while he was helpless without his Ro? How long would the ice last? She couldn't go running back in like this. She would never make it into the Sun Palace, let alone stand a chance in a fight with Yoichi. Not without advancing at the very least.

Lysander pressed a hot fish on a charred stick into Koida's hands. She looked up in time to see Hush taking her food into the forest, leaving them behind.

Still considering the sharp right turn her life had taken, Koida picked at the fish. It burned her fingertips, but what was a little pain compared to what her father or Shingti or Batsai had suffered on their way to death?

"I think Raijin knew this would happen," Koida said, turning the fish over in her hands. "Before the feast, he spoke of variations and deviations, and he said no matter who I was, he would always find me."

Lysander just shook his head. "If I had a link for every weird bit of nonsense Raijin's dropped since I met him, I would be swimming in silver."

"He spoke as if he knew me before he negotiated the treaty with Father," Koida insisted. "As if it was all intentional, from us meeting to the…to last night. But how could that be?"

Lysander sighed, his fish-on-a-stick poised halfway to his mouth.

"Last year, we went with Raijin to the Dead Waters Kingdom. He slipped us for a while, went off alone. When he came back, he wouldn't talk about what happened, but he was dead set on coming here. That was the first he ever mentioned the valley or your people."

Koida frowned. She had never even heard of the Dead Waters Kingdom. She didn't see how Raijin could have learned about her there.

"Where are we going now?" she asked.

"As far away from the empire as possible before you're captured and executed," Lysander answered. "Now eat your food so we can saddle up."

Koida nodded. That made good sense. Yoichi would be telling everyone that she had killed her family and Raijin. Maybe by now word had reached Raijin's tribe, and the Ji Yu would want her dead as well. A sudden wash of helplessness hit her. There were so many people in the world, so many more than she had ever even considered, and it felt as if everyone but Lysander and Hush wanted her dead.

Except maybe that wasn't true. There was one place, one allied tribe Yoichi might not even try to bring over to his side.

Koida looked at Lysander. "Which direction have we been riding?"

"South," he said around a bite of food. He swallowed. "Why?"

Half a day's ride south of the palace. Another day and a half would bring them to the lower reaches.

"With all of us dead or gone, Cousin Yoichi…" She grimaced, though there was no real emotion behind the expression. She just didn't want to call Yoichi her cousin anymore, didn't want to be associated with him at all. *Our family,* he'd said. *She poisoned our family.* "He's the next highest rank in all the empire and the only other blood relation to the emperor. The nobles love him. Power will fall to Yoichi, and all of our—the empire's— allies will become his allies. Except perhaps one tribe. Yoichi didn't like Raijin bringing the Uktena into allegiance with the empire. He called them filthy savages and suggested they were worthless." Koida held the charred stick between her fingers and twirled the rapidly cooling fish, picturing the barbaric delegation Raijin had seemed perfectly at home with. She glanced up at Lysander. "I know Raijin was acquainted with them before he brought them into the empire."

"He never said he didn't know them before the negotiations." Lysander tossed his stick into the fire, then wiped the grease from his hands onto his pants. "You people just assumed."

"I'm not accusing him of deception," Koida said. "I believe Yoichi won't think to convince the Uktena that I'm a murderer. He probably won't even uphold their agreement with the empire. That means they could be a potential ally. We should go to them first."

"We should eat our food," Lysander said, picking at his teeth with a thumbnail. "So we can get back on our horses and run for your life."

"Well, that's where I'm going," Koida said. "You and Hush are welcome to come with me or go off as you please." She raised her chin a touch as she would have with an insubordinate messenger or lady in waiting and switched to a formal tone. "You have done everything you were tasked with, Lysander, rescuing me from the massacre and getting me to safety. Gratitude."

He stared at her in disbelief. "Are you dismissing me?"

Hush came out of the tree line, her fish gone, and knelt next to the fire. Lysander reached over and slapped the silent woman's arm.

"This infant is dismissing me, Hush," he said. "Can you believe that?"

Hush rolled her dark almond eyes.

"Your responsibility to me is fulfilled," Koida said, looking from Hush to the soldier. "You are free to do as you see fit. I release you both from my service."

"Well, isn't that just as sweet as sugared violets?" Lysander snorted. "You release us! Kid, I don't work for you, and I'm sure as sunrise not one of your subjects."

"When the Ji Yu tribe joined the empire, all members became—"

"Ah, see, there you go making assumptions again. Did Raijin ever say I was a member of his tribe?"

Koida tried to remember, but everything before the massacre melted together once more. She couldn't pick any specific thing her almost-husband had said about Lysander from the soup of days and years.

"I'm not the joining type," Lysander said as if her confusion had proven his point. "Never joined the Ji Yu, never allied myself with the Shyong San Empire."

Koida shook her head, trying to make sense of his words.

"Does this mean you're leaving or not?" she asked.

"No, I'm not leaving!" Lysander crossed his arms over his wide chest. "I wouldn't trust you to use the necessary alone, much less keep yourself alive out here. Raijin told us to get you to safety, and you're a long way from anything resembling that." His lips twisted into a smirk. "Of course, I can't speak for Hush. She may want to leave us both behind."

From the glare on the silent woman's face, it was obvious Hush did not find this as funny as Lysander did. The woman shook her head sharply.

"It's settled then." Lysander shrugged. "We're staying with you."

Koida nodded slowly.

"I accept your protection," she said. "And your tutelage."

The smug smirk disappeared from Lysander's face.

"You what now?"

"Cous—Yoichi is a formidable Master of the Living Blade with a Heroic Record more decorated than even Shingti's. I'll have to train like mad and find a way to advance before I can repay him for his sins against my family. And my betrothed," she added belatedly, remembering that Lysander and Hush both thought Raijin was dead. She turned to the silent woman. "I'll need a master, and Raijin said you were master of many Paths. You already began by teaching me meditation. Would you continue?"

Hush's expression darkened above the cloth wrappings, her brows drawing low over her almond eyes. Lysander, however, was the one who answered.

"If this cousin of yours is the man behind everything, then he's more than another Master of the Living Blade. He's practicing the Path of the Water Lily as well, if not already a master of it. You don't just run into battle with these people. They can't see your attack coming or you'll be dead before you strike. You can train to your heart's content, but going after him is suicide—and not the honorable kind. If you think…"

Lysander went on, but Koida let his words dissipate into the crackling of the fire. Hush hadn't immediately refused. If the silent woman did later, however, that wouldn't matter. Koida would just find another master. Raijin had been certain that she could advance, had gone so far as to entrust his Ro to her. How could she be worthy of that responsibility if she gave up now?

Koida took a bite of the cold fish. It tasted like ashes, and it sat in her stomach like river stones, but she ate the entire thing. She would need all the energy she could get for the path ahead.

ΞPILOGUΞ

Present

RAIJIN OPΞNΞD HIS ΞYΞS TO A BLUΞ-gray world of smoke and shadow. Distortions danced and shimmered in the air like a heat haze. Nearby, a slate waterfall ran off a vertical cliffside into a shallow indigo pool, the water churning strangely. It was as if he could only see glimpses of its motion, and between these glimpses it froze, as still as a painting.

He looked down at himself. He wore nothing but the loose-fitting pants of a warrior artist, and his hands and body were rendered in the same bluish charcoal smears as the twin waterfalls. When he turned them over, they moved in the same skips and jumps as the roiling water in the pool.

The air smelled like burning incense. It felt thick, but a lungful of it barely satisfied his need to breathe. Within seconds, his shoulders were heaving.

Where was he, and why did he even need to breathe? He shouldn't be alive. He had drank Koida's poison, just as he'd done in each of the potential futures—the ones where both Koida and the world survived, anyway—and he had gifted her his Ro to keep it out of the Water Lily's

357

hands. He should be dead, the prophecy of the Thunderbird and the Dark Dragon fulfilled.

Was it because the Koida in this reality had been so different from the Koida in the others? Had he or she done something unintentionally to alter the outcome of the prophecy? Raijin had tried to stay within the confines laid out for the chosen one, but Koida kept surprising him. Maybe he had failed, and the Dark Dragon would crush the world.

Through the haze, a flickering near the pool caught Raijin's attention. The pale blue ghost of a woman, almost glowing against the dark blue-gray shades of this strange world, tossed some unseen object into the pool. She stared down into the depths for several long seconds before sinking into a martial pose Raijin had never seen before, her feet so wide that she was nearly sitting, right palm raised to the sky, left facing the ground. As Raijin watched, the woman rose up on one leg, thrusting her right hand forward and her left behind her.

Unlike the water and Raijin himself, the woman's movements were smooth and natural, no skips between. She flowed through the series of sinuous, graceful techniques like a snake sliding through the grass, focused unwaveringly on her every motion. The thin air didn't seem to have any effect on her.

High up on the cliff face, Raijin thought he saw a flash of red. He searched the rocks for any sign of movement, finally catching a glimpse of a long-fingered claw gripping a ledge. Something a shade lighter than blood was slinking down the cliff toward the woman. In the gaps between boulders, Raijin saw powerful arms and swaying folds of bright red skin.

Raijin tried to call out to the woman, but when he opened his mouth, no sound came out. She continued to flow through her techniques, oblivious to the thing's approach.

Though he could barely breathe, Raijin broke into a run. If he couldn't warn her, then he had to put himself between her and the creature. Unfortunately, the jerky, halting motion of his body in this world did not translate to swiftness. Out of habit, he triggered Straight Line Winds.

But the sudden burst of speed never came. He had no Ro to fuel it.

The woman sunk down into another deep, nearly seated stance and held the pose, her back to the cliff. She didn't even look Raijin's way as his stuttering gait took him past her. Perhaps she couldn't see him at all.

Just as he came to a stop between the woman and the cliff, the red creature emerged from the rocks. It was nearly twice Raijin's height, with the backward-jointed hind legs of a dog and the dragging, muscular arms of an ape. Folds of leathery red skin hung down from its equine jaw, slapping against its chest, and an apron of flesh reached from its belly to mid-thigh.

With a thought, Raijin tried to manifest the butterfly sword from the living lavaglass embedded in his left arm. Nothing. He glanced down. The twin lines of lavaglass sunk into his flesh were gone, replaced by unmarked skin.

Raijin raised his hands in Inviting Attack. There were any number of bare-handed fighting styles he could use to drive the creature away.

The red beast pounced, its needle-studded maw dripping with bloody strings of saliva. Raijin planted his feet, pulled both fists back to his hips, then threw them both forward simultaneously, high and low. One struck the creature in the leathery folds hanging from its jaw, and the other landed just above its swaying belly apron. It was a technique Lysander had taught him, often effective against a human opponent. Against the creature, however, neither punch did more than shake the fat inside its folds.

Undeterred, Raijin grabbed hold of the creature and, with a twist of his body, tried to turn the punches into the throw that was their natural conclusion. But the creature's huge arm slammed into his side like a battering ram. Raijin tumbled through the air and across the slate-blue grass, finally crashing into a shadowy tree trunk. His ribs cracked like dead branches, and he curled in on himself.

By the waterfall, the red creature crept toward the woman.

Raijin drew a painful, insufficient breath and tried to shout. Again, no sound came from his throat.

The red beast leapt, snapping at the back of the woman's head. Without looking, the woman slid aside and grabbed the creature by one long arm and its jaw flap. She slammed it to the ground so hard that the earth shook beneath Raijin, and dark blue-gray blood flew up in a fountain from the beast's needle-filled mouth.

It didn't rise again.

The ghostly woman turned to Raijin, her face tilting down as if she was looking at him. Where her eyes should have been, however, were only empty holes that showed the shadowy, smoky scenery behind her. She smiled.

"Welcome to the Land of the Immortals, chosen one," she said. "You're going to have to do better than that if you want to get back to her and finish this."

BOOKS, MAILING LIST, AND REVIEWS

If you enjoyed reading about Raijin and Koida and want to stay in the loop about the latest book releases, awesome promotional deals, and upcoming book giveaways be sure to subscribe to our email list at:

www.ShadowAlleyPress.com

Word-of-mouth and book reviews are crazy helpful for the success of any writer. If you *really* enjoyed reading *Darkening Skies*, please consider leaving a short, honest review—just a couple of lines about your overall reading experience. Thank you in advance!

ABOUT THE AUTHOR

I am invincible. I am a mutant. I have 3 hearts and was born with no eyes. I had eyes implanted later. I didn't have hands, either, just stumps. When my eyes were implanted they asked if I would like hands as well and I said, "Yes, I'll take those," and pointed with my stump. But sometimes I'm a hellbender peeking out from under a rock. When it rains, I live in a music box.

But I'm also a tattoo addict, coffee junkie, drummer, and aspiring skateboarder. Jesus actually is my homeboy.

ACKNOWLEDGEMENTS

Esteemed readers, *Darkening Skies* is the book of my heart. It combines everything I love and more, and I poured everything I had into writing it. But books don't get made just because the writer is passionate about them, and the ones that do don't always turn out good. Every mistake in this book is my fault, but everything awesome in it is the result of several amazing warrior artists and demon beasts from around the Horned Serpent Valley. They deserve all the credit and praise for *Darkening Skies's* existence, so let's give it to them:

God, Jesus, and the Holy Spirit, Who drank the cup of wrath so an untouchable like me could drink the cup of joy, so sweet and undeserved.

The Op boys and girl, Kensey, Ronny, and Will, the second most important trinity always in my heart.

Master Mark, Master Natalie, and everybody at the dojang for humoring my awkward flailing.

The Shadow Alley family, for the encouragement and support and for not tearing their hair out every time I come to them with another book of my heart. I'm just so very proud to be here.

Adam, Mark, Zack, and Tamara, for making me sound way smarter and cooler than I am.

The diehard readers and bleeders who make releasing new books into the world a never-ending thrill ride—Silvia, Mandy, Michael, Doc F, Rebecca, Sara, Anders, and The One Man Stand Against Man Buns & Man Purses.

Tim McBain and LT Vargus, for letting me splash around in their pool while we talked craft and literary theory to our hearts' content.

And my Joshua—sparring partner, beloved chieftain, pretty face, prettier brain, and living embodiment of the principles of our Path. Five years ago, when I published my first book, I made him a promise, and it's finally come true.

BOOKS FROM
SHADOW ALLEY PRESS

If you enjoyed *Darkening Skies*, you might also enjoy other awesome stories from Shadow Alley Press, such as Viridian Gate Online, Rogue Dungeon, the Yancy Lazarus Series, School of Swords and Serpents, American Dragons, or the Jubal Van Zandt Series. You can find all of our books listed at www.ShadowAlleyPress.com.

James A. Hunter

Viridian Gate Online: Cataclysm (Book 1)
Viridian Gate Online: Crimson Alliance (Book 2)
Viridian Gate Online: The Jade Lord (Book 3)
Viridian Gate Online: The Imperial Legion (Book 4)
Viridian Gate Online: The Lich Priest (Book 5)
Viridian Gate Online: Doom Forge (Book 6)
Viridian Gate Online: Darkling Siege (Book 7)

Darkening Skies

VGO: The Artificer (Imperial Initiative)

<<<>>>

VGO: Nomad Soul (Illusionist 1)
VGO: Dead Man's Tide (Illusionist 2)
VGO: Inquisitor's Foil (The Illusionist 3)

<<<>>>

VGO: Firebrand (Firebrand Series 1)
VGO: Embers of Rebellion (Firebrand Series 2)
VGO: Path of the Blood Phoenix (Firebrand Series 3)

<<<>>>

VGO: Vindication (The Alchemic Weaponeer 1)
VGO: Absolution (The Alchemic Weaponeer 2)
VGO: Insurrection (The Alchemic Weaponeer 3)

<<<>>>

Strange Magic: Yancy Lazarus Episode One
Cold Heatred: Yancy Lazarus Episode Two
Flashback: Siren Song (Episode 2.5)
Wendigo Rising: Yancy Lazarus Episode Three
Flashback: The Morrigan (Episode 3.5)
Savage Prophet: Yancy Lazarus Episode Four
Brimstone Blues: Yancy Lazarus Episode Five

<<<>>>

MudMan: A Lazarus World Novel

eden Hudson

<<<>>>

Two Faced: Legend of the Treesinger (Book 1)
Soul Game: Legend of the Treesinger (Book 2)

<<<>>>

Rogue Dungeon: Rogue Dungeon Series (Book 1)
Civil War: Rogue Dungeon Series (Book 2)
Troll Nation: Rogue Dungeon Series (Book 3)
Rogue Evolution: Rogue Dungeon Series (Book 4)

eden Hudson

Revenge of the Bloodslinger: A Jubal Van Zandt Novel
Beautiful Corpse: A Jubal Van Zandt Novel
Soul Jar: A Jubal Van Zandt Novel
Garden of Time: A Jubal Van Zandt Novel
Wasteside: A Jubal Van Zandt Novel

<<<>>>

Darkening Skies: Path of the Thunderbird 1
Stone Soul: Path of the Thunderbird 2
Demon Beast: Path of the Thunderbird 3

Aaron Ritchey

Armageddon Girls (The Juniper Wars 1)
Machine-Gun Girls (The Juniper Wars 2)
Inferno Girls (The Juniper Wars 3)
Storm Girls (The juniper Wars 4)

Sages of the Underpass (Battle Artists Book 1)

Gage Lee

Hollow Core: School of Swords and Serpents 1
Eclipse Core: School of Swords and Serpents 2
Chaos Core: School of Swords and Serpents 3
Burning Core: School of Swords and Serpents 4

Shadowbound: Ghostlight Academy Book 1

J.D. Astra

Neon Dark: Zero.Hero Book 1

Morgan Cole

Inheritance: The Last Enclave Book 1
Redemption: The Last Enclave Book 2

Kenneth Arant

A Snake's Life Book 1

eden Hudson

BOOKS FROM BLACK FORGE

Aaron Crash

War God's Mantle: Ascension (Book 1)
War God's Mantle: Descent (Book 2)
War God's Mantle: Underworld (Book 3)

Denver Fury: American Dragons Book 1
Cheyenne Magic: American Dragons Book 2
Montana Firestorm: American Dragons Book 3
Texas Showdown: American Dragons Book 4
California Imperium: American Dragons Book 5
Dodge City Knights: American Dragons Book 6
Leadville Crucible: American Dragons Book 7
Alamosa Arena: American Dragons Book 8
Alaska Kingdom: American Dragons Book 9
Wyoming Dynasty: American Dragons Book 10

Barbarian Outcast: Princesses of the Ironbound 1
Barbarian Assassin: Princesses of the Ironbound 2

Darkening Skies

Barbarian Alchemist: Princesses of the Ironbound 3

Raider Annihilation: Son of Fire Book 1
Kraken Killjoy: Son of Fire Book 2

Nick Harrow

Dungeon Bringer 1
Dungeon Bringer 2
Dungeon Bringer 3

Witch King 1
Witch King 2
Witch King 3

Made in the USA
Monee, IL
16 October 2022

16011484R00215